BONE PARK

SANDY ROBSON

Copyright © 2022 Sandy Robson

All rights reserved. No portion of this book may be reproduced in any form without permission from the publisher, except as permitted by U.S. copyright law. For permissions contact: sandyrobsonbooks.com

ISBN: 9798361496051

This is a work of fiction. Names, characters, businesses, places, events and situations are either the products of the author's imagination or are told in a fictitious manner. Any resemblance to actual persons, living or dead, or actual events is purely coincidental.

PUBLISHED BY: Sandy Robson Books
www.sandyrobsonbooks.com

Original cover design by Sandy Robson

A woman with no watch—lives forever.

CONTENTS

	Acknowledgments	i
1	Tequila Sunrise	1
2	Hustle	Pg. - 50
3	Champagne	Pg. - 88
4	Buffalo Girls	Pg. - 132
5	Under the B	Pg. - 184
6	Three Dames	Pg. - 231
7	An Eye for an Eye	Pg. - 267
8	The Lottery	Pg. - 307

ACKNOWLEDGMENTS

Thank you, to my Bernie and my Ruby. You were so much more than these characters. You made my childhood an adventure, so I created an adventure for you.

Thank you to New Smyrna and Daytona, for the fond memories I found on your beaches.

Thank you to Nicole, my artistic director, heavy critic and most trusted sounding board. Your love and belief in me continues to amaze and surprise me. I am grateful for your continued support on this insane road.

And as always…
Thank you Nanners. The only one who can hear the same voice I hear in my head. Without you, all these stories would still be locked away in the echoes of my racing mind.

CHAPTER 1

Tequila Sunrise

They found her.

She thought she'd escaped, snuck out at the crack of dawn and left them behind in the cold February winds of Buffalo—but they've found her. They've come right down the coast, B-lining it without pee breaks, like a hatchback packed full of horny spring breakers on a mission. They've hunted her, followed her scent along the interstate—ignored the cooler shores of the Outer Banks, the fat pensioned golfers of Myrtle Beach and the Budweiser-chugging bikers in Daytona—to find her here. Away from the A1A, miles from the shore, in the quiet mobile home retirement community of Cicada Hollow. This was supposed to be Bernie's oasis—the reflecting pond for her golden years—her time of relaxation, but this oasis is now on fire. Paradise is lost. The two bodies floating face down in the pool, less than fifty feet away from the rear of her trailer, have destroyed the mirage. But it's not the corpses that have found her, it's what accompanies them. It's what always travels with the dead, hand in hand, before and after the breath stops. This is what has followed her—the screams.

The desperate shrieks of loss have found her.

"Somebody call an ambulance!" Mullet screams again, but Bernie's not answering back. She never answers back—never has said a word to him other than good morning.

He does have a name, it's Tony, but the women of the Hollow refer to him as Mullet. The female residents here can be cruel, judgmental and vicious, it's like they are regressing to the petty values of their formal education. They also have ripened into pure, closet perverts. Ogling has become a legitimate pastime for the past prime. Long side glances of Mullet's tanned, sculpted, surfer muscles have become a staple around here, but he's only eye candy to them from the neck down. The greatest generation doesn't fancy men with long hair, and they certainly don't much care for the rebellious shaved sides and long tail of his 'Kentucky Waterfall'. He's all look and no talk. Not much of a scholar, more suited for shirtless, lawn mowing and pool skimming. He can't even tell the difference between drowning and dead. Bernie could tell those men floating in the drink needed body bags right away. Even from all the way back here, behind her trailer, but he's still screaming and fussing like it's Baywatch.

There are no back yards on this inner circle of Cicada Hollow. All of these 'single wides' lined up around this oval, back onto the same patch of rough St. Augustine grass. It's a common area shared by the park residents as well as a common back yard, shared by all the trailers that back onto it. This inner ring of corrugated-tin shotgun homes is not as quiet as some of the others on the outer lanes, but they are the most desirable. They are the highest priced and most coveted because they back onto all the action. They have front row seats and unfettered access to the bright-green, eight-lane shuffleboard courts, four pit-bowling greens, the activity center and the fenced-in, kidney-shaped pool. The normally placid pool that is right now white capping, with the thrashing and screaming of one young man triaging two dead bodies.

"Bernie! Call for help would ya? It's Stan!" Mullet shouts, splashing around, fighting to push back the blue, plastic, bubble blanket covering the other body. "Bernie?! Oh God—I think this one under the thermal here, is Brent!"

Bernie's not moving—her lips or her feet. She's just watching. Doing what she does—being stoic and stern. Sort of her M.O. in the park. The only reaction she musters is letting out a sigh. A long and unamused sigh which shakes the tight curls on her 'electric blue hued' perm a little.

"Bernie? Bernie?! Over here! Bernie?" Mullet is starting to sound like an attention-starved child and Bernie was done with rearing long before this tool was born.

So, like any slightly inebriated parent would do, Bernie continues to ignore his pleas and go about her business, which right now is trying to tighten the sash on her men's terry-cloth robe, without spilling her drink. Her very important drink—her morning tequila sunrise. This is more than ritual, it's medicine. The antithesis of coffee, which she only drinks in freeze-dried form. This is her little helper—which is always heavy on the grenadine.

With her robe secure and having had enough of the illegitimate, hyperactive child in the pool, Bernie turns her attention to her right. Far right, almost halfway around the circle of trailers, to the off-white one with the blue pinstripe. The one that Freda is standing behind.

Although their height and facial intensity are polar opposites, Freda and Bernie clearly go to the same hairstylist. They also share the same level of interest in this morning water show. Freda says nothing, offering no help to Mullet, she just continues to watch the commotion dressed in a baby-blue, quilted-polyester, floor-length dressing gown that is way too warm for this climate. She's way too wild-eyed for this early in the morning as well. She could probably use a cocktail, but instead, she's hauling on a fag as if it's life support.

BONE PARK

Bernie acknowledges Freda, slowly raising her sunflower-printed highball into the air, sending a subtle 'cheers' over to her—but she doesn't 'cheers' back. Instead, Freda purses her stress-lined lips together around the yellowed filter of her Lucky Strike and takes a long, hard, distressed drag. She holds eye contact as she slowly turns the corner of her mouth into a teardrop shape and keeping the lit lung rocket pinched in her wrinkled lips, she exhales out the port on the side of her mouth, like a bandito in some Spaghetti Western. As the white plume of anxiety clears, she breaks eyes with Bernie and looks over to the trailer across from hers. The one with the red pinstripe and awnings. The one that Ruby is standing behind.

Ruby is watching this quietly too, but her—everything—is anything but quiet. Her bright, long, wavy ginger hair that's perfectly placed on either side of the deep, wide V of her kimono, screams "look at me". It's not by accident, it's always open like this, to expose her ample, purchased cleavage. It's all a performance with her, even the length of the silk wrap is planned, it's short enough to lead the eyes into trouble, but long enough to avoid an indecent exposure charge. She'd go shorter if she could, but the park would be in an uproar, so she's compensated for the hem length with the six-inch, red stilettos. It's a coy, half smile that Ruby gives Freda. A snarky smirk with her magenta-stained lips accompanied with a nod. A directional nod, not a greeting, motioning to the trailer between Freda and Bernie.

All three of the women look over to the trailer with the pink awnings and window casings. The one that Opal is now suddenly standing behind. She's appeared out of nowhere, making no sound. Opal doesn't look anywhere but forward, straight ahead to the kidney-shaped pool. Rigid. Stunned. She's soft granite, unmovable in her pink-chiffon, full-length nightgown. She doesn't look scared per-se, more so like her body is frozen and her soul is trying to escape by turning inwards. She both stands out and fades away behind her slightly smeared makeup, tousled, loose curls and blank expression.

Bernie, Freda and Ruby watch her—watch the pool. The three are fixated on her. They barely have given each other the time of day—a listless 'cheers', a nod, a smirk—but they are intensely focused on Opal, and she doesn't even seem to realize they are there.

Four women standing behind their trailers, out in the open grass of the inner ring, in the early morning sun, is nothing to cause alarm. Most people over 60 beat the sunrise every day, like they're afraid the night will take them if they stay too long. There would be nothing suspicious about this arms-length gathering if Mullet wasn't desperately trying to pull the two, waterlogged bodies up onto the pool deck. But he is and it's alarming. These four old women are just standing in silence, watching as this macabre Marco Polo plays out in front of them and they're all relatively calm. Way too calm for the circumstances, for the optics of it all, for the witnesses and Bernie knows it. They've had their moment. She's let them indulge their inner, nosey neighbor, but now it's time to move on. Bernie gives them both a look. Freda first, then Ruby. It's just a look, to anyone watching. It's nothing but a glance, but for them it holds weight. It means more than the three seconds of eye contact—it means leave now. Freda and Ruby heed the order, immediately walking back to their trailers.

Bernie can hear the inevitable. They always work this way—a raven's caw attracting more. It's the second wave of screams—the screams of sirens. They've followed her too. They've heard the cries and are racing to join in on the kill, to pick the bones clean, so she knows that it's time for her to leave as well. She knows what these scavengers will do, but Opal doesn't. Opal is stuck in a state that will take more than a look or approaching sirens to snap out of. Bernie has no choice but to leave her. There is no time to reason with Opal. No time to coddle or soothe. There are too many eyes about to descend on this violent vignette. Bernie must—and so she does. She leaves her there, out in the thick-bladed grass, staring at the pool as the siren screams are joined by the screams of surprised park residents just waking up to this horror.

Now, I could tell you what happened, but that's not what's important. What really matters right now isn't the what, the why or the when—it's the how. How always matters. How is always the unanswered question. How is the missing piece of the school shooter's manifesto. How gnaws away at detectives pouring over their cold case files and keeps relatives up at night, long after the body is found. It baffles doctors and rages inside the prayers of parents kneeling at the foot of hospital beds. It is the missing link of creation and basis of all magic. I just told you what happened—so let's move on to the how.

This wasn't how it started.

This wasn't how it was supposed to be.

Bernie should have known better—known that the deals made in fire always burn, because that bitch, the devil, never has kept her end of the bargain. That's how she does business.

A year earlier, the deal was still fresh. The ink and the blood hadn't dried. Over the palms, the sun was just coming up as Bernie drove her brand-new dark-brown 1991 Lincoln down the dusty side road. It was like all other side roads this far back from the ocean. Less kept, less traveled, lined with dry, Floridian jungle that looked like it could either eat you alive or burst into flames at any moment. It's too early to warrant a speed reduction, no cops were patrolling this stretch of road when the sun wasn't high enough for the visor. So, Bernie laid into the gas a little more as she flew past the 'cigarette ad clad' gas station and bungalow biker bar at the four-way stop.

That was the final marker.

That was the gateway to her two weeks a year. The two weeks that became four weeks and now was going to be forever. She'd driven this road a hundred times and this was the end of the gauntlet that started at the crack of dawn in Bill's country and finished here. Just beyond the crushed armadillo carcasses and scampering geckos, at the white cinderblock walls. The hand-painted, concrete blocks that spread out on either side of the entrance, like angel's wings and were the base for the sign that spanned over the entrance. The arched sign that proudly declared your arrival at Cicada Hollow Mobile Home Park.

This was supposed to be the next chapter of her life—the next story in a very long book—but it was the last chapter of it all.

As she passed under the arch, past the bronze plaque bolted to the concrete wall that warned any lost spring breakers that this was a 55+ community, she felt the cold, heavy weight of upstate New York begin to melt away.

"Wake up. We're here." Bernie gave Ruby a gentle nudge on the shoulder. She'd almost slept the entire way. Although Bernie wanted to close her fingers into a fist and give Ruby a knuckle sandwich, she felt it wouldn't start things off on the right foot, so she went with the nudge instead.

It wasn't the drive that bothered her, Bernie was used to doing the seventeen hours straight by herself—it was the selfishness. The least Ruby could have done was offer. But that's how little sisters are, selfish and safe. Always looking out for themselves and always feeling safe to do it in the vicinity of their older sibling. Safe enough to nod off for seventeen hours and not fear being tossed out on the side of the road, somewhere in the hills of Pennsylvania.

Ruby slowly batted her false lashes and wistfully raised her head off of the door, releasing a breathy moan as if she'd been stirred by Prince Charming. That's how she was, always. Didn't matter what it was, she made everything slightly provocative.

"My word…here?" Ruby asked, in a precious, distasteful way.

Bernie chose to ignore the snootiness of her sister's tone as she brought the Lincoln down to a respectable five miles an hour, passing under the archway. That's the point where the dusty road changes into deep-black asphalt. Where the county meets private, and the road is painted with bright-yellow lines and authoritative commands. Arrows, speed limits and direction of flow, all ordering you into an enforced turtle's pace that only goes one way. Bernie was never one for rules, other than her own, but something about the park has always had her toeing the line. Wanting to mix in. Here she could be one of them, fade away into the cribbage boards, and the shuffleboards—and be bored. All she had to do was obey the signs. For a couple of weeks a year, it was a

BONE PARK

small sacrifice to make for sun-kissed skin, 24-7 happy hour and zero headaches.

Bernie obeyed the yellow lines, like she always did, following the road flanked with clusters of stubby palms into the community. This was the first time she'd come here in the Lincoln. It was a retirement gift, a little too flashy for her, but it was comfortable, and she knew it would send a buzz through the cackling crones at the canasta tables. A little buzz wasn't bad, it was the low wattage current that kept the park alive.

Bernie cruised slowly through the tiny streets of Cicada Hollow, taking Ruby on the scenic route, populated by permanently placed, 1960s' corrugated-metal mobile homes. It was a self-contained small town made of single wide trailers. They were all tightly packed together, perched perpendicular to the road, with manicured rough-grass lawns, large-screened lanai, open carports and frosted-glass louvered windows. A 'Pleasantville' of retirement, where the homes only vary slightly in awning choice, accent colors and whether or not the mailbox was 'stand-alone' or a 'light post combo' with hanging baskets.

After weaving through the quiet, one-way streets, passing a smattering of 'wake walkers' and the two elderly marathoners in the park—that were possibly running their last mile—ever, Bernie pulled into a driveway. It was short driveway. Just a slab of cement really, from the road to a yellow carport. A yellow carport that was attached to a white trailer with a matching yellow stripe. Bernie parked the Lincoln and within seconds of the car turning off, she was already getting out. Out, into the warm, humid, southern air. This air, the heat mixed with the faint fragrance of citrus trees and salt water, was her lost fountain. She had been stuck in the same position for the last seventeen hours, but one breath of this elixir and she was Ponce De Leon, erasing the aches and pains and the fact that she was now 60 years young.

Bernie stretched her long arms above her head—she could almost touch the ceiling of the carport. She had always stood out because of her height. She was easy to find in a crowd and worse, when she wished she could fade away. It was both her power and her curse. Besides being a target for jokes, it had become the epicenter of most of the pain that circled around her body for most of her life. But it was something she learned to deal with and use to her advantage. Something that didn't do well with being sedentary, so extending all of her 6'2" stature was essential to letting go of the thousand miles that had wrapped themselves around her joints.

She was an anomaly. Not only because she was a tall woman, but now, because she was a tall, elderly woman. Folks shrink with age, it's just a fact. Some even turn into the letter C under the pull of gravity or the weight of their sins, but she'd managed to stay upright. Only losing a few notches on the wall, making her tower even more over her elderly peers. She hated that word—elderly. It conjured up images of caskets and uselessness in her head, but like it or not, she was now part of that club. Forced into the guillotine of retirement early. She loved the way it had been—her life before the axe. How she could visit the park, a few weeks a year, pop in and pop out like a guest star, with another gig waiting in the wings. She had somewhere she was needed. It was rest, not retirement. She'd never admit it, but that made her feel superior to the rest of the residents here, because she was there by choice, not by classification. There were certainly worse places to be than the sun and serenity of Cicada Hollow. There were nightmares all across the USA, that retirees were dropped off at by their ne'er-do-well, ungrateful children. Prisons of pudding and chair aerobics that made hell look inviting. Bernie knew this was the golden ticket of the golden years, but this time was going to be a stretch. The park was doable when the dollars were rolling in, but now she was going to have to dig up all the nuts she had been able to squirrel away just to make ends meet. If she could make ends meet.

Ruby got out of the passenger side, opened the back door of the car and begun filling her arms with garbage bags of clothing. Bernie paid her sister's huffing and puffing no mind, grabbing her purse from between the front seats and walking away from the car, deeper into the carport, towards the small shed at the back.

"Bernie?! Aren't you going to help?" Ruby asked her, with that arcing whine that little sisters add to all their accusatory questions.

BONE PARK

"I believe you can handle it," Bernie said without an ounce of concern.

"Fine. What about your stuff? Is it in the trunk? If it is, I'm not helping you."

Bernie shook her head, then turned to a side door on the trailer.

"You didn't bring anything?"

"No, I didn't. Not a thing, Poob. Everything I need is right here," Bernie said, pulling out a ring of keys from her well-worn purse. She rifled through the dangling collection of copper, stopping on the one that had the bright, Florida-orange nail polish on it. She held the key up for a moment, thinking of all the times she'd opened this door, all the times she'd locked it and all the time spent back home yearning to return. Well, she'd returned, but not how she'd planned. She'd arrived empty-handed, with her sister in tow and something inside her was screaming that she would never lock it again.

The door opened up into a thin hallway lined with thin pressed-wood paneling, that was just big enough for one body at a time. Bernie turned to her right, heading for the small pocket door on the left, passing the odds and sods that were hung on the walls. They were the usual senior suspects, some religious symbols, a decorative barometer and a horrible velvet painting of a sad clown. These weren't Bernie's decorations; they came with the trailer. Most of the trailers here were sold furnished. Turnkey retirement with each new owner adding their own tchotchke to their tin can caskets. That's what these were—caskets. All the Hummels that were curated over the years, the commemorative plates, dolls and needlepoint, were for not. These trailers were generally sold furnished because most of the time the owners had died and their money-grubbing offspring wanted the cash, not the memories.

Bernie clicked on the switch inside of the pocket door. A duo of glass-tulip shades came to life, lighting up the Formica vanity with the haunting orange glow of forty-watt bulbs. She paused for a moment, scanning the tiny bathroom plastered in yellow wallpaper with silver cherubs. She looked around with contempt, as if someone might have been hiding in the nook with the white, wicker shelves or in the yellow tub-shower. When she was finally satisfied that she was alone in this topaz shoebox, she moved over to the tub's fraternal twin, the matching sunflower-colored toilet. Bernie stood in front of the dated 60s' commode—complete with a yellow shag lid-cover—and reached down for the three, off-brand Barbie dolls that stood on the back of the tank. Each of these dolls wore a handmade crocheted gown and were a staple in any respectable retiree's bathroom. Hot items among the Pepsodent People, they sold out at every Cicada Hollow craft fair. These import Barbies held a terrifying secret under their skirts—spare toilet paper rolls—because heaven forbid someone should find your extra rolls exposed.

Bernie lifted the shiny-skinned middle doll, that still held on to the sweet smell of the processed plastic it was made of, revealing what lay underneath. This cringe-worthy craft wasn't hiding the embarrassment of a roll of butt wipes, instead she was smuggling a large tin can underneath her bustle. Bernie looked back, over her shoulder towards the bathroom door, then opened her purse and pulled out a shiny stubby-barreled Ruger revolver. She set it into the tin can, handle up and quickly replaced the Polyethylene Princess over top of it. With her small hand cannon now safely stowed away, she then turned, undid her relaxed slacks and squatted down to do what most normal 'non gun smuggling' travelers do after a very long, road trip.

There really is nothing quite like that kind of relief. Sure, women are experts at holding it. Some can rock an entire concert, beers and all, without breaking the seal, but they usually suffer the cranberry curse for it. And that's different. Standing up and sitting down are different feats of strength. This was a long haul that was long overdue. The kind that sent shivers up her spine and made her head dizzy, as all of it tried to get off the ride at the same time, out through the poorly designed exit. It was exacerbated—the holding, not the release—by the rotating hot flashes and constant bubble gut that hadn't disappeared like her period did.

"Screw me? Screw you!" That familiar bellow, coming from outside, forced Bernie to push, bossing her bladder into pressure washer power.

Couldn't she have a moment of peace? Whatever was going on, all she needed was a few more seconds. A few more moments—

"Blow it out your ass, you dried up hag!" That was definitely Ruby.

"I'm going to call the police!" a very different voice shouted. A shriller one that immediately changed the look on Bernie's reddening face, forcing her to cut off the road relief in mid-stream and run out of the bathroom, while trying to hoist her sensible trousers up.

"You don't live here!" the shrill voice accused as Bernie burst out of the side door, looping the clasp on her waistband.

"Ruby?" Bernie was already on the offense before even seeing what was playing out beyond the carport.

Ruby had her hands on her hips, with an indignant S curve to her silhouette, standing at the edge of the road. She was facing an angry, finger-waving woman, wearing a skirted, one-piece swimsuit with a matching husband accessory.

The woman was surprised. "Bernie? You are here. But this isn't your car? This isn't the usual time."

"The car's new. A retirement gift. I came early."

"Retirement? Well, that explains it, congratu—"

Bernie cut her off, focused on Ruby. "What did you do?"

"I didn't do anything," Ruby huffed.

The woman snapped, "The hell you didn't…hussy—"

"Hussy?!" Ruby's hands raised off her hips and her posture straightened quickly, going from pissed off pinup to Rocky Balboa.

Bernie got between Ruby and the woman. "Connie, this is my little sister."

"Your sister?" This was a huge shock to this righteous resident. "I didn't know you had a sister."

"I do. This is her...Ruby."

"The black sheep I take it? You need to keep her on a leash. She practically propositioned Merle right here—"

"I did no such thing! Bernie, all I did was say hello and that I liked his swimming trunks." Ruby's attempt at feigning innocence was calculated, coy and insulting.

Merle said nothing, but his slightly nodding head was placing his impotent allegiance with Ruby. Connie was having none of it, which she accented with a swift slap to his bare sunburned curly white-haired chest.

"She said, and I quote, 'Hey hot stuff, you're going to need more material than that, to hide that concealed weapon'." Connie was irate, but behind her, Merle looked pretty proud of himself, like he'd just gotten a second shot of self-esteem.

It was ridiculous. Humorous even. The absurdity of cat-calling this sheepish man wasn't wasted on Bernie, but it was not the right place or the right time. "Ruby? We just got here," she said, fighting back both her smirk and her sneer.

"It was a joke," Ruby scoffed, deflating Merle's newfound flex.

Bernie's eyes went cold. Dark. Staring right into Ruby's. Nothing was said out loud, but whatever was sent silently, across the empty space between the two of them, had Ruby stepping backwards, dropping her shoulders and lowering her gaze.

"I'm sorry. I didn't mean to upset you," Ruby said to Connie with the sheepish sincerity of an apprehended, adolescent vandal.

"Well, thank you," Connie said, getting off of her heels. "I accept your apology. If it was a joke, then I accept it. It was crude, but you weren't entirely wrong. Merle keeps insisting on wearing those tennis shorts, even though they only fit him for one summer in '78. He thinks they make him look like some kind of John McEnroe. It's indecent." Connie turned to Merle again, giving him another slap. "See what you and those shorts have caused. Go back and change. And don't you dare put those back into the drawer…they go straight into the garbage."

Merle slowly turned and started walking away from the three women. He had no control over the wiggling of his 'tiny hiney' in those tiny shorts or the last strips of his dignity that he dragged behind him.

"I'll meet you at the pool," Connie shouted at him, then turned back to Ruby and Bernie. "Glad you've returned Bernie, you were missed. And Ruby…it's a shame we got off on the wrong foot. We here pride ourselves on our hospitality and kindness so let's start over. Let me be the first to welcome you to Cicada Hollow." Connie dug into her straw beach bag, pulled out an oversized pair of sunglasses and put them on in front of the sisters, as part of her 'Jackie O' exit. "Looking forward to you fitting in to our little slice of heaven."

Even though Ruby wanted to slap those cheap Walgreens' sun worshipers right off Connie's face in pure 'Dynasty" fashion, Ruby said nothing and the sisters let the henpecker strut away in the glow of her false victory.

"You can't do that here," Bernie said as Connie disappeared between two single wides, heading towards the pool.

"Do what?"

"I brought you here, because you said you wanted to get away. Just like me. I've left it all behind and that's what you're going to do."

"Leave what behind? I was just being friendly."

"Your friendly is most women's home run. You need to put a lid on it. Men are scarce around the Hollow. After slaving their whole lives, most die within the first few years of finally getting here. So, the women that still have their husbands, guard them like gold. I have managed to come down here for the last five years without incident and I don't plan on changing that. You are my guest here, so you will respect my wishes. You will fall in line and act like the others do. Or you can find…" Bernie stopped herself. Catching the next words coming out of her mouth, like fragile plates falling from a tray.

Ruby didn't need to hear them to know what they were. She paused for a moment then spoke up with an aching mixture of shame and anger. "Find what? With what? You know I'm not here because I wanted a vacation. That may be what you'll tell all your Ben Gay buddies, but that's not the truth. I've got nowhere else to go, Bern. I've got no one left but you. Everything I own is in your fancy car, that's not even that fancy. I used to have two Lincolns and a Porsche. Now all I have are those garbage bags and you telling me how to act as if I'm some kind of child. I may be down, but I'm not out. Tell the truth, you love this, don't you. Having me under your thumb finally. Falling into your line. Your little sister, under your rules."

"Yoo-hoo?!" the Heidi-esque call broke the tension and the frustrated tears building in Ruby's eyes.

The voice was coming from down the lane, a little further around the inner circle made of pristine, black asphalt. It was a little voice coming from the little woman standing silently out front of the trailer with the pink pinstripe and window casings, who was dressed head to toe in pink and was waving at Bernie.

"Bernie! Welcome back!" the woman called out, in her soft, faint voice, that conjured up images of angels and fluffy clouds.

"Glad to be back, Opal. This is my sister, Ruby!"

Ruby reluctantly raised her arm and waved back with the lackluster enthusiasm of a bronze medal athlete. "Hello…I…uh…love your pink visor."

Even from down the road, they could see Opal blush with the compliment, lowering her waving arm and recoiling with sheepish modesty.

BONE PARK

Bernie smiled at Opal as she whispered to Ruby, "That's the ticket. I guess you do know how to blend in." She then raised her voice and her arm, waving back to Opal, "We'll catch up later, okay Opal? We're pretty zonked and have a lot of unpacking to do."

Opal nodded with apologetic enthusiasm and went back into her tiny, tin trailer.

With no further discussion being entertained, Bernie went back into her trailer too. She left her still seething sister at the end of the driveway, contemplating what was left of her life. The life that was jammed into plastic bags and was stuffed in the back of the Lincoln. The Lincoln, that for your information, she used to have two of.

The layout of the trailer was simple, bow to stern; front bedroom, open sitting room to open kitchen, tiny hall down the right side of the kitchen that held the bathroom and lead to the master bedroom at the back. The sides of the trailer—one with the carport on it and the other with the large, screened-in lanai—were technically the front and back, but the park's orientation of these mid-century masterpieces, was always long ways. The trailers fit better this way, took up less frontage side by each, so that's how they sat. Modern, movable versions of the southern, shotgun shack. They were the perfect size for an elderly couple or a couple of sisters who were struggling with becoming elderly.

Bernie gave Ruby the front bedroom. It was smaller, had almost no closet space, but the bed was more comfortable. It's where Bernie usually slept when she came down and was one of the main reasons she couldn't wait to come back. It was the only bed she'd slept in, over the last twenty years, that didn't hurt her back. She dreamt about this bed when she was in Buffalo, sitting up through sleepless night, soothing her back and her worries with ever increasing amounts of tequila. That bed was her sarcophagus, her crypt of rejuvenation, that was crucial to her recharging, but she gave it to Ruby. That's Bernie—that's who she was. She cared more about family than anything else. About making them—

comfortable.

    Ruby had passed out long ago, disappearing under the flowered-print, quilted covers of the comfortable bed and Bernie was still awake. She was folded into the sand-colored La-Z-Boy in the main room. The one on the left. The one with the high back, and large, doughy armrests. Not the smaller one, beside the door to the lanai—the one by the couch. It was the one sold with a masculine gender attached to it, so men who fell asleep in it at three in the afternoon would feel virile. Between it and the couch was an octagon-shaped, faux-wood side table, that had ornate moldings on the two hinged front doors. It was late. The TV that backed onto the wall of Ruby's room, that was housed in a massive, wood cabinet for no functional reason, was on. It was playing a technicolored rerun of The Lawrence Welk Show. The bubbles floated by on the television screen and Norma Zimmer sang a striking rendition of Moon River, but Bernie missed it all. Her attention wasn't on the TV. It was focused on the soft-yellow telephone, sitting on top of the side table. She sat there in the blue flickering light of the big band broadcast, looking at the long, éclair-shaped phone with its two halves connected by a curly cord. She wasn't ready for the wireless one yet. Didn't like the look of the long aerials, thought they looked like some kind of army-surplus rejects. She didn't trust the privacy of her conversations traveling through the open air without the accompanying encoding of an enigma cipher. There were a lot of things that Bernie didn't trust anymore.

    She tutted, disappointed in herself and sat up a little straighter. Lifting the yellow receiver off its identical base, the square-white numbers on it weren't totally blurry, but blurry enough for her to make a mistake. Blurry enough for her to have to apologize to some stranger who shouted, 'Wrong number' at her, so she went for the cheaters. For years Bernie's eyes had been going and for the most part, she could fake it. She ate lunch at the same diner where she had the menu practically memorized, didn't look at paperwork in front of co-workers whenever possible. She even resorted to swearing at her computer, complaining that it was glitching, every time someone was waiting for the information that was on her screen. She saw needing glasses as a weakness. Another sign that the mileage on her motor was too high for resale. That she had gotten too old to be respected.

Right then though, in the safety of her trailer, she was alone. She was a thousand miles away from prying eyes and the need for excuses, so she put the footrest down on the La-Z-Boy. She opened the doors of the side table and pulled out a bright-orange pair of number two magnifiers. Twos were perfect for this kind of work—threes were too much, and ones still left room for error. As soon as she put them on, the white squares with black numbers on them shifted into clarity. She looked good in glasses. Smart. Attractive—she just didn't have anyone to tell her that.

Bernie punched in a methodical order of numbers. She wasn't calling anywhere local, the amount of long tones coming from the receiver attested to that. As she hit the last number, she took a very deep breath—the kind you take before asking for a raise or forgiveness. She held it in as the sound of ringing came out of the tiny cluster of holes in the phone.

The ringing came to an abrupt stop. "Yeah?!" a gruff man's voice snapped on the other end. "Who the hell is this?"

Bernie realized she was holding her breath and quickly let it out, followed by a throat-clearing swallow. "Hi…can I speak to Marcie please?"

"Who's this?"

This question or the way in which it was blurted out, took Bernie a second to process. "It's…Bernie."

"Who?"

"Verna," she corrected herself. "Is Marcie there?"

The pauses suddenly belonged to the other end. There was a lot of heavy breathing and what sounded like stalling, surrounded by faint ums and ahs.

"Yeah, uh…Verna? It's late. She's busy putting the kids down."

"Yes, that's why I called. I was hoping to—"

"It's late. I'll tell her you called." The dial tone that sharply followed his gruff words, removed any room for negotiations.

Bernie slowly pulled the receiver from her ear. She took off her glasses, put them back in the side table and laid the receiver down onto her lap, letting its haunting drone of disconnection fill the room.

She woke up in the La-Z-Boy. Not so much woke, but startled by the bronze-skinned, silver-haired evangelical that was screaming at her from the TV about debauchery and vice. Bernie dove into the latter last night after the call. Was this divine intervention? She felt like this false prophet was speaking right to her. Judging her. Condemning her. But there was no need to yell at her, dunk her in the witches' well or tie her to the stake because her piss-holes for eyes, mung-matted lips and empty highballs on the side table, had already confessed.

Sunshine came in hot and bright in New Smyrna. Not like the 'ol sol's slow rise in Buffalo. If you weren't getting shade or air conditioning by 11:00am, you were regretting your choices. Bernie was definitely questioning hers. The analog hands of the clock hanging beside the door to the lanai said it was nearly 9:00am—almost a whole day gone, in retired time.

Bernie peeled her sleep-sweat-soaked body from the plush chair and did her best to stand up. Even hunched over under the weight of a few tequila sunrises, she was tall. She looked over to the door of Ruby's room. It was still closed. She nodded a little, soothing herself, reassuring herself that all was okay. Not being able to see the completely flattened back of her permed head yet, she believed she could clean herself and this mess up before anyone was the wiser. Older sisters have an image to uphold, even older-older sisters. If their flaws are left on display, they could lose credibility and then would have nothing to hold over their underlings. Bernie had secrets and she liked to keep it that way. So, she hid her footsteps in the long piling of the carpet, shuffling her way to the bathroom, where she planned on secretly repairing the damage she'd done.

Looking into the triptych mirrored panels on the medicine cabinet, it was obvious that a face towel and some mouthwash weren't going to cut it. She was bearing witness to the deflated balloon that her face had turned into and the full glory of her headboard halo—the flat back of her head that looked like she had been hit by a serving tray. Her tiny, blue-hued curls were all matted and mangled. The brush kept getting stuck in it, pulling at the tight Shirley Temple's with every painful yank. After trying every variation of brush she could find in the drawers, she left the yellow-porcelain paradise and headed for the less reflective walls of the master bedroom.

She grabbed the first thing she saw, on the top rack of her closet. It was a foam-front baseball hat she'd won at the last shuffleboard tournament. It was an off-color hat. Bright yellow and across the front of it were the letters F.B.I. and under those letters were the words, "Female Body Inspector". This was the kind of souvenir that the office loudmouth wore with his favorite apron. The one that had a print of a naked woman's body on it—that he kept fondling, making homophobic and sexist jokes about, evoking uncomfortable laughter from his colleagues at the summer barbeque. It was the kind of hat you'd see at a gas station and wonder who the hell would ever wear one of those. Bernie thought that too when she won it. She wanted nothing to do with it, but didn't want to be rude, so she took it and stuck it in the back of the closet. The hat was tasteless, but it didn't pull her hair like the brush, and she was staying close to home, so it would do.

Bernie collected her shame from the side table and shuffled her way back into the kitchen to put her armful of dirty glasses into the sink. It was an open U-shaped kitchen, with sink and cupboards on the left wall that the lanai was on, stove and cupboards on the back wall and fridge and cupboards on the carport side. Bernie hand washed all the glasses and set them in the drying rack. It was a simple task, but not today. Her thoughts were scattered, foggy. There were flashes of last night. Strobes of moments she wished weren't real. That she wished were rare. Bernie could feel the plush, toilet cover under her butt and the back of her legs. She could see the gun, in her hands. The stubby Ruger. She could taste the metal of the barrel mixed with the salt of her tears. She could feel the tendons of her neck straining as she silenced her cry. She could sense the courage she was trying to muster, the thumb she was trying to convince to pull away from her. To put an end to all this pain. But they were just memories. Reminders of last night. Another night she didn't go through with it, leaving her with another day to make it through.

She knew it wasn't a good idea in the long run, but it was the only idea she had, so she opened the upper cupboard by the sink. She pulled down a tall, dry, sunflower-print highball glass and proceeded to go through the ritual. The ritual that led her here. Ice, then grenadine—heavy on the grenadine, until it caresses the top of the three large cubes—then tequila. The offering of the agave was measured by the fist she placed beside the glass, then topped with just enough orange juice to color it. To make it look morning friendly. This was not what she needed, but it would stop the thumping of her head, the flashes, steady her hands and get her through the next hour or so—and that's all she could do.

There was a laugh.

A loud laugh.

The kind that golden-age Hollywood starlets made in black and white. The fluttering sounds of flirting scenes shown on fifty-foot screens. Bernie ran, as best as her thick, hungover legs could, to the front bedroom where Ruby was sleeping. She opened the door, and her hunch became worry and that worry became real.

There was that laugh again. That Jane Mansfield' laugh, but now Bernie knew that was no Jane—it was Ruby.

The thin, metal door to the lanai, that rattled and twisted a little when it opened normally, nearly flew off its hinges as Bernie shot out of the trailer. She was on a mission. Following the sound of that put-on laughter, determined to put an end to whatever Ruby had started. She

BONE PARK

didn't have to travel far out into the hot sun, only fifty feet or so across the course grass of the inner circle, before she found her. Her little sister, sitting on one of the covered benches on the shuffleboard courts, surrounded by four, silver foxes. Truthfully, they weren't foxes, more like chicken hawks with bypass scars, knee high socks and sandals.

Bernie slowed her charge. What had gotten into her sister, she wondered. She thought they had an understanding, one made very clear in the driveway yesterday. It had been a long time since the two of them had been together, but could her sister have changed that much? Had she become that disrespectful, to just disregard her wishes, even when she had no alternative—no one to support her but Bernie?

As Bernie got closer to the commotion, it began to look different. Yes, Ruby was laughing. Loud and big and fake, but it wasn't flirting. Not any kind of flirting that Bernie had ever seen her do before. Something was wrong. Off. Ruby didn't look like she was holding court, feeding her ego like Bernie had thought—she appeared to be trying to placate these men. These wrinkly-skinned sharks that were circling her as if she were chum. Everything about Ruby's body language, tone and dismissals of their advances was saying "I'll be on my way now", but the men were playing deaf.

This wasn't like Ruby. Men were Ruby's specialty. She had their number. All of them. She could work the best of them and barely break a sweat, so what was this? Bernie had never seen her like this before. Ruby looked genuinely scared, confused even, but why?

Ruby was able to catch a glimpse of Bernie between the Hawaiian shirts of two of the men. Her eyes were pleading, there was even a little shake to her head. That's when it hit Bernie. What was actually going on here. Ruby wasn't in a pickle she couldn't get out of; she was in a pickle that she promised she wouldn't get out of. She was laying low, rolling over and playing dead. Doing what Bernie told her to do. The fear in Ruby's eyes, in the shaking of her head, wasn't about the men, it was about Bernie. It was the fear of upsetting her sister and being put out on the curb.

"Harold! Fred! Stan? I see you've met my sister!" Bernie shouted loud and clear so that there was no room for confusion.

The men turned around, startled.

"Merle? Is that you? I thought you'd already met yesterday." Bernie flew into the scrum, with her fresh tequila sunrise in hand, wedging her way into the middle, creating a little room for her sister to stand up finally.

Merle started to stutter, "Yes, that's true, Verna. I was just introducing her to the others."

"Is that so. Well, it looks like you've all met now. So that's that. We should be going. The board rules are strict about loitering on the courts. Don't want my sister to get into any trouble."

The largest man of the group, the only one that had any presence to him, Stan, piped up, "Oh relax Bernie, we were just being neighborly."

"Well thanks for that, Stan. Nice to have nice neighbors. But we really should be going—we have big plans today." While she was talking, Bernie was able to create an opening in the group for Ruby to slip out of.

Once she was saw that Ruby was free, she immediately stopped talking and left the presence of these predators, following her sister back towards the trailer.

"I look forward to getting to know you, Ruby," Stan said with a lecherous laugh, but the sisters kept on walking.

"Verna!" The call of Connie's macaw-sounding voice, bounced off the backs of the trailers, tearing through Bernie's hungover eardrums.

"You go back to the trailer," Bernie instructed Ruby, before turning back to cut off Connie, who was practically frothing.

"What in the Lord's name does you sister think she's doing?"

BONE PARK

"What seems to be the problem, Connie?"

"Seems? Nothing seems—it is! I see what's she's up to. We all saw it from the pool deck. Quite the spectacle she is. Throwing herself on my husband, on Opal's husband, on Maryanne's and Cecilia's too?"

Bernie stopped moving. She pulled the brim of her hat down low, over her eyebrows and dropped her chin, angling her face to better suit the stunted height of her charging assailant. Cool as a cucumber, she slowly raised her dewy, highball to her lips while she waited for Connie, whose short, stubby legs took a lot of moving to make up the distance. Bernie proceeded to take a long, refreshing drink, swallowing gulp after gulp of her orange-colored medication, until the cubes fell down against her teeth.

Connie slowed her pace, but not her mouth, unable to run both at the same time. "If you don't get that woman under control, I will be forced to file a complaint with the park board and have her removed!"

Bernie pulled the rim of her sunflower glass away from her lips and lowered it down by her side but said nothing.

Connie's nostrils were in full flare, starving for oxygen and perplexed by Bernie's silence. "Well, what are you going to do about it?!"

Bernie didn't break a word or a sweat. Didn't part her lips so much as a hair, she just stared at Connie from under the brim of her offensive hat.

"Verna?!" Connie did not like this silence, so she kept trudging her tubular torso towards her, pecking at Bernie with question marks. "What are you going to do? How long does she plan on visiting you? There is a limit to visitor stays you know. How old is she anyway? Do I need to remind you that this is a 55+ community? Do we need to get the board involved?" Connie reached Bernie, standing almost toe to toe with the geriatric giant looking down on her.

The two women stood there facing each other, between the

shuffleboard courts and the back of Bernie's trailer, out in the open St. Augustine grass of the inner ring.

"Verna? Are you just going to stand there or—"

As fast as the snap of a slingshot strap, Bernie's right hand swung upwards, smashing her sunflower glass against Connie's left temple.

Connie's legs went instantly weak, but Bernie had already swooped her left hand around Connie's back to hold her upright. It was all lightning fast. Even before the blood knew what happened, Bernie had moved Connie's left hand up to cover the new gash beside her eye.

Bernie pulled Connie in close, into a pseudo-sapphic tango, "I suggest you keep your hand over that. Lots of pressure or you'll cause a scene and trust me, you do not want to cause a scene."

"You attacked me—"

"Shut up!" Bernie spoke in soft, fast, dominant blasts. "You shut your gob—for once in your life—and listen. You're lucky that's all I did—or my sister did for that matter. Your husband is a limp-dick, spineless 'yes man'. If you want to yell at anyone, you yell at him. He went along with the other dried-up testicles who cornered my sister and made her feel very afraid. We should be the ones calling the police or telling the board, but that's not how we handle our affairs. The Hewton girls handle them like this. That glass was just a taste of what we're capable of. No more questions, no more yelling, no more nice. You are going to leave my sister alone and are not going to bother me or her ever again. You're not going to call the police or go to the board. And you most certainly will not tell all the little hens who are watching us right now from the pool. That gash above your eye—it's your fault. Your husband's fault and your mouths. You are going to say you fell. In your house, all alone. Because Connie, I am not who you think I am. I am far worse than you could ever imagine. That little red tear in your skin is to remind you that if you say anything, to anyone, I will kill you and your ball-less husband and mail your body parts back to your grandkids."

Connie wasn't just at a loss for words, she was absolutely fear stricken. Stiff in the sudden realization that this quiet woman was not who she thought she was. Frozen in the seriousness of Bernie's unwavering stare. This was far beyond some "Murder She Wrote" plot or "Matlock" season finale.

Stan, Merle, Fred and Harold, who had moved on to playing shuffleboard, were looking over at them. The odd sight of two women locked in an odd hug out in the open.

A very concerned Merle called out, "Connie? Everything alright?"

Before she could answer, Bernie shouted back to him, over Connie's shoulder, "She's fine Merle. Aren't we girls allowed to have our secrets?"

Merle looked confused. "I guess so…as long as it's not about me."

Bernie whispered to Connie, "Tell him to bugger off, or I'll slit your fucking throat right here."

"Bugger off, Merle!" Connie shouted, channeling the terror that had consumed her.

Merle may not have listened to Bernie, but his wife's instructions had him spinning on his heels and putting his attention back on the clay pucks that were sliding across the court.

Bernie tightened her grip around Connie. "That's what I'm talking about. You take instructions very well. That's good, because here are some more. Tonight, you are going to have sex with your husband. Trust me, I understand, I don't find him attractive either, but you married him, and he is very obviously in search of affection, so you're going to take one for your team. A little charity and punishment mixed together. That'll put a spring in his step and make what comes after a lot easier."

Connie stuttered, "What comes after?"

"Glad you asked. After you consummate your long-lost nuptials, you are going to tell your husband that you want to leave Cicada Hollow. That you miss the grandkids and want to go home. But not someday or after this season. Immediately. Do you understand?"

Connie froze, sullen and silent in the shock of being face to face with a maniac and trying to process all her demands.

"Connie!" Bernie's bark snapped her out of it. "Do you understand?"

Connie nodded and Bernie released the hold she had on the frightened woman's waist.

"Best that you go clean yourself up." Bernie stepped back from Connie, who saw her chance to escape and started to walk quickly away from her.

Bernie slowly bent down and picked up the pieces of her glass that were laying in the grass as she watched Connie speed walk away between the trailers. Mid-stride, Connie looked back. She had the fear in her. That's what fear does. It has you hearing footsteps behind you and feeling eyes on you. Connie was relieved to see that Bernie wasn't chasing her. Bernie could see the relief in her face, so she stood up quickly, spooking her and Connie quickened her stride.

As Connie reached the road, Bernie waved to her with her hand full of glass, calling out with the bright, well-wishes of Mr. Rogers, "Bye Connie. Have fun tonight!"

The metal screen door to the trailer opened and Bernie slowly stepped in.

"Damnit!" she shouted, skipping her back leg forward as if she'd been bit by something. "Goddamn screen door!" She looked down to the bare backside of her heel. There was a fresh strip of skin missing from it.

"It's the spring," Ruby said, standing by the sink. "It's too strong. Just take it off, or it'll keep doing it."

"I know it's the spring," Bernie snapped back. "But if I take the spring off, the door will stay open, and the no-see-ums will get in."

"I'm sorry," Ruby said quickly.

"It's okay. How could you know. You're not used to living down here. Those no-see-ums are no joke. Tiny little bloodthirsty bugs. Hand to heart, an ankle-biting door is well worth keeping them out."

"No, not that. I'm sorry about what happened out there. With those men."

Bernie took her attention off her heel and put it on her sister, who was now glassy-eyed. "Oh, Poob. You have nothing to be sorry about. I'm sorry. If I hadn't have come down on you, I know you would have taken care of them in a snap. You'd have never let them corner you like that."

"I just didn't want you to be mad."

"I'm not. Well, I'm mad at myself, but not you." Bernie walked over and put the broken pieces of glass into the trash bin under the sink.

"You broke your glass?" Ruby asked.

"Yeah, dropped it when Connie came in hot."

"My word, that woman was out for blood."

"Connie? No. She's all hiss, but no scratch. Nothing for you to worry about. She won't be a problem."

Ruby searched Bernie's face for the truth that seemed to be missing in her words, but Bernie just walked past her and down the hall to the bathroom. "I need a band-aid."

Ruby moved over and looked out through tiny window on the carport side of the trailer. Pulling back the scalloped bottom sheers that covered it. She could see Connie way down the road, walking quickly and holding her head.

"Hey, Poob?!" Bernie called from the bathroom.

"Yes," Ruby responded still watching Connie out the window.

"What do you say we head to the ocean?"

"The ocean? Why? The pool is right there." Ruby quickly turned away from the window as Bernie emerged from the bathroom.

"You don't come to Florida for the pools, Poob," Bernie said with a wink, taking the key ring off a hook on the wall beside the carport door. "No point in wasting a parade on these old prunes. A woman in her prime like you, should be allowed to strut and there is no better place to strut, than the beach."

Endless miles of beach stretched out in front of the Buffalo Girls. They walked along the edge of the undulating ocean, letting their toes kiss the dying waves as they judged and were judged by the spectators up on softer sand. Ruby proudly promoted herself in a high-hip, low-necked, one piece, while Bernie happily played second fiddle, covering her suit in a knee-length muumuu and 'clear plastic brimmed' visor. There were the occasional wolf whistles, that came from anonymous lips up on the patchwork of blankets that covered the busy beach like a quilt. Ruby enjoyed the trills of validation and Bernie let her. She couldn't remember how long it had been since the two of them had spent this much time together. A day and a bit was not long, but it was a record for recent years. When was the last time they were together long enough to pass the catch-up conversations and move on to silence? When was the last time they were anywhere together and when was the last time they were somewhere together that required swimsuits?

It had to have been back in high school. Before Gary. Before bright lights and VHS. It was probably on that trip to Canada. That first rap on their sheets. Bernie was just 18. Stole the funeral director's hearse to get them to Wasaga Beach. They didn't have a love of the macabre, the hearse was picked by elimination. The long vehicle was one of the only cars in town that wasn't under the constant watchful eye of its owner, so it was easy pickings to get them to the beaches of their northern neighbors. That was back when the two of them were thick as thieves. Their first trip after the war, when things had started to feel normal again. It was the trip where Ruby lost her virginity at 13 and Bernie met Sal. Two of the biggest mistakes of their lives were made on those sandy shores, so what was this? What was going to happen this time, on these shores?

The fond memories of the road trip to Wasaga quickly faded under the heavier consequences that followed it. Slipped under pressure of pummeling Connie. Bernie sighed. She was great at keeping her cool—outside ice, while inside was burning—but her deep sighs were her tell. Her nostril thrusts were the signal, the miniscule opening in her armor that her sister could pierce.

"He recognized me," Ruby said softly, still looking forward.

"Who did?" Bernie inquired, calmly.

"Stan...I believe that's what his name is...Stan?"

"That's Opal's husband. Make sure you keep your distance from him. Not because of Opal, she's a church mouse, but because of him. He has that corner energy."

"He does. Reminds me of the guys outside of Sal's place."

"Exactly. A blowhard. Blowhards are dangerous because they need to be seen. Stay away from him."

"Oh, I will. I just wanted you to know."

"Did any of the others recognize you?"

Ruby thought for a second. Going over the elderly men's eyes in her mind. Skimming over the looks they gave her. Most of their gazes were shifty. Nervous, like boys at the edge of the dance floor, not pointed like Stan's.

"I don't think so."

"Good. Then you've still got deniability."

"Do we?"

Bernie looked to her, taken off guard. "We? What's that supposed to mean?"

Ruby paused, silent for two of their slow beach steps, then answered, "Nothing, just don't want the entire park gossiping."

"That's impossible. They gossip about everything, but they won't be gossiping about you." Bernie turned and looked to her right, pointing up to the hotel behind the beached sunbathers. "That place has a great tiki bar by the pool. Let's get a drink. My head's killing me." Bernie wasn't really asking, she was telling and deflecting at the same time. She started walking away from the water, heading for the soft-pink hotel towers, behind the six-foot cement seawall.

Ruby followed and as they hit the transition from hard, wet sand to soft, white grains, they both began to hoot and hop uncontrollably. It was an instinctual, ankle-twisting, hot-sand dance, done by all tourists on all sun-scorched, rippled beaches everywhere. The events of the day were suddenly gone along with the pauses and silence. They were kids again, running up the hot sands of Wasaga, before the bad happened. When they were still carefree and belonged to no one. They were holding onto each other for balance and support, laughing, instantly erasing their age and the tension that followed them here.

The saltwater-softened wood of the outdoor tiki bar was covered with a sticky mix of spilled cocktails, sand and paper wristbands. Bernie liked sitting at the bar. At every bar. She liked the banter with the

BONE PARK

bartenders, the random people that bellied up to it and the 'fly on the wall' of it all. Ruby liked it too. It was a place she was very familiar with. A place her back was usually against. It was a place that many lips had leaned into, to whisper in her ear and where just as many compliments had been paid to her in the form of brightly colored concoctions.

It was well into the evening and our Buffalo Girls were well into the hooch. Bernie's hangover was long gone—as were Ruby's worries. They were doing what sisters are supposed to do when they hung out—catching up and letting loose. They were sharing drinks, stories and waves of heat. They were taking turns, fanning themselves with the drink menu—passing 'the change' back and forth between them, in a game of hormonal hot-potato. It was humorous and bonding. So much had changed since they saw each other last, and they had changed. Their bodies had been going through the whirlwind of time alone, but as the menu passed back and forth, they weren't alone anymore. There was support in the barbs and in the laughter. Respect and acknowledgement of the life lived to get here and the wisdom these waves represented.

The gusts of heat passing through their bodies weren't the only changes in the air. The grass roof over the tiki bar was blowing too with the changing evening breeze and the clientele was changing as well. Bloated businessmen, Harlequin-reading wives and 'virgin daiquiri seeking' kids were being steadily replaced by clean-cut college kids and tattooed bikers. It was a very odd mix, but not just there—around the little hut overlooking the ocean—it was everywhere in Daytona that time of year. A crossover of creatures in a kind of cultural eclipse.

A little over fifty years before, Daytona was the beach of speed. In 1937 motorcycles raced along the packed sands at the water's edge, pushing the limits of combustion engines and courage on two wheels. It was on January 24th, 1937, that the inaugural running of the Daytona 200 happened and continued for the next five years. After being halted by the war, it came back, but gradually morphed. It became more and more regulated and commercial, until it was moved to the new Daytona International Speedway in '61, away from the desirable and expensive real estate of ocean views. The race may have left the beach, but the gathering didn't. It was an established mecca of biker culture, that kept drawing in its followers to gather every year in comradery.

They weren't the only ones drawn to the white beach and blue ocean. In the mid-80s when Fort Lauderdale had had enough of destroyed hotel rooms, barfing frat boys and half naked co-eds, they kicked out the droves of spring breakers, pushing them and their dollars towards Daytona. They welcomed them and all the brands that financially supported their binge drinking, with open arms.

This was the birth of the eclipse. The month-long festival of motorcycles had been condensed down to one week, which happened to overlap college spring break. A miscalculated pandora's box of partying. But what could have been a powder keg of cultures, of coleslaw wrestling, wet t-shirt contests and burnouts, was actually, for the most part, a symbiotic existence, with both camps looking for the same thing—a good time. Generally, the two stayed to their own, respecting each other's 'right to party'.

The tiki bar was a slice of that. A microcosm of this week-long madhouse. Sitting at the bar was like watching the rec yard in a prison. Lots of mixing, lots of bravado, lots of loud talking and trading of 'things', but each gang sticking to their own.

There was a large group of heavily tattooed, bald bikers sitting at the tables over on the right side by the railing. They were straight out of a Woodstock security detail and every elderly person's nightmare. Beards, boisterous, earrings and chains and patches. All the stuff to make any self-respecting geezer call the cops. But Bernie wasn't interested in them, instead she was fascinated with the three boys who had come in after them. All three were fresh. Fresh out of the shower, fresh on spring break and wearing their freshest shirts over their fresh sunburns. They reeked of a CK One, Drakkar and Eternity soup, turning the air around them into a cologne bath. Bernie didn't find the youths attractive. She wasn't ogling them through her beer goggles—she was fascinated by their attitudes. It would take all three of them to make one of the bikers, but their arrogance was colossal. Candy-colored, candy-nosed, candy-assed kids of the baby boomers. They were entitled. Especially their apparent ringleader—the Lord of these Flies. He was demeaning the staff, complaining about everything and laughing at everyone. Bernie wasn't used to this kind of unkindness, not from a bunch of kids. She wasn't raised with a silver spoon in her mouth, never went to college or debutante balls, so she was in awe of their preppy gall. Where Bernie came from, respect was earned not demanded and a loudmouth was the quickest way to a fat lip.

Ruby tugged at the oversized arm of Bernie's muumuu. "Let's get out of here." She opened the top of her beach bag a little, revealing the full mickey inside. "Bartender and I are friends now."

Bernie looked back to the arrogant group of frat boys, who were now starting to snicker and bother the bikers. Those boys were in over their heads—out of their heads and were standing a good chance of losing them too.

"That's not him. It has nothing to do with us. Let's go," Ruby said, not waiting for the okay, pulling Bernie from her stool and guiding her away from the bar. "Bye Mike!" Ruby waved to the bartender. "Thanks for the traveler!"

White noise. That's the best way to describe the sound of the ocean as its waves roll onto the shore, turning foam and froth into the ether. It's soothing. No other inconsistent rhythm can soothe the soul the same way—not even rain. It's the ancient therapist of the human mind and tonight it was listening to Bernie.

As she and Ruby sat in the last rolls of soft sand at the water's edge, Bernie thought about me. Ruby knew it. That's what sisters do. They know things. They know you. That's why she pulled her away from the bar and why she was unscrewing the top of the bottle of rum and passing it to her.

"He looked just like him," Ruby stated watching her sister swig from the bottle. "But it wasn't him."

Bernie nodded as she pulled the bottle from her lips and passed it back to Ruby. "I know. But it could have been him."

The moon was almost full. It made a wavy ribbon of white on the waves, from horizon to shore, that lit up the girls, who were lit on pirates' blood and regret.

"Six years—almost seven. But I remember him that way. That young." Bernie let out one of her sighs.

Ruby laid back on the sand, taking a swig—giggling.

Bernie was insulted. "Is that humorous to you?"

"It isn't that. I was remembering when we were young. Sitting on a beach just like this, passing a mickey between the two of us."

"Wasaga?"

"Yes, Wasaga."

"I was thinking about that earlier today." Bernie's guard lowered.

"My word. Do you remember the look on the cop's face when he pulled us over in that funeral car."

"The hearse."

"Yes, and you made me lie in the back and pretend I was your cargo."

"I couldn't do it. I was driving."

"I held my breath forever. I thought I was going to pass out. What was it you said to him?"

Bernie grinned, "I simply told the man that I wasn't completely sure that you were fully dead. That's why I was speeding. I had to get you back to the undertaker and check. I swear he messed his drawers."

"That was a great trip—parts of it at least. I remember laying on my back on the beach just like this."

"I bet you remember laying on your back a lot." Bernie laughed at her own jab.

"No, most were completely forgettable." Ruby burst out laughing too, but then stopped suddenly, spying something coming down the beach towards them.

Bernie snatched the bottle from Ruby's hand and tucked it between her legs, making it disappear into the ample fabric of her muumuu. "What is it? The fuzz?" Bernie wasn't joking, she was really asking, she couldn't get a clear image through her booze-soaked eyes. "Last thing we need is a ticket. You're not allowed to drink on the beach down here."

"Don't touch me!" an angry, high-pitched male voice ordered. "Keep your dirty, fucking hands off me! Do you know who I am?!"

The shadows became clearer as they moved into the moonlight ribbon. At first, Bernie could only make out the person at the front. It was the college kid from the tiki bar, he was stumbling, shirt covered in vomit, shoes missing, slurring, shouting and barely able to stay upright.

"Do you have any idea who I am?!" he screamed out again as the other shadows stepped into the light.

The other shadows were three of the bikers from bar, all covered in tattoos. The two bigger bald guys in the back had their leather vests on, complete with colors. They were displaying full top and bottom rockers, front rank patches and fingers full of tenderizing rings. These were the real deal. Not the weekend warriors, the midlife crisis cruisers or the Easy Rider fan club, these were the one percent. The third one was not. His vest wasn't complete. He still had something to prove.

The college kid suddenly fell flat on his face, right into the water. The youngest of the three bikers, with the long brown hair and incomplete vest, ran over and pulled the kid up out of the waves.

Ruby shook her head. "Just like him," she said to Bernie under her breath.

The long-haired biker held the wavering, intoxicated jerk by the arms. "Listen kid. I don't care who you are, I just don't want to see you drown."

"Get your fucking hands off of me, you skidder!" the kid kept shouting.

"I will if you will stop falling into the ocean."

Without warning, the kid spit right into the biker's face.

As fast as Bernie smashed her glass into the side of Connie's head, the young biker clocked the kid in the jaw, knocking him out cold.

"A little help?" he grunted, struggling under the weight of the kid's suddenly limp body, pleading with the large bald bikers standing back, watching this all go down.

One of them snorted. "Fuck 'em! You tried, he yapped. Let 'em drown."

"You've done enough, Prospect. Time to go," the other biker ordered.

"I'll help," Bernie called out, getting to her feet and quickly moving towards them.

"Bernie!" Ruby tried to stop her, but she was already beyond arm's reach.

The long-haired biker took a second to assess who or what was approaching him. Seeing it was an elderly woman, he blew her off. "Thanks lady, but we got this."

"Is that so?" Bernie said with a dash of superiority. "Might want to tell them that."

The long-haired biker turned to see his two compadres walking away from him.

"Nice. Thanks!" he shouted to them, and they just raised their middle fingers into the air as a response.

"You hold him, I'll search his pockets for a room key," Bernie said, patting down the passed-out kid's pockets, like she was a cop on the frisk. "There we are," she announced proudly and pulled out a single key attached to flat, diamond-shaped, hotel key tag. She turned the key tag into the moonlight. 'Room #410, Tropical Winds Oceanfront Hotel' was written on it.

"Why do you need his room key? What are you gonna do lady? Rob him?" The long-haired biker seemed surprised and a little impressed.

"No. We're going walk him back to his room and lock him in it. He can't drown in there," Bernie reassured him as Ruby reluctantly reached them.

The biker moved around and got under the drunk kid's arm, supporting him like a wingman on an Irish pub crawl. "You know where that is?" he asked Bernie.

"It's not far, just a few hotels down from here. Come on," she said, getting under the kid's other arm and leading them away from the moonlight.

The long-haired biker was fresh out of breath by the time they made it to room 410. The hallway was covered in a heavily patterned sisal—dizzying for the drunk, but camouflage for the dirt. Bernie put the key into the lock on the soft-yellow door and opened it. A powerful waft of cologne and booze blew out of the room, as if they'd just opened the lid of an All-American's tomb. The biker took the full weight of the kid, took two steps inside the door of the hotel room and just let go of him. He dropped the dead weight onto the floor of the suite, just outside the bathroom.

The biker quickly stepped out into the hallway, stretching his back, trying to let go of the strain this good Samaritan act put on him.

Bernie closed the door and then slid the hotel key under it.

"You're a good man," Bernie said to the biker. "That kid would have died if it weren't for you."

"For us," the biker said, nodding to her and Ruby. "Thanks for your help…"

"Bernie," she answered his unasked question, helping him out one more time, "and this is my sister, Ruby."

"Daz," he smiled.

"Don't any of you fucking move!" a very loud, very assertive voice yelled, scaring the three of them.

They turned around quickly to see a group of men, moving towards them. These men were well-dressed—too well-dressed to be on spring break or riding Harleys—they had nice shoes, nice watches, gold chains, tans and muscles.

The one upfront in the suit jacket, the leader, continued to shout, "Where the fuck is Kenneth?"

"Who?" Daz asked, moving Bernie and Ruby behind him—becoming a gentleman's shield.

"You know who I'm talking about."

"No, I'm afraid I don't." Daz was still at a loss.

"Then why are you standing outside of his room?" the angry, well-dressed man said, pushing the three of them out of the way.

He snapped his fingers and another of the well-dressed men emerged from the group. He stepped up, kicked the door, right beside the handle and the entrance to room 410 flew open.

"Kenneth?!" The leader snapped his fingers again and two other men from the group, ran in and lifted the kid off the ground. He then turned his head to Bernie and the others. "You three, inside, now!"

This was not an invitation. They were pushed into the room before they could even choose to comply.

They closed the broken door behind them, leaving one of the men to guard it. The other goons split up, half directed Bernie, Ruby and Daz, to sit down on the queen-size bed, by the window and the other half, propping Kenneth up in a chair.

The leader, sat down across from Kenneth, in the other chair by the window. He gently slapped Kenneth's face until his eyes began to open. "Kenneth, wake up."

Kenneth's eye's fluttered and he moved his jaw a little, cracking the dried blood on his bottom lip, clearly feeling the pain of Daz's uppercut. "What are you doing here, Donnie?"

"What am I doing here? What are you doing here? Your father had us running around all of south Florida looking for you."

"Yeah, well you found me," Kenneth snarled, raising his hand to his jaw, which was now turning purple.

"What happened to you?" Donnie asked, just as Kenneth realized that Bernie, Ruby and Daz were sitting on the bed across from him.

"It was them," Kenneth grunted pointing at the three of them. "Punched me in the face. For no reason."

"I was trying to save your life!" Daz pushed back.

Donnie nodded and two of goons grabbed Daz, dragging him past Kenneth, out the sliding glass doors, onto the balcony.

"Whoa! Everyone slow down!" Bernie shouted, "He's telling the truth! We saw it. This kid was off his head. Falling into the ocean. He'd have drowned if it—"

"The old bitch is lying," Kenneth snapped with the same charm he had at the tiki bar.

Outside on the balcony, the goons were raising Daz over the railing.

"Stop!" Bernie stood up quickly.

Donnie drew a gun from his belt line just as fast and pointed it at Bernie.

"There's no need for that. Please." Bernie raised both her hands and leaned in slowly towards Donnie.

He looked very confused as she got close to his head, leaning down and whispering into his ear.

Ruby couldn't hear what she was saying, no one could but Donnie. Donnie's expression slowly changed, and he put his gun back into the waist of his pants, locking eyes with Bernie. Bernie didn't follow the gun; she kept her gaze on his green eyes.

"Put him down!" Donnie shouted to the goons on the balcony.

"What? He hit me!" Kenneth protested like a child having a tantrum.

"Go, take the other woman with you," Donnie said to Daz as he stumbled back into the room.

"Bernie?!" Ruby questioned, unsure of what was going on.

"It's alright, Poob. Just go," Bernie assured her, still locking eyes with Donnie.

"I can't leave you here." Ruby panicked as the goons got her to her feet, forcibly escorting her and Daz to the door.

BONE PARK

"Just go back to the park, Poob. I'll be right behind you." Bernie stayed calm.

"Go before I change my mind," Donnie started to raise his voice.

With that, Ruby and Daz were muscled out into the hallway, but before the door could close, Bernie caught her sister's eye and mouthed, "Go." Then shot Daz a look. It was a pointed, information-filled look, but Daz didn't get it. He didn't understand. He hadn't learned her shorthand. She looked at him like that because he looked like me.

SANDY ROBSON

CHAPTER 2

Hustle

    Ruby held on tight to Daz's waist as they flew down the dirt road on his Knucklehead. The dry jungle looked very different at night, foreboding and ominous, not like its morning doppelganger, that first welcomed her to Cicada Hollow. She was used to this, to the rumble coming through the seat, knowing where and where not to put her feet to save her calves from skin grafts. She would normally have leaned back against the sissy bar, only resting a hand on the waist or upper thigh of the daredevil holding the handlebars, but this wasn't normal. She'd just left her sister in a room surrounded by men with guns. She couldn't comprehend how it happened. How could she just walk away? She abandoned her sister.

    Ruby had to gather her thoughts quickly, regain her composure—while her face was still hidden, buried sideways into the back of Daz's vest. That's not how it had gone down. It wasn't like that though, was it? No. Bernie had told her to go. Insisted on it. She said she'd be right behind her. She'd given Ruby that look. The one they used to communicate with back when they were kids. She'd always obeyed the look. So, she did now. But they weren't kids anymore. It wasn't just her; Daz had pulled her away. Dragged her down the hallway, down the stairs, out the door and all the way back to his motel. He'd put her on the back of his bike and was driving before it all had really sunk in.

He only was doing what he thought was best. Following the lead of Bernie—doing what he could—saving her sister. There was a million to one chance that any of them would get out of that room alive. Hell, he was hanging over the balcony by his ankles, so two of them walking away was better than the odds, it was a miracle. But it wasn't without regret. He was raging at himself on the inside. He had gone against his own code to uphold the one of the clubs. He did what he was supposed to do as a prospect. He kept the club out of harm's way. Away from whoever those goons were and whatever heat they might attract. He took his regret and his moral code and bottled it, clenching his hands around the grips of the Harley's ape hangers so tight that they had gone numb.

Ruby tapped Daz on the shoulder as the loud "potato, potato" sound of the motorcycle got close to the white cinderblock walls of the park.

"I'll get off here," Ruby shouted over the engine and Daz slowed down, pulling the bike to the side of the dirt road.

The yellowish beam cast by the single Harley headlight, illuminated the sign on the right side of the wall. The sign that said, 'A 55+ Retirement Community'.

"A Bone Park?" Daz asked as he steadied the bike with two feet on the ground, so that Ruby could climb off.

"Sorry?" Ruby wasn't sure if she had heard him right over the popping exhaust.

Daz turned the key, shutting off the engine and repeated himself,

"Bone Park. That's what we call these retirement places."

"Why?"

"Because most of the people in there are about to croak—" He stopped himself, seeing the look on Ruby's face. "Oh, shit...I'm sorry."

"No, it's an accurate name." The humor and symbolism of the name wasn't lost on her, it was just bad timing. "Thank you for the ride," Ruby was obliged to say, even though she felt guilty that she was there without Bernie.

"She'll be alright, you know," Daz said. "That guy listened to her. She's tough."

"I know," Ruby asserted.

"You both are. You're not like most old people. You're cool." Daz could see his compliment was falling on stressed ears. "Hey—I'm sorry I got you two into that mess."

"She got us into it. Goodnight," Ruby said, turning away from Daz as he kicked life back into his sleeping monster.

As she walked under the arched sign of the gates, where the stony, dirty road matured into smooth pavement, Ruby took off her sandals. She put her feet into the thick grass that ran along the side of the lane, curling the toes of her sore feet around the cool, dewy, soothing blades. This could look like a walk of shame to any of the light sleepers in the park. A bashful return from a day turned night by a woman with loose morals. The new hussy who was still in her revealing one piece, with her sandals in her hand, stumbling along the side of the drive. This was a walk of shame, of sorts—the shame of returning without her sister, but Ruby's stumbles were shock induced, not rum. The buzz of the booze wore off when the gun came out.

Ruby could hear the motorcycle getting further away, popping and rumbling until it faded into the hum of the cicadas. What was it that she'd said? Bernie? What had she whispered into that man's ear that changed the course of that sinking ship? Ruby kept trying to figure it out. Trying to remember what she heard, if she had heard anything at all at that moment. It was like a Vegas act. Like Bernie had whispered into the ear of a roaring, rare, white tiger and it magically rolled over. Her big sister had always been a giant to her. Not just in height, in presence. Bernie had always been a force to be reckoned with. A silent power, that needed no fanfare, no showboating. She was a woman that quietly demanded respect, but what had happened in that hotel room was something else.

Ruby opened the screen door of the lanai, slowly and quietly, not wanting to attract any attention or questions, because she could handle neither. She set her bag down on one of the white wicker chairs at the far end and flopped down into the other. She thought about calling the police, but that's not what Buffalo Girls did. The police had not been a positive part of their lives. They took their daddy and broke their mom. They'd harassed her and killed Sal. The police were a totally other species as far as she was concerned, so she just sat there. She sat in the dark, mesh-wrapped room, staring out towards the lane. The only person she could call, hadn't picked up in a long time. A cast aside sidekick from her youth she thought she would never, ever turn to again. But she had no one else to turn to, so she prayed.

"Forget what I am. What I've done. That's between you and me. But not her. She's not like me, you know that. She has nothing to do with us. If you're up there. If you can hear me. Please bring her back, safe."

Mullet pulled the ripcord on the push mower hard, sending the steely sound of the motor out into the inner circle. For him, there was barely no sound to it at all—his ears were being assaulted by the 90s' dance music coming through his headphones. He lifted his Oakley-wrapped eyes up, away from the rattling mower's motor and began to push the machine towards Bernie's trailer.

Ruby's eyes shot open.

She'd fallen asleep in the wicker chair, but none of the morning walkers could tell, because she was still in her swimsuit. As far as they were concerned, she was just another early bird, ready for another sunny day in the Hollow.

It took a second for Ruby to realize where she was, and that Bernie had not come back last night. Ruby's bag was still in the chair and her sandals right in front of the door to the lanai. She knew Bernie would never have left those there, she would have placed them neatly to the side—if she had seen them. This was when her worry turned to panic. For most people, that would have happened hours ago, a few miles from here, in that beachfront hotel, but Ruby wasn't most. She was forged in fires others could never get close to and this phoenix had reached her melting point.

As Mullet moved the rotating-gas guillotine away from the trailer, Ruby could hear voices. Loud voices. Standing up, after spending hours slumped in the wicker wingback, she instantly felt pain. Not from the hunched form of her sleeping skeleton, but from the bas relief of the chair's woven stick pattern that was carved into the backs of her arms and thighs. Sleep marks of any kind were never for public consumption, but self-consciousness was not top of mind—Bernie was—so she pushed through the tingling sensations of returning circulation and ran out of the lanai.

Ruby moved briskly towards the lane, placing her feet carefully on the separate, cement pavers, as if she were playing a sneaky game of hopscotch. At the edge of the trailer, she slowed her movements, tucking in close to the trailer's rippled wall. At the front of the trailer, the voices were louder, accompanied by the sounds of movement and something else. A nervous kinetic energy that she could feel. Images of the goons from last night and the last look on Bernie's face raced through Ruby's head—turning Ruby's feet into anchors. Unsure if it was her body warning her or just the freezing effect of fear—she stayed put and slowly peeked around the corner.

Way down the road, at the far end of the curve, where it begins to bend so far to the left that it disappears, there was a gathering of people. They were standing at the end of the driveway, at the side of the trailer with the blue metal awnings. Ruby didn't recognize any of them, except for Stan and Opal. Stan was right in the middle of it all, while Opal was hanging well back from the group. Ruby searched the faraway figures but couldn't see Bernie. It was possible that she was there. Somewhere in the group. Maybe in the middle? Maybe on the ground?

Ruby pulled up her anchors and started to move. She was barefoot, cutting across from lawn to lawn in her high cut swimsuit, publicly displaying her wicker sleep-lines and night-worn makeup. A couple of trailer plots closer to the gathering and the group suddenly opened. There was no Bernie. Not in the scrum, not on the ground, nowhere in sight. The crowd was standing around something, but it wasn't someone, it was the front of a huge Oldsmobile.

Merle emerged from deep in the shadow of the carport, carrying a box and handed it to Stan.

"Oh, come on, Merle. Not your bocce. I can't take these," Stan showboated. "These are the only balls you have left!"

"Good one, Stan. But they're yours now," Merle said, giving Stan a strangely confident slap on the shoulder. "Not a lot of bocce back in Alaska."

Alaska? Ruby was perplexed. Why would he be going to Alaska now? It's barely spring here so it must still be a freezer in Alaska. There was something different about Merle. Ruby couldn't quite put her finger on it, but he seemed different. His back was straighter, his chin was higher. Not at all like the weasel who ran home in his tennis shorts a day ago because his wife told him to. His wife? Right, Connie—where the hell was she?

As if Ruby's thought were a spell, Connie appeared, walking out of the carport, handing a box to a woman, who seemed humbled by whatever it was. Connie was different too. It wasn't the large bandage she had just above her eye, on the left side of her head—it was her aura. She was radiant. She was smiling. Not a fake smile, a real smile—and laughing.

The woman she gave the box to was crying. Connie put her arm around her. "Don't cry. We'll stay in touch and if you're ever in Alaska, you have somewhere to stay."

"Yoo-hoo, Ruby!" Without looking she knew that was the buttercream call of Opal.

She was waving her hand high above her head, from the safety of her own lawn, away from the hubbub. Opal seemed very happy to see Ruby. Calling to her as if she were a dear friend, not wanting Ruby to feel left out.

Looking back to the farewell that was underway, Ruby saw Connie's whole demeaner had changed. She let go of the crying woman instantly and stepped back towards the Oldsmobile slowly, keeping her eyes on Ruby the whole way.

"Merle! Time to go!" Connie ordered getting into the driver's seat, forcing Merle to stop shaking hands.

"Don't you want me to drive?" Merle asked, as if his masculinity were attached to the steering wheel.

"Just get in the car!" Connie screamed and a very startled Merle slipped back into his sheep's clothing and took shotgun.

The car started up and launched out of the carport so fast, it almost clipped Stan. There may have even been a slight chirp to the tires too. The Oldsmobile peeled down the thin lane, towards Ruby, going the wrong way and way too fast. As the old boat passed Ruby, Connie looked over to her and nodded. Ruby was confused by it all, but especially by what was in Connie's eyes. It was not a "hello" nod, not a "nice to see you" nod or a "goodbye" nod—it was an acknowledgement. A nod that said, I see you, seeing me and we see each other. The kind of nod you give someone you both fear and respect and that can order a shanking in the world of orange jumpsuits. So why was this old bird giving it to her, she questioned, and did she even know what it was?

The crowd that had become a mix of criers and fist wavers,

began to disperse and Ruby was brought back to reality. To the whole reason she was even out there to witness it all. Bernie. Her sister still hadn't come home, and panic once again took over the phoenix.

Ruby rushed into the lanai and up the three cement steps on the side of the trailer to open the outer screen door. It only took a half turn of the knob, because like all the rest of the doors, it was unlocked. Every door to every trailer was. Unless the owners were snowbirds and had gone home for the required months to collect their free health care.

Ruby stepped into the trailer holding onto the tiniest sliver of hope. A miniscule wish that her prayer had been answered. That somehow Bernie had slipped inside while she was outside watching the big bon voyage. She went straight to the back of the trailer, only to find Bernie's bed empty, still crisply made. It was the same for the bathroom, the main room and her room. All empty, all hopeless. With no one there but herself and no one in the park that she trusted, her eyes turned to her only option. The last resort. The yellow phone on the side table. She knew what she had to do. Even though her heart rate was staccato, practically ripping through her chest, she picked up the receiver and started to push the square white buttons. She wasn't sure if the new emergency numbers worked down here yet, but she tried them anyways. 9-1-1.

There was a pause. A moment of disconnection, where she considered hanging up, but she considered too long—

"911, what's your emergency?"

Ruby was sullen. Her mouth suddenly dry. Her mind suddenly blank.

"Hello? 911, what's your emergency?" the female voice on the other end repeated, a little more forcibly this time.

"It's my sister," Ruby blurted out, like a bad actress on camera for the first time. "She's missing."

"Okay, ma'am. What's your name?"

"Ruby Hewton." She said it without processing, instantly realizing that this was already more information than she wanted to give.

"The computer tells me that you're calling from unit 512, in Cicada Hollow retirement park, is that correct?"

"Yes? I've been up all night waiting for her, but she's not here."

The woman's tone changed, from concerned and attentive, to placating.

"Alright, Ruby, is it? What you need to do is take a nice, deep breath. Okay? Can you do that? Let me hear you breathe."

Ruby breathed into the phone, uncomfortable with the request.

"That's better now, isn't it?"

"No, it is not. My sister is missing."

"Okay, tell me then, how long has your sister been missing?"

"Since last night."

"Okay and how long have you and your sister been living together?"

Ruby stumbled. "A day."

"And before a day or two ago, when was the last time you saw your sister?"

"Uh...thirty years ago."

The dispatcher cleared her voice. "Thirty years? That is a very long time, was she missing then?"

"Absolutely not. We just weren't speaking." Ruby was becoming very frustrated with these idiotic questions.

"No need to get upset, I'm just trying to help. Okay, when you last saw her, was she in distress? Do you have any reason to believe she would hurt herself or others?"

"No. But..." Ruby caught her tongue, hearing the words in her head before they made it to her lips. This woman wasn't helping at all, she was condescending and even if she told her the truth, Ruby had a strong feeling she wouldn't believe her.

"Well, Ruby, if there is nothing else you can tell me, there is not a lot I can do until she has been missing for at least twenty-four hours. I am sure she's alright. You try and stay calm. Maybe a cool glass of water and a nap. I'm sure things will be clearer when you're rested. But if you haven't heard from her by tomorrow, you can call back, okay?"

"Yes, I understand."

"Cool drink and a nap, it works wonders."

"I'm sure you're right."

"That's better. You take care now, Ruby. Bye for now."

The dial tone took over, forced in by the dispatcher, but welcomed by Ruby. What was she thinking? If Bernie knew she'd called the police, she'd lose her mind. Bernie was right. Cops were nothing but criminals with a badge.

"Morning," Bernie said matter-of-factly as she walked in the door. "Shit!" she suddenly shouted, hopping on one foot, looking down at a 'fresh screen door scraped' Achilles on her other heel. "Don't say it. I know it's the spring!"

Ruby ran over and wrapped her arms around Bernie who stiffened instantly, but Ruby didn't care. She squeezed her tight, burying her makeup-smeared face into the chest of Bernie's muumuu. As awkward as Bernie felt, she didn't pull away. She just tilted her head down a little and let it happen. This was new. This was needed. It had taken thirty years full of pain and hardship, a gun and a man held over a railing to get here. This hug, this concern, was more than Big Pharma or Jose Cuervo could ever provide.

Bernie slowly lifted her arms and put them around Ruby. "I'm alright, Poob—I'm alright." Silent, invisible tears fell from nowhere, but they felt real to her. They were the closest she could come to letting go. The thought of crying was the nearest she could step to the edge and had very little to do with the hotel room or the events of last night.

Bernie fought back the quiver in her breath, the shaking in her body and the threatening avalanche of emotion before Ruby pulled her head off her chest.

"Where have you been?" Ruby questioned with the concern and hurt of a sleepless parent.

"I've been in that hotel room. But I'm back. That's all that matters," Bernie answered, releasing her arms from Ruby and walking into the kitchen, as if the night or that hug had never happened.

"The hell it is!" Ruby followed her.

Bernie went straight to the cupboard with the sunflower tumblers and pulled one out. As she walked to the fridge, Ruby kept on her.

"Those men were going to kill Daz, probably kill us all!"

"Probably," Bernie calmly agreed, placing three large ice cubes into the glass and reaching for the almost empty bottle of tequila.

"What did you say to him?"

"To whom?"

"You know who. You whispered something into the ringleader's ear, and he let us go."

"I asked him to let you go. Said I was the one that hit the boy. Told him I'd stay, make things right, but only if he let you both go."

"And I'm supposed to believe that? That he believed that? How could you make it right?"

"I apologized—all night."

"You'll get a canker sore telling that many lies. What did you really say? What really happened?"

"I just told you."

"Bernie—" Ruby stopped. She was angry, but not angry enough, not blind with enough rage to miss the violent shaking of her sister's hands. She laid off the gas and watched as Bernie shook, pouring the last of the yellow fuel into the glass. She'd never seen this before, not in her sister, but she knew what it was, and it was bad. "Did they feed you?"

Bernie shook her head.

"You must be starving. How 'bout some eggs?" Ruby suggested with a cautious olive branch extended in her voice. "I haven't eaten anything since the tiki bar. What do you say?"

Bernie put the empty bottle down on the counter and paused, looking down at her shaking hands. "I'd love some, but there's nothing in the fridge."

Ruby smiled. "I'm sure Opal has some. I could ask her. We can replace them when we get some. Alright?"

Bernie nodded, still not turning to face her sister.

Ruby left the trailer as fast as she could, not wanting to give Bernie a chance to think too much about it. The sound of the outside lanai door slamming shut, was the green light—the signal that released the pin in Bernie. She exploded. Body shaking, mouth dropping open, choking to catch her breath as she leaned over the counter and wept, clutching the sunflower glass in her hand. This was the wizard behind her curtain, lost in her reality without the plumes of brave green smoke to hide behind. Bernie stared through her blurry tear-filled eyes into the yellowy cactus liquid for a long, painful moment, then turned and poured it out into the sink. Her hands settled almost immediately. These weren't the shakes of detoxing, the jitters of a raging alcoholic, this was her body releasing whatever she had been fighting back. What she let make a brief cameo moments ago—silently—while she held her sister in tight, so it would stay out of her view. It was possible that it was the manifestation of what transpired last night, after Ruby and Daz were kicked out. But this was deep, not the surface shakes of immediate fear. This was organic, an exposure of something far greater than what could have transpired in that beachfront hotel room.

The Buffalo Girls rolled up to the front of the bank in the long Lincoln and got out of the car. They were primped for paparazzi—dressed to see and be seen—primed for a day in the shops. Ruby was wearing a red-flowered shorts and halter one piece with her hair up on her head, under a silk scarf. She was flashing fresh polish on her nails and exposing the matching set through the open toe of her heels. Bernie was much more conservative, but just as well put together, wearing a flowing, summer sundress, yellow kerchief and matching yellow flats. It had been almost forty-eight hours since the hotel incident and at least twenty-four since Bernie had her last drink. They had been able to mooch off Opal's groceries until now, but enough was enough. Bernie knew it was time to shake off the clouds that were hanging over her and get on with life.

"Once I'm done here, I think we should go to Walgreens, then the salon and end with the Pick and Save. Sound good?"

"Sounds good. I can't wait to have my hair colored and styled. It's been too long." Ruby 'Monroed' her words, posing against the hood of the Lincoln, already catching glances from men pulling into the parking lot.

"Please don't pick up any strays while I'm gone. You can't afford to feed them," Bernie teased.

BONE PARK

"Catch and release only." Ruby smiled. "I promise."

"I'll only be a minute." Bernie started for the bank doors.

"Why don't you just use the ATM, you old biddy?" Ruby teased back.

"Because I don't trust them—and you shouldn't either," she snapped back, but with a curl of a smile. "Now just stay put and hold onto your britches—that is if you're wearing any, you hussy," Bernie jabbed, leaving her sister at the car and went inside.

Ruby put on her big, plastic, heart-shaped sunglasses and tilted her head back towards the sun. It felt good on her face. This warmth was free and right above her head all day long. She thought about how rough things had been before that week. How rough they had been for such a long time, but how she'd landed on her feet once again. A cat.

"Jesus Christ!" The sacrilegious swears of Bernie coming out of the bank were heard by everyone in the parking lot.

"What's wrong?" Ruby tried to get a hold of the situation.

"This is!" Bernie waved a small piece of white paper and a wad of cash in the air.

"What?" The paper was too small to tell what it was, but the cash was clearly making her outrage even more confusing.

"Get in the car!" Bernie snapped.

Ruby immediately complied. Bernie always kept her cool, so whatever was happening must be monumental—definitely not the time to argue.

Inside the sweltering brown-on-brown car, Bernie handed Ruby the cash and the piece of paper. The paper was a bank receipt.

"I don't understand." Ruby searched the paper for the source of the outrage. "Okay, the disappointment with the zeros on the bank

63

statement I understand, but you've got two thousand dollars in cash here. You're no Rockefeller, but it's a hell of a lot more than I have."

Bernie snatched the paper from Ruby's hand. "It's all I have. The cash was from a safety deposit box I had here. I'd forgotten about it. The teller brought it to my attention. This is all I have—they took everything else."

"Who did?"

Bernie pulled back. "Doesn't matter."

"The hell it doesn't! If someone took something from you, then we—"

Bernie slammed her hand against the brown vinyl dash. "It doesn't matter. There's nothing we can do."

Ruby retreated—then, "You're right…it doesn't matter…because you've still got your pension." Ruby brought her tone up.

"No, I don't."

"How can that be? No one can take that from you. You worked for the City of Buffalo for over thirty years! The whole point of that job was the pension. That's what you always said."

"Yeah, well I don't have one…anymore." Bernie wouldn't look at her. "How much do you have?"

Ruby's face went long. "Four hundred and sixty-five dollars and seventy-two cents—in cash. It's wrapped up at the bottom of my unmentionables. I don't have a bank account. Well, I do, but there hasn't been anything in it for years."

"So, we're buggered! It's barely enough to get us to summer. We'll be out on the streets, in the hottest months of the year." Bernie slumped over the steering wheel of the Lincoln. "I worked my whole life for this? To be left with nothing, but two thousand dollars?"

BONE PARK

"So, I'm guessing we can forget about getting are hair done today?" Ruby placed her hands against the side of the silk scarf that was wrapped around her head, realizing that even the smallest joys had instantly vanished. That they too had slipped through her fingers, like her dreams and the years had.

"Can't even get your hair done. What was it all for?" Bernie's defeat slowly built into anger. "Everything I've done, everything I've lost, what was it for?! Jesus Christ! You're 60 years old, Verna, and you can't even afford to get your hair done. They're stealing our dignity. Two thousand dollars? The pad fee alone at the park is five hundred a month! With two mouths to feed, medications, doctors' appointments, the insurance on this car—" Bernie stopped, lifted her head from the steering wheel and turned to Ruby. "Get out."

"What? Bernie, come on. We can figure this out. You can have all the cash I have."

"Get out," Bernie said again with a very disturbing look on her face—a possessed smile, something akin to the killer's look in a low-budget horror movie—involving clowns.

Ruby wasn't sure what to do, other than to follow Bernie's sudden and slightly terrifying instructions. She reluctantly opened her door, keeping her eye on her sister and stepped out of the sweltering car.

Bernie turned the engine over.

"Please, Bernie, I know you're upset, but—"

"Step back," Bernie said, slamming the car into reverse, launching the shiny, brown mob-mobile backwards with Ruby's passenger door still open.

Ruby jumped out of the way, stepping quickly up onto the raised walkway in front of the stores. In the middle of the parking lot, Bernie screeched to a stop and then thrust the car into drive, slamming the passenger door shut, like a stunt driver.

She shouted out through the driver's side window, "Keep your four hundred dollars."

Bernie stomped on the gas before Ruby could open her lips to question. A few onlookers had stopped their Saturday shopping to witness the old woman doing some Dukes of Hazzard stunts in the parking lot. Ruby did her best to blend into the disturbed crowd while they were distracted by the insane retiree flying out into traffic and speeding away.

As Ruby faded into the consumers, who returned to their hurried capitalism as quickly as they were distracted, she realized this was a 'puppy moment'. She had plenty of them, but never one done by her sister. She worried that she'd just been discarded, an unloaded burden, tossed out of the car, like a bag of puppies on an old dirt road. For most of her fifty-five years it had been men who cast her burlap heart into the ditch—romantically, professionally, personally. The first time was unbearable, like having a triple bypass without anesthesia. After that— each time she was cast aside, sent tumbling down the shoulder of life— she built up her calluses and killed another nerve. It dulled the pain a little more until she felt almost nothing and expected almost nothing from everyone.

Bernie and Ruby hadn't seen each other in thirty years, but they had spoken—on the phone, at least once a month. The calls were brief, filled with just enough pleasantries and 'catch up check lists' to fulfill the family quota. The socially acceptable minimum contact needed so they could both continue carrying the family card, the one we pull out to prove we aren't alone. And she wasn't alone. Bernie did come to get her. Just a few days ago, she took her out of that hotel room, brought her all the way here and offered her this last chapter. Compared to where Ruby was, Cicada Hollow was a fairy tale, only her white knight was her sister who arrived in a brown Lincoln. This seemed to be the perfect end to the story. They began together, as kids in Grand Island, then Buffalo and would cross the finish line in New Smyrna the same way. What happened in the middle didn't matter—the years of empty phone calls— because the start and the end of the book was wonderful. Or was that just a fairytale too? If by chance that was a puppy moment—if Bernie had just thrown her away, then that would be it. She didn't know if Bernie realized it or not, but Bernie was all that mattered to her. Ever. The brief phone calls may have been empty, but they were everything to her. They brought her back to her big sister once a month and that brought Ruby back from the brink more often than that. So, if Bernie had abandoned her, right there in that parking lot, seeing her as trash—like she saw herself—then Ruby was done. There were no more monthly phone calls for her. There would be no need to fill the last chapter because she knew the ending already and she would write it herself.

It had been four hours since Bernie took off—three hours since Ruby made her decision. She came to the understanding that she was done for. That she was going to be out on the streets, without a pot to piss in or a hope in hell and if that was her fate, then she was going to go out looking her best. Ruby had put too many years into cultivating her image, to let some beauty school dropout working graveyards at the morgue create her last look.

There isn't much in this world that can lift the spirits like a new 'do. Nothing that soothes the soul quite like the chatter of a busy salon. Nothing can compare to the laughter and buzz of other people's gossip, the smell of the bleach and color, the undivided attention of the stylist, the fingers of the shampoo boy and the first look in the mirror at the new and improved you. It's a religious experience—a baptism of sorts. A transformation of your shameful neglect into a virgin version of yourself. The emergence of a new you that you make a silent promise to in the mirror. A promise to be that person looking back at you and maintain your mane, only to watch it disintegrate with every step you take back into the chaos of real life.

Ruby had forty of her four hundred and sixty-five dollars with her. Two twenties, folded up in her tiny, heart-shaped purse. It was definitely not enough for what she wanted, but she'd be able to tip along the way and make some fantastic looking mug shots. Ruby figured that when she couldn't pay, they'd call the police. This outcome had two benefits; one, she'd get her new 'do for free and two, she'd have a warm meal and a bed to sleep in that night. She didn't have an appointment, but she rectified that by playing the high roller—asking for the full work over. It was like ordering everything on the menu so that the maître d' had to give her a table. She got more than the table—she got the whole restaurant. Ruby was getting a cut, color, brows, mani, pedi and facial. This was a significant drop of coin for anyone on a Saturday afternoon, let alone a woman with only forty dollars in her clutch. But in true Ruby fashion, if she was going to go out, then she was going to go out with a bang!

Three hours in and she already had her hands and feet properly pampered, had her face steamed and creamed and she was onto the cut and color portion of this gauntlet. Ruby sat under a hair dryer, over in 'rumor row'; the long line of dryers where women sit under the heat of plastic domes, waiting for the chemical reactions to take place, while exchanging endorphins in the form of gossip. Within a few minutes under the dome—that was just really a way for the stylists to take a smoke break—she had made two new friends. Left and Right, she called them, because she couldn't hear their names over the roaring dryers when they introduced themselves and she didn't really want to know them either. Women—in general—were not her friends. She was the 'other' to most of them. The one that they gossiped about in salons like this all over the country. The one whose name carried the blame for their cold beds. Not there though. There, in that 'rumor row' she was just another old biddy, under a dryer, and it was nice to be included. They made her feel like one of them, even though the whole thing was a lie and was most definitely going to end with her in handcuffs.

"Where did you say y'all are staying?" Left asked again, because she missed it the first time.

Ruby wasn't sure if it was because Left was hard of hearing or if it was just the din of the dryer, but Left asked so nicely in her southern accent, that Ruby repeated herself. "Cicada Hollow."

"Oh, right here in New Smyrna?" Right responded happily. "Oh, we're both over in Quails Hollow, not far from you. We play cards with a group over there once a month!"

"You have to join us next time, sugar," Left added and Ruby suddenly regretted divulging.

"Cicada has a far nicer pool than ours, but our shuffleboard courts definitely outshine yours," Right bragged.

Ruby remembered that it didn't matter. What they said, what she said, none of it, because she wouldn't be seeing that place or them ever again. She felt the freedom of vacation take over her. The devilish spark that turns PTA moms into CIA operatives while on adult holidays. They can be anyone they want. They can tell any bartender or casual conversationalist that they are a million times more interesting and make plans to boot. Plans they have no intention of ever keeping, because they aren't really pilots or doctors or CEOs.

"I tell you what girls." Ruby perked up, lifting the hood on the dryer a little so she didn't have to shout. "To hell with waiting for your card game. Life's short, clock's ticking, we should pack all the fun and gin we can into what we got left, right?! Why don't the two of you come over for happy hour."

"Well, aren't you a cinnamon stick," Right cheered.

Left laughed, "Life is short, darlin'."

Ruby's stylist, a cute little woman in her forties, wearing a baby-blue salon smock, came over to the row.

"Mrs. Hewton."

"Miss." Ruby, quickly and proudly corrected her.

"Sorry. Miss Hewton, it's time to rinse you out."

The stylist lifted the dryer hood up and back, away from Ruby's head. As Ruby stood up, she turned back to Left and Right. "Tonight! You two are coming over tonight. We got new hair to flaunt, conversation to continue and trouble to start!"

Left and Right both agreed, they seemed excited, but Ruby didn't really care, because Ruby wasn't going to be there. It wasn't malicious, Ruby liked being liked. It felt nice to play the part of someone who her peers enjoyed. She knew that if they knew who she really was, this whole interaction would never have happened. They may have not even let her in the salon, so this was nice.

"Tonight!" Ruby cheered again and the two old ladies lit up like they were planning a bank robbery.

A long shampoo, stretched out on the reclining vinyl chair with her head leaning back into the sink. This was the money—the young, male mane-mechanic's fingers pressed deep into her scalp. This was as close to chocolate or the little death as you could get. When your head was in the hands of an expert hair-custodian like him, it was heaven. He was making the rounds, playing all the favorites. Pressure points, long dragging motions, squeezing the muscles at the base of her skull, stimulating every possible nerve on her cranium, behind her ear and jaw until she was convinced they were all connected directly to her crotch. It was a sustained orgasm that never peaked or waned, all conducted by the master of her follicles. This was pampering. Nothing asked of her but to enjoy. This was what she came for. This would be the perfect end to a less than perfect life.

"Take it all off!" Ruby said with conviction, looking into the mirror. "I want it all gone."

The stylist looking back at her in the reflection, ran her hands through Ruby's long, wet, freshly-dyed red hair. "All of it? I think you should think about it."

Ruby sat, looking at herself. At her long, curly locks. A bombshell. That's what the boys used to call her. Jane Mansfield. Her hair had always been her calling card and as she got older, it made her stand out even more. Older women didn't have long hair. Not unless they were hippies, or homeless. Homeless? That's what she was now. If her hair was her calling card, then it needed to go. She didn't want anyone to recognize her. To put two and two together when she was found.

"I don't need it anymore. I won't be able to take care of it. So, take it all off!"

"Don't you dare." Ruby looked up from her own reflection—it was Bernie. She was standing behind the stylist, casually peeling a fifty-dollar bill off the huge wad of cash she had in her hand. She gave the fifty to the stylist and instructed, "That's for you—so your scissors don't go anywhere near her."

"What are you doing here?" Ruby was elated and lost.

"Came to get my hair done, same as you. That was the plan, wasn't it?"

"But, how?"

"Lincoln's dead."

"Lincoln?"

"Dead to me at least. Got a great price for it."

Ruby's eyes welled up.

"No need for that. Looks like you're almost done. I was hoping to get a wash and set—that is if you don't mind waiting," Bernie continued.

"Don't mind at all," Ruby answered, holding back her tears as best she could.

"Not an inch!" Bernie waved her finger at the stylist and then walked over to the wash sink, where the 'miracle fingered' wash boy was waiting.

Ruby looked back into the mirror and beaming at the stylist, "That's my sister. Isn't she something?"

Bernie, in her newly tightened curls and Ruby with her flowing red curls, got out of a taxi and walked through the gates of the park. They strutted into the Bone Park like celebrities, carrying their bags of groceries as if they were parcels of overvalued vanity from Rodeo Drive.

"I still can't believe you sold the car." Ruby shook her head, taking in the glares from the women outside the activity center.

"I didn't like it anyways. Too flashy for me." Bernie blew it off, turning to the gawking women. "Hey Patty, Cecilia, Barb—Maryanne. Nice evening, isn't it?"

Caught in their judgmental glares, the women tried to cover their rudeness by politely waving to Bernie and spreading insincere smiles across their faces.

Maryanne spoke for the group, "It is, Bernie, we were just saying that."

"Well enjoy," Bernie said, not breaking her stride, moving her sister past the cluster of curmudgeons. "Cunts," she uttered in a sigh.

"What did you say?" Ruby turned quickly to Bernie. Ruby wasn't sure if she'd heard it, imagined it or if it were her own thoughts slipping out her own mouth. "Did you say something?"

"No." Bernie played her poker face.

"Okay." Ruby accepted her answer, because Bernie didn't talk like that. It wasn't that she was a prude, she just wasn't crass. Not one to throw around slurs and swears so easily—or at least that's how she remembered her.

"Look at that!" Quick to change the subject, Bernie motioned with her head towards the end of the road.

The sight of a small U-Haul trailer attached to a blue station wagon with wood panels, out front of Connie's trailer, was a surprise to Ruby as well. "That was fast. They only moved out a couple of days ago."

"I told you, this place flips over like hospital beds."

"Well, I hope the new people are nicer than the old ones."

"Impossible. Old people are never nice," Bernie said with a smirk and Ruby snorted, enjoying her sister's stupid joke.

Ruby came out of her room to find Bernie in the kitchen—making a drink. The usual, a tequila sunrise, heavy on the grenadine, in a sunflower-print glass. Ruby was about to say something, but then thought twice. It had been almost a week since she saw her sister imbibe and it had been one hell of a day. There is a time and place for everything and one of Ruby's greatest gifts was being able to read the room. So, she bit her lip and walked out into the main room, in her red, velour tracksuit, as if it were none of her business. And it wasn't. Pot and kettle. She was the last person who should be telling people to abstain. Besides, she knew that no one stops unless they want to. Unless their *why* is stronger than their *want*. The intention was pure—the concern well placed, but it was moot. Ruby couldn't kick it for Bernie any more than Bernie could do it for her. If loved ones were the key to sobriety then the world would be all tea, but the truth is that women leave their babies every day for the monkeys.

"Don't suppose there's a beer anywhere in that icebox?" Ruby asked.

"Yes, I believe there is. I..." Bernie made quote signs with her fingers. "I 'borrowed' a couple from Opal when," Bernie made the quotes signs again. "I 'borrowed' some bread and lunch meat. Help yourself."

As Ruby opened the fridge in search of the borrowed brew, Bernie went out to the lanai. The night was young. A soft hue of orange still lingered in the sky. The air was warm, and the park was peaceful. This is what the elderly came here for. This slice of paradise.

Inside the trailer, Ruby opened the found can of Budweiser. The cracking sound of an American beer can is unmistakable. The snap, followed by a crisp hiss and the clicks of the widening mouth—sounds like a small rocket is being shot into the air. It's an ingeniously designed sound that subliminally excites the addicted masses and sends fearful trigger shivers up the spines of the sober.

Ruby stepped out of the trailer and down the steps into the lanai. Off in the distance, there was an odd sound. Well, odd to Ruby. It was a chorus of clicking.

"What's that?" Ruby asked.

Bernie leaned forward, looking through the screen door to the clock inside the trailer. "Is it 8:00 already?"

"What happens at 8:00?"

Bernie pointed to the road out front of the trailer. The clicking got louder and a white glow began to build on the dark pavement. "The trikes," she announced forebodingly.

Suddenly, a mass of senior citizens appeared, riding large, three-wheeled bicycles. There were so many of them that they took up the entire road, riding in tandem—a prehistoric, pedal-powered gang. Each trike was decorated differently, adorned with personal flair to reflect the interests and needs of the rider. These were the hot rods of the aged. There were flags, aerials, streamers, baskets, spoke covers and bead-clickers, stickers and decals, reflectors, lights, horns and bells. Lots and lots of bells.

Bernie called out to the pack, "Good evening, ladies!" The gang erupted into an explosion of bell rings, like an ice cream man desperate to unload the goods in one stop.

Even though the 'tainted Tour de France' was a little over the top, it intrigued Ruby. "My word, that looks like fun."

"Really? You think so?"

"They seem to be enjoying themselves," Ruby said, defending her interest.

Bernie set her drink down, stood up and headed for the front screen door of the lanai.

"What's wrong?" Ruby asked, but Bernie didn't reply.

Ruby quickly set her beer down too and followed. She chased after her sister, around the front of the trailer, all the way to the carport on the other side. Bernie was moving so fast that by the time Ruby got to the carport, Bernie was already at the back of it, standing in front of the shed.

"Bern, where's the fire?!" Ruby said, catching her breath, both from the sudden exertion and excitement.

Bernie swung the large, single door on the shed open, stepped inside and pulled down on the cord that was dangling from the ceiling. Suddenly the shed was filled with light from the pigtail bulb and Ruby could see what had gotten into Bernie. Behind her big sister, parked one beside the other, were two trikes.

"That one's mine," Bernie said pointing to the one on the right, with the large rear basket, drink holder and Buffalo Bills' pennant atop a long aerial. She carefully wheeled the trike out of the shed and stood aside. "You can have that one if you want?"

Ruby stepped into the shed. The trike sitting inside wasn't as clean or as taken care of as Bernie's. In fact, it was pretty rusty. It didn't have any of the bells or whistles on it that the ones that just passed had. It was basic.

Bernie said, "The trailer came with two when I bought it. Never had anyone to give it to—until now."

Ruby's eyes lit up. "I want it."

"It could use some TLC, but it's all there."

Ruby grunted, muscling the trike out into carport. The tires were flat and so were Ruby's hopes.

Bernie could see the cloud that had come over her sister's excitement. "I do have a pump in there somewhere. If we inflate them quick, we can catch the group."

Ruby's eyes lit up again. "I got it," she said and went back into the shed in search of the pump.

Bernie chuckled to herself. "Okay. You get the pump and I'll go get you another beer."

The smile on Ruby's face was wider than her chariot's stance, as she and Bernie pedaled through the park, behind the gang of 'Healthcare's Angels'. Ruby was right. This was fun. She hadn't been on a bike in decades. Most of these retirees hadn't, hence the three wheels. Safer and much more comfortable than their two-wheel relatives. They weren't built for hills, even Lance Armstrong would struggle to get one of these tanks up a slight knoll, but the park was flat and perfect for cruising.

"Yoo-hoo." The girls didn't even turn to look, they knew it was Opal.

The quick brrring, brrring of a bicycle bell that followed had the sisters opening up the space between them for the Crazy Canuck.

"Scooch up, Opal," Bernie gently commanded.

BONE PARK

Opal pedaled a little faster to get her pink trike in between them. "Oh, hi. Thanks," Opal said in her breathy way, that always had some sort of apology to it.

"I thought you usually rode with the dusk crowd. A little late tonight, aren't you?" Bernie asked.

"Oh, dear, yes. Stan didn't want me to ride tonight at all. But he fell asleep during Jeopardy—and I saw you two ride by—so here I am," she said shrugging her shoulders, adding a cute curl to her nose.

"You got the groceries?" Ruby asked. "Stan said you weren't home, so we left them with him."

"Oh, yes. Thank you."

"I'm sorry if we forgot anything. We only could carry so much," Bernie humbly apologized.

"Oh, heavens, you two replaced them and then some. You have to take some of those groceries back."

"Wouldn't hear of it. Consider it interest." Bernie put an end to that. "Did you see that someone moved into Connie and Merle's place?"

"Oh, yes, I did. I met them today in fact. They're from Massachusetts," Opal said with wonder, as if the state were some exotic destination. "They have the accent and everything. Sound just like JFK."

Bernie found this hilarious, because Opal had an accent, a sweet, east coast Canadian accent. "And who do you sound like?"

Poor Opal hadn't the foggiest what Bernie meant.

While Bernie continued to snicker, Ruby jumped in, "Did you get their names?"

Opal instantly dropped her confusion over Bernie's teasing, changing focus like an infant distracted by dangling keys. "Oh, yes, I did. Reg and Freda." Opal lowered her already soft voice. "She smokes,"

Opal said, as if she'd just outed a heroin addict. "Didn't smile much—"

The triple, repeating beeps coming from the pink plastic Casio on Opal's wrist startled her. The look of concern on her face was a little more than the benign alarm should have caused.

"Past your bedtime?" Bernie teased.

"Oh, no. That's my 'Stan alarm'. He likes a sandwich when he wakes up."

"You know when his naps are over?" Ruby was both bothered and curious.

"Oh, heavens yes. Stan's my job. Has been for fifty years. When you're married to someone for that long, you know the answer before they've thought of the question." Opal squeezed the brake levers on her handlebars to slow down, dropping her trike back behind the girls. "It was short, but sweet. Night, night. See you tomorrow."

It was foreign for the two single women to comprehend the life that Opal described, but it was expected of most of her contemporaries. Service without celebration. Homemaker and caretaker was the life for most married women her age, a life that continued well into retirement, even after the children were reared, raised and released and the career husband had come home to roost. There was no retirement for the matrimonial slave.

As Opal turned around and headed in the opposite direction, Bernie and Ruby picked up their pace to catch up with the pack. What a pleasant night Ruby thought. Pleasant? It wasn't a word she could ever remember using, but it fit this. Pedaling down the road, part of a group, ringing bells, waving at neighbors and doing it all beside her sister. This is not something she thought she'd ever do, let alone see her sister doing. The Bernie she knew was too uptight, too put together to be seen riding around on a giant tricycle, with open alcohol and waving at people. She was once like this, long ago. Back when they were teens, before Sal and me. She was a fireball. She was fun.

BONE PARK

So, this is what happens here, Ruby thought. Old people pass under the arch and leave the race to get here behind them. Leave the stress and budget, responsibilities and consequences, for the reward of regression. They stop racing forward and start to go back. They form cliques and gossip like they were in high school. They drink and play games all day as if the last line of judgment, their own parental supervision, had been lifted and they ride bicycles. They ride bikes by their friend's houses, ring their bells and ask if they can come out and play? Ruby finally got it. She got why Bernie had been coming here for years and why she had brought her here too. To play. To leave the worries of the world at the arch and go back to Wasaga Beach. If this was what the last chapter was going to be like, then she accepted it. The adult world had taken enough of her, it was time for simpler things. Fun things, but first, she had a trike to decorate.

Bernie had fallen asleep in the La-Z-Boy again, less grenadine-smeared sunflower highballs on the side table than the last time, but enough to make the honking coming from outside annoying.

Ruby opened her bedroom door and walked out into the main room, "You been there all night?"

Bernie nodded with a mix of shame and none of your business. "What time is it?"

"11:00." Ruby walked over to the bank of windows that looked out onto the lanai and opened the louvers. "My word, Bern. Take a shower today, will ya. It's starting to smell like palliative care in here."

After a bout of momentary blindness, from the morning sun coming in the window, Bernie was able to stop blinking enough to take in the vision that was 'very Ruby'. She was wearing a very short red cocktail dress, very high heels and very red lipstick.

"What's all this?" Bernie said standing up from her plush prison as the honking continued outside.

"That's for me. I have go," Ruby said walking back into her room and emerging with a slim red leather attaché case.

"Go? Where are you going?" Bernie was having trouble processing the speed of Ruby's movements, the lack of information and the overwhelming visual stimulus.

"I like it here. I understand now why you do too. So, we need to stay here. You and I are in this together. Just like when we were kids. You sold the Lincoln, so it's my turn."

"What are you selling?"

"Myself," Ruby said with a confident smile.

Bernie raised a labored eyebrow.

"Not like that," Ruby scolded her. "Although it is my plan B," she smirked.

"What's plan A?"

"Oh relax. Nothing I can't handle. Shouldn't be too hard with my resume." Ruby winked at Bernie. "Just like riding a bicycle," she said, then opened the door and rushed out through the lanai.

A very pasty Bernie moved over to the louvers and watched as her dolled-up sister got into the waiting taxi. Hustle. That's what Bernie thought, hustle. They didn't have much growing up, but hustle was something the Buffalo Girls always had—and apparently hadn't lost.

Shakers was not what Ruby expected. Had she been able to see the place first, she would never have come, but all she had to go on was an address she'd found in the back of New Smyrna Daily. Even though this was not what she hoped for, she believed the 'help wanted' ad was a sign. Right ad, right time. Ruby was into that sort of thing. Signs, fortune tellers, tea leaves, hexes and potions. Women like her always are. The

BONE PARK

wise ones, who realize their power early on in life. Who understand the spell they can hold over their oppressors and cultivate it to survive in a hostile world.

The small building was barely the size of a medium, corner store. It was all brick with the front windows blacked out and the words, 'Come and get it' plastered across them. It was just off the A1A, somewhere between New Smyrna and Edgewater, on a cracked and pothole-filled parking lot. It stood alone, between the rubble of former foundations. It was as if the buildings that were on either side of it had committed suicide, just to distance themselves from this shithole. Ruby wasn't second guessing her decision to come—she was third, fourth and fifth guessing it. This wasn't the sketchiest place she'd ever seen, but it was up there. In her mind's eye, it was a much larger establishment. Something with clout, a packed parking lot and fat pockets. A place with prestige and potential, but all this place had was a busted Mazda out front, slim pickings and desperation.

The heavy, single door opened, letting blinding sunlight in to the dark, dank, drinking hole. It smelled. Ruby was hit first by the musty, hoppy wave from the beer-soaked burgundy carpet under her feet. Riding on the back of that bittersweet scent was a warm waft of vanilla. A very distinct kind of vanilla that seemed to stick to dancers and their patrons like their sins. The dark space thumped with the pounding sound of hair metal. A topless woman with peroxide-faded hair, gyrated on the stage that thrust out from the left wall. A balding man in a dress shirt, with a loosened tie, was sitting in perverts' row watching the lackluster performance. He clearly was the only customer in there and the proud owner of the Mazda in the parking lot.

Ruby wanted to turn around and walk out, but that cab cost money. Money Bernie and Ruby didn't have to blow on 'signs'. Part of it was the money and the other part was that the old, rough-looking man, standing behind the bar on the opposite wall, was staring at her. Ruby coveted the bird in the hand rule, it went hand in hand with signs. So, she lifted her head, made eye contact with the old man and headed to the bar. She made sure to use her signature walk, weaving her strides, forward grapevine fashion, turning a simple A to B into a calculated, hip-swaying strut.

Ruby smiled, shouting over the music, "Hi, I'm here to see Sugar."

The old barnacled bartender ran his sty-covered eyes up and down over Ruby. His silence was infuriating. She hadn't come all this way to be scrutinized by a lumpy, long-bearded, old man who looked like he'd just crawled out from under a rock.

"Are you Sugar?" Ruby did her best not to lose her shit.

The bartender shook his head and pointed behind her.

"Is he in the office? Could you tell him I'm here please?"

The bartender shook his head again and kept pointing.

"What do you mean, no? Now you listen here. I am a very important person. He most definitely will want to talk to me and will be very angry with you for getting in the way of that happening."

The bartender stopped pointing, leaned forward over the bar and pressed a cylindrical, metal tube to his throat. "She—knows—you're—here." A grinding effort-filled robotic voice came out of the device.

Ruby turned around and realized that the bartender hadn't been pointing to an office door, he'd been pointing to the waif dancing on the stage.

"Take—any—booth you—want," the bartender emitted. "She'll come—to you—when—this song's—over."

The old man smiled, with what teeth he still had, pulling the electrolarynx away from his throat. Trying to mask how mortified she was about threatening this poor man, Ruby returned the grin and then walked over to one of the round burgundy tufted vinyl booths that took up the back wall.

'Pour Some Sugar on Me' came to an end, eliciting a rousing, standing ovation from the balding man in perverts' row and the bony dancer to collect the three singles sadly spaced out on the stage. Once she'd rounded up her mis-fortune—and Def Leppard had finished serenading her—Sugar strutted over to the bar. Still topless, with nothing else on but a G-string, she exchanged words with the bartender, took a beer from him and then headed towards Ruby. The red attaché case was already out on top of the sticky table in anticipation. Ruby snapped the latches open, in a practiced, power-business move, readying herself for the approaching negotiations.

"Is it really you?! Quincy said it was. He was sure of it," Sugar asked, squinting her eyes.

"Depends on who you think I am?" Ruby said as Sugar sat her bare ass down onto the vinyl bench beside Ruby, studying her face as if Ruby were a living forgery.

"No way."

Ruby pulled an 8"x10", black and white print of her much younger self out of the attaché case and handed it to Sugar.

"Holy shit, it is you! You're her!" Sugar jumped to her feet, waving the 8"x10" to Quincy back at the bar. "It's her!" She could hardly contain herself as she bounced her way back onto the bench. "My God. Ruby Rain. You're like my idol!"

Ruby slowly lowered the lid on her case. "Oh, go on. Flattery will get you everywhere."

"I'm not fucking with you. You were in the first porn I ever saw. You inspired me!"

"I'm sorry about that," Ruby chuckled, half joking, half not.

"I can't believe you're here. I thought you were…" Sugar stopped herself.

"My word." As Ruby spoke, a sudden wave of heat rushed up her back, over her chest and through her cheeks. Perfect timing for a goddamn hot flash. They seemed to have a knack for making appearances at the worst possible moment these days. She knew her cheeks had to be as red as tomatoes, but there was nothing she could do about it. She couldn't fan herself in front of this yearling; she didn't want this girl's idol to turn into a crone and melt right before her eyes. She couldn't excuse herself either, she didn't want to show her age or weakness right at the beginning of her pitch, so she pressed on. "Well as you can see, I am very alive, very well and certainly not dead."

"No, you're not. You're here. Ruby fucking Rain is here! Wait, why are you here?" Sugar stuck her arms out, panning them from left to right, presenting the shithole to Ruby as if she hadn't realized where she was.

"I'm here about the job," Ruby said, trying to put a smile on her face, without losing face.

"A job?"

Ruby lifted the lid on her case again and pulled out the New Smyrna Daily. It was folded to the want ads, with a big red circle around the 'Help Wanted' for Shakers.

"Oh, that. That ad's for dancers," Sugar scoffed.

"I know. That's why I'm here. I thought your establishment could use a boost. I could headline, maybe Fridays or Saturdays—maybe both if you want. You said you know me from my films, but did you know that this is how I started? In small venues just like this." Ruby's shoulders dropped a little, letting go of jitters, because she had shown some of her cards. She looked around the dark, empty bar. What seconds ago was a dump, was now nostalgic. She was remembering the past and remembering her place in it.

"I know you did. Like I told you, you're my idol. I actually had a friend send me some flyers and a front-of-house poster of you—from when you did those shows in Reno."

"Reno? Wow, that was a long time ago."

BONE PARK

"They're going to be worth a lot of money someday."

"I don't know about that. Not sure how collectable peelers are. They're not baseball cards."

"They are to me."

"Well then, what do you think about the gig? Should we do an encore of Reno?"

Sugar, who had been all talk and flattery, was all of a sudden quiet. Avoiding Ruby's eyes. "Miss Rain, I don't know."

"It's Ruby—and it doesn't have to be a feature, per se." Ruby started scrambling. "If it's about the money, don't worry. You could pay me what you pay the other girls, until word gets out and I start packing them in. I wouldn't normally appear anywhere for less than my rate, but you're a true fan, so we'll call it a favor."

"Ah, fuck," Sugar said, setting her beer down on the table. "You're really doing this?"

"Well, yes. That's why I came down here."

Sugar turned and looked at Ruby, the adoration was suddenly gone from her eyes. "How old are you?"

"Excuse me?" Ruby was taken aback by the brashness of this young woman. From men she expected it, but not one of her kind.

"Fuck, Ruby, you shouldn't be up on that stage at this point in your life."

"This point in my life? Thank you but I am more than capable, and I'm excited too."

"But you shouldn't be."

"Why not?"

"Because it's not right!" Sugar snapped.

Ruby was at a loss, confused by Sugar's sudden anger.

The half-naked dancer took a moment to calm herself down before she continued. "I respect you, Ruby. I don't want you embarrassing yourself, going to strip bars up and down the I-95, pitching this. So, if you can't see the truth, then I'm just going to tell you. No one comes into places like this to watch their grandmother dance. I know who you are and some of them will probably remember who you *were*, but they don't want to see you like this. It's hard, but that's the truth."

Twenty years ago, Ruby would have smacked the lips off of her face. But that was twenty years ago, and Ruby didn't need the money back then. Maybe Sugar might be right. It's not like she hadn't thought about this. Hadn't locked herself in hotel bathrooms, crying over lines of powdery white, terrified that this day would come. Hadn't spiraled, becoming the 'naked Nostradamus', prophesizing her plummeting value with every leaving man and with every passing year. It's part of the reason she disappeared—and she'd have stayed a memory if it all had played out differently.

"I need a job," Ruby stated, humbly.

Sugar looked angry, "You? Don't go shitting me just to tickle your fancy one last time."

"I'm not lying. I really do need a job."

"But Rain videos? You owned all that. It was in People magazine. You're a millionaire."

"Was," Ruby said, unwavering and defeated.

Sugar sat back into the booth. "Fuck me. Really? How?"

"What you'd expect from a fortune made off of porn. Everyone who couldn't screw me physically, screwed me financially. Including myself."

Sugar was watching her Superwoman fall back down to earth. "That's not right."

"Well, you'll learn—if you haven't already—none of it's right."

"I'll help you," Sugar said, her voice thick with pity.

Although she had to practically beg for it, Ruby felt relieved. "Thank you."

"Can you serve drinks?"

Ruby didn't quite catch that, or maybe she didn't want to. "Say again, the music's a little loud."

Sugar sighed, "It's always loud. It's a strip bar, Ruby. Do you think you can serve drinks? Can you carry a tray? Count cash? Stay on your feet all night?"

A waitress? How could the famous Ruby Rain do that and still keep her dignity? This was not the offer she came in for. This was not dancing. No feature or pole spins. No dollars to fill her G-string and no adoration to fill her ego.

"That's what I can do for you, Ruby. If you think you can handle it."

Ruby looked around the empty bar. It couldn't be that hard. This place didn't look like it ever got packed. With so few people coming in, who would know? And wouldn't have to tell Bernie. As far as she was concerned, Ruby would just tell her that she was working in a strip club. If she didn't say anything else, the logical assumption would be that she was working as a stripper. Who knows, by mingling with the customers, flirting, reminding them of who she was, she'd be able to make some money and maybe created a buzz. Create a demand for her to get back on the stage, maybe even feature. Ruby had hustled her whole life, that's what Buffalo Girls did, hustle. So, why would this be any different? Maybe this was the sign. The real reason for coming here. The sign telling her that she needed to keep fighting. To remind her that she was a hustler. That there were a few rounds left and that her life wasn't over—yet. "When can I start?"

CHAPTER 3

Champagne

It was local season. The rumble of Harleys and bass-rattling hatchbacks of spring breakers had passed on—cremated in the hot, early days of summer. It was the beginning of the heat that tourists found unpalatable and offensive, like the real hot sauce, consumed in the staffroom of every all-inclusive resort. It was June and the mobile home with the yellow stripe was still inhabited by the Buffalo Girls. They'd been able to pull in their purse strings and survive on the money from the Lincoln and Ruby's tips. It wasn't glamourous, but they were still holding onto their piece of paradise. They still had their mornings poolside, their afternoons in the lanai and their rides around the park on their trikes—when Ruby wasn't working of course. But it all came at a cost, everything always does.

Shakers was far busier when the sun came down than Ruby had

expected, but the strip bar clientele weren't as generous as she remembered them being. That could have had something to do with her holding onto a tray, not a pole. The cash thrown at the stage was not the same kind of financial gratitude that came with slinging drinks. Her small hauls also could have had something to do with her uniform. Her bra top and short shorts didn't look the same on her as they did on the other, younger waitresses. Whatever the reason was, she was being run off her feet, having to fight for every quarter that they left on her cork-topped tray. The past three months hadn't reaped the droves of fans she had hoped for. There were no clamoring patrons demanding to see Ruby Rain back on the stage. Most of the guys in there barely looked at her when ordering or receiving their drinks, but they were nothing to look at either. She'd miscalculated the demographic for this hole in the wall. This dump was full of cheap ugly washed-up sex addicts and cheating husbands in their late forties. They were rude, angry and dismissive. They sucked back drinks like their redemption might be found at the bottom of the next one and kept their change to fund it. And it wasn't only the guys that were giving her the gears, it was the girls too.

"Ruby!" the scarlet-haired stripper on the stage barked, as Ruby was trying to take a drink order from the two jerks sitting in perverts' row, who had snapped their fingers at her. "Piss off until my set's done and stop bugging my fans!" the stripper snarled, then spread her legs and blew a kiss to the jerks.

"They called me over, Sparkle!" Ruby defended herself.

"You want me get Sugar?"

Ruby backed down immediately, stepping away from the stage. Sparkle winked and blew her a kiss too, from between her legs.

Sparkle? Ruby grunted her name inside her head. She knew her real name was probably Margret or Ursula. She was a cheap rhythmically-challenged skank who smelled of fried onions and had probably given herself that name. Ruby never used a stage name. She was born Ruby and got naked as Ruby. She was proud of her profession. She loved the adoration of her crowd and didn't want to give any of that away, even to a stage name. The Rain came later, away from the stage and close to the camera. It was given to her by her first and only agent Hiram Goldblatt. He gave it to her because of a 'special talent' she possessed, and it stuck. It followed her from 16mm to VHS and worldwide distribution. Sparkle was just some meth-smoking bitch, from the Florida swamps who would never amount to anything. That stage was the peak of Sparkle's career and even though Ruby wanted so desperately to smack her off it, she couldn't because she was on her last chance with Sugar.

"Ruby!" a voice shouted, but this one came from over at the bar, not the stage. It was Sugar.

Ruby acknowledged her with the finger. Not the middle one, although she thought about it, it was the index finger, the universal sign for 'just a sec'. Sugar was not fond of waiting, Ruby had learned that, so she soothed the impatient child by holding up her finger as she weaved her way through the slalom course of cocktail tables towards her.

"What was that with Sparkle?" Sugar prodded, not hiding her accusatory tone. It had been months since she fan-girled over Ruby and for Sugar, Ruby had lost her sparkle.

"She wanted me to have a drink ready for her in the dressing room when her slow song's done," Ruby answered. "Why?"

"Because you have a habit of stirring up shit," Sugar said, matter of fact.

"No shit here," Ruby said with a smile.

"Better not be. If you're pulling the same shit you did with Diamond and Candy, you know I'll have to let you go."

"I know."

"Ruby. Look, I love ya—but I don't need ya. You're not the main attraction anymore."

"I know." Tried to keep her chin up.

BONE PARK

"Do you? You're the slowest waitress I've ever seen, and you have a real talent for pissing off my dancers. Not personal, just basic dollars and cents. Sparkle, Candy, Diamond—they make me money—you don't. Remember that!" Sugar said, with the backhand warning of a pimp.

Ruby fought to keep the pleasant half smile on her face, because if she let go of it, she'd have turned into tears. Ruby carried this indignity all by herself. The stripping away of her final, thin layer of worth—the last barrier holding onto her self-respect. Bernie had no idea that this was how it was going. She thought Ruby was dancing. She didn't approve of it, but she believed her sister was making ends meet, the best way she knew how and doing it with the adoration of men. This was partly true, but not how Ruby wanted or deserved.

Over the shoulder of Sugar, a tall, dark-haired man, in a silky, large-collared shirt, casually waved to Ruby from the back booths of the room.

Ruby made eye contact with him and set her tray down on the bar. "Sugar, is it okay if I take my break now?"

Sugar was blown away. "Are you fucking with me? I just finish telling you that it basically costs me money to have you here and you ask me to go on a break? You know the other girls don't get breaks."

"I know, but the other girls don't have as many miles on them as me. It's my feet…these heels are…"

Sugar waved her off. "Fuck, just go. I can't have you collapsing on the floor—but I'm giving anyone who comes in, to Cammy, even if they sit in your section—so hurry up!"

"Thanks. I'll just be a few minutes. Let my corns rest…"

"Gross! And you wanted to go on my stage with that shit? Fuck me—just go!" Sugar put her hand on Ruby's shoulder, physically pushing her out of her eyeline.

Ruby walked over to the double, glassless doors with the big warning sign above them that said Employees Only. She shot a look over to the dark-haired man in the back, then pushed the swinging doors open and entered.

The dressing room of a strip club is a completely different world. A subculture of a subversive culture, but it isn't the sexual slumber party men have cooked up in their misogynistic minds. It's their boring staffroom, their pre and post performance hangout, their green room full of nerves, their gossip chamber, their gym, their boxing ring, their drugstore, their therapist's office and their bank.

Diamond, Candy and a couple of the other dancers were in there when Ruby entered. They were bartering and trading outfits, going over floorwork, doing sit ups, makeup and lines. Candy looked up from a powder-covered mirror on the counter to glare at Ruby's reflection in the makeup mirror of her station. Ruby ignored her and kept walking towards the bouncer-guarded, steel door at the back of the room. She had to ignore Candy—and the other girls too. If she didn't, she and Bernie would be out on the streets in a matter of weeks—a wonderful realization that hung over her every step. Many things had come to light in the months since she started there; like that jobs for people over 60 were as rare as a virgin stripper, that Sugar was an asshole, but she occasionally was right. Ruby *was* a horrible waitress. While the rest of the servers were clearing a few hundred a week, she could barely make enough money for groceries. But something else came to light. This job offered other means of income, you just had to look for them. Desperation is the mother of means. Means she wasn't proud of, but she had turned to in the past and these means had always come through and kept the lights on.

The back door of the strip club opened, and a big, tattooed man held the door for Ruby.

"Thanks, Kurt. I'm just going out to have a cigarette," Ruby said to the imposing bouncer.

"But you don't smoke, Miss Ruby," Kurt stated.

"Must you do this every time." Ruby raised her eyebrow.

BONE PARK

"Must you?"

Ruby sighed, "Mind your business, Kurt. I'll knock when I need back in."

"You knock, Miss Ruby, if you need anything. Anything at all," Kurt said to her with the kind concern of a grandson, before shooting an evil eye out into the parking lot.

Ruby gently tapped Kurt on his huge shoulder, reassuring him and the ink-covered crusader stepped inside, closing the steel door behind him.

On the edge of the lot, a dark car flashed its lights and Ruby headed for it. Dark parking lots, dark cars and women do not go well together. They're on a long list of places that women don't tend to stroll around in alone. A growing list of dangerous spaces that is added to by the day in a world that continues to grow more hostile to them at the same alarming rate. It's astonishing that any woman would wander anywhere in the world anymore. Surprising that they continue to emerge from their captivity knowing the whole time they are being hunted. No man would risk the same fate. That's why their invisible barriers continue to go up, trying to build smaller and smaller corrals. Men rule and are ruled by fear—but women are not men. In this world just moving freely is a massive show of bravery. Women merely going about their day, doing their desired tasks, is in fact an act of defiance and protest. Walking into the boardroom or across a dark parking lot, is a usurpation of the polite society that sexualizes, brutalizes, vilifies and denies their power and their right to choose their own path.

Ruby got closer to the dark car and through the windshield she could see the face of the dark-haired man behind the wheel. He leaned over, unlocked the passenger door and then smiled, taking some of the danger out of the air—but not all of it.

Ruby opened the door and got inside. "Hey. I haven't got a lot of time."

The smile faded from his face. He looked let down. "Okay, so what then?"

"Well, I don't have time for a full, but I can give you a half?"

"My friend said you give fulls."

"Not tonight honey, my boss is on my back. Just a half."

"How much is that?"

Ruby looked around the lot. But it wasn't to see if the coast was clear, it was to gather her pride. "Thirty."

"Forty," the dark-haired man said. "Without a condom."

"Forty, with a condom," Ruby quickly countered.

"What? It was thirty."

"It was." Ruby reached for the door handle.

"Okay, fine. Forty. With a condom," the dark-haired man pleaded.

Ruby sized up his demeanor. His desperation. His eyes that kept glancing up and down her chest.

"Fifty. Up front, and if you're not done in two minutes, you're on your own."

The man cowered a little, uncomfortably put in his place. He dug into his pants and pulled out the cash. "Fifty," he said handing it to her. "Is it true you're a porn star?"

Ruby pulled her long, wavy, red hair back. "You're goddamn right I am."

Bernie and Ruby were sprawled out on two of the white-plastic-strapped chaise lounges that littered the deck around the park's kidney-shaped pool. It was pre-noon—10:30am or so—and all the regulars were in their respective plastic plots as well. The placement of your pool chair was earned in Cicada Hollow, unofficially assigned in a sort of seniority of seniors. The ones who'd been there the longest, had their dibs on chairs and placement and the rest chose theirs in descending order of residency. This system worked very well for those who had been here the longest, that were still alive, but for 'newcomers' it was an uphill climb.

Bernie had been in the park for five years, which wasn't a long time, but in that time, there had been a lot of attrition. William Morris and the wear and tear of WWII had a lot to do with that. So, with cancer running rampant and after a particularly bad winter of the flu, the sisters had arrived. Bernie—and by association, Ruby's chair—had finally made it to the south side of the pool and were proudly facing north. This was prime property, full sun arc, no shadows from the pool house, near Maryanne, Cecilia and the other of the park's matriarchy.

Ruby was sawing logs, snoring face down on the flattened lounge. She was a beautiful golden-brown by then, seasoned to perfection after months turning over on this poolside rotisserie. Bernie however was only a shade or two darker than a ghost. She was a devotee of sunscreen and wide-brimmed hats. She liked the warmth and buzz of the sun-soaked pool deck, just not the leather-making burns of it. She always thought it was ironic that 'sun worship' and hide processing were both called tanning.

Bernie was paying close attention to the two new members in the park who were walking across the thick grass towards the pool. They'd been in Cicada Hollow for a few months, but still hadn't gotten the hang of heat timing. Tourists always had difficulty with heat timing, the delicate dance of doing activities in the hottest months of the year. Florida in June, July and August didn't have to be oppressive, you just had to learn how to schedule your movements around the placement of the sun. As the newcomers approached the pool, the seasoned seniors were starting to leave. It was time to move on to shadier activities. Maryanne and her litter were packing up and Bernie should have been too, but she still hadn't met these newbies—the ones that bought Connie and Merle's place. Most newcomers were on a first-name basis in the first week, but not these two. That's what made them so intriguing. Bernie liked having a bead on everyone, and these beads were missing from her string. What were they hiding? Maybe they weren't hiding anything. Maybe they were just very private people. Whatever the reason, Bernie saw the pool exodus as the perfect time to find out. If they were private, she could get to know these new neighbors, without the curious ears of Maryanne and the Canasta Club.

Maryanne and her dark, greasy, Coppertone skin stopped on her way past Bernie's chair. "You know, if your sister wants to sleep, maybe she should do it in your trailer?" she said with a condescending smirk, using her long, coral-painted nails to point at Ruby. "No offence, but the snoring is quite unsettling. Couldn't read a page of my book and trust me, Dean Koontz is hard to distract me from. Do you read Dean Koontz? He's really gripping—anyhoo, the point is, Bernie, this pool is a quiet zone."

"I know, Maryanne."

"I know you know, that's why I'm so shocked. Wouldn't want to have to make a noise complaint about her. For snoring? Can you imagine? Honestly, how mortifying would it be to have that in the minutes of the next park meeting?"

"I'll take care of it," Bernie assured her, politely, wanting to move Maryanne along so she could get back to the fresh meat that was approaching.

"Wonderful." Maryanne seemed satiated enough to be on her way, but not before shelling out one last shot. "You might want to get some shade, Bernie, sun's a little high for your complexion."

Bernie was well aware of her pale palette so this didn't insult her the way Maryanne had hoped it would, instead she just smiled and turned her attention to the couple that had almost reached the pool gate. As they were about to enter, the man suddenly stopped his wife, pointing to the 'No Smoking' sign on the side of the pool house. The woman rolled her eyes, but stayed outside the gate, where she hauled hard on her cigarette, trying to get the last few precious puffs out of it.

"Morning!" Bernie said. "Or should I say afternoon?" At this point in the introduction, she needed to play it safe, so she joked in that palatable, Midwest, ham and cheese fashion.

"Afternoon?" the short woman responded in a thick, Bostonian accent, throwing her cigarette to the ground and grinding it into the grass under her blue flip-flop.

"No, it's still morning." Bernie put away the Bible Belt standup routine. "I was joking."

The woman was unproportionally offended. "Why?"

"Reg," the man behind her stepped forward, speaking far more friendly, but with the same Boston sound, "and this here is my wife, Freda."

Bernie stood up and closed the distance between them, with her hand extended.

Reg was the first to take it. "Wow. That's a firm handshake. I'm willing to bet that you weren't just some schlep's secretary, were you?"

Bernie let go of his hand to take the barely offered hand of Freda. "I was a Union Rep," Bernie said quickly, while keeping her eyes on Freda. "Nice to meet you, Freda. I'm Verna, but my friends call me Bernie."

"Nice to meet you, Verna," Freda responded, pulling her hand from the shake, having spent an acceptable amount of time holding a stranger's hand. She took her freed hand and starting to walk towards the chairs on the other side of the pool deck.

"Where you going, Freda?" Reg sort of chuckled, having dropped his towel and bag down on the lounges beside Bernie and Ruby.

Freda stopped and turned back—reluctantly.

Ruby suddenly snored, loudly, choking a little.

Freda looked both disgusted and concerned. "Is she okay?"

"She's fine. That's my sister, Ruby. She works nights."

"Works? Still?" Freda seemed put off.

"What's wrong with that? I'd still be on the road with Prudential if you hadn't made me retire," Reg said, then tried to turn an obvious truth into a joke. "She wanted me all to herself."

"Oh, stop it." Freda blushed and set her stuff down on the lounge beside his, surrendering to his charm.

Bernie paid very close attention to this small but powerful moment between these two. Freda, from first impressions, was a pill. Bernie was positive Freda had the remnants of a broom handle permanently placed in her posterior, but one little word from Reg and she was butter. Reg was nice. Not flirty, or inappropriate, just sociable. This was an interesting dynamic, a peek behind the curtains of their relationship psychology. What made people tick or a not tick was of particular interest and importance to Bernie. So, this little display made waiting out in the hot sun to introduce herself worthwhile.

Reg dove into the pool. Not a huge stunt for most people, but it was Evil Knievel territory for the over 65 crowd. With that splash, it appeared that Bernie had a rebel on her hands. Reg was breaking all the rules. The ones written in tile all around the deck that said 'No Diving' as well as the unwritten ones. The socially acceptable rules that governed the behaviors of the retired. Men were supposed to use the cement stairs in the shallow end. They were to hold onto the handrail that ran down the middle of them, complaining all the way, until their enlarged prostates broke the surface. At that point they lean forward, like 'old growth forest' falling into the water, extending their hand out so they'd be ready to turn their fall into a breaststroke. Women were to make a slow descent down the metal-tube ladder, one plastic rung at a time, to introduce themselves into the chlorinated liquid. They were to pause as soon as the water had reached swimsuit-skirt level. This was to let the blood adjust and to display the majesty of their suit frills as they floated around them. For some women, the half dunk was the whole swim, while others would continue down the ladder, submerging themselves in the brine, but none of them would let their heads go below the water. Never—ever. Those were the rules around the Bone Park, but this James Dean apparently played by his own.

"So where are you from, Freda?" Bernie did already know, not just from the heavy accent, but from Opal's first report. Even though she knew, she needed a way in.

"Worchester. Mass." Freda kept it short.

"We're from Buffalo. Well, Grand Island originally. But we grew up in Buffalo. I spent most of my life there. Ruby…she spent a little time in just about everywhere."

"Union woman you said?" Reg joined in, swimming up to the edge of the pool and then resting his crossed arms on the deck. "What union?"

"SEIU 1199."

"Healthcare, isn't it?"

"It is." Bernie seemed surprised that he knew that.

"They have a chapter in Mass. Did some work for them in the early eighties. Remember, Freda?"

Freda shook her head, less enthused about the topic than him.

"Sure you do. Worked on term life for them."

"If you say so, Reg." Freda was still not into this.

"Isn't 1199 the biggest healthcare union in the USA?"

"Uh, huh." Bernie was pulling back too, suddenly as put off by this line of questioning as Freda.

"What did you do?" Bernie shifted the spotlight onto Freda.

"I worked for Reg. From home. Bookkeeping mostly," she said a little withdrawn.

Reg wouldn't let her hide behind modesty. "Without her, we'd have been dead in the water. Certainly wouldn't have been able to move down here." Reg leaned back into the pool and shouted her praise, "She's a goddamn abacus!"

"What's all the shouting about?" Ruby snapped awake, flipped over and sat straight up.

"Ruby, this is—RUBY!" Bernie jumped up from her chair, throwing her arms in front of Ruby, who had forgotten that she had undone her top for strapless tanning purposes.

"Oh my God!" Freda shouted.

Ruby looked down at her bare chest, barely being covered by Bernie's arms, struggling to do some kind of nipple-blocking semaphore. Of course, Ruby wasn't shy, not bothered in the least about her exposure. She'd spent half her life with both of the girls out. She was proud of her attributes, and they were practically unicorns in the greater senior citizen community. No one in the park, or in any retiree park along the A1A for that matter, had her famous curves and they were famous for a reason.

Reg let out a boisterous, belly jiggling laugh. "You certainly know how to make one hell of an entrance, don't you, Ruby?"

***

The sun had just set. It was Ruby's night off at Shakers, so Bernie and Ruby did what they always did on her nights off—they pedaled their trikes around the park. Ruby's trike had changed. Along with using things she found, she'd managed to scrounge a bit of her earnings here and there to make it her own. It had a red seat, red grips with streamers coming out of them, an aerial with silk scarfs tied to it and she'd replaced her rear basket with an old cooler. She was very proud of her handiwork, but she wouldn't be showing it off this evening, no, this evening they were riding alone. Bernie couldn't handle facing Maryanne and the others on the off chance that Freda or Reg had told them what had happened at the pool. She was a little surprised it had taken this long for Ruby's girls to make an appearance in the park, but regardless, it was going to be a very hard pill to swallow, when it was force fed to her by Maryanne.

"It was an accident, Bern," Ruby said.

Bernie had been quiet all afternoon. She wasn't ignoring Ruby, just the topic and unfortunately Ruby was guilty by association.

"What was?" Bernie replied, playing dumb.

"Boobie Gate," Ruby stated.

"Boobie Gate?" Bernie, couldn't help herself, snorting a laugh that wouldn't be held in.

"Yes, the scandal of the century. The upper half of my body was exposed to daylight. So was Reg's. I don't know why you're so uptight about it. Why do you even care what these people think?"

They continued to pedal their trikes down the road, side by each.

"It's not that I care." Bernie let her chuckle subside. "It's that I can't stand the look on Maryanne's face. Her and her school of piranhas feed off this kind of thing."

"So, let them feed. It was just my boobs. Hell, half the USA and most of Asia have seen them by now. Well, maybe not this version, but one of their predecessors most definitely."

"Yoo-hoo!" The dinging of her bell was unnecessary, it was Opal. The Buffalo Girls parted to make room for her. "Sorry if I'm interrupting."

"It's okay, Opal. You're always welcome," Bernie reassured her listlessly, slightly put off by the polite interruption.

Ruby had grown to like this, having Opal around, tagging along, always on their tail. It was like they had another sister. A little sister. Even though Opal was ten years older than Ruby, she finally had someone below her, taking her place on the roster and moving her up a notch.

"You two are early," Opal pointed out, with a slight accusation to her observation.

"Yes, sorry. We wanted to get a ride in before The Wheel," Bernie said, slightly apologetically.

"You like The Wheel? You've never mentioned it?"

"Well, we're beginning to take a shine to it." Bernie did her best to back up this ridiculous lie.

"I hate The Wheel," Opal blurted out. This was unlike her. For Opal, hate may as well have been the f-word. "Stan loves it. Always making googly eyes at that Vanna White. I think it's indecent. The way she parades herself around in those, barely-there outfits—"

"You know what was barely there?" Ruby scoffed.

"Zip it!" Bernie snapped.

"She's going to hear about it sooner or later."

"Hear what?" Opal's ears perked up.

"Fine," Bernie sighed.

"I accidently flashed the Boston couple," Ruby laughed.

"Flashed?" Opal didn't understand.

"Yes, I was sunbathing, face down, with my straps untied and when I sat up, I flashed them," Ruby kept laughing.

Opal started to giggle, but it was weird. It was put on, only laughing to seem in on it. "Really? That's funny."

Ruby saw right through what she was doing. "My word, Opal, did you grow up in a convent? I sat up and my tits popped out!"

"Ruby!" Bernie snapped.

"What? Tits? Why can't I say tits?"

Opal's jaw was practically dragging on the pavement behind her pink trike.

Bernie snapped again, "Ruby. Dial it back a little. Remember where you are!"

"I know where I am, and this place needs to loosen up. Don't you think, Opal?"

Opal didn't know what to think, caught in the middle of this argument between her two surrogate sisters, so she just smiled.

"See there? Opal agrees." Ruby took her hands off the handlebars and raised them above her head. "Tits, tits, tits," she cheered out into the air. "Tits, tits, tits! Come on, Opal, say it, it feels good."

"Stop it, Ruby," Bernie pleaded.

"No. You should say it too. Tits, tits, tits! It's like a Band-Aid. Let's just rip it off. Come on." Ruby was still a cheering section of one, but that didn't stop her, she just kept on cheering, "Tits, tits, tits. Who cares? It's just a word. And they are just tits! We are the ones who have them, so we should be allowed to say it. It's our word. Tits! Opal, you know what Stan's looking at when he watches The Wheel?"

Opal was even more confused. "Vanna White?"

"No, he's looking at her tits. You have tits, don't you?"

Opal didn't know what to do or say.

"Well, don't you?" Ruby kept on her.

"Yes. I guess," Opal nodded.

"Then own 'em! Tell Stan to stop looking at hers and look at yours! Own 'em! Tits, tits, tits!"

Opal mumbled under her breath, "T—its, t-its."

"You can do better than that. Who cares what people think? They are a part of our body! They are *ours* to celebrate! Tits, tits, tits!"

Opal started to lose herself in Ruby's hoopla. "Tits, tits, tits!"

"Yes, Opal! Tits, tits, tits!"

The two women shouted out, over the clicking of their trikes and the whining cicadas. It was ridiculous and loud and somehow wonderful. Bernie didn't join in, but she didn't try to stop them either. They kept saying the swear over and over and it soon turned into a sort of chant. A repetitive song, like you'd hear in the stands of a game. Funny thing was, that as it became a chant, it also lost its bite. The word lost its taboo and just became another word.

"Opal?!" A woman shouted, barging out of her lanai screen door with her arms crossed. Offended.

Opal clammed up immediately and the three slowed their trikes to a stop.

"What in the Lord's name are you doing, riding around shouting obscenities like some juvenile delinquent?" The woman kept storming towards the road.

"Calm down, Cecilia," Bernie piped up.

Right behind Cecilia, Maryanne emerged from the same lanai. "Bernie? What is—"

"Oh great. You're both here. They were just having fun, ladies."

"Do you remember fun?" Ruby mocked.

"That did not sound like fun," Maryanne chirped.

BONE PARK

"It's not that bad really. Actually, it's the name of a bird in New Zealand," Opal said as bright as a kindergarten teacher.

"Shut up, Opal," Maryanne snapped.

"Hey!" Bernie's eyes changed. "Don't talk to her like that."

"Oh, it's okay." Opal withdrew.

"No, it's not," Bernie said, with her eyes locked on Maryanne.

Ruby took notice of the change in Bernie and acted quickly. "Okay, this has gotten way out of hand. We're all women here. We should be supporting each other, not bickering. What I think is needed here is for you, Maryanne, and you, Cecilia, to get off your broomsticks and just celebrate your tits!"

Cecilia was totally blindsided. Maryanne however was now fuming, she couldn't believe the audacity, the gall, the…

Bernie saw the anger on Maryanne's face and in that look, she began to understand exactly what Ruby had been saying. What did it matter? They weren't breaking any law. Nothing that would warrant or could warrant any kind of police interaction. All they were doing was swearing—if that. Why did the opinions of these people matter, especially around something so silly as this? Bernie realized that by keeping up appearances she hadn't been blending in, she was bending over, becoming them. The camouflage of normality she had covered herself in was starting to stain her skin and she did not like the color.

Bernie stared right into Maryanne's eyes and started singing, "Tits, tits, tits."

Ruby jumped in with her. "Tits, tits, tits."

Opal started laughing so hard, mostly out of nervousness, that she could barely pronounce the T's, but started saying it too. "T-its, its, its."

Maryanne and Cecilia were beside themselves with outrage, but the rheumatoid riders didn't care. They kept on chanting as they pedaled away, filling the Hollow with a chorus of mammary celebration, announcing their freedom and their cemented, united sisterhood.

Word travels fast, even in the Bone Park where most of the residents are hard of hearing. The word that morning wasn't just the usual cold gossip, it was ablaze. With the raging wildfire of opinions burning its way around the Hollow, Bernie and Ruby thought it best to stay put and drink their instant coffee in the lanai. Normally they would be moseying over to the activity center where there was always fresh baked treats on Saturday mornings. It was a fierce, delicious competition that the residents kept stoked. They never would declare a clear winner for fear the bakers might lose their competitive drive and the sweets would be cut off. Out of all the competitors, Gladys' turnovers were the best, but Dasha's Babkas were no slouch. The sisters usually headed straight for their tables and got one of each. But this Saturday morning the Buffalo Girls would have to sip their Sanka sans sweets and put off developing "type two" for another week.

Ruby was sitting under the trailer's side window, at the wicker table, reading the Daytona Beach News-Journal. Bernie, like always, was in her throne. The high back wicker chair, at the far end of the screened porch, that faced the road. It was her woven, wooden place of power, hidden right there, under the park's elderly, upturned noses. It was the secret helm of her stealthy ship where she silently reigned over her kingdom for the last five years—until that morning. The silent queen's secret name was now on all the subjects' lips and Bernie knew better than anyone, what happens when the people are aware of the crown.

Bernie kept her eye on the road, watching the obvious uptick of early morning traffic. There were the rhythmic swish-swish of the K-Way suited speed walkers who passed by, looking directly into the lanai, not even trying to hide their surveillance. There were the trikes that made their fourth, fifth, even sixth drive-bys and there were the few, brave, single pedestrians, that gave slow waves, pretending they were on their way to get the mail, even though it was a Saturday.

"Pathetic," Bernie sighed, causing Ruby to raise her eyes above the newspaper.

"I told you."

"I knew they were uptight but Jesus, Poob."

Ruby lowered the paper. "Give it time. You're not used to this, but I am. I spread shock around like VD."

"Ruby."

"It's a joke, Bern. Like last night. Who cares? I learned my lesson long ago. That's why I never pretend to be someone I'm not. They always end up finding out anyway, so why bother. I'm proud of what you did last night, finally letting your real self out."

"My real self? We were being foolish."

"Foolish, precisely. That's the Bernie I remember. We used to do things like that all the time when we were young. Never cared who was around." Ruby stood up and started to sing, "Buffalo Girls won't you come out tonight, come out tonight, come out tonight—"

"Ruby." Bernie cut her off, glaring past her at the old couple walking by who were watching Ruby dance around like a Bathtub Gin Flapper.

"Oh, Bern, I've got a newsflash for you, you don't need to protect me. Try and cover up who I am. That guy out there already knows. Most of the men here do, well the ones who aren't 'a friend of Judy's'. The husbands here saw my sins the moment they laid eyes on me, or at least they suspected it. The women don't know though. That's how it usually goes. Husbands keep them in the dark, so they don't have to admit how they know who I am. It's more than likely that there is a tape or two of my work right here in Cicada Hollow, hidden up in a false ceiling or stashed in the shed along with one of my spreads. Other than the couple of 'lezi's' I've clocked who most certainly already know, the rest of the women will find out sooner or later. And that's okay. It will be a hot topic for a week or so, then it will be yesterday's Daytona Journal. It always works like that, so stop hiding it. Stop pretending. You be you and let me be me. I'm not embarrassed about what I've done in my life, so why would you be?"

"Poob. I'm not embarrassed. To tell the truth, I was a little jealous. I was tied up and knocked up while you were living the dream in the Hollywood Hills. You stopped being my sister and became a fantasy. So many people's fantasy. My fantasy. You had fans, while the rest of us had bills, and diapers and grumpy husbands. You were every woman's other woman. You built an empire—"

"I lost an empire."

"But you built it. In a man's world, in man's media; you took what was yours."

"And they took it back."

"They always do. But some girl out there saw you. Saw it was possible and will do it again. Because of you. I'm not ashamed of you, not at all."

"Then what is it? Why are you hiding here, in this park? Afraid of what those sour tarts think?"

Bernie looked at her. Looked deep into her eyes. There was so much to say that could never be said. So much to tell her, to warn her about; but that was not how it was done. Bernie broke her eye contact, looking away for something to change the subject too.

"I thought you had a job?" she said, taking Ruby completely off guard.

"Pardon?"

Bernie pointed to the paper Ruby had put down onto the wicker table. "Did you get fired?"

BONE PARK

Ruby looked down to the paper and saw the ad she had circled in red marker. "No. Just keeping my options open." Ruby thought about the words that just left her lips. About the lies buried in them. Hypocrite. She had just berated Bernie about hiding who she was, touting herself as never wearing a mask, but she was. "I hate it there," Ruby blurted out, pulling the cork from the bottled-up emotions she'd been hiding for months. "They treat me—like shit."

Bernie sat forward on the edge of her seat, as if there were a physical threat in the lanai that she could lunge for. "Who does? The boss? The men? Other dancers?"

"All of the above. Everyone there except Quincy and Kurt; the bartender and the bouncer."

"But I thought you were loving it? Up on stage, your encore, being featured again?"

"I'm not dancing. They won't even let me near the stage. I'm a waitress and I'm horrible at it." Ruby's eyes teared up.

"Oh, Poob. It's okay. Why didn't you tell me?"

"I guess, I was pretending too. I don't care what anyone thinks—except you. I didn't want you to be disappointed." Ruby wanted to tell her more. Tell her about what was happening in the parking lot. How she was really paying the bills, but she couldn't bring herself to. She feared that would undo the pride her big sister had just bestowed upon her. The approval she had been showered with. She could live with it; the shame that came with the tricks' cash. She was hardened to it decades ago, but it was her shame, and she couldn't bear burdening her sister with it.

"To hell with them. Just quit!"

"How? How will we survive?"

"We'll find a way. We always do."

Just like she had always done, in every other overwhelming situation, Ruby dried her eyes, put her shoulders back and lifted her chin.

"This is the only way. The best option I have. We won't make it long on what you have. That's the truth and you know it. Bird in the hand, Bern—no one else wants to hire us. Not at our age. We're past due. Rotten fruit that no one wants around, because they think we're stinking up the joint."

It wasn't untrue. Bernie knew it. She'd seen it for herself. She searched her head for the encouraging words her sister needed to hear, but she couldn't find any. This hard truth was unavoidable and undeniable. It had forced her out of her former world and followed her into this one.

"If you'll excuse me, I think I'm going to lay down for a bit," Ruby said, rising from her chair.

"Okay," Bernie agreed, offering no resistance. "Are you alright?"

"We have to be," Ruby replied stepping up into the trailer. "Can you make sure I'm up by 11:00? They've moved me to the afternoon shift. Part of the perk of being the worst waitress there," she said as the metal screen door closed and she faded into the day-dark trailer.

Bernie sat back into her large wicker chair, alone in the lanai. A new wake of buzzards had gathered during Ruby's confession and were now circling their plot. She watched them as she sipped her lukewarm instant coffee, wishing it tasted more like tequila and grenadine. This was not the worst situation she had ever been in, but it was caused by it. The worst of her, led to the least of her; made her less and opened the door for scavengers. Her wits had always gotten her to shore, but she had suppressed them along with herself. To stay safe, she had to lay low. The plan was to disappear. Fade into the golden years crowd, as a different person. But was she? What she had her heart set on had not disappeared. Ruby still wore her past, her true self like a full-patch biker, for all the road to see, so why wouldn't she? This next-door Nancy routine had worked for her holidays, her establishing visits, but it wasn't working anymore. That was it. Her sister had made it abundantly clear. Bernie needed to be who she was. This was not what she was down here for.

BONE PARK

Suddenly, the blind could see. As if her surrender to true self had let the light into her darkened mind, she saw things differently. Well, one thing in particular. The paper. She stood up from her chair and snatched it off the table where Ruby had left it. But it wasn't the want ads that piqued her interest. There was no 'help wanted' square that caught her eye, it's what was on the other part of it. On the front page, that Ruby had set to the side. It was in the large headline. Something in the bold, black letters lit the fire in her eyes.

Dade County Wrapped In Deadly Drug War, While Volusia County Boasts Record Arrests Made Using Sheriff's New Profiling Program.

Bernie sat patiently in the lanai, looking at the watch on her wrist. It was an old watch. A man's watch. It had a slim profile, simple face and smooth leather band. It had been buried in the bottom of her purse, one of the only things she brought with her from Buffalo. Brought from her past. It was Sal's watch. His pride and joy. The one thing he counted on as much as her.

She waited until the minute hand had grazed the three, giving a good fifteen-minute buffer, in case Ruby forgot something and her taxi had to double back. With no sign of the yellow top returning, she turned her attention to the inner circle. The open grassy area behind her trailer that held the pool, shuffleboard, lawn bowling and activity center. The activity center was over on the far left-hand side of the circle, by the entrance to the park. The large, flat-roofed building with the tan siding, was home to all the indoor events of the park, including today's poker game. Every Saturday the game kicked off at noon and in the summer months it was packed. Not because the geezers in the park had more money to burn in June, July and August, but because the activity center had incredible air conditioning. There were other poker games during the week at night, at different trailers around the park, but none of them drew the sun-weary crowd in like the Saturday game. And that Saturday's game had the added incentive of spicy gossip. Bernie knew the poker game would be all abuzz with the events of yesterday, specifically discussions centered around her sister's nudity because men were drawn to titillation like flies to shit.

Even though the elderly are known for being punctual, actually pre-punctual, there were still a few stragglers crossing the open grass. It was these stragglers that Bernie was interested in. One straggler in particular—Stan. He was a drinker. A rise and shine sort of drinker. Everyone in the park knew it, but he was the life of the party, every party, so no one cared. They were all cut from the same cloth. All businessmen forged in that time were like that. It was an unhealthy helping of work with a side of booze. All of them had a wet bar in their offices, did meetings over drinks at lunch, golf games with drinks, dinner with drinks, everything with drinks. Stan was just more committed to it than the others, bringing the work ethic of drinking into retirement. He was always late to everything and would have missed everything entirely if it weren't for his wife, Opal.

"Come on, Stan." And there she was, gently guiding a rather pickled Stan out into the open grass. Her hands full, carrying his poker chip carrier and a small cooler with a few cold ones in it to keep him level for the game—because nothing kills a good poker game like a man going through withdrawals.

A few wobbly steps out into the grass, Stan finally found his sea legs, snatching his arm away from Opal and taking her care packages from her hands. As Stan continued on his way, solo, Opal watched him intently, with the worried concern of a preschooler's mother.

Once Stan had opened the sliding glass door to the activity center and stepped inside, Bernie called out, "Hello, Opal!"

Opal turned abruptly—a little startled—but then again, Opal was always a little startled. "Oh, hi Bernie, good afternoon!"

"It is, isn't it. Say, Opal, can you come over?" Bernie asked, lightly.

"Oh, why? Is there something wrong?" Opal's 'Tweety Bird'

panic appeared.

"Of course not," Bernie giggled, fake but effective. "I just have a question for you."

"Why sure, be right there." Opal smiled, but her shoulders were still up near her ears. She was worried that Bernie was going to ask her what the park was saying about Ruby's flashing.

Opal was not good at lying. In fact, she was horrible at it. The moment she tried to do it, the corners of her mouth would uncontrollably frown, and her left eye would twitch, like there was a rough grain of pepper dancing around in it. She could try and fake a stroke, but then she remembered that she'd disclosed her allergic reaction to untruths to Bernie years ago, when she couldn't bluff during their brief Euchre partnership. But what if it wasn't that? Bernie could just want to ask her about the weather or want to borrow some groceries, again. That could be it, or maybe it was worse? What if Bernie was asking her over for an encore, trying to get her to chant swear words again?

Opal was as rigid as an armadillo as she walked around the side of the screened-in lanai to the door at the front. This was exactly how Opal looked every year for the entire month of December. She was stiff with anticipation of what the jolly, fat man might leave for her under the tree. Bernie could see her discomfort. She knew that Opal didn't do well with the unknown and Bernie knew what she was worried about.

"Opal, relax. I'm not going to ask you what people are saying about my sister."

Opal let out an audible exhale; she had apparently been holding her breath the whole time. "Oh, good. That would have been awkward."

"Not as awkward as it was for Freda. And how about Maryanne last night, huh? I thought she was going to pop a blood vessel."

Opal smiled.

Bernie was great at reading the room and writing the mood. "I love your pink sundress, is that new?"

Opal looked down at the conservatively cut sundress, with the perfectly pressed pleats. "Yes. Yes, it is." Her face beamed. "Stanley bought it for me."

"Was it your anniversary? I'm sorry if I missed it?"

"Oh no, our anniversary isn't until November. It was sort of an apology gift. For being a grump."

"Wow. Better than flowers."

"Yeah. He can be pretty prickly, but he always apologizes."

That sentence was something Bernie had heard before. It didn't quite sit right, but it would have to be put on the backburner, because Bernie had an agenda.

"Opal, do you think I could borrow your car?" Bernie tossed this request out like she was asking to borrow sugar.

Opal wasn't as casual, struggling with her answer. "Our car? I...don't...know. Stan doesn't—"

"Oh, it's just to run an errand. You know I sold mine, right? We just need a few things, errands; I'd be back before Stan was done poker."

"Bernie, I don't think Stan would want you taking it without—"

"Without you? No, that's why I was asking. If you're not busy, I was hoping you could take me. It's your car. I just need a ride."

Opal's wheels were spinning, thinking hard about the request and the repercussions.

Bernie could see the lowering of her drawbridge, so she advanced. "When was the last time you drove? I read an article that said that as we age, if we don't keep up with our skills, we stand the chance of losing them."

BONE PARK

Opal couldn't remember when the last time was.

"If Stan needed to go to the doctors or something, you'd want to make sure you're still up to snuff, right? Practice." Opal was still searching her mind for answers, so Bernie laid it on thick. "I wouldn't ask but we're running low on things and with Ruby taking taxis to and from work, we really can't afford to call one for errands as well."

Opal felt for her friend. She felt for everyone. That's what her huge heart did. "Well, if I come with you, I don't see where there would be a problem. And we'd be back before Stan's done?"

"Absolutely."

Opal gave in. "Oh, alright. If you're truly in a jam, Stan will have to understand. Give me a few minutes. I'll meet you at my place."

Bernie was antsy, checking her watch over and over after Opal left. She was already prepared for their outing; her huge yellow purse and sunglasses were on the wicker table ready to go, assuming that Opal would oblige her request. And she did, but Bernie paced. Back and forth in the lanai, watching the hands of her modest watch spin by. It was when the minute hand had gotten a little too close to the six for her liking, that she put on her sunglasses, grabbed her purse and left.

She walked briskly down the road, ignoring the looks of the neighbors still gossiping and marched right up to the trailer with the pink awnings. Normally, that was about as close as she got, because Opal would have cut her off at the end of the drive, intercepted her, to limit the amount of 'Stan time' she had. This wasn't just for Bernie, she did it with everyone. Opal was the buffer; his silent social agent managing his movements and engagements. She monitored his time at events and with individuals, like she was wrangling interviewers on a press junket; and she did it all without him ever knowing. But this time, Opal didn't cut her off, she didn't have time to. She had just stepped out into the carport after frantically searching for the keys, which she finally found in a pair of Stan's slacks that were set for the wash. Still, this would have been the moment she guided the visitor away from the trailer, towards the road, or their own trailer, in polite Canadian fashion, but this time Stan wasn't home. It couldn't have happened if he was. Bernie knew that. She knew it was all about timing. That's how she was able to catch her in the carport, standing beside the gold-colored, four-door Toyota Corolla.

"Ready to go?" Bernie said cheerfully.

Opal was once again startled, but she quickly pulled it together. "Bernie. I wasn't expecting you so quickly."

"Gold? Nice choice," Bernie said looking at the car.

"It's not gold, it's actually champagne." Opal had heard that rebuttal straight from the horse's mouth enough times to choke on it. "Stan insisted," she added.

"Champagne? Wow. Even better," Bernie flattered, walking farther into the carport.

Opal moved around the front of the car and towards the driver's door. "I almost couldn't find the keys. Stan was out last night at the theatre."

Bernie bit her tongue; she knew that the 'theatre' Stan went to alone at night had nothing to do with Shakespeare, however there was a lot of 'shaking' involved. Opal knew it too. Theatre was just another of the spins that she put on his transgressions. They weren't lies, nothing that would send her face into palsy. They were just sugar coating, to paint the perfect picture, although everyone could see it was a forgery.

"I guess we should get going. Hop in. It's open," Opal said, happily.

Bernie opened the passenger door, then looked down at her watch. "Say Opal, on second thought, why don't I drive?"

Opal already was sitting behind the wheel. "But you said I was supposed to practice my skills?"

"You should and you will, on the way back. It's just, there isn't a lot of time before the poker game is over and I know the way. Besides, when was the last time you drove?"

"Well, I'm not—"

"I imagine you are pretty nervous about taking Stan's precious champagne car out. You shouldn't drive when you're stressed. I'll drive first so you can get the feel for it again, watching me and then you can take over." Bernie had already made her way around to the other side of the car and led Opal out of the driver's seat. "That poker game isn't going to last forever. Get in," Bernie said, slamming the driver's side door shut, startling Opal who was still trying to formulate a response.

Bernie turned the car on, which caused Opal to run around to the passenger side and jump in, afraid that she was going to leave without her. Inside the champagne-colored car, that had champagne-colored vinyl, champagne-colored carpet and champagne-colored seats, Bernie looked at the watch once again. She then looked up at the dash, to the small black numbers on the grey digital clock that was buried in the instrument panel.

"Your clock's off by two minutes," she said, then put the car in reverse.

The Corolla backed out fast and smooth, without Bernie so much as glancing into the rearview mirror, as if it were on autopilot. Unable to get her belt on in time, Opal was thrown around a little in the passenger seat, from dash to headrest. As the car slid into the dead center of the road, Bernie gently put her foot on the brake, giving Opal a break to buckle up. She clearly had let her lead foot take over.

"Sorry, Opal, the gas is a little touchy on this."

"Why don't I drive then." Opal couldn't hide her discomfort and disapproval.

"No, I think I got it," Bernie said sliding the car into drive before Opal could protest.

Bernie restrained herself, pulling away from the trailer slowly, being careful to obey the park signs so Opal could gather her nerves. After all the years with Stan, she only had a few of them left. They were raw, thin and sat just below the surface, but for what lie ahead, Bernie knew she was going to need every single one of them.

Bernie kept the speed down to a respectable limit as they drove away from the park and towards the ocean. By the time they reached the A1A, Opal seemed to have relaxed, no longer perched up near the dash; she was sitting back in her seat, looking out the side window. Taking in the scenery.

"This is nice," Opal said. "Can't remember the last time I went anywhere without Stan."

"You should do it more often," Bernie said, looking over at Opal with an encouraging smile.

"Maybe. He does play poker every Saturday, so maybe we could make this a date."

"Maybe," Bernie said, taking her eyes off the road for a second, to look down at her watch and over at Opal. Seeing that Opal was lost in thought, staring out the window, Bernie seized the opportunity to step on the gas a little more.

Outside, the scenery started to pass by a little faster, but Opal didn't notice, she was too caught up in this strange feeling. This lightening of her breath, this excitement that she couldn't put a name to, but the rest of us know it as freedom. Opal suddenly felt hopeful, ignited by the prospect of adventure, of a bigger world outside of Cicada Hollow, outside of Stan, even though she would never admit it. No, Opal would never do that, it sounded like disrespect. Not a word. She would just keep this excitement to herself. Lock it away in that back storage room inside her, where she kept her other, happy things.

Bernie made a hard left, jostling Opal a little, pulling her out of her daydream.

As the car took a new direction, Opal became concerned. "Bernie, the Pick and Save's right there. You missed it."

"I didn't miss it. We'll hit it on the way back. I have another errand to run first."

"Errand? I thought you needed groceries."

"I never said groceries." Bernie kept pushing on, driving away from the water.

Opal tried to hide her concern, while she searched her brain, trying to recall what was actually agreed upon back in the lanai. Bernie turned on her blinker and pointed the nose of the car towards the I-95 onramp. As calm as Opal was trying to be, trying to seem cool in front of her friend, this new direction had her freaking out. The car began to pick up speed, racing up the incline and launching out of the merge onto the interstate. She let go for as long as she could. Gripping her hands so tightly they were turning white, but as the champagne Corolla passed a road sign stating MIAMI 261 Miles, Opal could no longer contain her cool.

"Where are we going?"

"Did you miss the sign?"

"Miami?! Bernie, we can't go to Miami. It's like four hours away."

"Not the way I drive," Bernie said, stomping on the gas, thrusting Opal back into her seat.

"What about Stan?"

"I'll tell him it was my idea, okay? But trust me Opal, when we get back, he'll be tickled pink that you went to Miami."

Opal wasn't one for confrontation and while she was worried about what Stan was going to think, it was out of her control. Bernie had the wheel and had all the answers. So, all she could do was watch as the world passing by got more and more unfamiliar.

Saturday afternoons at Shakers were the equivalent of the pews at a pedophile's funeral—empty. It wasn't the worst shift. Monday through Wednesday afternoons were the worst shifts, but Ruby was now working those too. Other than Quincy over at the bar reading a paper, Diamond barely swaying on stage and the two guys in perverts' row who had been waving the same singles the whole time they'd been there, it was just Ruby. The cab ride here and back was once again going to put her in the negative. Some days she could at least make enough for the ride and something to eat, but that wasn't happening today. She could probably mooch a ride home off Quincy, but food was another issue. Nothing in this place was free. Even though the shitty, premade and deep-fried food coming out of the kitchen should have been, Sugar made them all pay full price. Ruby hadn't felt much like eating after her confession to Bernie and because Bernie let her sleep too long, she didn't have time to put anything in her mouth before she left. She couldn't tell if it was boredom or if she was actually hungry, but either way her stomach felt like it was eating itself.

Just as Ruby sat down on a stool by the bar, Diamond waved at her. Ruby had been there since noon and the whole time, Diamond hadn't so much as blinked at her, but the moment she sat down, Diamond suddenly needed something. It wasn't a secret that everyone except Quincy wanted her gone. She thought they were trying to starve her out of there, taking away any evening shifts she had, but now it seemed like their attack was two pronged, cutting off her income and the blood supply to her feet.

Ruby got up off the stool and slowly walked towards the stage, answering the beck and call of her superior. Superior? What a joke. Ruby was twice that twig's age and a hundred times more talented. She should have just quit, like Bernie said, but Ruby was many things and stubborn was top of that list. If they were going to get rid of her, they were going to have to fire her, because at least then she could apply for welfare or sue them for age discrimination.

As Ruby got to the stage, Diamond squatted down to talk to her. Looking at Diamond up close, she was amazed that she could get the lap dances she did. The whole industry had changed since her day. Diamond, like most of the other girls, was covered in tattoos. Ruby liked tattoos, even had gotten a couple herself when the whole Pam Anderson craze hit, but Diamond's tattoos were horrible. No plan or reason to them. She was plastered everywhere with them, even the inside of Diamond's thighs looked like casts that had been signed by the whole senior class. Ruby knew what these markings meant. They weren't symbols of freedom; they were marks of ownership. Made by men who had or still did, own her. These weren't the expressions of feminism and celebration of autonomy that they should have been. These were the ink version of brandings. Markers of territory and property. Ruby felt bad for the girl, for most of them that wore these labels. She wanted to reach out to them, to help them and she would have if each and every one of them weren't a—

"Bitch," Diamond snapped. "Don't be sitting your raggedy ass down. Just 'cause Sugar's out, don't mean you're not being watched," Diamond scolded, as if Ruby was walking the block for her.

Ruby buried her true response. "Diamond, there's no one to serve. I've already wiped everything down and refilled every condiment."

"You ain't getting paid to sit down."

"I ain't getting paid at all."

"You're making minimum. Which is more than me right now."

"Barely."

"Whatever—make yourself useful. Go wait at the door. I got a pizza coming."

Diamond stood up right away and pointed to the front doors. Ruby did what she'd been doing every shift for the last three months, she put her tail between her legs to keep her minimum wage and walked away. On the surface she was doing what she was told, but underneath she was boiling over with thoughts of murder, dismemberment and fantasies about where she would scatter the body.

The contrast between a world that is forever night and the afternoon Floridian sun, is jarring. Ruby squinted as she made her way out the front door and over to the side, leaning on one of the blacked-out windows of the bar. It took her a moment to realize there was no one around and that she could sit down finally, without the harassment of the painted lady.

Knees, hips, ankles—basically every joint does not approve of getting down or up from the ground after 50. Ruby was doing exceptionally well in the aging department but had definitely reached the anti-squatting age. Regardless of her screaming knees, she sat down on the cement ground anyways. It wasn't very ladylike, but it sure beat standing. With her back against the wall and her legs out in front of her, she was sure that those driving by with good eyesight were catching a glimpse of her thong—that is if she was wearing one. That was a thinker. She couldn't remember if she put any on today under her short skirt, but it didn't bother her, because resting her legs and feet trumped a peek-a-boo.

It didn't take long for the sun to go from blinding to feeling good, settling into her skin, resting on her face. It helped her let go of her contempt for the witch inside and had her hoping that the pizza man would never come. She was happy to just soak up the sun, collect her $4.25 an hour and drift away into a memory. The sun can do that. It can wrap a person in its warmth and take them away to better days. At that moment, Ruby was sunning herself on a rock. Twenty years in the past, in Jamaica. Her hair was still wet from climbing Dunn River Falls, she had gold on every finger and beads in her hair, like Bo Derek. It was a great trip. The first trip she took after making her first major distribution deal. She felt like a queen. Paid for the whole thing herself and traveled there by herself. It was before all the cocaine and snakes. It was her reward. Nights filled with different lovers, that she chose, and days spent alone, exploring whatever she wanted to explore. After all the years of being told what to do, she was finally calling the shots. In charge of her own career and her own life. But it was also there, on the rocks below the falls, that she realized that there was something still missing. Some*one* missing. All the success was empty without the one person she really wanted to share it with. To celebrate it with. Her sister.

"Everything alright?" A young man's voice pulled her out of time travel and back into the blinding sunlight of reality.

"Why wouldn't it be?" Ruby blinked trying to get a clearer picture of who was asking.

Even with the sun behind him, casting his face in shadows, she could make out that the t-shirt and matching baseball hat he had on said Domino's. That meant that her break was over, so Ruby started to get up.

"Wait, let me help you," the young man said, quickly setting the pizza warming bag down on the ground so he could take hold of her arm.

"Thank you," Ruby said, happily accepting the help, taking the possible fall out of her rise to eye level.

As she got to her feet, the young man gasped, "Hi."

Ruby pulled back a little to allow her eyes to focus, trying to make out his face. He was cute. Clean cut, mahogany skinned, probably mid-twenties.

"Do I know you?" Ruby wondered if he had been in on a busy night, and she'd forgotten his face. All the faces start to blend together when you're slinging drinks for a quarter tip.

"No, I'd remember meeting someone as beautiful as you," the young man said smiling.

Ruby would have blushed, but she knew it was bullshit. She was decades off his radar. "My word. Thanks for saying that. You're a real charmer."

"Didn't know this place was open during the day."

"Neither do the customers," Ruby joked. "12:00 till 2:00, every day."

"You work fourteen hours every day?"

"No, just the afternoon shift. 12:00 to 8:00." Ruby was enjoying the banter but realized she may be enjoying it too much. Taking up this young man's time. "I'm sorry. Thirty minutes or it's free—got to Avoid the Noid." She was overcompensating.

"Right, you've seen the commercials. But technically, that would make you the Noid." The young man chuckled.

"My word. Well then, what does this Noid owe you?" Ruby stuck her hand down into the front pockets of her small waitress apron. "Oh shit." The pockets were empty.

Diamond hadn't given her any money for the pizza and Ruby didn't even have a float. She hadn't had one since they moved her to afternoons. She spent her float and didn't make enough money to replace it. Quincy had been making change for her and not telling Sugar. But this young man needed to be paid and her pockets were bare.

"Nothing," the young man said, taking the pizza box out of the warming bag. "Forget about it. It's on me."

"That's kind, but I can't let you do that. Just wait here a second." Ruby turned to leave.

"No. I insist. Please," he said, holding the small pizza box out in front of him with two hands like he was offering frankincense to the

BONE PARK

Messiah. "You deserve roses, but this is all I've got right now."

Ruby didn't know if she could take him seriously. Was he serious? Did he feel sorry for her because of the lack of people in the parking lot? Did he think she was broke? Hang on, she was broke. Then it dawned on her that maybe this was a blessing. If Ruby took the free pizza from him, she could still hit Diamond up for the cash and maybe break even on today. A sign? This could have been the universe throwing her a bone. It had been a while since the powers that be shed some light on her. Maybe this was a little reward for coming clean with Bernie.

"You're very sweet. I'll make you a deal. Next time you come in, the drinks are on me," Ruby caught herself, "within reason."

"Deal, but how can I ask for you, if I don't know your name?"

She had just assumed he knew it. She wasn't used to men not knowing who she was, well if they saw her in the light of day and not the darkness of the bar. She also wasn't used to the way he looked at her. He wasn't leering, looking over her body, up and down, like he was reliving what he'd just seen on his TV; he was looking into her eyes. Listening to her words and beaming from both.

Ruby pulled out a matchbook from her apron, wrote her name on the inside cover and handed it to him. "Ruby," she said, expecting his eyes to change, maybe remembering one of her spreads in Playboy or Hustler.

"Ruby?" he said gently. "Oh, I get it. Just like your lipstick. Ruby red."

Ruby blushed, he was really flirting, but politely. "And you?"

The young man blushed too. "Benny."

"Okay, Benny, it's a deal then, next time you're in, beers are on me." Ruby took the pizza from him.

"Next time huh? That sucks. I'll have to wait a year for that. I just turned 20."

Ruby was getting bad at clocking ages, but then again, everyone looks like a kid, once you pass 45. "You're just a pup. Can't make any promises, but if I'm still here in a year, the offer stands." She wasn't sure what his angle was, but it felt nice to be treated nice. It had been a long time since anyone treated her this way, so she played along. "Thanks again, Benny. It was nice to meet you."

Ruby giggled a little as she said her goodbyes, that unconscious flutter that happens when we can't hide our joy. But as she stepped through the door, her giggle was stolen by the heavy air and darkness of that bar where joy and flattery went to die.

"Two hours and fifty-five minutes!" Bernie exclaimed as she steered the champagne Corolla down Ocean Drive.

This was the iconic Miami promenade, painted with pastel hotels and palm trees, neon signs and almost-naked singles. It was a confectionery for the eyes and Opal was devouring all of it, through the open window of the sensible sedan. Opal's grocery-getter was attracting lots of looks, most of which were concerned because Ocean Drive was not the street that economy cars frequented. It was the cruising route for vehicles that cost more than most people's houses and convertibles that put their roasted occupants on display like rolling chafing dishes.

Bernie pulled the car over to the side of the busy road just in front of the Marlin Hotel. This yellow art deco building, looked like a giant jukebox. It was a masterpiece of style and design, flashy and tasteful, drawing a crowd of cocktail sipping admirers to the sun-soaked patio that flanked its shiny, chrome entrance.

"I'm going to let you out here," Bernie said to Opal who was not expecting it.

"Out here? Why?"

"This place is easy to find, for you and for me, when I come back around to pick you up."

"Back around from where?"

"Never you mind. The less you know the better, Opal."

"I don't know anything, Bernie. I haven't the foggiest idea why we're in Miami—"

"Exactly. Now get out and I'll be back for you in around twenty minutes."

Opal hesitated, grabbing for the door handle, her mind racing with worry.

Bernie looked down at her watch, "Opal, please get out. I have somewhere to be in exactly five minutes."

"Bernie, I can't just leave you with Stan's car."

"Opal, please!" Bernie cut her off, but her eyes and tone weren't angry, they were pleading.

Opal caved to the sight of her friend in need, because that's what Opal did for people she cared about. She caved. She bent over backwards and trusted them. Opal got out of the car and stood on the sidewalk out front of the hip hotel. Although her pink sundress matched the palette of Ocean Drive, her innocence and age clashed with it, making her look like a lost child.

Opal leaned into the car and begged through a whisper, "I know you and your sister are having money troubles, but please tell you're not going to rob a bank?"

Bernie smiled, "Opal, I'm 60, the only thing I'm robbing is time. It's just an errand, an errand I'd like to keep private. Don't worry. I'll be back in twenty minutes."

Bernie pulled away from the curb and out into traffic, just missing a rollerblader in a bright-yellow speedo. After almost committing vehicular manslaughter, on one of the busiest strips in the state, Bernie took the next side street, leaving the mayhem of the Miami Mardi Gras and a newly orphaned Opal behind her.

Even though it was after 4:00pm, the heat didn't dissipate this far south and the last twenty minutes for Opal had become a survival exercise. She felt like she'd been dropped into a foreign country, with no food or water, where she didn't speak the language or know the customs. She hadn't budged. Standing in the exact same spot she was dropped off at. She was stuck. Afraid to venture away from there and afraid of what Bernie was possibly doing. All Opal could do was pray that Bernie returned for her soon, that she kept her word and wouldn't leave her there all alone.

She was spiraling and rightfully so. She was standing in the bright sun, but she was totally in the dark. How well did she know Bernie? Bernie? What kind of name was that even? Did she steal the car? How would she ever explain this to Stan? So stupid, Opal. Stan was always saying how naive she was and by letting Bernie steal the car, she'd proved it. She'd never live this down. Stan would hold this over her head forever.

Two quick beeps.

That's all it took to get her attention. Two short blasts and her fears were calmed. It was Bernie. She was pulling the car over to the curb, right in front of Opal and Opal couldn't contain her relief.

"Oh, thank goodness, you came back," she said to Bernie through the open window.

"Why do you sound surprised? I told you I would be," Bernie looked at her watch, "and right on time. Twenty minutes."

Opal went to open the passenger door.

"Hold on, Opal," Bernie said putting the car in park and undoing her seatbelt. "You're driving."

"What? Me?"

"Yes, you. That was our deal. I drive here, you drive home."

Opal looked worried. "But it's so busy here."

"Don't worry about it. Once you turn right up there, it's easy peasy."

Opal suddenly looked excited. "Okay."

Bernie got out and Opal ran around to the driver's side.

After adjusting the seat, a lot, she turned to Bernie, "Buckle up."

"Roger that," Bernie said, showing her the fastened belt around her waist. "You can do this, Opal."

Opal took a deep breath and put the car in drive.

Bernie gave her some last-minute advice. "Just watch out for the guy in the yellow speedo."

Ruby said goodbye to Quincy, he was staying to work a double, to make up for the financial void of the afternoon shift. Ruby would have too, but that was not an option given to her. She stopped and gave Quincy a friendly kiss on the cheek which made him smile. She always made a point of saying goodbye to him, not just because he was nice to her, but because other than Kurt, who only worked nights, there was no one else to say goodbye to. The bar had started to fill up, but with the young girls taking over for the evening shift, she was invisible to them. Old wallpaper in a room filled with new toys. Didn't matter anyway, because she was not on the clock anymore. Ruby was so happy to be done. Eight hours of nothing, feels more like twenty-four, but the day wasn't a total wash. Ruby had gotten the pizza money from Diamond, so she was leaving with enough money in her right hand for a taxi home and maybe even a small nachos from the 7-11. There was an art to getting the most out of your corner store nachos. A layering process of cheese that only the seasoned night owls knew. It took two containers. One empty and one with the chips. First you filled the bottom of the empty one with the orange, mostly petroleum, cheese-like substance. Then a sprinkling of nachos. Then more cheese and you repeated it. You knew when you were finished when every chip was evenly covered. But just covered enough to leave a small untouched dry cornmeal corner for you to pinch between two fingers for extraction.

Ruby opened the heavy door to freedom with nachos on her mind. The sun was setting, and the outside world smelled of warm pavement and citrus trees; a small payoff for the punishment she'd endured. There was a group of rowdy men walking across the parking lot. The typical horde of horny husbands who had arrived at the bar already well sauced. This was normal. The evening clients generally chose to prime ahead of time, to save money on the marked-up spirits which made them very obnoxious and handsy. Ruby wanted to move away from the door as quickly as she could, to avoid their inevitable rude comments and advances, so she sought the shielding of the parked cars immediately to the right. She stepped down off the raised cement walkway and into the gap between an Astro van and a station wagon, just in time to miss the detection of the inebriated inbreds as they passed.

Ruby thought it was just her, that she was on top of it, having spent her life dealing with men, but every woman does it. This risk assessment and adjustment to this parkour of penises. Women spend their entire lives developing survival skills to navigate a world not designed by them. Our world. Always on alert, looking and planning ten steps ahead of their predators; and every man could be a predator. Sure, not every man is one, but they are all on the prowl in one way or another. Just getting through an average day or night is impossible without having to swat away the flies. We are the gnats, the no-see-ums, the blackflies that constantly hover around their existence. They move through this lifetime perfecting their ability to deal with our prodding, prying,

BONE PARK

watching, judging, asking, begging and blaming. It is a miracle that every woman on earth is not completely and utterly insane and those who are, have every right to be. Men crumble under the pressures of war, but very few men serve. Every woman is born into the warzone and their tour ends at the tombstone.

Ruby waited for a second, crouched down a little to make sure the men didn't see her, countering their movements through the many windows of the station wagon. As the men reached the front doors of the bar, she started to stand up straight—but she couldn't—an arm had snatched her around the waist. She couldn't scream either; a hand was slapped across her mouth. She was being pulled backwards, away from the front doors of the bar—disappearing into the darkening parking lot.

CHAPTER 4

Buffalo Girls

    The back of her heels were being scuffed, her kicking feet skipping across the uneven ground, moving fast, being dragged with intention. There was no need to guess where she was being taken, she knew what this was, what this was leading to, and there was no way in hell she was going to go.

    She was terrified but she knew she had to upset the balance of power. Tilt it any way she could into her favor or at least upset the power that the attacker thought they had over her. Ruby bit down hard into the hand that was clasped over her mouth. It didn't let go, but she could taste blood, so she knew she'd made an impression. While the sting of her teeth was fresh, she thrashed around hard, twisting and turning, jerking her body up and down; one of her arms came free! She had a chance, a way to defend herself, so she started swinging at anything and everything she could reach behind her. She was hitting the attacker with awkward, devastating blows, focusing above her head to where their face might be. Breaking free should have been the only thing that mattered, but as she pummeled her attacker with blind, overhead punches, she kept her right hand clenched tight, holding onto the pizza money inside it. It wasn't worth her life, but it was the only money she had, and she wasn't about to let this asshole take a single thing from her.

"Stop! Stop it! Stop fighting me—you'll only make this worse." He spoke!

Letting her hand get free was his first mistake and this was his second, speaking, because she knew that voice. There was strength in this discovery. A lessening of fear, the difference between what could be at the bottom of Crystal Lake and actually seeing the hockey mask. The unknown is always far more terrifying. She was still scared, but knowing who had her in their grasp helped bury that fear under an intense burst of infuriation. Ruby threw both of her hands up fast, breaking the hold around her waist while twisting her body around at the same time, like she was trying to do a triple salchow. The fast motion caused the attacker to lose his grip entirely and as she spun free, she fell backwards onto the ground. Looking up from pavement between a row of cars, she confirmed that she was right. It was him, the dark-haired man in the silk shirt. One of the men she'd serviced in the lot. Why? She couldn't understand. He'd had her; could have her again for another fifty dollars. Hell, he could have the whole kit and kaboodle for a hundred, so why attack her? What was it with men and this need to destroy everything they couldn't completely own?

He stepped towards her, bending down to try and grab her again. It was a very bad idea, because sadly this wasn't Ruby's first tango in a parking lot. Sleazeballs and pieces of shit like him had a thing with picking on her. Fans, friends, former lovers and plain old creeps. She's been tossed around and worse before. She learned from every untrustworthy, manipulative, abusive man along the way and was ten steps ahead—expecting the unexpected.

She waited until the dark-haired man's face had gotten down to almost eye level with hers, then she used her free hand to pull the keys to the trailer out from her purse and jammed them right into his left eye.

"FUUUUUUUUUCK!" The dark-haired man, with the newly punctured left eye, stumbled backwards, trying to cover the gushing blood, shooting out of his left looker.

As he shuffled backwards, screaming the whole time, Ruby slowly got to her feet. She took her time getting up, not because she was cocky, but because some of the soreness from the attack had started to set in.

As Ruby stood up straight, wobbling a little on her broken heels, bright headlights washed across the darkened lane of the parking lot.

"Hey!" someone shouted, pointed and aggressive. "Get the fuck away from her!"

Ruby thought it might be Kurt, but the voice was too high, and Kurt didn't start till 10:00pm.

"Ruby?!" the voice shouted again as the car screeched to a stop a few feet away from her.

The driver's side door flew open and the dark-haired, one-eyed man took off, running into the woods on the far side of the lot, like the spineless, limp-dick loser he was.

"Benny?" Ruby inquired, with her strained, raspy voice, trying to make out the form running towards her in the headlights.

"Holy shit, Ruby, what happened?" It *was* Benny and he was amped.

Ruby looked towards the direction her attacker ran off in. "Some creep grabbed me."

"Are you hurt?"

"Just my heels and a few scrapes."

BONE PARK

"Fuck, Ruby. Did you get a look at him? Do you know who it was?" Benny asked with a sudden dose of angry, macho concern.

"No idea," Ruby said, even though his face had been permanently burnt into the mugshot wall of her mind.

"Okay. You can wait in my car, lock the doors. I'm going inside to call the police."

Ruby shook her head. "Don't bother, Benny. There's no point."

"Yes, there is, we have to catch the fucker!"

"Benny—I work in a strip club. Unless I'm dead, they won't even fill out the paperwork. Besides, I got my justice right here." She raised her hand that was still gripping the bloody keys. "An eye for an eye."

Benny was both afraid and impressed. "His eyes?"

"His left one, specifically. He'll be easy to spot. Karma has a way of sorting these things out."

Her calm, confident demeanor after just going through all of that, was miraculous and kept Benny in his own lane. "You can take care of yourself, huh?"

"You're goddamn right I can. Been doing it for three of your lifetimes."

He looked her up and down, not in a creepy way, but with attention. "Are you hurt at all?"

"No. Just sore. I think the adrenaline is starting to wear off. Nothing a stiff drink can't fix." Ruby was finally able to take in the young man. He'd changed, it wasn't the Benny she met earlier. He wasn't wearing his Domino's uniform anymore and he didn't smell like pizza. His hair was freshly brushed, flattop with faded sides, he smelled like a CK One display and was wearing a bright teal Polo shirt and clean jeans, with a goofy smile on his face. "What are you doing here? You're not delivering dressed like that. Were you planning on going in there? I thought you said you were only 20. If you got some fake ID, you better let me look at it. Kurt takes the term 'bouncer' literally."

"I am only 20 and no ID. You said your shift was over at 8:00. I would have been here sooner, but I wanted to clean up a little first."

"For what?" Ruby's mind went straight for the obvious, the worst possible reason, the most logical reason. "Benny, I don't know what you've heard about me, but the shop's closed, if you know what I mean."

"I have no idea what you're talking about." Benny's face was pure bewilderment. Ruby had a lifetime of reading men and this one was being completely honest.

"So why are you here?"

"For you," Benny said with the same honesty. "I came back to see you. I know you said to come back when I was 21, but I couldn't wait a year."

Ruby was blindsided. It all came together, the clothes, the cologne, the goofy smile, but it didn't make sense. She was almost forty years older than him. She was a waitress at a dive peeler bar, so what was his angle? What did this sweet boy want with a worn-out woman? He wasn't in any way being pervy. He was looking at her with silver screen modesty, like the boys in the movies did, standing at the door with a corsage in hand, ready to take her to the prom.

"You came back for me?"

"Uh, huh. Wanted to be here when you got off." Benny suddenly turned on himself. "Shit, I'm so sorry. I just realized that if I hadn't taken so long changing, I would have been here on time—and what happened to you—would never have happened."

Ruby stepped forward, placing her hand on his shoulder. "Benny, don't do that?"

BONE PARK

"I'm just so mad at myself."

"Yes, well don't be; don't make this about yourself. You seem like a sweet young man, so don't do that. That's what those guys in there would do. Turn my attack into an attack on them. It wasn't. It was an attack on me. Only me. Men get mad about property being damaged and I am no man's property. So, don't make this about you, I think you're better than that."

Benny snapped out of it, sucking back the tears and rage that were cresting.

"That's better. Women don't need you to save them, just support them," Ruby said leaning in and kissing him on the cheek, "but I *am* glad you showed up."

Benny took a deep breath, taking it all in and letting his anxiety out. "I sort of had a whole night planned for us, but that was before…can I drive you home?"

There was no mistaking what was looking at Ruby; it was the rare breed known as a gentleman. It did exist and it was in this boy. Ruby nodded and Benny walked quickly back to his beat-up Mercury Sable, so he could open the door for her. As he closed the door, she looked down at her hands. After everything that had happened, everything that could have been lost, this cat had landed on her feet once again. She had a free ride home, with a safe young gentleman and a fistful of Diamond's dollars.

Opal hadn't asked. She wanted to ask, but she hadn't, instead she spent the last four hours concentrating on the road. Once they got away from Ocean Drive and hit the highway, it was like riding a bicycle. Bernie let her do what she wanted. Let her pick the radio station, change lanes, speed up, slow down, stop for a pee—three times—and never said a mean word about it. This was a whole new world for Opal. A world of choices and possibilities and none of it had the undertone of Stan's cruel comments or controlling hands. Sure, she wanted to know why they had gone to Miami, but part of her liked the mystery. The only thing that truly was troubling her was the time. It was well past 8:00pm and she knew that Stan had finished his poker game hours ago. Bernie had made her call home and leave a message on her machine for Stan, telling him that she was out with Bernie. She had also called Cecilia and asked her if she could take a hot plate over for Stan, so he had something to eat. Opal knew there would still be hell to pay when she got back, but maybe, just maybe this tame adventure had been worth it—like Bernie said it would be.

As they pulled off the interstate into New Smyrna, Bernie started to make requests. "Opal, could you take a left up here?" Opal obliged. "And now a right?"

Opal obliged again, steering the car towards the ocean. Although they weren't heading in the direction of the Hollow, they were at least close to it, back driving the roads that Opal was familiar with.

"That's great, Opal, and if you can pull in up here, I'd really appreciate it." Opal was loving these polite, friendly requests. They were nothing like the barks Stan gave.

"Sea Harvest?" Opal exclaimed, seeing the shack that sat on top of stilts, up ahead, at the water's edge.

"You know this place?"

"Oh, yes. Stan just loves their conch fritters!" she said with excitement. "Do you?"

"Sure do," Bernie said, scanning the lot as they drove in.

"Oh, good. It's late, but I think they're still open. I'll get a half dozen of them for Stan, and I bet he'll forget all about our little outing."

"Could you back up over there?" Bernie asked, pointing to an empty spot over to the side, away from the well-lit front of the wooden shack.

"Good idea," Opal giggled. "The driving I've got down, but I never was very good with the parking."

Opal pulled the Corolla over to the far side of the lot and did her best to back up into one of the many empty spots. Although she landed a little cockeyed, it really didn't matter because there was nothing for her to hit.

"Oh, dear. They're turning off the lights, I think they're closing," Opal said with a bit of panic. "Come on!"

Bernie leaned over and took the keys from the ignition, "You go ahead. I'll wait here."

"Aren't you hungry?"

"I'll eat when I get home," Bernie said calmly as across the lot, a large, white SUV flashed its lights. "You should go, Opal."

The white SUV started its engine and began moving towards them.

"Is this another errand I don't need to know about?" Opal worried, but she found the answer in the seriousness of Bernie's eyes. "Okay, then. I'll be back with fritters."

Opal got out of the car and walked briskly towards the waterfront, seafood shack. Her head was racing with the possibilities of what was going on behind her, but none of them entertained concern for Bernie's well-being. She didn't know why, she just felt that deep down Bernie had it under control. It felt dangerous and she was a little excited. Titillated even. It was a spark she hadn't realized was missing. Opal wanted to peek. To look back over her shoulder, like peeking over the seats on a double date, when the front seats were frigid, but the sounds coming from the back seats were hot and heavy. She didn't though. She kept walking, facing forward. The unknown wasn't just safer, it was invigorating.

As she stepped off the pavement and onto the boardwalk, the one that led to both the shack and down to the boats that kept the deep-fried phenomenon stocked with fresh fish, the lights on the sign turned off. They were indeed closing. The kid working behind the open order window finished handing a woman a paper bag, then reached up for the rope that was attached to the heavy shutter.

"Wait!" Opal called out. "Please!" She shuffled her fastest down the boardwalk to get to him.

"Sorry ma'am but we're closed," the kid said.

"Oh, my. I just want a few of your amazing conch fritters. That's all," she said with a smile.

"Yeah, sorry. We're closed."

"Not really though, right? Your window is still open. And you just served that girl."

"Yeah, but we're closed."

"It would only take a minute. I'll take any fritters you have left."

"We don't have any fritters left."

Opal did her best grandma smile. "Couldn't you make a couple, dear?"

"You want me to fire up the deep fryers and whip up a batch of batter just for you?"

Opal looked over the kid's shoulder and could see the bin of batter still sitting on the edge of the deep fryer full of bubbling grease. "I will throw a little something extra in it for you. For your troubles. I can't go home to my husband without these." Opal rummaged through her purse, pulling out a crisp five-dollar bill.

The pimple-faced kid, chuckled. "Are you trying to bribe me?"

"Oh, my…well, yes? I think I am."

"That's funny. My grandma puts fivers in my birthday cards."

"Does she? Well, isn't that nice."

"My grandma's a bitch."

Opal was shocked, not sure how to respond.

"You think you can have whatever you want. Pushing us locals out of our homes, complaining about everything. You old people are wrecking the beach—you're the reason my family had to move inland. Keep your five dollars lady. I told you we don't have any fritters left," the kid snapped. "Now buzz off."

The kid pulled the rope. Opal jumped back just in time, to avoid getting struck by the hatch that slammed down over the window. The rest of the lights across the top of the shack quickly turned off, emphasizing the point. Opal hung her head, offended, her feelings hurt. Sure, it was about the way the kid spoke to her and about not having a peace offering to distract Stan with, but it was more than that. It was about that girl. The double standard. It was that Opal, and her business, weren't worth what the girl's was. The fryer was still on; the batter was right there, but that kid couldn't care less about her feelings. He hated her and said as much.

Opal walked back to the champagne-colored Corolla empty handed. The white SUV was gone, and Bernie was sitting in the driver's seat. She didn't bother asking or arguing about why she wasn't driving, she just got into the passenger side and closed the door.

"No fritters?" Bernie asked, sounding surprised.

Opal shook her head and said defeated, "No. They were closed. Stan's going to be very disappointed."

"Don't be so sure about that. Here." Bernie reached behind the seat, pulling out a brown paper bag, covered in grease stains, and dropped it into Opal's lap.

"You got me fritters? How?"

"Look inside."

Opal opened the crumpled bag, excited—then stopped in the middle of unrolling the top of it. "Oh, my! What's this?" Opal slowly pulled out a small stack of cash. "Bernie, what is this?"

"Well, it's no conch fritters, but I'm pretty sure it will put a smile on Stan's face."

"No, Bernie, where is it from?" The wonder and excitement of the day now felt very strange and serious.

"What do you mean, where is it from? It's what I won at bingo. Your portion for taking me there," Bernie said with a straight face.

"But we didn't go to bingo."

"I did and I did great. Trust me, when you give that to Stan, he's going to love that you took me out today."

"Where did it come from?"

"Bingo, Opal. That's all you need to know."

"Bernie, you know I can't lie. I twitch and it—"

"You don't have to. I'll tell him."

"But I'll know."

"No, you don't. You don't know what I was doing when I dropped you off in Miami or while you were over trying to get fritters, do you?"

"Well…no?"

"So, I could have been playing bingo at either of those times, couldn't I?"

"But there isn't a bingo hall—"

"That's not what I asked. I asked you, if while you were away from me, I could have been playing bingo?"

Opal struggled with her conscience and the concept. "I guess so?"

"Good enough for me! Now, it's getting late, so let's take you and that wad home to Stan." Bernie turned the car on and pulled out of the parking spot, proud as a peacock, playing the part as if she had just cleaned up under the B, dabbing numbers. "Always feels so good to win at bingo, doesn't it?"

Opal watched her closely, enjoying Bernie's performance—the theater of pretend. She found the façade of victory alluring and began smiling too. Heading back towards the Hollow she became an innocent mime, mimicking Bernie's joy, letting go of her own worry, stress and doubt, trading it happily for the fantasy that Bernie kept creating.

It had been an interesting trip back from the edge of Edgewater, with Benny splitting his time looking at the road and looking over to check on her. Had Ruby been thirty-five years younger, the two of them could very well have been on their way to the hospital, to deliver their third wheel, given the nurturing way he was doting over her. Ruby didn't normally like that kind of attention. The *kind* kind. It was unfamiliar from men, so therefore it was untrustworthy. It's a feeling many women share—and part of the reason that 'nice guys finish last'. If men weren't taught by their mentors that coarse hands and coarse hearts were mandatory, then women would be swooning over the lover, not the fighter.

The rusted red Sable turned the corner at the four-way stop, the one with the gas station and biker bar, and started heading down Pioneer Trail, towards Cicada Hollow. Even the way Benny drove was nice, easy on the gas, smooth on the brakes and gentle on the turns. He had the velvety touch of a Meals on Wheels' driver.

"Pioneer Trail? You sure?" Benny asked looking around. "The

only thing down here is the Bone Park."

"That's where I live," Ruby said, a little embarrassed.

"Shit. I'm sorry. I shouldn't have called it that."

"Oh, don't worry. You're not the first." Ruby tried to lighten the mood, for both of them.

"You know, I used to party down here, back in high school."

"You mean last year?" Ruby smirked

"Ha, ha. Very funny." Benny started to slow the car down, about a half a mile from the park gates. "Yeah, pretty sure the entrance is around here somewhere." Benny scanned the dark jungle on the left side of the road.

"It's alright, Benny, I believe you. No need to show me the woods where you gave Cindy Lou your sacred flower," Ruby joked, but she was serious, she really just wanted to get home.

"There it is." Benny turned the wheel, crossing the dirt road, driving towards the two ruts that disappeared into the dark forest. "I think you're going to want to see this."

They were already going down the overgrown path before Ruby could assess if this was going to be a really bad decision or not. The jungle was thick on either side, growing out from and even over the path at some points. It had gotten so thick, so fast that there was nowhere to turn around. Even if she did protest, the two ruts were so rough, they turned this cruise in the woods into a sadistic chiropractor session. If Ruby wasn't sore enough already, this ride into the everglades was going to have her laid out for weeks.

Just when she had reached her breaking point on this redneck roller-coaster, holding onto both the 'Oh-shit' handle and the center console for dear life, the thick jungle suddenly opened up. The car settled down, no longer rocking them both to death and they pulled out into a flat, dirt clearing. The moon was high in the night sky by then, a celestial chandelier, hanging over the trees that encapsulated the area in a green, thatched dome. The Spanish moss dangling from the branches overhead, twinkled in the moonlight, dripping an air of fantasy over this secret hideaway.

"My word!" Ruby gasped, looking up through the front window. "What's that?" she asked, referring to the structure at the other side of the clearing.

"That's what I wanted to show you," Benny said, pulling the car up to the strange building.

The headlights of the Sable filled the darkness ahead, shining an intrusive glow onto the old, metal Quonset hut. It was an arch-shaped building, like a barrel had been buried and half of it was left above the ground. The huge hut was made out of corrugated steel strips that were riveted together and it had a wooden front door with a small window beside it.

Benny shut the car off but left the lights on and got out. Ruby reluctantly followed his lead as he went up to the door of the building and opened it.

"It's not locked?" Ruby questioned.

"We broke the lock on it in freshman year, no one ever replaced it. If you think this is cool, you gotta see the inside," he said as he stepped into the dark building, backlit by his car's headlights.

No longer in her busted heels, Ruby stepped carefully across the dirt ground in her bare feet, and over the threshold of the building. The inside was bigger than she expected. There were a few pieces of furniture scattered around the place. Old couches, chairs and tables, things that looked like they were originally destined for the dump. The walls were spray painted in layers of graffiti, colorful and interesting and some of it was quite beautiful.

"So, this is where you lost your flower?" Ruby said with a wonderful, playful lilt of sarcasm.

"No, I'm still holding the bouquet. My friends and I would just get high in here and talk about how bad we wanted to get out of this shithole."

"Did you do this?" Ruby asked, pointing to some of the graffiti.

"Most of it, but not that one." Benny ran over to right side of the arched building. "I did this one."

Ruby carefully walked over to the humongous painting that spanned at least ten feet of wall space. It was a stunning, modern, chaotic depiction of three angels. A tall, naked, ebony female in the middle, with large, outstretched wings and two smaller sexless cherubs on either side of her.

"My word, Benny, this is beautiful!" Ruby was honestly awestruck. "Absolutely beautiful."

"I did that a long time ago," Benny responded bashfully. "I was just messing around."

"If this is your messing, then I must see your serious. You shouldn't be delivering pizzas; you should be doing this! The snobs in New York would flip their wigs for this! The sunset strip too."

Benny stood silently, listening awkwardly to her praise.

"Honestly, Benny, it is incredible. One of the most stunning paintings I've ever seen. And you did this with spray paint?"

Benny smiled, still silent.

"Come on Picasso, tell me about it." Ruby grabbed him by the arm and brought him closer to it.

"Well…" Benny seemed suddenly uncomfortable. "It's a…kind of a family portrait. That's my mom in the middle and my sister and I on either side."

Ruby walked up even closer to it. "How come your sister and

BONE PARK

you don't have wings?"

Benny shuffled his feet a little on the dusty floor. "Cause we're still alive."

Ruby turned back to the young man, who was clearly fighting with this admission. "Oh, Benny, I'm sorry."

"It's okay. Happened my senior year. Time and wounds, right? Painting got me through a lot back then. I haven't been back here since, haven't been able to draw much either. Of course, I'd love to do this instead of pizzas, but I have to work—so my sister can stay in school. I got to graduate; she deserves to graduate too."

Ruby's heart nearly broke under the weight of this young man's character. Never before had she met such a dynamic, talented, caring member of the opposite sex. He was the unicorn. The fabled good guy and this magical realm, in the middle of nowhere, was his Ark.

The champagne Corolla pulled into the carport of the trailer with the pink casings, quietly. Bernie and Opal were very careful to open and close their doors gently, holding the handles up as they did, so only the faintest click was heard. Opal looked across the hood of the car to Bernie, worried.

"Breathe," Bernie whispered. "Like I said, I'll handle it."

Opal took a big breath then opened the side door of the trailer with surgical precision.

Bernie stopped her before she could step inside. "Just follow my lead," she whispered, nodding her head quickly in time with her words. "You don't have to say anything—just do as I do." Bernie pushed past Opal and went up into the trailer. She started to laugh loudly. "Ah, ha, ha, ha. What are the chances! I still can't believe it!"

"Opal!" A booming, angry yell came from the back bedroom.

"Where the f—"

"Stan!" Bernie shouted as a very drunk, very angry-looking Stan came barging towards them in a dirty undershirt and stained underwear.

"Bernie—what are you doing here?" Stan pulled back, disoriented, unable to see Opal who had hidden herself behind Bernie's long body.

"I'm here to see the look on your face when Opal gives you the good news!" Bernie reached behind her, pulling Opal out from hiding.

"Gives me the what?" This was all moving too fast for the grumpy, groggy old man.

"Show him, Opal!" Bernie motioned with her head, and Opal nervously thrust the grease-stained paper bag out in front of her.

Stan snatched the paper bag from her. "Leftovers?" Stan was not impressed. His brow started to furrow as he unrolled the soggy bag. "Holy Christ!" he exclaimed, pulling out the small wad of twenty-dollar bills and relaxing his brow.

"BINGO!" Bernie cheered, reliving the exact moment she won all this imaginary moola.

"Bingo?" Stan was still wincing from the volume of Bernie's cheer. "Opal, you won this money at bingo?"

Bernie jumped in before Opal's twitches could start. "No, I won! This is her cut. Fifty-fifty because she drove me there."

Stan was fixated on the cash. "There's hundreds of dollars here."

"I have never had such a good night! Opal's my lucky charm! Now, Stan, I need you know that this was all my fault. She said she needed to be here for you, but I insisted she take me to bingo. I practically kidnapped her."

Stan's entire energy changed; his anger was replaced with

drunken joy. "Oh, don't listen to her. I'm glad the two of you got out and about. I was fine. You know, Cecilia's not a bad cook."

"Maybe you could get those new golf clubs you wanted?" Opal chimed in, smiling, but still testing his waters.

"My God you're right!" Stan stepped up and wrapped Opal in a big hug. "I can't wait to see the look on Norman's face when I tee off with my new PING driver!" Stan started to nibble on Opal's neck, squeezing her sides, making her squeal.

"Well, that's my cue to leave," Bernie joked, winking at Opal, who was smiling devilishly back at her. "Night, Opal. Night, Stan," she said, as she excused herself, closing the trailer door behind her.

From the carport, she could hear the giggles and squeals of Opal inside, moving down the trailer, towards the rear bedroom. Bernie sighed, shaking her head a little at the whole thing. It was moments like this that reminded her of her freedom. She didn't have to answer to anyone, steer around their moods or whims. She had spent enough time playing puppet master in her own life to revel in the retirement of her marionettes.

While the R-rated celebration of her pretend bingo victory continued in the trailer behind her, Bernie opened the driver's door of the champagne Corolla and retrieved her purse. She stood there for a moment and looked around. She scanned the lane, Opal's next door neighbor's lanai and the darkness of the inner circle out back. After a very quiet, observant moment, she reached back into the car, down under the driver's seat and pulled out a gun. It was the snub nose, 38 revolver, which she quickly tucked into the waist of her slacks. She closed the driver's door softly, then moved down a few inches, stopping at the rear door. Bernie scanned the street again, then opened the door, bent down and pulled out a tiny, black, gym bag from under the back of the driver's seat. She stood up slowly and closed the door as gently as she had the others. Bernie looked down at the small, nylon bag with reverence. She paused, staring at it as if she were contemplating its fate—or maybe, it was her own she was pondering over. Whatever answer she was seeking in that deep silence, she must have found it, because she suddenly stood up straight, tucked the bag under her arm and left the carport, walking out into the black of the inner circle.

Ruby would have preferred it if Benny had let her out at the arched gate, but that wasn't in Benny's DNA. He was a purist, a door-to-door gentleman. As the old Sable crept through the park, obeying all the signs and painted instructions, Ruby couldn't shake the feeling that had taken over her. Although it should have been the anxiety, fear and outrage from her attack, it was something entirely different. The antithesis of that. It was happy. More so, it was that she felt happy. It probably began the moment they pulled away from the strip club, but it really took over when he brought her to the hut. When she saw so much beauty hidden inside such a dilapidated, forgotten relic.

"It's that one. With the yellow stripe around it," Ruby directed Benny who pulled up to it as smoothly as he had done everything prior and put the car in park. "Thank you, Benny. For everything."

"It's not the night I had planned, but it—"

"It was perfect. And you are a perfect gentleman. A talented, sweet, perfect gentleman." Ruby leaned over and kissed him on the cheek.

Benny turned slowly, just in time to catch her lips with his before she pulled away—but Ruby didn't pull away. She knew she should, that he was so young, that this could never work, but she didn't pull away. His hand found the line of her jaw and held her head there, held her lips in that kiss, but it wasn't to lock her there. It was a rest for her cheek, not a grasp for control. A few heartbeats of held breath and it was over. Both of them pulling away from each other at the same time. Happy with what it was, not pushing for what it wasn't—what it could never be.

"Goodnight, Benny."

BONE PARK

"Could you call me Ben? It sounds more mature than Benny."

"Goodnight, Ben," Ruby said, as a long-lost twinkle came to her eye.

"Goodnight," Benny responded with the smile of their great secret strung across his face.

Ruby got out of the old Mercury, with her busted shoes dangling from her hand and walked up towards the dark lanai of the trailer. As she opened the screen door, to the meshed-in patio, she turned around and looked back. It was an old habit, not one she'd employed in a long, long time, but when she turned around, her hunch was right. Benny, was of course still there, waiting at the side of the road to make sure she got in alright. Her heart fluttered, and she waved to him, the signal he needed to pull away. As the redness of his taillights faded away, she turned back to the porch—

"Who was that?" Bernie spoke softly, but coming out of the darkness, her soft was scary.

"Jesus!" Ruby shouted, finding her sister coming towards her from the shadows of the inner circle. "What are you doing out here? I thought you'd be asleep?"

"No, I was just out for a walk." Bernie approached her, having already moved the black bag down to her side, blocking it from Ruby's view. "So, who was that? A little young—even for you, don't you think?"

"That was Ben. A customer from the bar. He gave me a ride home," Ruby said brushing it off.

Bernie didn't stop, she kept moving, through the lanai and into the trailer. "And what did you give him?"

"I beg your pardon?" Ruby was insulted. She stormed into the lanai after her. "What are you suggesting?" Ruby's bare feet slapped against the thin AstroTurf-covered cement steps, emphasizing her disdain as she stormed up into the trailer.

"What is the problem?" Bernie asked from the back bedroom of the trailer. "That you didn't hear me, or you didn't understand the question?"

"I understood it, I just can't believe you asked it—or thought it for that matter!" Ruby was shouting.

Bernie came out from the back bedroom to meet her in the main room. "No need to yell. I saw the two of you kissing in the car. It was a logical assumption."

Ruby lowered her voice, but not her blood pressure. "Yes, an assumption. What is it you assume exactly? Do you think I sold myself for ride home? Pulled over along the way here and let him ravage me?"

Bernie looked her up and down. Ruby's hair was tussled, her outfit askew, makeup messed up, barefoot, holding onto her broken heels. "Ruby, maybe you should look in a mirror before you try and play Mary."

Ruby moved over a little, looking past Bernie, into the six stacked mirror panels attached to the wall. For the first time since she left work, she saw herself.

"I was attacked," she said stunned, fixated on her reflection.

"By that kid! Oh my God, Ruby, why didn't you—"

"No. He helped me—he chased the guy away."

"Are you alright? Did the guy…" Bernie couldn't fill in her own blanks, ashamed of her assumption and terrified of the answer.

"All he got was my teeth marks in his hand and my keys in his eye."

Bernie breathed, but it wasn't relief, just a breath she could finally release. "What did the police say?"

Ruby's lock on her own reflection broke and she turned her gaze to Bernie. "Nothing, because I didn't call them."

"Why?"

"Because, Bernie. That's not what we do. And they wouldn't believe me if I did—I knew the guy."

"Ruby—"

"No!" Ruby couldn't hold it in any longer. "I can't call them! I can't tell anyone, because he was a trick."

"What?"

"Yes, Bern, your little sister has sex with men for money. That asshole was just one of the johns I've been flipping in the parking lot at night to keep us going. To keep food on the table and the lights on."

"Oh, Poob." All of Bernie's defenses dissolved instantly, crumbling along with her sister's façade. "You didn't have to do that. You never have to do that."

"You don't know what I've had to do to get by, this was old hat. I've done worse for less. But at least now, I have someone worth doing it for. You need my help, so I'm helping. Doing what I know how to do—the only thing I have left to do, that I can make any kind of living from. What happened tonight was just a work-related injury, a risk that comes with the job."

Bernie grabbed Ruby's face in both of her hands. "No, it's not—and you quit. As of right goddamn now, you quit. You don't call them to tell them, you don't go back there, you just quit."

"How?"

Bernie paused, then put on the happiest face she could muster. "They found my money."

"Who did?"

"The bank. Called just after you went to work. I was so excited, that's why I couldn't sleep."

Ruby couldn't tell if she was lying or not. It was way too convenient. "Bern, if you want me to stop working there fine, but—"

Bernie could see the distrust in her sister's eyes. "But nothing. We are fine again. Just like I had planned all along. They even said they're looking into my pension."

"What does the bank have to do with your pension?" Ruby was still not buying it.

"That's beyond me but said they're looking into it. Seems it has something to do with whoever was messing with my savings. Don't you see? It's a sign. The hocus pocus you keep telling me about."

"How do you figure?"

"It's a pretty strange coincidence that the day you're attacked, my savings are suddenly returned?"

Ruby's overworked mind was trying to process this ironic chain of events, and Bernie knew it.

"You've been given a way out, just when it was telling you to get out!"

Ruby looked up at her sister. "You're not lying? You promise you have enough? For both of us?"

Bernie nodded, "More than enough."

Ruby suddenly looked like the entire world had been lifted off her shoulders. "Then I guess I can quit? I quit?"

"You're goddamn right you quit."

"I quit!" Ruby smiled. "I quit! Sugar and Diamond and Sparkle and all the perverts can kiss my ass because I quit!"

BONE PARK

Bernie's broken sister jumped around in tearful joy. She felt good being able to protect her, to have set her free from the horror she had been unaware of. The admission didn't change the way she saw her sister at all, but it definitely has bloodied the water for the rest of the world. As Bernie watched her sister walk down the thin hallway, to the shared bathroom, to wash off the day and the shackles that had been holding her down for months, she realized that it wasn't over. Because of Bernie, Ruby may have been freed from her cuffs, but the binds had not been destroyed, not at all—Bernie had just transferred the restraints.

Ruby went straight from her hot bath to the bed. No more was said or asked about it. Bernie had even tucked her in. She did that every night when they were young. That was part of the role she didn't sign up for—having a child that was only five years younger than her. Ruby wasn't her daughter, but Bernie raised her and tucking her into the comfortable front bed, seemed to bring things back into alignment. Putting their roles into place and Ruby into a slumber where Bernie knew she was safe.

It made her think of her other role. The one stolen from her—that was irreplaceable.

The numbers on the yellow phone were now 'pushable' by memory. She had dialed them at least once a week since she got to Florida but had yet to get the response she so desperately desired. It was late. Very late to be calling anyone. But all the other times hadn't yielded any fruit, so she thought she'd change tactics. Hoping that the rings would make it past the gatekeeper. Hoping, because she needed hope.

As the rings repeated, Bernie's anxiousness grew.

"Uh, hello?" It was a woman.

"Hi, Marcie?" Bernie was elated. "It's Bernie."

"Bernie?" The woman sounded very groggy. "Jeez, it's a—

what's happened? Why are you calling so—"

Another voice came in, behind the woman's, shouting in the background. "Who the hell is it?"

"Go back to sleep, Brent," the woman urged.

"Who is it!?" the man insisted.

"It's Bernie."

"Bernie? Bernie! For Christ's sake," he grumbled

Bernie spoke quickly, "Have you gotten my messages?"

"Your messages? No," the woman responded, confused.

"I've called a few times now. I spoke with Brent."

"He didn't say anything. What's wrong?"

"Everything is fine, I just wanted to—"

"It's midnight, Marcie. I have to work in the morning." The man's tone had grown angrier.

"Bernie. Brent's right. It's late, can we talk tomorrow?" The woman hurried her words.

"Yeah. Tomorrow's fine."

"Bernie, what number are you at? I don't think I have a current one for you."

Bernie paused, "Don't worry about it. I'll call you."

"Alright. Goodnight," the woman said. "It's nice to hear your voice." Suddenly the phone went dead. Cut off from the other end.

The large, cabinet TV was on low, and Opal was in her pink-chiffon nightgown. She had pulled one of the kitchen chairs and a TV tray up close to it, so she could hear what the tanned, silver-haired preacher was saying. She was hanging on his every word as she scooped the sections of grapefruit from their fleshy bowls, one by one. Stan was nowhere in sight, but still the TV was hovering just above a whisper. It made the whole interaction seem somehow more intimate, a one-sided conversation just between the two of them.

"It is our charge," the preacher condemned, "our duty to live our lives according to his example. We must be beyond reproach, beyond sin and Satan. We must use our tongues for truth, not lies and any among you who do, must seek his forgiveness." The preacher on screen moved over to a different part of the set, to where a large reading chair sat beside a table with a telephone on it. "Our lines are now open." The phone on the table rang immediately following his announcement and he picked it up. "Hello, this is Reverend Kind, what weighs on your heart?" the preacher asked, then covered the phone and spoke to the camera. "Set yourself free, call the number on your screen."

A bright 1-800 number flashed on the bottom of the screen, like it was advertising a 'one day only' sale. Opal pushed the TV tray out a little and got up, moving back to the small, round kitchen table that sat just beside the door to the lanai. She reached for the telephone that hung on the wall above the table and held the receiver out in front of her. She refocused her eyes, reading the numbers off the TV. Opal jammed her finger into one of the holes of the rotary dial on the receiver and spun. She continued to spin, inputting the digits on the screen, number after number until the long line of them had been satisfied. There was only one brief ring and then—

"Hello, Reverend Kind Ministry, what's heavy in your heart?" a young woman's voice asked.

"Oh, hi. Hello." Opal was taken aback by the dive into the deep end without any wading. "I was…actually calling to speak to…Reverend Kind?"

"I am one of Reverend Kind's helpers, the Reverend is very busy as you can imagine, but I am here to listen and will convey your troubles to him."

"Oh, alright." Opal did not seem very pleased with this.

"This call is charged at a rate of two dollars a minute," the young woman said quickly. "Now how can the Reverend free you from the weight that's on your heart?"

Opal looked to the television, to the handsome, kind-looking man on the screen, who was pretending to talk with a caller. So, she began to pretend as well. Staring at the TV, talking to this young woman as if it were him. "Well, Reverend, you see…I think I may have sinned?"

"Alright. And what's your name?"

"Ah, Opal. Opal Rose Murdy."

"Okay, Opal Rose, tell me your transgression, so you can let go of your burden."

"Well, Reverend, I lied to my husband," Opal said, spilling her worry into the receiver while the young woman on the other end lapped it up, "and I accepted money that I think may be the fruits of the devil's work."

That confession flicked a switch. "Oh, I understand, Opal. How much money exactly?"

"Opal! Is there coffee ready?" Stan's voice bellowed from the back bedroom.

Opal jumped clear out of her skin, immediately hanging up the phone. "Coffee? Yes, Stan. On my way!"

The eager early-morning sun made the metal trailer creak,

expanding as it warmed up, ready for another hot June day. Bernie sat in her wicker throne, sipping Sanka and holding court for one. Her knee was bouncing a bit, anxious and out of character for her. It was partly the conversation of last night, partly the conversation that was cut off and partly her watch. She was looking down at it with the same intensity as she did with Opal. Whatever the placement of the hands represented today, it was unsettling.

Bernie took a break from watching the second hand to look at her little sister who was quietly sipping her crucible of morning magic. Ruby was out, but Bernie was in. The chess board had been set and she had started the long game. She pondered what was next. So much had happened already. What was she going to do? How would Bernie keep this going and how long could she lie? There were new complications that she thought she had time to sort out, but she'd opened her mouth last night. She'd went off script—against her plan—made promises to make things better for Ruby and now she'd have to make good on them.

Ruby sighed in that light, wonderful way that fills the air on mornings away from the grind. The sound that accompanies your mind drifting off into one of those delicious post wake-up stares.

"So, what's on the agenda for today?" Bernie asked, interrupting her paralyses.

"Sorry, Bern, I drifted off for a moment. What did you say?

"Any plans for today?"

"Um, today? I don't know."

"Well, it is your first day as an officially retired woman, so you should do something."

Ruby perked up. "Well alright then, what do you have in mind?"

"Not me. I'm sorry but I already promised Opal that I'd help her today."

"That's okay, I'll help too."

Bernie had to think fast. "You sure? It's pretty boring stuff; she needs me to help sort through her slides."

"My word, slides? I despise slides! They're visual Valium."

"She needs my help labeling each of them. Putting them into dividers and then putting those dividers into binders and—"

"You are not doing a very good job at selling it. Thank you but no thank you. I'll pass. Maybe I'll just spend the day by the pool."

"Really? Do you think people are still buzzing about the show you put on for Reg and Freda?"

Ruby looked surprised. "I thought you were over that?"

"I am. Just not sure if they are. Not sure if you need the hassle. What about the beach?"

"I'd love to, but we don't have a car."

"Take a taxi. It's on me. Consider it a retirement gift."

"Are you trying to get rid of me?"

"Don't be foolish. Of course not."

"Who's your lover?"

"I beg your pardon?" Bernie was blindsided.

"Come on, Bern. I am the last person you need to lie to. If you want the place to yourself, just say it."

Bernie looked very unamused. "I don't have a lover. I'm helping Opal with—"

"Slides. I know. Bern, it's okay you know. To have needs. I was starting to wonder about you. It's the 1990s not the 1960s. You have every right. You're not disrespecting Sal."

This was not a conversation she ever planned on having with

anyone, let alone her sister. It wasn't even true, but it was an opportunity. As much as it went against her code, it was a bird in the hand.

Bernie stared Ruby dead in the eyes, "He'll be here at 9:30."

Ruby chortled, "There you go! That was easy, wasn't it? I'm happy for you! Of course I'll bugger off. After the last twenty-four hours, a day at the beach sounds like fun. Not as fun as what you'll be doing—but fun." She stopped herself. "You're still paying for the taxi, right?"

Bernie awkwardly smiled back. "Absolutely."

"What time is it now?"

Bernie looked down at her watch. "8:15."

Ruby snorted. "My word. When were you going to muster up the courage to ask me to leave? When he was on top of you? Thanks for the short notice," Ruby said standing up and gulping her coffee. "I should have gotten this to go." She laughed again. "Don't worry, I'll pack up and be on my way in plenty of time for you to feather your love nest," she jabbed at Bernie, because she knew it bugged her. "Do you remember how to?"

"Go on," Bernie said through her teeth, which only delighted her little sister even more.

Only seven flowers could fit into the slim neck of the vase, but it was all Bernie had. She'd secretly picked them from Opal's back garden. Opal's garden was tiny; it ran around the trailer, in the skinny foot of legal lot space allowed by the park, but it was manicured and perfectly curated, just like Opal. Bernie knocked three times, with a force somewhere between hello and I'm not going away. She had opted for the side door of the carport, instead of the cordial lanai entrance, so it required a different kind of knock.

The side door opened slowly. "Yes?" It was Freda, and she did not look happy to see Bernie standing there.

"Good morning, Freda." Bernie raised the tiny vase with stolen flowers in it. "These are for you."

"For what?" Freda scoffed, physically moving back a little, as if she were afraid of blooms.

"Just a little something. To say we are sorry for the other day."

"We? Where's Mae West? You didn't show my husband your breasts, so why are you apologizing?" Freda wasn't making this easy at all.

"Yes. Well, she's a little embarrassed about the whole thing so I came, but with her knowledge and hope that you'd accept."

Freda stuck her head out a little, looking through the carport and down the lane. She then looked back at the flowers. "Is Opal apologizing as well?"

Bernie was shocked, this woman was a firecracker. She was no turnip-truck castaway like all the others here. "Opal's a saint. She'd apologizes for breathing, but these are from us, we just borrowed them from her."

Freda's frown lessened a little. "Borrowed? That's an interesting use of the word."

"Actually, that's the other reason I'm here," Bernie said, shifting gears.

"You want to steal some of my flowers? Believe you me, you can go ahead, half are dead, and the other half are ugly. Came with the place," Freda snarled.

"Connie was a horrible gardener, I'm in agreeance on that, but I'm not here for the flowers. I wanted to ask if I could borrow your car?" Bernie opened up her body a little, motioning to the long, blue, wood-paneled station wagon behind her.

"I think not," Freda stated, straight away.

"Oh, let her use the car, Freda," Reg called out from somewhere deep inside the trailer.

"Reg? We don't even know what it's for?" Freda shouted back to him but kept her eyes on Bernie.

"You're not very good at playing in the sandbox, are you?" Reg appeared in the doorway, behind Freda, wrapping his arms around her waist.

Freda's whole body instantly softened.

Bernie saw the window created by Reg. "I just have a bunch of errands to do. They've been piling up and now I have a mountain of them."

It was night and day, how Freda changed. He was like a muscle relaxer for her, it was not only incredible to see, it was also envy inducing.

"It's a '72 wagon, Freda. If something did happen to it, she'd be doing us a favor," Reg said gently over the shoulder of Freda. "Come to think of it, could you make something happen to it?" he said, grinning at Bernie.

"After the errands maybe," Bernie joked back.

Freda reached over to the wall beside the door, unhooking a set of keys from a nail in the wall and reluctantly traded them for the vase in Bernie's hand.

"I will make sure to fill it with gas when I bring it back," Bernie said gratefully.

"Or you could just pour the gas over it and light a match?" Reg chuckled and so did Freda—a little.

Bernie stepped back from the door, walked back and opened the big station wagon's front door. Reg and Freda watched, standing in the doorway, observing their big girl leaving, like happy parents.

"Now you make sure to have her back by curfew." Reg was on a roll.

"What's curfew?" Bernie played along.

"When the kissing turns to heavy petting!" Reg laughed and Freda gave him a playful slap on his chest, sending him back into the trailer.

As Reg left the doorway, Freda's eyes changed, fixing on Bernie with a stern stare. Bernie returned the look and the two women stayed locked onto each other, in animal-like intensity, until Bernie finally relented, giving the win to Freda and her the window to drive away.

The beach was busy, but then again it always was. The numbers never really changed, only just the bathers. Sunny or cloudy, local or tourist. The swimsuits and cars always showed up. Daytona has always been known as a driving beach. Cars of every kind make their way up and down the beach all day long. The locals watch the tides and the high-water parking lines. They know the differing consistencies of the sand and what cars should stay off the grains, but not the tourists. Every afternoon the beach went from see and be seen to slapstick comedy. It was a folly of tourists trying to dig their cars out of the soft sand, others who raced to save their sedans from the approaching tide and some who struggled to pilot their ponies saturated in a long day of adult soda pops. This spectator sport was a favorite amongst the Dayton-ites and also provided them with a side hustle, pulling Pennsylvania plated cars to safety for cash.

Ruby had made her way down the sandy chute, one of the many 'two car wide' ramps that lead to the beach. She made sure not to go where the out-of-towners were parking, but to stay behind the cars that had local plates. They knew the tides and knew the code of the beach.

BONE PARK

The respect given to other locals, not the entitlement of the out-of-towners. This wasn't Ruby's intuition guiding her, it was on Bernie's instruction.

Ruby found a great spot to spread out her blanket behind a group of Jeep-driving hot bodies. She had brought an umbrella, little cooler and AM radio this time and she was tickled pink about her set up. She also didn't mind the view. Not the ocean, but the young 'Bucks and Does' who were sunning themselves just a few feet away. Ruby chose her bikini on purpose. It had very little fabric, it was red with white polka dots. It was statement suit that screamed 'I am here'. After last night, her natural tendency was to hide. She had curled up on couches with the blinds closed before, but not today. Today, she celebrated what he didn't take. What she fought off. That she was a survivor not a victim. A queen of her own destiny and this little red number was her victory cry.

The young women with the group in front of her seemed friendly. Waving and smiling at her as they went around their business of setting up chairs and blankets and slathering oil all over their elastic skins. Ruby was a prime specimen of mature beauty, but she wasn't immune to the comparison. She used the covert shade of her lenses to look over her body and take note of the wrinkles. The spots that had set in on her once even skin tone and the ripples that gathered at her joints. It wasn't that she was upset with her appearance. She wasn't hateful of what time had massaged her into, she was just aware. Aware of her earned and maintained attraction and their youthful beauty. Ruby was an admirer of the vain. Male, female and anywhere in between, she was a customer of appeal. Her life had been entangled with every form of it and she enjoyed being in its presence.

Happily, Ruby was able to find a 70s' rock station with a good signal on her tiny radio. It was a little sharp, but it was clear. The sun and the Rolling Stones, the ocean and The Who, the sky and Skynyrd.

"Hey, could you turn that up?" one of the blonde beach bunnies shouted to her.

Ruby noticed that they were all bobbing their heads to her music.

This was odd, because the beach was constantly bombarded with the pounding bass of the passing cars. Hip hop and dance music were the thing. To the MTV generation, she was a fossil, playing music that was made with real instruments, by men in tight pants and long hair.

"Your tunes are great!" another girl added. "Please?"

Ruby looked down at her tiny, palm-sized radio. The dial was already all the way up. She looked up at the girls and shook her head. "Sorry honey, it's as loud as it goes."

"What station is it?" The blonde girl smiled.

Ruby searched the numbers along the analog tuning panel to find the spot where the red line was resting. "680?"

"FM?"

"AM," Ruby shouted back, and the girl quickly walked away.

Ruby knew that AM was absolutely inferior to FM, but that snub was totally unnecessary.

Suddenly the beach in front of her erupted into a blast of rock. It was The Who. The blonde girl appeared again, running back towards Ruby.

"I got my boyfriend to put it on his stereo. Now we can all hear it. I'm Tammy."

"Ruby."

"You're beautiful, Ruby," Tammy said, then turned and ran back to the group.

Ruby sat basking in the sound bath of her heyday and the unsolicited adoration of stunning, fleeting youth. Between the compliment and the 70s' compilation, the day couldn't have been any better.

BONE PARK

Bernie arrived at the base of the pale-pink tower just after noon. It was a very tall condo building, built in the early 80s, that still held its modern, fashionable appeal. The 70s' wagon however did not. It clashed with the modern, sky mansions, not blending in well with geometric landscaping as she pulled it into one of the visitor's spots out front. The stylish resident who hovered around the glass-encased entrance shot her disapproving glances as she made her way to the large glass front doors. The snooty doorman did hold the door for her, but only out of professional obligation.

The concierge sitting behind the bright-white, pink-veined, marble podium, motioned her over, with an impatient limp wrist and frustrated look. "Can I help you?" the concierge asked rhetorically.

"I'm here to see Vergil."

"Who?" the concierge snarked.

"Mr. Bennet?"

"Really?" He looked her up and down. "You are here for Mr. Bennet?"

"I am and you don't want to make me late." Bernie gave every ounce of attitude right back to him.

The concierge picked up the phone on the Miami marble desk and dialed it. "Hello, Mr. Bennet, sorry to trouble you but there is a—" he looked her up and down again, "—woman, who says she is here to see you. I would never have disturbed you for this, but our new protocols require that—" Bernie was unable to hear what was said on the other end of the phone, but the concierge adjusted his attitude immediately. "Yes, sir. I am aware that the lobby camera is visible to you. No, sir. Yes, sir. Yes, sir. I'm so sorry, sir. Yes, sir. Right away, sir." The freshly humbled help hung up the phone and looked up at Bernie with a plastered 'possessed' smile across his face. "I am so sorry about that. Our doorman confused you with a woman we've been having issues with." He glared at the doorman, who clearly had no idea what it was about. He then returned to showering Bernie with smiles. "Mr. Bennet is expecting you. You can take the elevators right over there. PH1."

"PH what?"

The concierge overcompensated with a fake laugh, like Bernie was the funniest woman in south Florida. "Oh, you're hilarious! Penthouse One. It has its own elevator."

The doors of the elevator opened, but not into a common vestibule or hallway, they opened up right onto the foyer of a palace. A palace in the sky made of clouds. Everything was white. White marble floors, white walls, white sculptures, white furniture, even a yappy little white dog that rushed at Bernie's feet. This penthouse was open concept, spreading out in all directions, guiding the eye to the spectacular wraparound balcony and the incredible views of the ocean.

"Holy shit! As I live and breathe!" A happy gritty-sounding voice echoed throughout the massive stone cloud.

The little dog kept barking relentlessly, furious with Bernie's ankles apparently.

"Shut up, Tina!" A bald, portly man, wearing a white, designer robe, came in from the balcony.

"Vergil," Bernie said happily, but with far less vigor than his greeting.

Vergil was the kind of man who looked like he always wore that robe, comfortable in a perpetual state of pre and post dip. He bent down and picked up the mouthy dog, still yelping at Bernie's feet, flashing the massive ring on the middle finger of his right hand. The gaudy ring was made out of sparkling, yellow gold in the shape of a bison's head.

"This little crap machine hasn't shut up since Dovey left us," he said as the bony pup wriggled in his thick arms.

"I'm sorry, Vergil. I wanted to be there. I would have come but—"

"But nothing. It's the job. You don't have to make excuses with me. Besides you two never really saw eye to eye." He turned and screamed out into the empty condo, "Cliff! Come and get Tina!"

A very tall, thick man in a black suit appeared behind Bernie. She had no idea where he had come from, or if he'd been behind her the whole time. The silent giant nodded an acknowledgment to Bernie then quickly snatched the pooch from Vergil's arms.

"Thank you, Cliff, and could you bring two tequila sunrises out to the deck." He winked at Bernie. "Make sure one is heavy on the grenadine."

Cliff turned and walked away from the foyer and Vergil lead Bernie towards the open deck that wrapped around the massive glass palace.

"Jesus Christ, Vergil, retirement looks good on you. You're doing alright."

"I bought early. I told you to do the same. Prebuild, that's the only way to buy. This place has doubled in the last ten years," he bragged, stepping out into the blinding sun as he put on a pair of gold-rimmed sunglasses and plopped down onto a white, linen couch.

The unobstructed Miami sky allowed the sun to bounce off his massive gold ring, like a mirror, practically blinding Bernie. "Speaking of living large—has that bull on your hand gotten bigger too?"

"It's a bison. How many times have I had to tell you that?" Vergil stopped, seeing the grin on her face—Bernie had pressed a familiar button, getting his goat. "Never gets old for you, does it?"

"Never," she chortled, pleased with her nudge.

"So, New Smyrna, is it? Why the hell did you pick that shithole?"

"It's quiet. Unlike you, I thought less flash meant less bullshit."

He looked over his sunglasses. "How'd that work out for you."

"Well, I still have the place, don't I? Something like this would have been one of the first things to go."

"They took everything, huh? Fucking bastards."

"Basically, but not the trailer."

"Trailer? What the hell are you doing in a trailer?"

"I'm surviving. It's quiet and they didn't take it. It's still in the park owner's name. We have an understanding."

"Mother fuckers. Do you know who?" Vergil asked her quietly.

Bernie sighed and shook her head as Cliff came out onto the deck with two tequila sunrises on a tray.

"I know which one's mine," Bernie said reaching for the one with the thick layer of red at the bottom of it. "Thank you, Cliff."

The big, strong man showed his teeth in a sheepish smile. "Nice to see you again, Ms. Hewton."

She winked. "You as well."

As Cliff left, Vergil sat back, settling into the visit. "I was surprised you called."

"I was surprised you answered." Bernie leaned back too, getting comfortable on the large white linen chair opposite him.

"Even for you, Bernie, it was a ballsy ask."

"What can I say? I have big ones."

BONE PARK

"Yes, you do. My guys said it went off without a hitch."

"What did you expect?" Bernie feigned an insult.

"I didn't expect that you'd be doing this, that's for sure. This isn't your game, not even in your ballpark. It's below you."

"No, it's not. It's survival. Me or them, and I plan on surviving."

"It's that! That right there! That's what made them love you so much. I had their loyalty, Bernie, but I never had their love."

"I love ya, Vergil. I've just never been above heavy lifting. Less penthouse, more trailer. You and I both know that contractors become punchlines if they can't lay a brick."

"That's the only reason I answered. I shouldn't be talking to you at all, let alone entertaining your proposal, but this little plan of yours seems like it will work."

"It will, as long as we keep it like the trailer. Small. Quiet. That's the key to the whole thing," Bernie told him flat out.

"Suits me just fine. I may have been a whale in our world but I'm just a goldfish in theirs," Vergil said, reaching into the pocket of his robe. "This is for you." He handed her a small black plastic square.

"What's this?" Bernie asked, dangling the box out in front of her as if it were contagious.

"It's a pager, Bernie. Haven't you ever seen one before?"

"Pager? Like a doctor?"

"Yes, just like that. One way communication. I'll send you the locations on it. Pick-ups and drop-offs."

"Thank you, but I don't deal with wireless things."

"Well, you can't be calling me like you did. You know that. And you're shacked up in New Smyrna, so?"

Bernie stared at the strange plastic contraption with a visible, hesitant fear.

"Oh, come on now, Bernie. It's not a bomb. You strong-armed your way into the union and made it one of the biggest in the country. That's just a little black box." Vergil made light of her discomfort. "You telling me that the Buffalo Banshee is afraid of that? The world's changed, Bernie, and this is just part of doing business in it now. There's nothing to fret over. Look, it's already on. All you have to do is just change the batteries when they run out and show up where it tells you to. Here, it's got a clip on the back of it," he said, standing up, moving over and taking it from her hands. "Allow me," Vergil said flirtatiously, sliding it slickly into the waistband of her slacks. "There. Now it will only bother you three times a week."

"Three times a week? That's not small." Bernie wasn't ready for that.

"Compared to what they're asking for, it's a pimple on a squirrel's dick. Bernie, you're the one who pulled me out of retirement for this. Now, overnight, I have a boss. A boss with expectations."

"But three a week? I was thinking three a month—at most. I don't have the manpower or transportation for three a week."

"You'll figure it out, just like you figured this out."

"I don't want to figure it out."

"You're going to have to, because we're both in this now. Good news is that they're impressed."

"What did you tell them?" Bernie sat forward, concerned and accusing.

"Nothing about you. As far as they know, I'm handling this all in-house. Sorry, Bernie, but I took all the credit. I promise you, your name was never brought up, for both of our safety. Not sure if you realize it, but the word's out, Bernie—you're a liability."

"I never said a word." Bernie glared at him.

"I know you didn't, but I am now in business with these people because of your request, so it's going to be three a week. Okay?"

Bernie could see the facts building up around her and her options disappearing. "Okay."

There was a sudden alarm—a high pitched 'beeping' sound—Bernie stood straight up.

Vergil laughed, "It's the beeper, Bernie!"

Bernie looked down at the raisin-box-sized technology hanging from her waistband. Across the top of it, in the green backlit display panel, a series of letters and numbers appeared.

Vergil stood up and took the drink from her hand. "Looks like you have somewhere to be."

Ruby was surrounded by college kids. Beautiful, bronzed and buff. She was sitting with them, in front of their Jeeps, with her new best friend, Tammy and another young girl. Tammy was wearing Ruby's sunglasses and Ruby had someone's American flag bandana wrapped around her head. The music that was blasting out of the Jeep's stereo had changed from 70s' rock to repetitive dance music, but Ruby was feeling no pain.

"Hey, grab two more of those beers," Ruby said to Tammy. "I want to show you something."

Tammy whistled to one of the boys and they tossed her two cold ones from a cooler in the open back of the Jeep.

Tammy handed Ruby one of the dew-covered cans as Ruby reached behind her and dug around in her beach bag. "This is how we Buffalo Girls do it back home," Ruby announced to the eager group of tanned idols watching her. "Three small shakes," she said, moving the can up and down slowly, three times. "Remind you of anything?" she teased the boys, who were paying close attention. "Then you pop and unlock!" Ruby whipped her hand out of her beach bag and slammed it against the bottom of the can. "Pop!" A little beer sprayed onto her and Tammy, but Ruby put her thumb over the hole fast, bringing the can up to her mouth. "And unlock." She wrenched the tab on the top of the can back, placing her mouth over the hole in the bottom of it, to accept the rush of beer that instantly shot down the back of her throat.

The crowd of kids watched in awe as this woman chugged the entire can of beer in seconds.

"Back home, we call that a backfire!" Ruby announced and her oiled-up groupies exploded in cheers, applauding her bikini-clad vaudevillian act.

"Let me try!" Tammy was all excited.

Ruby turned to her. "Okay, shake the can slowly, three times."

Tammy locked eyes with the dark-haired boy on her left, taunting him with her hand movements. "One, two, three."

"Okay, now poke this through the side of it." Ruby handed her the keys that she used for hers.

Tammy hesitated.

"It's easy, Tammy. Just slam it right in there. Don't worry about the key," Ruby encouraged her.

Tammy still hesitated, raising the key up to Ruby. "Is that—blood?" The entire key was covered in it. Tip to bow. Some of it was wet, reconstituted by the beer and it was dripping onto Tammy's hand.

Ruby snatched the keys from her. "No—that's just paint. I opened a can of paint with it this morning. I forgot. Probably don't want to use that." She shouted over to the boy that Tammy had locked eyes with, "Hey, make yourself useful and give her your keys!"

BONE PARK

The boy tossed his keys and Ruby did her best to carry on, getting Tammy to refocus on the task. "Just slam it into the beer."

As Tammy went for it, sending beer shooting out all over Ruby and the others. Ruby pulled inside herself—tucking the blood-stained keys back into her bag and her spirit back into its hiding place. She didn't whip them off, didn't try to clean them at all. She actually placed them carefully into the small, zippered pocket inside, like they were a precious shell she had found on the shoreline.

Watching this crowd of kids celebrate Tammy choking back beer, cheering as it shot out of her nose and ran down the front of her, Ruby suddenly wanted to be anywhere else but there. Somewhere that was meant for her. Where she wasn't trying to impress or keep up or fit in. Where she was beautiful for being her, not because she was the least weathered of the hulls. She looked around at the kids. She became suddenly aware of the annoying music and the childish laughter. She could see their lack of life experiences, their smooth, callus-free spirits and mettle that had yet to be tested. They were sweet, but they were innocent of character.

Ruby bent down and slowly gathered her things, tucking them into her beach bag then stepped back towards the rear of the Jeeps, to where her folded up umbrella and blanket were left—and no one noticed. Ruby picked up her things without alarm and was able to walk away from the group without so much as a question. Youth is fleeting and so is their attention. Without her stories and tricks, they had already made her into a memory. No one chased after her or begged her to stay, she was now just a funny tale for them to tell about the beer-chugging granny they met that one day on the beach.

Bernie was taking the off ramp from the I-95 when a startling mix of vibration and beeping coming from her slacks made her almost drive straight into the guard rail. As urgent as all the ruckus made it seem, she was sure to complete the curve and head towards the A1A before she unclipped the beeper from her waistband. The display was very small, so it was hard to read without cheaters and the blinking cryptic message didn't make it any easier. The first message was simple. It wasn't in code and the location was actually the parking garage of Vergil's building. That's when he told her that they'd be using an old school method of communication from there on out. They couldn't just put place and time out into the air for anyone to find. This did calm Bernie's nerves a little about the whole wireless thing, but now she needed to remember how the hell they used to do it. How this code worked. It wasn't used very often back in the day—on the job—but when it was used, it was spoken, or sent by letter or eventually, by telephone. They were means of communication that Bernie was familiar with, not a devil's box that displayed it on a screen the size of a *tic tac* lid and in digital black letters to boot.

"Stop AGT sleep NAA" was all she got.

This was a real mind fuck for her, real 'rub the belly while tapping the head' shit. This 60-year-old woman was trying to wield a rusty old wood-paneled behemoth down the road, with a special delivery in the back, avoiding making any police-alerting infractions, all while attempting to decipher Vergil hieroglyphics. The first part she knew. *Stop* had always meant parking lot. That was basic and the third, *sleep*, came to her fast as well. *Sleep* meant hotel. The other capped letters were tougher. The fourth block was the route and the second block used to be a landmark, but she had no clue what AGT was. Back home in Buffalo, this was easy. She knew every nook and cranny of the city, but New Smyrna was her vacation spot. She knew most things, but not in a 'doing business' kind of way. So, she focused on the fourth block, NAA. NAA? She spun the letters around her head, taking left and right turns at the same time, making sure to keep up with traffic, but staying geriatric enough to piss a few people off. She couldn't drive too smooth, the key to this whole plan was authenticity. NAA? What the hell was NAA? She rolled it around a few more times until—

"North Atlantic Avenue!" she shouted, as if Pat Sajak were waiting for her to solve the puzzle.

BONE PARK

She was proud of herself. It was a major street in New Smyrna, not the toughest guess, but she was still proud of herself. It gave her the confidence to dive into the remaining block, the second one, AGT. This was a very blind guess. Landmarks are tricky because they are mostly buildings in urban settings. Bernie went through the lexicon of beach attractions in her head and came up empty. She was getting very close to Atlantic Avenue. Two things these messages didn't have were date and time, but that's because both were immediate. In this type of work, you never give the heat time to see you coming or going. The pressure was on. AGT? She thought about every letter but couldn't crack it. She wished the pager was two way or that she had caved in and bought one of those cool flip phones. She'd seen the kids with them. They reminded her of Bones, her Star Trek crush from the 60s, but there was no time for that. AGT? Why would Vergil make it so hard for her? The code itself was basically 'bread crumb' free for any eavesdroppers, so why make it harder for her. Why couldn't he have picked something she'd know.

She kept going over the letters in her head as she pulled onto Atlantic Ave. The letters by then had jumbled all up, mixed and reconfigured in her noodle, not making sense anymore, dyslexic from it all. Dyslexic?

She slammed her hand against the steering wheel. "Goddamn it!" she yelled, putting her blinker on and pulling a U-turn in the middle of the busy street.

This was not blending in, this was standing out, but so were the letters. It was the jumbling up of them in her mind that had made it clearer. That was the key to it. She suddenly remembered. It was the way they used to hide the most obvious part of the code. The landmark letters were sent in reverse. A small but important fact that she had forgotten. It wasn't AGT, it was TGA and the sign she had just passed, had them all lit up on it.

Bernie pulled into the parking lot of The Golden Arms condominiums and headed straight for the back. Everything always happened in the back. With this problem figured out, her mind went straight to the next one. How was she going to do the next one and the next? How could she possibly carry this out three times a week?

She had enough sun and fun for one day, so Ruby found a nice little hole in the wall where she could sip on something that didn't taste like suntan lotion and misspent youth. It was the kind of place people went to disappear and the few people that were in there, gave her that courtesy. A courtesy that she respectfully gave back them.

Bernie had given her more than enough money to drink the rest of the afternoon away and still get home by taxi. She was set up to get plastered, but after the keys, Ruby didn't feel much like getting off her face drunk. She just wanted to be surrounded by adults. Surrounded by relics, reflective seasoned veterans of life, close to her own generation. Close to understanding the feeling she was having. The aching of invisibility. It wasn't attention she wanted; it was acknowledgment. A certain kind of acknowledgement, the awareness that you exist. That the world around you sees that, and is glad that you do, not annoyed that you're still taking up space or expecting you to entertain them. The corporate world had been doing it for years, mandatory retirement—not wanting you to take up jobs that the young people should have. This whole Floridian fantasy was that. Even last night was a fantasy. Not the attack, but the kiss. Benny really saw her. In a way the rest of the world hadn't. Was that why it felt so good, she wondered? Or was it something more? How could it be? He's a kid, just like the ones on the beach, so why was she thinking about him right now?

Ruby pulled a few crumpled bills from her bag and set them down onto the bar. As she stood up, an older, brown-haired woman sitting at a table all by herself, nursing a sadly empty beer, looked up at her. They made eye contact briefly, causing the woman to tilt her head a little.

"Ruby? Ruby Hewton?" questioned the brown-haired woman.

Ruby wasn't ready for that. To be talked to in this sad shack and especially not ready to be called by her last name.

"Do I know you?" she asked hesitantly, while trying not to show it.

"You did. I'm sure I've changed, but shit, you certainly have not. Darcy. Darcy Patterson. We used to dance together, on the upstate circuit."

Ruby was a sudden wash of emotion. "Darcy Dimples?"

The brown-haired woman smiled, revealing the deep crescent grooves on her cheeks.

"My word, I haven't seen you since Magog!" Ruby pulled out the empty seat across the table from Darcy and sat down.

"Magog! That church place, right? The old clock."

"Le Vieux Clocher. Old bell tower."

"Well, well, well. Par-dony moi!"

"I remember it because I begged the French dancers to teach me how to say it. It's still the only French I know to this day."

"My God. What a hell of route, New York to Quebec." Darcy snorted.

"Hey, can we get another round here!?" Ruby shouted to the bartender, who was not happy about the sudden loud break in this mirthless monastery.

"Thirty years?"

"More like thirty-five."

Darcy shook her head. "What the hell are the chances of you and I meeting up again?"

"I don't owe you money, do I?" Ruby laughed, just as the

bartender set down the drinks in front of them. "Run a tab for me," she said to him, suddenly very comfortable there.

"This beer should make it even," Darcy joked back. "What are you doing here? Are you on vacation?"

"No. I live here."

"Really? Me too. Been here since '78." Darcy coughed. It was one of those thick coughs, the kind that doesn't come with a cold and never goes away.

"I just came in a few months ago—with my sister."

"I guess we all end up down here, don't we?" Darcy pontificated. "Did you know that Cathy Buckner and Nola Banks were here too?"

"Who?"

"Cathy Cutie and Naughty Nola."

Ruby lit up. "Get out!"

"I kid you not. Cathy is just down the beach in the Sun Setter condos and Nola's in one of those trailer parks inland."

"I'm in one of those. Cicada Hollow."

"Ah, so you've gone from Beverly Hills to trailer trash," Darcy joked, but it didn't land well, and she could see it. "Oh heavens, Ruby. I didn't mean it like that."

"I'm sure you didn't."

"Cross my heart. I watched all the news on you. I couldn't believe what they said. They did you wrong."

"Some of it was right."

"Well to hell with them, huh?" Darcy raised her beer. "We're here now."

Ruby raised her glass to cheers. "We are."

"What have you been up to? You're looking at what I've been doing. Monday to Saturday, 11:00 to 4:00." She shouted over to the bartender, "Ain't that right, Tim?!"

Tim was, again, not impressed with the noise.

"Well, I was working at a bar, over near Edgewater."

"Working? What bar?"

Ruby was hesitant. "Shakers."

"Shakers!" That struck a chord. "The strip club?"

"Yeah, that's the one—but I quit."

"Were you on stage? Holy Dinah, I'd love to have seen that."

"I wasn't performing. I was a waitress."

"Stop the presses. Ruby Rain serving cocktails? That's sacrilege. How did they not know who you are?"

"Oh, they knew—the manager did anyway. She said she was a huge fan. But she didn't want me messing up their scenery. Apparently, I am past my prime."

"We should torch the place," Darcy whispered as she leaned in, over the table, serious about her pyromania.

"Not worth it."

"They don't know what they're missing. You always put on a hell of a show, could have taught the young ones a thing or two."

Ruby's memory was jogged. "Hey, do you remember that bar in Peterborough? It had a red and black sign?"

Darcy's head was spinning with memories. "Peterborough? Oh, Ruby, that's going back a ways."

"Come on, it had a Scottish lion on the sign. I think it was called the Miss Danny or—"

"The Miss Diana!" Darcy was excited.

"That's it. That's the one. Remember all the dancers from Quebec at the Miss Diana?"

"Christ, do I. They weren't the ones from Magog. Those broads were tough."

"Tough and old."

"Yes, they were. There was that one, Bijou?! She was really old, as old as—" Darcy caught herself.

"As old as we are now? That bar was the end of the line for most of them, but they still danced. And they were great."

"Sideshow girls. That's what one of the Frogs called them. They said the real old ones started in the circus. In sideshow tents at night." It was as if Darcy was describing some archeological find in the Valley of the Kings. "Burlesque. When dancing was teasing, not all prep for the champagne room and hand jobs. Professionals who knew how to put on a show."

"Like Flaming Mame in the Catskills."

"Yes, just like Flaming Mame, only older and with an accent."

"That's where I learned my tricks. We were the next ones right after them. I may never have danced in a circus tent, but I danced in my share of Legion Halls and Shriners' Clubs."

"It was a different time then. We were the last of the professionals. A dead art form." Darcy raised her glass again to cheers, just this time more solemnly.

BONE PARK

Ruby raised her glass to meet it, with a twinkle in her eye. "Dying, but not dead."

CHAPTER

5

Under the B

       Bernie pulled the station wagon over to the side of the lane, out front of the trailer and left it running while she ran into the carport with something. Freda couldn't make out what Bernie had tucked under her arm, even using Reg's high-powered binoculars. It was almost time for the evening news, but she'd been on block watch all day waiting for Bernie to return. She was committed to it, really committed to it. She had the front bedroom all set up like an FBI stakeout. The sheers were closed, and the lights were off to prevent her shadow from being exposed. She had folding TV trays on both sides of her, with her gear spread out all over them. There was a collection of different powered binoculars, the wireless telephone, a note pad with a surprising number of notes in it, a clock, an ashtray full of smoldering butts and a few dirty dishes from snacks Reg had brought her to get through.

Still peering through the binoculars, Freda called back to Reg, clenching a lit cigarette between her lips, "She's back, Reg. But she's made a stop at her place."

"Is the car on fire?" Reg shouted back with a jovial lilt.

"What? No. But she's stopped at her place."

"Freda, you've been in there all day. She's back, case solved. For the love of God, get out of the window. You look like some kind of pervert," Reg chuckled, "and I'd like to keep that our little secret."

"Believe you me, Reg, that woman is up to something," Freda answered, keeping her eyes on her suspect and the smoke in her mouth. "Who runs errands for eight hours?"

Reg opened the door of the dark bedroom, "Someone—"

"Close the door!" Freda ducked down immediately, shouting at him.

Reg obliged, playing along with his wife. "Right. Sorry, Columbo." He closed the door and continued, "She said she had a lot of errands to do. I don't think it's that strange at all."

"Then what is she dropping off at her house?"

Reg tilted his head. "Errands, Freda. That's how they work."

Freda shot him a glare then turned her attention back to the window. "Code red, code red! She's on the move!" Freda got up fast—a little too fast for her circulation's liking, causing her to fall forward, knocking over one of the TV trays and Reg as well.

Luckily, he was able to catch her in his arms and cradled her down to the ground, protecting her from the hard landing and laughing the whole way. Reg was like that. Always supporting her, protecting her, indulging her. She may have been a pit bull in the yard, but she was a kitten in his arms.

Headlights suddenly washed across the ceiling above them.

"Reg, this is no time for Booma, Booma! That's her." She playfully slapped him, and he released her from his arms.

Freda got to her feet, a little more carefully this time and straightened herself up. She made her way into the main room, taking up a posed position on the sofa, with her back to the carport door just in time for the knocking.

"Reg!" she called out as if she had no idea who it was, where he was, and she was too busy to deal with either. "Could you please get that?"

Reg came out from the front bedroom, looking at her as if she'd lost her mind. "Sure thing pumpkin," he said walking towards the carport door. "Say, darling, did you get all that mustache bleach off?" he joked loudly, getting the death stare he was hoping for from her and opening the door quickly before she could retort.

"Hello, Reg," Bernie said from the bottom step. "I'm a bit later than I thought I'd be. My apologies."

"No bother at all," Reg smiled kindly. "We weren't needing it today anyway. Did it give you any trouble?"

Freda casually came over to join him at the door.

"No trouble at all, ran like a charm," Bernie answered.

"Ran?" Freda questioned. "I would have thought errands were more of a jog, than a run."

Bernie grinned, "Jogged like a charm." She held out the keys to Reg. "It's got a full tank of gas, like I promised and now I need one as well. Time for me to make some dinner. Thank you both again." Bernie turned and started to walk away.

"Anytime," Reg tossed out and Freda jabbed him in the gut with her elbow.

BONE PARK

Bernie stopped at the edge of the driveway and turned back. "Thanks, Reg, I just might take you up on that," she said making sure to shoot Freda an overly sweet look before turning back.

As the six foot plus woman walked away, Freda snatched the keys from Reg.

"What are you doing?" Reg sighed. "The car's back safe and sound and with a full tank of gas."

"Fishy." Freda turned her nose up. "Believe you me, I have a way about these things."

Freda watched and waited until Bernie had made it back to her own place, then stepped down into the carport and opened the doors of the wagon.

"What was the mileage?"

"I don't know. I stopped looking at it when it broke 200,000."

"Well how the hell am I supposed to figure out where she went if I don't know the mileage?"

"Okay, you're in a way. I'll be inside when your done your forensics, Perry Mason." Reg sighed as he faded away, back into the main room.

Freda ignored him. She was on a mission. She opened all the doors on the wagon, one by one. Everything looked as it should be, but she kept on looking. Searching the seats, the floormats, the door handles, even the headliner. Finally, she made it to the back of the wagon, swinging open the large back door. She combed the massive, carpeted floor of the cargo area with her hands, but nothing was amiss. As she closed the door, her hands passed by her face, and she winced a little. Freda slowly raised her hands to her nose and smelled them. There was something there. A smell, a subtle one, just above the burning odor of the Lucky Strike that was permanently attached to her fingers. It was familiar, but she couldn't quite figure it out. Whatever it was, it wasn't supposed to be in the back of her wagon. That much she knew. That much was what she had waited all day for. It made sense to her, proving her hunch right, if only in her mind.

The warmed TV dinner—consisting of a dried-up slab of turkey, gelatin gravy, powdered mash potatoes and some slop pretending to be apple crumble—tasted like a hundred-dollar entree at Le Cordon Bleu to Bernie right now. She was scooping up mouthful after mouthful and this was not her typical dinner. This was all solid, with the exception of the gravy. In fact, there were no liquids anywhere near her other than a tall glass of milk. Shit had gotten real. She needed all her wits about her now. A full stomach was going to keep her levelheaded and a level head might just keep her alive. Might.

Bernie had issues to sort out and the first of them was transportation. She had none and she couldn't just go out and buy one either. She had no ID. No way to license one or get insurance. Her Lincoln was a gift—kept in a dear old friend's name. If only she had known that things would go this way. Even though the Lincoln was a little too flashy for what she needed, the grinding of her teeth on the tough chunk of turkey in her mouth, said she regretted selling it. Of course, the money from the Lincoln had helped get them through and the 'errands' she was now doing required more subtle transportation, but she was in a jam. A conundrum of her own making that could not be solved with 'could haves' so, she bore down on the fowl and chewed through the remorse, until she'd processed her unhelpful druthers.

With the past and the turkey swallowed, she took a bit of the mash potatoes from the right compartment and dragged them through the gravy on her way to her mouth. They had that odd, cardboard flavor to them that all packaged dinners from the frozen section have and she was finally able to taste it now that her hunger was satiated a little. As she swallowed the lump of starchy mush she returned to the facts. She had no car. She needed a car. Actually, she needed a few cars. If she couldn't buy one herself, then she would have to keep borrowing other peoples.

BONE PARK

But three times a week? She practically had to kidnap Opal and Freda was acting weird. Weirder than weird. So, what was her deal? Bernie didn't know much about Reg and Freda, other than they were from Boston. For all she knew, they were sent to the park to keep an eye on her; regardless though, Freda seemed like a risk.

"Yoo-hoo?!" Opal's Heidi routine broke Bernie's concentration.

"In here, Opal!" Bernie shouted back, not bothering to get up.

Opal opened the screen door and stepped up into the trailer. "Oh, hi Bernie." She stopped herself, seeing the formed cardboard plate in front of Bernie. "I didn't know you were eating."

Bernie spoke through her full mouth, "I know, peculiar isn't it—to see me with a fork in my hand instead of a highball?"

"Oh, dear, that's not at all what I meant."

"I know. I'm teasing, Opal. You're fine. I was just finishing up."

"No need to rush on my account."

"I'm not rushing. What is it you want, Opal? Ruby and I were planning on joining the trikes tonight as soon as she gets home, if that's what you're wondering."

"Oh, that's wonderful," she replied, but she shuffled a bit as she said it.

Bernie saw her struggling. "Opal, what is it? Is Stan drunk? Is he okay?"

Opal hemmed and hawed a little, then said softly, "When can we play again?"

"Play?" Opal was sweet, but this was odd. Play? She was taking the pink outfits and gumdrop smiles a little far. Sure, riding around the park on bicycles, playing games on the grass, swimming and the rest of the activities in the park were technically 'playing' but it was disturbing to Bernie to hear it requested like that.

"Bingo?" Opal added. "I was wondering when you might, if you might, be heading back to play bingo?"

"Oh." Bernie set her fork down and ruminated on this. She had thought that she might be able to use Opal again, sometime in the future, just not so soon. "You want to go to bingo again?" Bernie knew Opal was a straight shooter. Until recently she had gone to Sunday services in town every Sunday morning. Opal definitely didn't know where the money came from, but she had to know it wasn't from bingo.

"Stan wanted me to ask," Opal said.

Now it made sense. He was the bargaining chip that Bernie had used to make it happen in the first place. She hadn't played Opal, she'd played Stan through Opal, and played him like a Stradivarius.

"Why does Stan want you to go back to bingo?" Bernie already knew it was about the money and she wasn't being cruel, she was just doing what she did best—negotiating. "Did he get the golf clubs he wanted?" Bernie already knew the answer to that too.

"Oh…ah, no. Not exactly. He still wants them, but he went out the other night. Cards and the like. Not the best night for him."

This was what she was counting on—what she knew would happen eventually, just not that fast. It was the certainty of Stan's little gambling problem. Technically it was his drinking problem mixed with his gambling problem that made it a big problem.

"You told him I was your lucky charm, so maybe we could go again sometime?" Opal was embarrassed.

"You *are* my lucky charm. We can definitely go again. Soon."

"Will the game be in Miami again?"

"Yes. But I might have to tell you on short notice. Really short notice."

"Oh, that's okay. Stan really wants me to go with you."

"Alright then, I'll let you know as soon as a good bingo game comes up!" Bernie assured her and Opal seemed pleased. Pleased but a little troubled.

"Bingo?" Ruby's voice entered the trailer before she did. "I love bingo!"

Loose lips sink ships and loud voices free felines—that's how that cat gets out of the bag.

Bernie and Ruby were bringing up the back of the pack yet again. Lazily pedaling behind an oblivious Opal. The pack up front, led by Maryanne and Cecilia, couldn't care less. In fact, they were happy that the two, less desirable residents of the park, were far enough behind them that they could be seen as not being a part of the group at all.

"So, you just ran into her?" Bernie was into what Ruby was dishing out.

"I know, hard to believe. Over thirty years later and she's sitting right there. And two other girls I used to dance with are down here too. Nola and Cathy."

"Small world."

"Or big signs?" Ruby gave her a witchy raised eyebrow.

Bernie lowered her voice, "Look, I'm sorry about the whole bingo thing. It's just that Opal really wants it to be a 'me and her' kind of thing."

"It's alright," Ruby said a little let down. "I always lose anyway. Gambling has never been good to me."

"Me either. It's really just for Opal. She doesn't get out much.

It's good for her."

"I suppose so. Can't be easy being locked up all the time with that brute of a husband."

"To say the least."

Ruby thought for a few pedals. "I see it though. He does give off a certain Stanley Kowalski energy, doesn't he?"

"Don't you even think about it." Bernie glared at her.

"I was just saying."

"Well don't." Bernie wasn't hanging around for this to get any racier, so she pedaled a little faster to catch up with Opal.

Ruby let her make her exit, leaving her trailing behind. She was joking about Stan, but her mind was on a man. Benny. The warm night air felt romantic, the kind of ambiance that beach blankets are laid out in. Where lovers cuddle facing the dying sun, waiting to steal a kiss before the day disappears. She had stolen one, in the front seat of his car and as she moved towards the setting sun, all she wanted was to be a thief.

There was a loud thump in the back of the trunk. Bernie didn't drop her off this time. She didn't leave her standing on the side of Ocean Drive like before, there wasn't time. Opal was kind of looking forward to it though, once she knew that Bernie would come back. Opal had been tricky, tucking a couple of the 'bingo' dollars away, keeping them from Stan, just in case. Truth be told, it was not 'in case' it was 'in fact', because when he said he was heading out that night, to play cards, she knew he'd come home empty handed, so she socked some away. When Bernie called bright and early that morning to take her on another 'bingo' run, the one she had requested, the petty cash she had squirreled away was hers to squander. Opal was excited for a do over, she wanted to stroll through a few of the shops near the Marlin Hotel, maybe even pick up a new hat or bag. She couldn't remember the last time she bought something for herself, by herself, with her own money, but that would have to wait, because there were no fancy shops in this underground parking lot.

The car shook from side to side. Opal couldn't see what the two large men were putting into the trunk of the champagne-colored Corolla, because the image in the rearview mirror was blocked by the raised trunk lid. Whatever the cargo was, it was heavy, and the two healthy men were having a hard time making it fit in. Opal was naive, but she was not stupid. She knew what it most likely was, but she wouldn't let her mind think about it for too long, because Jesus was listening. He was always listening. Opal wasn't trying to put one over on the big man, she had just found a loophole. Honor thy husband was at the top of that amendment, followed by the forgiveness she would pursue and the good she could do with a few donated dollars. Her intentions were good, but there was a definite war going on inside her, good and evil and a lot of questions. The main one being how Bernie had gotten into this and why she'd asked her along in the first place?

The trunk slammed shut. Thank goodness Stan wasn't there or there would have been hell to pay for slamming it that hard. Opal made sure to look forward and try to appear as calm as possible, even though her hands in her lap had gone completely white from squeezing them together so tightly.

Bernie opened the door and scrunched her tall body into the driver's seat. "All set?"

Opal used sounds, not words. "Uh, huh."

"I should drive until we get out of here."

"Uh, huh."

"Hey. Everything's all right, Opal. Just a quick drive home and we're done. Next time I'll drop you off. Traffic was just tough this time."

"Uh, huh."

Bernie started the car and began to pull out. "Do you know what these errands are?"

"Yes, it's bingo," Opal snapped. "You are really good at bingo and I'm your lucky charm."

Bernie backed off. "Well then you'll be pleased to know that once we finish this game, the jackpot is going to be significantly bigger than the last one."

"You are very lucky, Bernie." Opal continued with her storyline.

"Yes I am."

Although Opal was being selectively honest with herself, she didn't seem all that upset. She was a 'goody-goody' after all, so what was her motive? Good God-fearing women didn't go along with this kind of thing knowingly. Bernie didn't push it any further, however. She started the Corolla, pulled out of the underground parking lot and headed for the interstate.

Good God-fearing women? She couldn't get the term out of her head. Bernie had many questions about God and just as many bones to pick with him. Hearing Opal pretend didn't help the tabernacle's case much. She felt bad for dragging Opal into this and putting her in a situation where she had to bend her faith. But it always happened that way. Faith always bent to meet the parishioners' needs; she had never seen it work the other way around. She had never seen the good, God-fearing believer bending for the belief. Sweet Opal was just the next to fold. So, Bernie let her look out the window, wrapped up in her fantasy, while she pondered the outstanding bill that the devil still owed her for. The one Opal had just been added to.

Ruby had dragged one of the folding, plastic-strapped lounges out from the shed and placed it just off to the side of the lawn bowling greens. The match that day was far more interesting than most professional sporting events. Ruby was set with her small cooler of cold beer by her side, a bag of chips by her feet and head to toe Coppertone coverage; she was the one-woman VIP section of this heated tournament.

Stan and Harold were facing off against Fred and Chuck. The wives that had kept their distance at the start of the match, staying over by the pool, were now making their way over to join Ruby in her impromptu cheering section. Maryanne, Cecilia and Gertie were being careful not to cheer too loudly, clap too vigorously or do anything to stir the pot too much, because this match was about to boil over.

"Horse shit!" Stan shouted, running over to the small, white ball, while pointing at the large, red ball that Fred had just rolled. "It's not closer at all! Your ball is a solid horse cock away from the Jack!"

The other wives shuddered a bit at the obscenities coming out of Stan's mouth, but Ruby was laughing, she'd never heard of a horse's member used as a measurement of distance before.

Fred stepped up to Stan. "Your eyes must be having a tough day, because it is definitely closer. Come on Stan, we let you play that other Jack, and it wasn't fully over the hog line."

"The hell it wasn't!" Stan stepped up to Fred.

Chuck, Gertie's short, skinny husband piped up. "Maybe if you didn't drink through the whole game, you'd—"

"I'd what?!" Stan stormed over to him. "You should be thanking your lucky stars that I'm lubricated, or I'd be making you see stars."

"Okay!" Gertie had seen enough. "Chuck, time for lunch!" she shouted walking over and taking him by the arm, dragging him away from certain destiny with a knuckle sandwich.

"You leave and you forfeit! Game is ours!" Stan taunted.

"Sleep it off, Stan!" Gertie shouted back over her shoulder.

"Undefeated!" Stan cheered to a crowd that wasn't cheering with him. Even Harold had clammed up and started to pack the balls away.

Ruby turned to Maryanne and Cecilia. "Damn, and it was just getting good."

Maryanne did not like the sass that Ruby was giving off and quickly followed Gertie's lead, gathering up her husband and slipping away into the gaps between the trailers. Ruby found the whole production amusing, especially the climax, she had come for the lawn bowling but almost got a boxing match as well. She marveled at what had happened to men. When did they all become so spineless? They weren't the men she grew up around back in Grand Island and Buffalo. These men didn't have callouses on their hands or a bite to their barks. They were dolls for their wives. Things to pose and position at events, but they weren't men. They were shells of what they were. The evidence wasn't just in their pussy-footing personalities, it was on display for all to see—it had become a part of their anatomy. Their wrinkled skin was the finished sculpture made from years of shaping by the displeased opinions of their wives and the medication from their multiple bypasses. Breasts—they had breasts. Most of the men in the park and the ones who walked the beaches of Florida did. Boobs. Gynecomastia. A side effect of the cardiology prescriptions that were saving their lives. Ruby wasn't condemning them for their physical appearance any more than their personalities. They were being what they thought they should be. Agreeable. Keeping the peace. After all, it's the hypertension they were afraid of. The boiling blood of manhood that they should avoid. So, they took their meds, and they became agreeable. Livable at an age when their vocations had dissolved along with their daily vacations from their wives. It was retirement, so being agreeable worked when all their time would be spent with their sculptor. To be otherwise would only cause undo friction in the last few years of their life. Ruby didn't blame them; she just lamented the death of the kind of man she used to swoon over.

Ruby folded her chair up and bent down to pick up her cooler.

"Feel like sharing?" Stan asked.

Ruby spun around, realizing her swimsuit covered behind was up in the air.

"I meant the beer. Is there one in that cooler for me?" Stan asked nicely.

This wasn't the Stan that she just saw ready to tear Fred limb from limb or the one that cornered her over at the shuffleboard court months ago. Contrary to his opponents, he seemed relatively sober—for him—and was asking nicely.

"Sure," Ruby said, sliding the peaked roof of her tiny cooler over to the side and pulling out a cold can of Coors.

"Thank you," Stan said, cracking it open. "We're fresh out at home. Hopefully Opal picks some up on her way back." Stan made his way down to the grass, with grunts and groans along the way.

"Don't sit down there, you'll never get up," Ruby scolded him and unfolded the overlapping ends of her lounge. "Here."

Stan took her up on the offer, crawling over the two feet of grass between him and it. Ruby was standing at the end of it, watching as this galoot dragged his body up onto the lounge.

"Have a seat." Stan patted the strung plastic tubes of the chair beside him.

"I'm fine standing. I sat for most of your game." Ruby held her position.

"I won't bite. But thank you for the seat. You're right, I'd never have gotten up. Probably die out here on the grass. Bad knees from college."

Ruby's heard this lead in before. "Football?" she played along.

"Nope. Just repetitive weakness—softening of the knees caused by too many beautiful women." He laughed and took a big swig of his beer.

It was corny, but it was familiar. This was the kind of man she was used to. "So, my sister and Opal are at bingo."

"Yup. Hopefully it's a good game today. Got my eyes on a new set of clubs."

"Clubs?"

"Yeah, nice set of PING drivers and a bag at the pro shop right now with my name on them."

"My word, that sounds expensive. Takes a lot of blue hairs dabbing numbers to pay for that."

"Not with your sister. She cleaned up last time."

"Last time?" Ruby wasn't sure if he was spinning a yarn or if she was missing something.

"Yeah, last time they went, she sent Opal home with wad of cash. Her cut for driving. I told Opal anytime your sister wants to play bingo, she can take her. Let's hope today's as good as the last haul."

Bernie didn't say anything to Ruby about winning or even playing bingo before. This was all news to her. Why would she have kept that a secret?

"How much did she give Opal—she never did tell me."

Stan beamed with joy. "Almost a grand. Not bad for being a chauffeur."

"I'll say." Ruby bent down and grabbed a beer for herself from cooler. "Shove over," she said to Stan as she plopped down onto the lounge beside him. Ruby's mind, a flurry of activity, spinning through all the unanswered questions, all the avoided conversations, all the missing years and all that she didn't know about her big sister. She couldn't understand why her sister was being so secretive. Ruby was the one who had been wrapped up in scandal since they were in their twenties, not Bernie. Bernie had turned over a new leaf, she'd been the responsible one. The dutiful wife, the doting mother. Was it pride?

Her wonder turned to worry. Ruby was wise to this underbelly of society, to the bottom feeders who will give you what you need and take three times as much in return. The sudden weight of this whole mess came crashing down on her shoulders. The root cause of all this secrecy. What scam or loan shark had Bernie gotten in bed with? That's the only way Ruby could think of. The only possibility for her to have gotten that kind of money that fast. Was that it? The dirty grease that sticks to the wheels of commerce—loves desperation—and who is more desperate than a broke, old woman? Ruby's guilt was heavier than the humid ocean air, trapped in the inner circle by the corral of trailers. That desperation was Bernie's self-imposed duty, the older sibling's charge from birth, to take care of her little sister.

Bernie spoke loud and firm from the behind the car. "Do I look like I was born yesterday?"

The beeper had gone off long ago, negotiations had happened, the drop had been made and all with Opal in the car. Bernie had given her the option on this end of the run to get out. They were parked outside of the pride of Port Orange—the world-famous Aunt Catfish's restaurant. The landmark had a plethora of seafood delights ready for take-out. Plenty to fill her man's belly and fill her guilty conscience with a deniably blind story, but Opal stayed put in the Corolla. She stayed put and stayed remarkably calm. Even all the way down at the end of the parking lot, away from the lights of the entrance and help if needed, she was as cool as a shrimp cocktail.

Behind the car, Bernie shot a look back, catching Opal's eyes in the side mirror and Opal quickly looked away.

"You boys must be stupid. Are you stupid?" Bernie continued her loud questions, holding a tiny black duffel bag open in her hands.

The two men in leather jackets shook their heads.

"No? You have to be stupid. Please tell me you're stupid, because if you're not stupid, then that would mean that you tried to steal from me."

The two men looked at each other.

In a flash, Bernie pulled out the snub-nosed revolver from the back of her slacks and jammed the barrel of it into the man's forehead.

"Hold this!" she said, handing the stunned man she had at gunpoint the small duffel bag. "Hold it open," she instructed firmly, and he complied, pulling the two straps he was holding onto apart, widening the partially unzipped opening. "I make sure to know what the drop price is before I get here, and I always count my bread first. So…you were stupid, weren't you?"

The man with the gun barrel digging into his brow quickly nodded.

"Okay—that's alright. I have taught many simple-minded boys in my time, and I'd be happy to tutor you both as well." Bernie raised the thumb up on her gun-holding hand and slowly cocked the hammer back. "Would you like that?"

It was hard for Opal to tell in these shadows, but it appeared that the man at the end of the gun had started to cry. Silent, but there was a shimmer of something rolling down his face.

Bernie turned to the other man. "Lesson One. Go get the rest of my fee."

He turned tail and rushed back to the front of the truck they came in. A second later he rushed right back, with a swollen manila envelope in his hand and placed it into the open bag his frightened friend was still holding.

"Lesson Two. Never, ever do that again. You messed up once, that's alright. That's a mistake. Everyone makes mistakes, don't they? But if you do it again, then you're stupid and this world has no use for stupid people." Bernie slowly pulled the gun away from the man's head and took the bag from his hands. "Okay, now hurry up. We've been here far too long already."

The men turned and opened the back of the truck. Bernie opened up the trunk of the Corolla as well. Again, Opal's view was blocked by the trunk lid and again the car shook a little as the men took out whatever was in there. They closed the tailgate of the truck and pulled a tarp over it concealing what was underneath.

As the one man got into the driver's side of the truck, Bernie called the man she had just had at gunpoint over to her. "Would you be a doll and put this in the trunk for me?" she said, gesturing the black duffel bag of money in her hands.

The man snarled, "Why can't you do it?"

"It's called manners, young man. I am trying to teach you some. Lesson Three. Respect your elders." Bernie sighed.

The man huffed and walked back the few steps, reluctantly, taking the bag from her hands. He rolled his eyes as he bent down and placed the tiny bag into the trunk. "Fuuuuuuuck!" he suddenly screamed.

Bernie had slammed the trunk lid down onto his hand as fast as she had drawn her gun on him.

"SHHHHHHH!" She got right up into his face, leaning on the trunk lid with all her weight and whispered, "You shut up. You shut up right now or I'll put a bullet in your temple. That's only one of your hands, you little baby. It's barely in there and I'm sure it will heal up in a couple of days. But the scars? The scars that will be left on it, those are what are important. Those are your notes. Something for you to remember our little class by and for you to reference whenever you forget your place."

Bernie lifted the trunk lid, releasing the man and he snatched his bleeding hand free. She stood stoically watching as he ran back to the passenger side of the waiting truck and got in. Bernie waited for them to drive off, then closed the lid of the trunk gently and walked around to the driver's side of the Corolla, as if nothing had happened. As she got into the car, she looked over to Opal, who was staring forward, pretending to be oblivious to the mayhem that had just transpired at the back of the car.

"You know, when we normally come to Aunt Catfish's, we like to come early and walk around the wharfs for a bit. Watch the boats come in and unload their catches, have you ever seen them come in?" Opal said as sweet as Key Lime pie.

Bernie noticed that Opal's window was open a crack and that her side mirror had been adjusted just enough to see everything that had transpired.

"Why are you here?" Bernie was done playing.

"I am taking you to bingo. Your lucky charm. I'm helping you out and by doing so, I'm helping Stan get his new clubs," she said a little too quick and rehearsed to be truthful.

"Bingo? I know you heard every word and saw just about as much. What's really in it for you? And don't bullshit me."

Opal turned to her, angry. "Who are you?"

Bernie turned the car on. "You don't want to know that."

"Yes, I do. Who are you? I did hear a lot of things. I don't know what we are transporting from Miami to here on these drives, and that I don't want to know, but I do want to know who you are. You have a gun, Bernie, and the way you talked to those thugs? How do you even know those kinds of people?"

"I know too many of those kinds of people, Opal, and I wanted to forget them. I tried, believe me, but we're broke, and this is the only way I know how to keep us afloat."

Opal backed off and looked forward again. "That's what's in it for me. Whatever you are or were, I like being close to it. It makes me feel strong, Bernie. Makes me a little more like you."

Somewhere between the empty cooler out in the inner circle with Stan and this bed covered with sweat and regret, Ruby had managed to mess up huge. This was how she always dealt with her problems, and it always led to more problems. As she lie there, completely naked, arms behind her head, staring up at the faintly mildewed ceiling tiles of the trailer, she contemplated why? It wasn't the sex she needed, or was it? Was it being wanted, losing herself in the endorphins of being wrapped around another or was it punishment? Letting someone take what they wanted of her, to distract her from herself?

"That was wonderful," Benny's voice fluttered a little, like he was holding back a tear or wave of emotion.

"It was great," Ruby said back, still staring up, spread eagle like an offering to the gods.

Benny propped himself up onto his arm, leaning towards her, while modestly covering up his exposed lower half with the tousled sheets. "I was surprised that you called. I mean—I thought—I hoped you'd call me, but I never expected this—so soon. I want you to know that—"

"You respect me. I know, Benny. You kept saying it the whole time." Ruby sighed.

"Well, I do." Benny over confirmed, then paused, hearing his own voice. "Did I ruin it? I did, didn't I? My ex-girlfriend said I talked too much. It was actually the reason she broke up with me."

"It was great." Ruby turned her head to him. "Yes, Ben, you could talk a little less, but you made up for it with enthusiasm," she said quickly reaching over and grabbing his crotch through the sheets, "and that secret you're hiding? Seriously, Ben, that is a gift. I have seen a lot of those in my life and yours is gossip worthy. If I still had my business, I could make you famous with that thing."

Benny blushed. "Glad you liked it."

"There is a lot to like." Ruby smiled and Benny went in for a kiss. "Whoa." Ruby pulled back. "We should slow this down."

"Slow what down? We just made love." Benny looked hurt and confused.

"We had sex, Ben. Hot and heavy, sweaty sex."

"Okay, whatever you want to call it, but it happened, so what's this?"

Ruby slid over to the side of the bed and looked for her panties. "This was what it was. And it was good. And who knows, it might very well happen again…" She found her red underwear and stood up to pull them on. "My word, who am I kidding, it will happen again, but it was sex. I don't want you going and getting feelings for me."

"Too late," Benny sort of snapped at her as he searched for his own underwear.

Ruby picked up her red bra from the floor. "That's what I thought. Ben, I am old enough to be your—"

"Girlfriend?" Benny cut her off, with a stern look on his face and frustration in his voice. "You are old enough to be my girlfriend and I am old enough to be your boyfriend. I want to be your boyfriend. I wanted to ask you that night, but it wasn't right."

"You just met me, Benny."

"Ben," he corrected her. "Yeah, you just met me, and you called me over to sleep with me. Things happen."

Ruby did up her bra and stepped towards him. "Well, Ben, I am flattered. Believe me. You are a catch, both your heart and what you're packing, but I am way past the girlfriend expiry date."

"Says who?"

Ruby sat down on the edge of the bed. "I've been on this spinning rock a lot longer than you have and what you are talking about doesn't jive with the world."

"Do you not like me?" Benny practically pulled his heart out and laid it at her feet. "What's wrong with me?"

"Nothing, Ben. Nothing is wrong with you. But there is a lot wrong with me."

"I don't care. The moment I saw you, I felt this. This pain inside me that only went away when I got to see you again and now? Now that we've done this. That I've felt this, the pain of being without you is only going to be worse. How can I ever go back?"

"I shouldn't have called you. This was so unfair, I'm sorry."

"Why?"

"Don't you see it, Ben? You're a very smart young man, you have to be able to see it."

"See what?"

Ruby struggled with the words. "See me. I'm a springboard. A worn-out bike that everyone has ridden."

"You are the most beautiful woman I have ever seen, and I don't care where you've been or what you've done. I just want you."

"Ben, it's more than that. It's what I am. What I represent to you. I don't want to be that. This was all my fault. I took advantage of that."

Benny searched her face and his head for answers. "I don't know what you're going on about, but whatever it is, it's in your head, not mine. If you need a reason why I like you, I don't have just one—"

"Your mother!" Ruby let it out and the air was sucked out of the room with it. "I have had young lovers in my life. Different ages, colors, religions, and sides of the law, I know what makes you all tick. What drives you. I made my living from it. And a young man with an older woman only means one thing.

Benny looked torn apart. "What kind of sicko do you think I am? Why would you sleep with me if that's what you thought?"

"It's basic psychology, Ben. I don't think you're any sicker than I am—I wanted you because I knew you wanted me."

Benny sat still, breathing heavily, filling his lungs with anger and hurt—then he stopped. He stopped working it all out and stood up.

He settled his eyes on hers. His soft, brown eyes with the roasted cinnamon tone that sat on and under his lids. "Is that so bad? I do want you and if you like me wanting you, then what's the harm in that?"

Maybe it was his eyes, his words or the fact that he looked so hot standing in front of her in his loose boxers. Burly men had always come for her, but she had always, secretly preferred the skinny ones. That sinewy mix of muscle and bone, tight skin and carved obliques. Ben was a vision, a masterpiece cut out of hematite—the perfect combination of all that she preferred.

"There is a concert, on the beach tomorrow night. I want you to go with me." He leaned in and kissed her. "Will you go with me?"

Ruby liked this strength in him. This unwavering fight for her. He was skinny, but his character made him an Adonis. His persistence was exciting—that, and she still hadn't shaken the images of him on top of her yet. "What time?"

"I'll pick you up at 8:00," he stated. No smile, just confident confirmation as he started to put on his jeans and t-shirt.

It was a reverse voyeur moment. Both in that he was dressing instead of undressing and that it was her watching him. They had landed in bed in such a frenzy, that this whole ritual was skipped. He didn't know it, but this little moment, this normal—private moment, was making his case more solid by the second.

Benny did up his woven leather belt and went to open the bedroom door. "Don't know if I've ever been someone's girlfriend," Ruby said in a soft whisper of surrender.

"You are now," Benny said, opening the door, claiming his heart and borrowing the one she was offering.

"You're back," Bernie said, from the main room. She was sitting in the La-Z-Boy, over by the end table. "I thought I saw your Sable in one of the visitor's spots."

Ruby rushed out behind Benny, still doing up her robe. "Bernie, I didn't know you were home?"

"Don't fret, I just got in and didn't hear anything—I swear."

"This is Ben," Ruby said, mortified by this postcoital introduction.

Bernie nodded to Benny. "Nice to meet you, Benny. Isn't it past your bedtime?"

"Isn't it past yours?" he gently barbed back.

Bernie cracked a smile, "Touché. The cub has claws."

Benny turned back to Ruby, "See you tomorrow." He went in for a kiss and the whole thing got really awkward, really fast. Lots of missed lips and embarrassed head bobbing.

Bernie was loving it. She let the whole exchange play out in front of her and let him leave without adding anything. No joke or dig was necessary because it was already a perfect mess—and you don't mess with perfection.

"What's tomorrow?" Bernie asked, still holding that condescending smile on her face.

"We're uh—going out." Ruby tried to find the courage in her words.

"Is that so? Do you think that's a good idea?"

Ruby paused, "I don't know."

Ruby and Bernie had stumbled into a ring. They were both at their wits' end for different reasons, at the end of very different days and were ready to face off and go toe to toe with all the words left unsaid.

"I think you do." Bernie belittled her. "But then again, you like the scenic route."

"It's always more entertaining. How was bingo?"

"Good."

"Did you win?"

"A bit."

"But that's not why you went, is it?"

"What do you mean?"

"You didn't go to win, you went for Opal, right?"

"Right."

They both held their ground, Bernie with her feet up on the chair's footrest, Ruby standing in the doorway of her bedroom, barely dressed.

"Been a busy day. I'm a little tired," Ruby said, suggestively.

"Me too." Bernie matched her insinuations. "Just so you know, I probably won't be here when you get up," she added.

"I'm planning on getting up at 8:00."

"I won't be here."

"Bingo again? I didn't know they had games that early."

Bernie held her composure. "They do."

Even though they were in the same room, the sisters suddenly felt miles apart. As Ruby went back into her room and closed her door, that distance got even greater. A divide for no reason, when what they both really needed was each other, but that is what secrets do.

It was an odd message that blinked on Bernie's pager that morning. She had gotten a heads up the night before, just before Benny popped his head out of Ruby's room, but it was just a heads up. All the page said was, **No MSG 6**.

No, meant it wasn't a run. **MSG** was obvious and because they used military time she knew when the instructions would follow. No errand meant she didn't need to bother Opal, or deal with the skeptical questions of Freda, but a sudden change of protocol was unnerving. The message that came in promptly at 6:00am was, **In WB sleep SBS**. Like she had figured, a taxi would do for that, but she had it pick her up just outside the gates. Besides Ruby hearing, she'd been moving around a lot lately and she knew eyes were on her. Old people are like owls, they are particularly drawn to movement. Bernie needed to slow down the movement around her trailer and keep their prying eyes out of her business.

The Breakwater Hotel was slice right out of 50s Daytona. Mid-century modern design. The pristine black tarmac at the front, had wisps of sand dancing around it in the ocean breeze. It sloped steeply down to meet South Beach Street, like a time traveling ramp leading into another decade. Curved glass wrapped around the entire front office, which sat under a curved, cantilevered, second level, kept in place by a beam jetting up out of the ground at a 45-degree angle. This was a Jetsons' entrance. Cliff, Vergil's man, was waiting there for Bernie when she arrived. It had to have been eighty degrees by then, but he was standing right there, in the bright morning sunshine, wearing his black suit and not sweating a drop.

"Morning, Cliff. Nice to see you," Bernie said, relieved to see a friendly face. It's not that she expected a hostile one, you just never know.

"Nice to see you again, Ms. Hewton." Cliff tipped his head—that respectful, forgotten pleasantry, that never gets old.

"Bernie," she insisted.

"Please follow me—Bernie." Cliff turned and led Bernie under the space age overhang and out into the open pool area just beyond it.

Vergil was laid out on a chair, on the other side of the pool. He was not in his typical uniform of white robe and cigar. He was wearing dark sunglasses, a bright Hawaiian shirt and a yellow speedo. The sunglasses were fine, but the clothing was not the most flattering for a man of his sturdy build.

"Bernie!" Vergil got to his feet and so did his ankle-biting purebred, yapping its god-loving head off. "Shut up Tina!" he shouted down at the indignant K-9 imp, then went back to his greetings. "Punctuality is a lost virtue and I love that you are the last to have it!" He rushed his flip flop flapping feet over to her. "Come on. I have a room over here."

"Jesus, Vergil, I hope to hell that is not why you brought me here." Bernie didn't budge.

"To talk. I got us a room to talk. Trust me, I'd love to have rented the entire joint just for this, but I am not that flush or that foolish. It may not look like it now, but this hotel is packed. You and I are just early risers. In a few minutes this pool deck will look a Black Friday sale."

Tina kept barking.

"Cliff, can you take Tina, please?" Vergil pleaded and the big bodyguard bent down to pick up the teacup pup, who immediately stopped barking.

As Cliff took the dog away, cradled in his massive arms, Bernie was feeling a little foolish for suggesting that this was some kind of rendezvous.

Vergil took notice. "Don't get me wrong, the idea had crossed my mind. But I know how you operate. Not that the offer isn't open. Cause it is. Always open." He smiled and she blushed a little at the proposition.

"Go on." Bernie pretended to be put off by it, keeping her flattered smile under check.

Vergil led the way to a hotel room just a few feet away from the pool, on the ground level. Inside it was more of the same fantastic, forgotten design as the entrance, only it was translated into the furniture. Slim-legged teak chairs, bright teal and orange accents, macrame and swag lamps.

"You know, our nest didn't look that much different than this," Vergil said, suddenly reminiscing.

"Yes, it did. It was in Pennsylvania, and it was freezing," Bernie reminded him.

"Well, we warmed the place up." He grinned.

"That was a long time ago."

"Why did we stop?" Vergil asked, sincerely.

"Because Sal would have killed you if he found out. Probably would have killed me too."

"Right, there was that."

"And there was Dovey."

That name seemed to put an abrupt end to his advances and Vergil walked to the small table beside the door and sat down. He was acting strange. All the reminiscing, this hotel room—not quite the confident man that held court with her on his deck in Miami.

"What brings you all the way down here, Vergil? Is it the slap on the wrist I gave your pick-up boy?"

Vergil shook his head. "No, that boy needed a wake up. He's Dovey's nephew. I inherited him, but after she passed, I could never bring myself to do what you did."

"Sure you could. You used to."

"Used to? Bernie, how the hell did I ever let you talk me into this?"

"Didn't take much talking, Vergil. You seemed pretty excited to dip your toe back into the pond."

"Dip?" Vergil scoffed.

"What's the problem, Vergil?" Bernie wasn't one for pussyfooting. "Why all the cloak and dagger?"

Vergil slowly pulled his sunglasses down. His right eye was as purple as an aged steak.

"Christ, Vergil, who did this? How did Cliff not—"

"They did this. I invited them in. There was nothing Cliff could have done. Five of them. They all had guns."

"Why?"

"A message—for you. They know it's you. I don't know how, but they do. And because it's you and you're doing such a great job, our boss wants six a week now."

"There's no way."

"Listen!" Vergil leaned in, across the table—he was not finished. "This is not open for negotiations, Bernie. They like what we're doing, so they've upped their production. With a safe route out of Miami, they're able to settle their competition. That means that there is a lot more to move. This eye is just them signing off on the order."

"Six?"

"And not a penny more for the extra runs."

"To hell with that!" Bernie got up.

"Sit down!" Vergil snapped at her in a very uncharacteristic way. "You know how this works. It's not just us. It's everyone we know and everyone that they know. This eye is them saying that they are watching. We do, or they do. No other way."

Bernie's thoughts went straight to Ruby, to Marcie, Gemma, Greg, Gwen and me. "Vergil, I never wanted—"

"Stop. I wanted to dip my toe, remember? We just need to figure out how we're not going to drown."

Stan was out on the shuffleboard courts. Fred knew that booking the earliest game was the best way to get the best out of his partner. If he scheduled anything past noon it was a total crapshoot. 'Morning Stan' was good, with enough coffee and a full belly of full English, he was a hell of a competitor. Opal had sent him on his way with a few minutes to spare for herself before her show started. The silence of an empty trailer was soothing for her. The pleasant sounds of park life that blew through the screened windows did make one feel like they were never fully alone. The clicking of trike wheels, the buzz of Mullet's landscaping, the clacking of shuffleboard pucks, all became a symphony around her as she opened the door to the freezer.

It was in the back, behind the solid pre-portioned, Ziploc-bagged meats. It was in a frozen orange juice cannister that had taken her some time and ingenuity to create. She had to meticulously cut around the metal end on one side, making the incision as close to surgical standards as she could. She then had to secretly thaw the concentrated juice inside the cardboard cylinder just enough, so that she could slide it out in one solid chunk, leaving nothing behind but a little sticky residue. The key to the whole operation was that Stan hated orange juice. Even screwdrivers. They were the only cocktails he would turn down.

Opal pulled out the pop-can-size-cylinder and gently lifted the almost invisible, thin band of scotch tape she had wrapped around the end. She slid her fingernail under the lip of the metal lid and pried it off the cardboard can. The lid was so frozen that it stuck to her fingers, like a tongue to a pole in a Detroit December. She blew on her fingers right where they met the metal lid, setting them free, allowing her to concentrate on what was inside the can—her buried treasure—a small roll of bills. A few twenties and tens. Opal slipped her hand in through the cleavage opening of her sundress, into her bra and pulled out another roll of bills. This roll was substantially larger than the one she had in the can already. Thicker and rounder and when she married the two of them together, the combined roll had real clout. Opal looked into the can for a moment, admiring her treasure until something on the TV pulled her away from her pirate's gaze. She quickly replaced the lid on the 'No-J' and buried it back into the bowels of the freezer.

As she rushed into the main sitting room, her evangelical stud's full face was on the screen. Opal didn't bother to pull up a chair or sit down on any of the comfortable furniture, she just stood stiff, at attention in the middle of the room and listened. She was all ears as Reverend Kind chastised her for all her sins, for all the wrongs in the world and all the financial shortfalls of his ministry. She stood and took in the sermon, a child before the picture tube altar, desperate for absolution. And it came. It came in the form of the 1-800 number once again—the flashing 'pay to pray' at the bottom of the screen, that caused Opal to dive for the phone on the wall.

Once all the numbers were twisted into the finger-hole dial on the receiver, one by one, the ringing on the other end began. The drawn out, repetitive ring seemed to be causing Opal physical pain, as she winced and shifted her weight with every whir of it. It was an anxious pain, the discomfort that manifests from impatience.

There was a click.

"Hello?! Reverend Kind?" She didn't even wait for the connection to finish or put any of her Canadian kindness on it.

"Yes, this is the Reverend Kind's Ministry, what's heavy on your heart?" a woman's voice asked, oozing with sweet, southern-Christian concern.

"I need to speak to the Reverend," Opal demanded, as sternly as Opal could.

"Well, as I'm sure you know, the Reverend is busy doing God's work on the television right now. But I am here on his behalf. So, tell me what's heavy on your heart."

"No." Opal said a word that didn't have a card in the rolodex of her vocabulary. "My name is Opal Rose Murdy, and I have a donation to make—a large donation, but I need to speak with the Reverend first."

The woman on the other end hesitated for a second. "How very generous of you, Opal Rose, but the Reverend can only accept calls on air from *certain* generous donors. Would you mind telling me how generous the donation is?"

Opal's eyebrows tilted down like a viper ready to strike. "Very. Generous."

"Let me see what I can do." The woman immediately put Opal on hold, leaving her listening to a butchered acoustic Christian rendition of George Michaels' *Faith*, which was mostly just repeating the chorus.

"Praise the Lord, is this Opal Rose I am speaking to?" It was the Reverend's voice, clear as a bell and for certain.

Opal had to steady herself with her non-phone-holding hand. "Yes, Father—it's Opal Rose Murdy."

The Reverend gently chuckled, "There is only one Father, and he resides in heaven, I am merely his servant, the Reverend."

"Oh, dear, yes. Reverend."

"My helper told me that you wanted to lighten your heart today and help our ministry continue to provide its much-needed message."

"Oh, my, I do Reverend. I want to give you my money—to help."

"That's very kind of you, Opal. And can you share with me what your contribution to our calling will be? It goes a long way to help inspire others, to help them look inside their hearts and realize what is possible for them to give."

"I think it's three thousand dollars," Opal said, looking like she was doing mental math at the same time.

"Praise the Lord, Opal! That is very generous indeed. So, what is it that you wanted to tell me? To lighten your heart. How can I be of service to you, in the name of Jesus?"

"Oh, right. You see, Reverend, it's the money. The money I have is…" Opal's words faded into breath as she looked at the television in the main room. On the floor height screen, she saw the Reverend sitting in his calling chair, with the phone held up to his ear.

"Opal? Are you there?" the Reverend said through the phone and then after a slight delay, he said it on the TV.

"Yes, Reverend." She was suddenly a doomed racoon—on the road—in front of a racing car.

"You were saying something about the donation?"

"I was?"

The Reverend put on his best television laugh. "Yes, you were. Opal, is your television on by any chance?"

"Yes," Opal answered, still completely comatose, except for her lips.

"Opal, it's alright. A lot of folks find being on TV daunting. That's why the Lord asked me to do it, to be his messenger on the airwaves, so you don't have to. But he is watching. He is watching us every day, like we are on his television, and he is very happy that you called today and are making such a wonderful contribution to the spreading of his word." The Reverend shot a look over to the side, nodded, then looked back into the camera. "We have another caller on the line now, Margaret from Myrtle Beach."

Opal hung up the phone.

The sounds of the park danced around the trailer, but she couldn't hear them because the Reverend's words consumed her mind. "He's watching us every day—we are on his television."

She looked to the fridge, then up, above herself as if her eyes could see through the false ceiling, through the corrugated tin roof and right up into heaven.

The phone beside her suddenly rang and Opal practically jumped out of her skin, rushed out of the trailer barefoot, as if she were being chased by the Holy Ghost itself.

Freda had gotten a jump on the day as well—coffee, grapefruit, swimsuit and out the door. She had been eavesdropping on the neighbors the night before and heard their plans for deck chairs in the morning. Freda hadn't had much pool time since she arrived at the park, mostly because of the heat, but she knew the secret to summer living now and was sure as shit going to get her laps in before the sun became malignant.

Breaststroke was her jam. Head always above water, blue swim cap on with blue flowers that fluttered with the passing splashes. Maryanne and her gang were already there when she arrived, sitting over at their end of the pool. They giggled more than they should for people their age and held their end of the pool deck like popular kids in a cafeteria. Cecilia, Gertie and Barb hung on Maryanne's every word.

They gossiped openly and loudly about anyone and everyone that wasn't present at the pool. Ten laps so far. Ten laps all under the watchful, judgmental eyes of Maryanne and her horde. They all had sunglasses on, but she could see their contempt through them, catching their glares and smirks between snide comments about others.

Freda loved it. She loved every goddamn ounce of it. There was something about Freda's wiring that loved getting others fired up. It was like getting under their skin gave her life, ambrosia that intoxicated her and kept her going. In her mind, she was getting revenge on these bitches with every stroke, sweating into this pool that they will eventually have to step in to cool off. She was soiling their bathwater like a vengeful eldest sibling. Freda wasn't evil—exactly—she just hadn't had a smoke in a bit. She was Jekyll and Hyde, satiated and unsatiated. A dash smoker, not a chain smoker. Unlike the chain smokers, Freda would actually finish one before lighting the other, leaving a brief pause between them, like morse code. A smokeless gap in her constant pursuit of nicotine, but this pause was getting long in the tooth and Freda was feeling feisty.

Maryanne had turned to say something to one of the other women, something that was said low enough that Freda couldn't hear and that was when Freda decided that her pool perspiration wasn't enough. She had decided to sweeten the pot, so to speak, and began to relieve her bladder while in mid-stroke.

"Freda? Is it?" Maryanne called out, walking over to the edge of the pool deck, crouching down and waving Freda over.

Freda was in the throes of vandalism, in full release, making it very difficult to pinch it off, so she had to think fast. She had a lot of coffee earlier, so her donation to the pool might very well be visible! Is that what Maryanne was calling her over for? Anarchy is fun when it's anonymous but getting caught is not. Freda clenched down hard on what 'Kegels' she could muster and started to swim aggressively, making large, violent strokes in the water to hopefully stir up what urine wake might be following her.

"I hear that you and Bernie have become friends?" Maryanne asked, sitting down on the pool deck and dangling her legs into the water.

"You hear?" Freda snarled and calmed her kicks, realizing this was gossip, not urine related.

"You lent her your car, didn't you? That's what the park's saying," Maryanne clarified as Cecilia, Gertie and Barb came and sat down beside her, mimicking her posture.

"I didn't realize the park could speak," Freda said sarcastically.

"You're funny, Freda," Maryanne said, throwing in a healthy layer of fake laughter. "You know, I read an article on how to remember people's names and it said to use word association. That's how I'll remember yours. Funny Freda. That's what I will call you."

"Please don't," Freda said, swimming over to the edge of the pool where they were sitting. "What does it matter if I was friends with Bernie?"

Maryanne shrugged it off. "It doesn't. Bernie is a friend of mine. Has been for almost five years. We all love Bernie. It's just…"

Freda wanted to scream. She didn't want to play along, she didn't want to bite but she had her own questions about Bernie, so this pageantry might pay off. "It's just—what?"

Maryanne looked to the other women, then back to her. "Her sister. You know, she is not a legal resident here. Bernie said she was visiting, but that was months ago. I heard she was working at the gentleman's club over in Edgewater and I heard what she did to your husband."

"*Did* to him?"

"Her—you know—exposing herself."

"Yes, that did happen, but not exactly *to* him. It happened *near* him, but it also happened *near* me."

"It's appalling." Maryanne clutched her imaginary pearls.

"It *was* shocking, but they were impressive. Mine have never looked like that."

"That's because they're fake of course. All those sex workers have them bought and paid for."

"She's a sex worker?" Freda was ready for the juice, the real deal, true info on what had been going on over at Bernie's place, but this was just childish gossip. Slander for no other reason but to make people feel small.

"Aren't they all?" Maryanne stuttered a little. "Strippers and hookers. Home wreckers and blackmailers."

"Have you tried talking to her? Have you asked her?"

"Ask her if she's a prostitute?"

"If that's what you want to know, then yes. I don't know anything about that. All I know is that she was nice to me, and my husband and she has a very nice rack."

"You should watch that," Cecilia jumped in. "Her being friendly. She's been friendly with lots of the men around here."

"Is being friendly a crime in this park?" Freda hadn't planned on defending anyone, least of all Bernie and her sister, but these gossipmongers were leaving her no choice. "From the sound of things, it might be you all that I should be careful of. I'd hate to think what you'd say about me when I'm not around to defend myself."

"Excuse me? We are not the problem here. We were trying to do you, our new park member, a favor and help you by giving you the lay of the land." Maryanne was appalled.

Freda started to laugh, not a fake one, a real 'F-you' one. "A favor? You are a piece of work, aren't you? Lay of the land—you're like a gang of clucking hens, looking for new chickens to help you peck. Thanks for giving me the lay of the land. I can see it all much clearer now!"

Maryanne looked absolutely beside herself, which made Freda laugh even harder.

"Oh my God!" Cecilia screamed, pulling her legs out of the pool and pointing at Freda. "What are you doing?"

Freda looked down into the water around her which had become a dark cloud of off-yellow. She looked back up at the women who had all pulled their legs out and jumped back from the water's edge, with disgusted, even nauseous looks on their faces. "I believe this is what the British call, taking the piss."

She'd gotten all dolled up. It took longer than her usual spit and polish, because this time she cared. This time she wanted to fit in more than stand out. This time she was on a date—with her boyfriend.

She paid a lot of attention to MTV that afternoon, watching all the videos her ears and eyes could consume, but it wasn't just for the music, it was for the fashion. Her clothes were risqué for the park, but basic and lame in Benny's world. Thankfully, all her years as a dancer had trained her to do more than shake her assets, she also learned how to be her own stylist. Long before the studio sets and costume departments, she was a magician of making something out of nothing. That's how you had to be back in the day, out on the road. You needed to dazzle the audience and they didn't want to see the same outfit every dance, so you got very good at sewing and recycling.

Ruby had borrowed a small tabletop Singer from Opal and whipped together what she thought was a very subdued outfit. She'd cut and stitched a crop top out of an old slip, made a vest out of strips from brightly colored dresses she hadn't worn in a while and managed to get a pair of baggy jeans from Mullet. He didn't ask questions, just took the twenty she had in her hand and pulled the beat-up pair of Levi's out of his trunk. She put her hair in curlers then pulled most of it up on top of her head, just letting a few curly strands dangle down on the sides, to frame her face. She could have been a guest star on Friends. That is if they were progressive and gave one of the men on the show an older lover, instead of just Monica's misogynistic romp with Magnum P.I.

The beach was packed, so was the entire deck of the hotel that had been turned into a stage with standing room only for the concert.

"This way," Benny said, leading a very self-conscious Ruby through the crowd of kids on the beach, over to a set of cement stairs that went up the seawall to the hotel deck. There was a large bouncer standing at the bottom of the stairs, who looked like he ate concert kids for lunch. This was clearly not an official way in, rather a back door of sorts, a target of opportunity for the ticketless, that needed to be guarded.

Ruby had nothing to be self-conscious about, she looked fantastic, fit right in with the girls there, her hair, her clothes, even her age was blending in because of the sheer number of people on the beach to blend in with. But not to Benny. To Benny, she stood out. She was the only person there—well other than the bouncer that was a few rows of people away, standing between them and the pounding music above.

"Don't worry. I got this," Benny leaned in and said into Ruby's ear, having to shout a little to make his words heard over the blasting music above.

He raised his hand, high above the people crowding the bottom of the stairs. He waved it, vigorously, until the giant guarding the steps noticed. At first the ogre grimaced, but then, as if his contacts had found focus, he smiled and started pushing people aside, making a clear path for them to walk through.

"What did I tell you?" Benny looked proud.

Ruby stopped him. "The beach is fine. We don't need to go up there."

"What are you talking about? We can see the band from up there."

"I don't want you to spend that kind of money. I'm sure tipping this guy isn't going to be cheap. You have your sister—we don't need to go up there."

He took her face in his hands and kissed her. "I love that you thought of her. But this isn't costing me a penny. Phil's a friend—well a business friend—he owes me."

"Hey, you coming?" the massive bouncer stuffed into a tiny polo shirt yelled, so Benny took her by the hand and led her to the steps.

"Thanks, Phil!" Benny said, as the two of them passed by the 'non-entrance' and up towards the sounds of thumping bass. "Are you excited?"

Ruby nervously shrugged, "I guess so. Who is it?"

"Arrested Development," Benny said with a huge grin, before seeing the confused look on Ruby's face. "Trust me. You'll love them."

The two of them reached the top of the steps where another angry bouncer was waiting. All it took was a quick look down to Phil, who gave him the thumbs up, and they were let out into the fray. They moved out into the middle of the crowd, a few rows back from the stage and claimed a little space for themselves. It was tight, so Benny moved around behind her and wrapped his arms around her waist, keeping them together and making them one. She had never heard of them before, but they were good. Really good and as a dancer, Ruby couldn't help but bounce along to the beat—and Benny bounced right along with her. She felt great. His subtle kisses on her neck here and there, the two of them moving together to the high energy, rhythmic sounds and Benny putting her in front of him—showing her off—was a dream. She was somebody's girlfriend.

The night was wonderful, even though Ruby's ears were ringing all the way to the parking lot across the street, where Benny had left his red Sable. Ruby had been noticed a few times at the concert, but every time she was asked, Benny just puffed his chest out with pride as she answered yes, owning her identity. The people were nice, fans really and most of them younger. She thought she was nefarious, infamous, a forgotten trollop, but the few that noticed her didn't treat her as such. She was treated with reverence, sort of like how Sugar did when they first met, like a retired baseball Hall of Famer. The glow of the night, of Benny's attention and pride, of the fans' respect and reverence, made the relentless tinnitus bearable.

When they reached his car, Benny opened the passenger door for her, and she got in. "You are like moonlight, Ruby," he said, eyes full of awe.

Ruby was taken by this poetic yarn. "My word, moonlight?"

His eyes widened. "Yes. Moonlight. You took my heart and lit up my dark little world."

She reached up and pulled him down to her, kissing him. Deeply, lovingly, connecting the butterflies in her stomach with his. "Let's go," she said in that gravelly tone that resonates specifically below the waist.

"Just a second, okay? Someone's meeting me here—then we can go."

"Who?"

"Phil. The bouncer. I have something for him. He should be here any second. You can just wait in the car. I promise, it won't be long."

Ruby's sultry face turned cold. "Drugs? Ben, are you selling drugs?"

Benny pulled back. "No, not at all. I don't sell drugs. I just move supplements."

"Supplements?"

Benny lowered his voice. "Steroids. I deliver them to guys like Phil. There's a veterinarian over in Daytona who has me do the runs for him. It helps with the bills."

Steroids? Ruby wasn't sure if he was telling the truth, but if it was a lie, it was odd enough to be believable.

"Aren't steroids drugs?" Ruby asked, both making her point and wondering at the same time.

"I suppose. But nothing I could really get in trouble for. I don't take money from anyone but the Doctor, so it's not like I'm slinging, and it doesn't feel dirty. The guys I deliver to are cool. Hell, one of them got us in tonight."

Ruby thought about it. It did sound like a pretty good gig, with low risk and she knew he needed the money. Hell, she had taken her clothes off and had sex with men for cash her whole life, so this was kindergarten.

"Shit. There he is. Look I should have told you sooner, I just…" Benny struggled, worried about cutting this difficult conversation short with someone he truly cared about. Someone he did not want to lose.

"You handle your business, Ben," Ruby said coldly, then hit him with that gravelly tone, "and then you can handle me."

Benny watched as she slowly closed the door, teasing him with just her eyes. She was that good and he knew just how lucky he was.

Bernie knocked on the carport door, lightly. She could see lights on in the trailer, but she wanted to be careful which occupant she enticed to open the door. She knocked again, but no one came, so she made her way through the carport and around the back of the trailer. The louvers were open, everyone's were this time of year. Besides being lulled to sleep by the hum of the cicadas, it was the only way to get air into the tin sweat boxes that they all had chosen to ferment in.

Bernie didn't have to stand on her tiptoes to reach the wide window across the back of the trailer like everyone else would have. She was tall enough to just lean in and whisper into the gap between the glass panels. "Opal!"

She took a breath, looked around and then did it again. "Opal!" This time the whisper was stronger. A little deeper.

"Stan?" Opal muttered from inside the trailer, in that raspy, half asleep, inquiring whimper.

Bernie was a little insulted by the question, sure her voice was deep, but come on. "No, Opal, it's Bernie."

"Bernie? Are you dead?" Opal gasped.

Bernie looked in through the louvers and could see Opal sitting straight up in bed, talking out into the air, like she was being visited by Jacob Marley.

"Oh, Bernie. I didn't get to say goodbye. Is that why you're haunting me?"

Bernie spoke in her normal voice. "Jesus, Opal, I'm alive. I'm standing outside your window."

Opal spun around and seeing Bernie's shadow outside the glass panels, she yelped.

"Keep it down!" Bernie instructed. "Meet me in the lanai."

Opal looked around the room and realized Stan wasn't there, he hadn't made it to bed. As she got out of bed and wrapped herself in her pink-chiffon dressing gown, she tried to shake off the startle and the fog of sleep.

She walked out into the main area of the trailer to find Stan passed out on the couch. The TV was hissing, the sound that accompanies the static snow on the screen. Opal went over and turned it off, then pulled a blanket up over Stan and turned off the end table lamp, before stepping down into the lanai.

Bernie was waiting, standing in the dark of the screened porch. Even in the shadow of night, Opal's pink plastic furniture was still pink. So were the plastic flamingos that stood just outside the screens, dotting the long flower beds that framed the netted porch.

"What are you doing here, Bernie?"

"I saw the light on."

"Stan's on the couch."

"I need you for an errand tomorrow."

"An errand? So soon."

"Yes, and they are going to be happening a lot more frequently."

"What will I tell Stan? I can't be away that much."

"Let me worry about that."

"What time tomorrow?"

"You leave at 8:00."

"I leave?"

"You. You're going to do the run on your own, I have another run to do at the same time." Bernie held out her hand. "Take this."

"What is it?" Opal asked, looking down at the pink square in Bernie's hand.

"It's a beeper. You just go to where it tells you. It's easy. Just like we did. Drive the speed limit, pick-up, drop-off and collect the money."

"But I can't."

"Yes, you can, Opal. There is a *me* inside you. You know it and you like how it feels."

"I can't"

"I need you to. This is our way of doing something big with our lives. Haven't you always wanted to do something big? Be more. You will make enough money to buy Stan anything he wants. Make him the happiest man in the world."

Opal's mind went straight to a man, but not to Stan—to the Reverend. "Happiest man in the world? Oh, my. I suppose I could do a lot of good with a lot of money."

"Yes, you could, Opal. I'm sure your kids back home could use a little help?"

"They don't talk to us much."

"I'm willing to bet that would change if checks started coming in the mail."

Opal's head was swimming. "But I can't do what you did. To that man's hand—in the trunk. I'm not like that."

"You don't have to do that. That's why I did it. None of them will try any of that again. Just don't look at the package. Let them put it in and take it out. Just drive the speed limit, pick-up, drop-off and collect."

Opal looked down at the beeper. "It's pink."

"I painted it with some of Ruby's nail polish for you. Thought you'd like it."

"Okay."

Bernie nearly fainted. "Okay?" She had planned on far more manipulation. More bargaining and guilt, but the church mouse just said okay.

"Alright, 8:00. But you talk to Stan."

"I will." Bernie took the beeper from Opal's hand and clipped it onto her pink robe. "Just watch for my message." Bernie handed Opal a small piece of paper that she had written on. "This is a key to decode the messages on your pager. I'll stay here with you until you know it like the back of your hand. Then we'll burn it."

"Burn it?"

"Of course, we can't let anyone find it. I'll let you burn, but only when we're done here."

This was all so exciting for Opal. A real-life caper and the burning of the secret code was the icing on the cake.

Ruby's crop top was dangling by a thread, her hair had fallen from her partial updo, and her vest was off. Benny wasn't looking any fresher, the Quonset hut had been hot, heavy and urgent. She hated it—not the hut, but the rush inside her. The new information about him, his slightly bad side, had turned him from a seven into a ten. Ruby had always liked the bad boys, so a few dashes of hot sauce on this meal was almost too much for her.

Benny was barely able to keep his eyes on the road as they drove into the park, partially from being so infatuated with her and the fact that her hand was resting high on his thigh. She knew he was buzzing, because she was too. Her hope was that wherever Bernie had been all day, she hadn't come back from yet, because this evening needed an encore.

The old Sable came to a stop and Benny put it in park. He turned to Ruby, about to start his goodbye routine.

"Don't bother. You're coming in," Ruby told him, giving orders that he was happy to receive. There were no lights on in the trailer, so she leaned in to seal the deal with a kiss that had been building since they left that old Quonset hut in the forest.

"Ruby!"

Benny jumped back, his heart stopping at the sight of the Bernie outside the car, behind Ruby.

"Jesus, Bern, what the hell are you doing?" Ruby said angrily rolling down her passenger side window. "Creeping around out here in the dark—is this your idea of joke?"

Bernie was hyper focused on Ruby but didn't forget her manners. "Hello, Benny."

Benny awkwardly responded, "Hello."

Bernie was deadpan, troubled. She swallowed hard as if she were trying to swallow the words, but they wouldn't stay in. "Ruby—I need your help."

CHAPTER 6

Three Dames

Bernie paced back and forth along the length of the main room in the trailer. From kitchen to front bedroom door and back again, while Ruby and Benny sat on the couch, witnessing the moving breakdown.

"I don't think he should be here for this," Bernie cautioned, revealing an old habit that had resurfaced, nail biting.

"He's not going anywhere. He's my—boyfriend."

Bernie scoffed, "Your what? Ruby, this is no time for your—"

"My what? My help? If I'm here, so is he."

"55 going on 18," Bernie snarled, under her breath.

"I'm not sitting here to be insulted. And neither is he. You pounded on the car window like a crazy woman asking for my help. So, we're here. You should probably just spit out what's got you so riled up, before all that gnawing leaves you with nothing but nubs."

Bernie stopped pacing. "Does he really have to be here?"

Benny wanted to keep the peace. "Obviously, my presence is bothering your sister so…"

He went to get up, but Ruby pulled him back down. "Stay—please."

"So be it." Bernie relented, lowering her raw finger from her lips. "The bank didn't find the money that was missing from my account, and I haven't been playing bingo."

"So, where did it come from?" Ruby asked, not fazed at all.

"Why do I get the feeling you already know?" Bern paused.

"I know some of it—not all of it. You're a great liar, but you're my sister. Go on."

"When I found out that you were so unhappy at the bar, I reached out to an old colleague of mine and proposed a business opportunity to him. He liked it and that's where the money has been coming from."

"From thin air? Because that's what's passing out of your mouth and through all the holes in that story of yours."

"Ruby, I know you've been around the block." She looked to Benny. "No offense." Benny just shrugged and she focused back on Ruby. "So, I am sure you know that this isn't what you'd call a legit business."

"I gathered that, Bern." Ruby was getting annoyed.

"I didn't tell you because with this kind of business, the less people that know about it, the better it is for all concerned."

"I gathered that too. But what I don't understand is what it is, why you need my help and how in the world you got wrapped up in it? You're straight and narrow, Bernie. I know that Sal was a little salty, but you? You're the pension woman. The union secretary lady. All of this isn't you."

"Yes, it is. This is me—the real me. This is why my money is gone. It's why I came here and brought you with me." Bernie was different. Softer than her sister had seen before, open and honest.

The weight of Bernie's emotions sat heavy in the room and there was suddenly no room in there for three of them.

"Ben, maybe you *should* give us a minute," Ruby said gently to Benny

"No problem. I'll be outside," he replied, getting up and heading to the lanai.

"And close the door," Bernie said, and Benny understood, making sure to close the solid, inside door of the trailer behind him.

"Why are we here?" Ruby asked with a fusion of emotions attached.

"Short answer? Because I'm under investigation."

Ruby sat back on the couch. "You? By whom? For what?"

"The FBI. I'm not the paper pushing secretary you thought I was. Well not for the last ten years of my work—at least. I started there, when my boy was little, after Sal, but I worked my way up. For those last few years, I ran the union. Not on paper, but in presence. I did a lot of things, Ruby, any one of which could get me put away for life—multiple lives, that is if they could prove it. I don't know who the rat was, but they had to have been close to me. I was very, very careful. Up to and after I retired. Which was a farce in itself. They forced me out. Politely. Said it was time for new blood and I was tired. So, I stepped aside. Things weren't the same after my boy. The day before I picked you up bright and early, before I'd had a drop of Sanka, the Feds swarmed my home, pulled me into their offices and drilled me for hours. I don't know how many hours, but when they let me out, I came looking for you and brought us here. They hadn't charged me with anything yet, so I took the window. I took the only person left that I cared about, the only one I had left, and I disappeared. This place—the trailer—it isn't in my name, never has been. I was always careful. Always prepared. The car wasn't either, but it's gone now. When they seized my bank accounts and pension, I knew we had to get rid of it. I made sure the numbers were changed by the shop I sold it to; that was part of the deal, part of the lowball offer they gave me too. Chop shops always lowball, but it can't be traced back to anyone now. The Feds are trying to squeeze me. Cut off my means of providing for myself so that I surface, and they can make me roll over. But I won't ever roll over. That's not me, but the rest is.

"Who are you?" Ruby was dumbfounded, frightened and needing something to cling to.

"I'm your big sister, Poob."

"No, not the one I knew."

"Yes, I am. When we were young, I was the same, just more hot headed and with smaller risks. How do you think I was able to raise you? Feed the both of us and keep the roof over our heads after mom? Hewton girls, Buffalo Girls are hustlers."

"Is that how you got us out of that hotel room? With those gangsters?"

"I just told him who I was. Apparently, they knew my name."

"Enough to just let us walk? He was afraid of you! I saw it then, just didn't understand it. He had a gun, so did the rest of them and he was afraid of you—are you in the mafia?"

"I'm not in the mafia. First of all, that's an Italian name and they stick to family. Sal ran with a certain crowd, but I let go of his name when he passed, and they stick to blood."

"Sal was in the mob?"

"Come on, Ruby—like you didn't know."

Ruby lowered her head, admitting her ignorance was a front for her gut.

Bernie nodded. "He was a horrible husband, but I learned a lot before he died and left me with nothing. I was a single mother and I saw a way out of the slum he'd left me and our son in. I saw opportunity. I clawed my way up, digging respect out from under my fingernails until I had no one left to climb over. Then I ran that organization like a family. Fair, smooth and loyal. I loved them all, but someone clearly didn't see it that way eventually. Didn't see the family I had built, because family would never betray me like that."

"So, what have you gotten into down here? If you're retired, if we are supposed to be in hiding, why would you come out of it?"

"We need money, the Feds have seen to that, but it's not a big deal. It's just doing deliveries. Miami to New Smyrna. That's all. Sure, there are other ways of making ends meet. But they don't pay what this pays—and like you said, I can't be what I am not. If the FBI knew anything for certain, if they had found anything concrete on me, I'd already be in cuffs. But I am not."

"My word, Bern, why risk it? I'm no angel in the Feds' eyes either. They have rooms full of paperwork on me. Why put a target on your head now and why make it bigger by risking it with me?"

"You and I lost a lot of years, but it isn't over. Just like you, I have lived ten lifetimes in those years, but I'm not ready to roll over and die. I won't. I won't just shrivel and melt, down here in the sun like the rest of these 'vanilla wafer sucking' seniors. Let my pride be squeezed out of me—my strength—my worth—until I'm forced into the ground to fertilize more orange trees for these snowbirds to slurp on. I ran away from Buffalo, but I can't run away from who I am—anymore than you can. And there is no one in the world I trust more than you."

Ruby saw her sister in a million new spotlights. All the years of silence and distance started to make a little more sense, because Bernie was finally real. Instead of being afraid or appalled by her admissions, she was relieved. All those years that she had felt like the bad apple, the one who danced so far outside the lines of morality that she needed to stay away, she really had been closer to Bernie than she realized. They weren't so different after all. Two bookends of same underworld. Ruby felt closer to her big sister in that moment, than she had in a very long time. "What do you need me to do?"

Six runs a week and only one car. The champagne-colored Corolla had just left with Opal in it, as another message came in on Bernie's pager. Another run. Every run now was life and/or death and she had only one car. Benny had stayed the night in the trailer and although the constant canoodling between him and Ruby was annoying to her, she was ultimately glad he had stuck around. Not because she could see how happy he made her sister, which he did, but because he had a possible solution.

It was a shady-looking car dealership over in Port Orange. The quintessential used car lot found on every major drag, in every small town across the USA. There was a small, one room, office-slash-showroom-slash-trailer-slash-shipping container at the back of a paved lot that was packed with parked, polished turds. From the flat roofline of the temporary building to the flag lines and pigtail lightbulbs that spread out over the lot in a starburst of color, it all screamed cheap! The name painted on the vinyl sign strung across the front of the building, screamed the same thing, it was just spelled differently. **Daryl's Deals on Wheels.**

Daryl was a delivery client of Benny's. A man in his late forties who stopped lifting weights six years ago, but still took steroids. He was swollen, everywhere, giving the illusion of muscle by packing all that Pillsbury into a polyester suit and tie. He looked eternally uncomfortable, red faced, sweating, the neck of his shirt digging into his throat and was constantly licking his lips, trying to get those white things out of the corner of his mouth—but never did. You could definitely judge this book by its cover, and he was exactly what Bernie needed right now.

"If Benny recommends you, then you are alright in my books. Take any one you want," Daryl said, licking deep into the left corner of his chapped maw.

"And you have plates?" Bernie asked, her volume and delivery filled with hesitation.

"Never did the dishes, but I have plates. Registered and legit."

"Are they dealer plates?"

"Fuck no. Sorry, excuse my language. Rentals can't use dealer plates. That's illegal. My plates are legal—registered to wonderful old women from right here in Port Orange."

"And they let you borrow them? Why would these women be looking the other way?"

"They aren't looking this way, that way or any way, tough to see anything from six feet under. He resorted to the over-used and under-inspired 'air quotes'. "I 'acquire' the plates from the newly departed's family members. To help them with funeral and other miscellaneous expenses. Do you have any idea how expensive it is to die these days? I like to think of it as my way of easing the burden on their loved ones while keeping their memory alive for just a while longer. That is until the DMV gets around to canceling them. Which they do, eventually."

"How much?"

"Well, because the risk falls on me, it's five hundred a day. That's car rental with plates—taxes included," Daryl said smiling, revealing that he was the curator of a very yellow set of teeth.

"Five hundred? A day?" Benny was blown away. "Just borrow mine for your errands. I'll do it for free."

"You need your car for work," Bernie said to Benny before turning back to Daryl. "We may be able to swing five hundred."

"Great," Daryl said walking back into the lot office. "Can't say I've ever had someone borrow a vehicle that was of your—vintage." Bernie followed him in, and he continued his spiel, "Don't get me wrong, I'm an equal opportunity lender, just not used to dealing with people close to my plate donors' ages. So, what happened? Did they take away your license? Was it for cataracts? Or did you have a little fender bender?" Daryl went behind the tan metal and wood veneer desk to unlock one of its filing-cabinet-type drawers.

"Just let my insurance lapse—that's all," Bernie said in the most unconvincing way. "Can't be bothered with the required physical."

Daryl pulled a plate from the desk drawer and held it out to Bernie. "Okay. Now I only accept—"

Bernie had the wad of hundreds already in front of him before he could say the word.

"Wow, you came prepared. No wonder you want to avoid the physical, your eyes are worse than you think lady, that's more than five hundred."

"I'll take two."

"Two?" Daryl was both impressed and a little unnerved.

"Yes. One for me and one for my sister—she also let her insurance lapse."

"Okay then. Two it is. Always happy to help out our seniors." Daryl sat down into his desk chair, leaning back in a posture of negotiation, as if this were a legitimate transaction. "There are a few things we should go over. With this type of arrangement, the kind on the greyer side of the law, there isn't any paperwork, so I'll just give you the terms of the rental verbally. You can keep the vehicle for twenty-four hours from the time you leave my lot. As stated, the plates are legit and live, they are insured for auxiliary drivers, so you are legally allowed to be in said vehicle. Now, that works for traffic infractions, speeding tickets, license plate runs or any other minor run-in with Johnny Law. But—and this is the fine print—if you do not return my property within the agreed upon twenty-four hours or you get in an accident or are caught doing any illegal activity in said vehicle, it will have been reported stolen. By me. You look like a nice lady, so I don't expect any issues with Volusia County's finest, but just drive carefully and make sure you bring it back before the twenty-four hours. Agreed?"

Bernie nodded and Daryl happily snatched the cash from her hand. "Go ahead and pick any cars out there, just let me know which ones."

"Alright," Bernie said, turning to leave the tiny, sweaty office.

"Oh," Daryl added, "and thank your grandson for recommending me."

"Benny? He's not my grandson," Bernie said with a dash of venom. "He's my sister's boyfriend."

Daryl's red and bloated face went blank, trying to figure out this sudden May-December riddle and what exactly he had just gotten himself into.

Ruby was the last to return to the trailer, pulling her red rented Nissan Micra into the carport just behind the tan Honda Accord Bernie had used. They had them for twenty-four hours, so decided to come home after their runs and take them back the next day. After all, they had paid a lot for them, so there was no need to rush their return.

Opal and Bernie were waiting in the lanai for Ruby, with the patio lanterns on and a tequila sunrise in Bernie's hand. She looked relaxed. So did Opal, who was nursing a rum and Fresca. To be honest, it was all Fresca, but Bernie played along to make Opal happy.

"How'd it go?" Bernie said, speaking from her high back wicker chair.

"Smooth," Ruby said, as if she had just been out to pick up the dry cleaning, not the tiny black duffel bag that was under her arm. "Wasn't a fan of Miami traffic, but the rest was easy."

"What was the package?"

"I have no idea—you told me not to look."

"Good. Just checking."

"You know the boys on this end, at the drop-off, were very nice."

"Don't." Bernie shot her a glare.

"My word, I'm just saying that I was surprised. I expected the same type of galoots as the hotel room," Ruby defended.

"What hotel room?" Opal asked, feeling left out.

"It's nothing, Opal. Grab yourself a drink, Poob, you earned it," Bernie said, deflecting from a story she really did not want to get into.

Ruby went inside and quickly returned with cold beer in her hand. "To us?" she proposed, standing in the open screen doorway of the trailer.

"To us!" Bernie raised her glass and the corners of her mouth.

Ruby cracked her beer and took a huge swig.

"To us!" Opal joined in, taking a big gulp of her cloudy, lime-flavored cocktail which made her eyes instantly tear from all the carbonation.

BONE PARK

"Now get out here and close the door, you're letting all the no-see-ums in." Bernie went from cheers, right back to big sister mode.

Ruby closed the door on her orders and came down into the lanai.

"Time to tally up?" Bernie suggested with a slightly festive peak to her voice.

Ruby handed Bernie her small duffel bag. "You want us to leave while you do it? Opal and I could go for a walk?"

"No. That's not how we do this. We do this part together. Always. You see what I see, that way you never second guess my honesty and I never have to second guess your loyalty."

"Oh, I would never—" Opal shook her finger.

"Opal, you'd be surprised what happens to people, all people, when money's involved. It pits brother against brother, father against son, but I will not let it pit sister against sister. And you're our sister now."

Hearing nothing other than her inclusion into the sisterhood, Opal was overcome with joy.

"Shouldn't we at least go inside?" Ruby said as Bernie moved over to the wicker table where Opal's duffel bag was waiting.

"Peter and Penny knock out at 8:00 sharp," she replied motioning with her head to the trailer on the other side of the screens, "They're earplug sleepers too and the trikes have all parked for the night, so I think we can expect a certain level of privacy." Bernie unzipped her tiny bag, dumped it out on the table and then did the same with the other two.

It was impressive. A football-sized mound of yellow banded bills. Each bag contributed a slightly different amount to the pile, but combined it was a hell of a haul for one day's work.

"Equal," Bernie said. "We divide it equally—always."

"In all fairness, there was less in Opal's bag," Ruby stated.

"She's right. I don't mind." Opal backed her up.

"I do." Bernie was nipping buds. "Ruby, some days there'll be less in yours or in mine, but we do this equally, always. We benefit from the work and from our trust in each other. All of us succeed or none of us do, understand?"

Ruby and Opal gave small nods and then Bernie began divvying up the spoils, giving each of them four bands of bills.

"Four thousand dollars? Each?" Ruby said, keeping her voice down, which was unusual for her.

"Yes, minus your rental fee of course."

Ruby counted out fifty ten-dollar bills and took them out from one of her banded stacks.

"Oh, how much was that?" Opal asked concerned.

"Nothing for you, Opal. You used your own car."

"But I'd like to contribute to the group. Like you said, always equal."

"You did say that," Ruby added.

Bernie shot her a look. "Equal pay and equal fees for equal expenses. She's not paying for us." Bernie snatched the five hundred dollars Ruby was holding in her hand.

Ruby laughed, "My word. Thirty-five hundred dollars, in one day. And I kept my clothes on the whole time. I'm glad you asked for my help."

"This is just the beginning. Like I said, each of us is going to need to do two runs a week."

"Fine by me," Ruby said sitting down to drink in the windfall and her beer.

"What about Stan?" Opal was hesitant.

"Well, Opal, that's up to you. I told him that we had started a little business, the three of us. That business needs to use the car twice a week, but there is no way it pays four thousand dollars a day. So, because we know you have difficulty with stretching the truth, I suggest you create a little slush fund for yourself. A little nest egg to pull from, for your kids and grandkids, and for your future. No need to explain any of it to Stan. Just leave him a little stack on his bedside table, two hundred dollars each time you work, and I think it will all be just fine."

"I can't lie to him."

"You don't have to. When he asks how was work, you tell the truth. Fine. If he asks how much money you made, you say it's on the side table. I told him the business was a delivery business, going from here to Miami and back. That is also true. So, there is nothing for you to lie about."

Opal let all this devious information sink in. Her shoulders were heavy with angels and devils talking over the other, vying for her attention and fighting for her soul.

Bernie kept speaking for the red team. "That's why the most important rule is that you never look at the package. What you don't see, isn't there. No need to lie to anyone; to Stan, to the police—anyone. If you don't see it, you don't sweat it. You don't make mistakes worrying about it. *It* is whatever you say *it* is."

Opal looked up to the two women, figuratively and literally. The two women who embodied what she longed for, the two women who were staring right back at her with encouraging eyes.

"*It* is what you say *it* is. Okay, so what did you tell Stan it was? What's the name of our delivery business?" Opal asked hesitantly.

Bernie walked slowly back, sat down onto her wicker throne and said, "We are providing a service between two communities. Simple, sweet and unsuspected. We are Three Dames' Dinner Delivery."

Reg had gotten up for round two of his nightly bladder dance. He was a solid five 'tinkler' a night now. No dress rehearsals, all shows, from 8:30pm to 5:00am. It was a musical number that had been increasing its choreography more and more over the last few years. What started out as a simple rumba had now become an elaborate Danny Kaye number. It was torture. At his age, his aches and pains made sleeping hard enough without the constant alarm bells of wetting himself going off in his head. But this growing old business wasn't for wimps and Reg was no wimp. It was what it was. That's what he had come to understand about this growing old business. It was a constant progression of acceptance. In his early fifties, he had spent a lot of time lamenting about what was starting to wear out on him. Feeling angry about his thinning hair, his worsening golf swing, his unbearable hangovers, his chronic sciatica and his bum hip. There was also his incredible, unstoppable ear growth, his wild eyebrows that seemed to be feeding off a steady stream of Miracle Grow and his increasingly unresponsive little best friend. He had worked far too hard for far too long to have it all crumble around him. But after years of doctors' appointments, that only led to referrals, which only led to specialists, that only led to more appointments, which only led to prescriptions and follow up appointments—he decided to let go. He said to hell with it all. He accepted the changing winds. Funny thing was that as soon as he did, everything started to feel better. Sure, there were still aches and pains and midnight trips to the bathroom. His ear hairs were continuing to grow, and his feet had corns, but it all just became normal. And he lightened up as well. Reg found out how nice it was to be a part of his own life, rather than fighting it and he discovered how nice it was to be sharing it with Freda.

Her side of the bed was empty. He always checked on her, every time he got up at night. He always looked over when he reached the foot of the bed, to see her in the sliver of moonlight that came in through the louvers. He always waited there for one breath. One rise and fall of her silhouette before he answered his calling, but right then, she wasn't there.

He walked out into the thin hallway. It was the same one all the single wides had, the skinny one that ran from the back bedroom to the kitchen. The one with the entrance to bathroom in it. From the hallway he could see out into the rest of the trailer. Out through the main room and even into the front bedroom. That's where he found her. He might have missed her if it weren't for the red glow coming off the heater at the end of her cigarette.

Freda was perched once again at the window, in the darkness of the front room, on the other side of the bed looking out through the sheers. Sure, he thought she was nuts hanging out in the darkness, late at night spying on the neighbors, but it made her tick. She got all worked up by this sort of thing but worked up in the positive sense. She was abuzz with all sorts of conspiracies. She woke up with a spring in her step, ready to crack the case, ready to take on another day and that was just fine with him.

"Any update Columbo?" Reg whispered from the hallway.

"Shhh," she hissed back. "What are you doing up?"

"Bagpipes are full. How 'bout you?"

"Lots going on tonight. Can't talk. I'll tell you in the morning."

"You going to sit there all night?"

"If I have to."

She couldn't see it, but a grin came to his face. "Alright honey, I look forward to your report." Reg walked into the bathroom and carried on with the task at hand. It was odd, his wife sitting at the window, but she was happy and when it came to Freda, he was behind anything that kept the dark cloud away from his girl.

Outside there was movement. Freda was lucky that Reg had stopped bugging her at the right moment or she would have missed it.

She reminded herself of this, how all the hours of waiting would be for not, if she let distractions get in her way, but right then the runway was clear, and Opal was on it. She was walking down the road, towards her house. Not all that suspicious, even though it was late, but she had come from Bernie's place. Freda grabbed the big binoculars and aimed them at Opal. Nighttime was not the best for using them. What she really needed were some of those night vision goggles. The kind she'd seen in that Steven Seagal movie Reg made her watch. Those would be perfect, but right now she would have to settle for the slim bands of illumination, that came off each trailer's porch light. She missed the first few ribbons of illumination between Bernie and Opal's house, and there were only a few left. In the shadows she could tell that Opal had something in her hand, she just couldn't tell what. Opal walked through the next band of light, but as she did, she shifted what she was carrying into her other hand. Freda got bubkes through the lenses—she was focused on the right hand, but at the wrong time. There were only two strips of light left. Two chances to see what Opal had and maybe shed light on what she was doing over at Bernie's so late.

Freda steadied her hands, placing her elbows securely on the window ledge. With the high-powered lenses in the binoculars, the slightest move makes everything blurry and can shift away from the target by a foot or more. Opal took two more steps, moving into the light. Freda studied the image coming in through the lenses, but it was still too dark as the porch light on the Murphy's trailer was dim. All Freda could make out was that it was rectangular. A little longer than her hand and about as thick as a brick of butter. Was it butter? Freda nearly flipped out. She pulled her eyes away from the binoculars. How could it be just butter? Did Opal go over to just borrow butter? Freda's zest for the all-night stakeout began to fizzle. She suddenly could see herself from the outside in. What had she become? A crazy old lady, looking through the curtains at night. What the hell was she doing? How could her gut be so wrong?

Opal crossed into the light coming from her own porch and stopped. She paused, just standing there, facing her own trailer for a moment, and for no reason. That caught Freda's eye. Why was she

BONE PARK

stopping? Freda moved her eyes back down to the binoculars. Looking through them, she could see Opal's face. It looked pensive. The pink wafer woman appeared troubled and was looking down at her hands. Freda followed her gaze with the binoculars, down from her eyes, to her shoulders, to her arms, elbows, wrists—

"Holy shit!" Freda exclaimed.

Through the lenses, clear as a rock at the bottom of a still pond, she could see the banded brick of cash in Opal's hands.

Opal suddenly looked around, as if she could sense she was being watched, then hustled her way into the carport—out of Freda's view. It all paid off finally. All the hours and speculation, the second guessing of her sanity and the teasing from Reg. Freda had gotten what she was waiting for, what she knew was there—she just had no idea what it meant, or what to do with it.

The Buffalo Girls rolled into the car lot at exactly 9:55am the next morning. Bernie made sure of it. She watched the hands on her watch the whole way there, with Ruby following closely behind her, speeding up and slowing down so that her wheels didn't touch the lot until exactly 9:55am. Could have been 10:00am, but she wanted to leave a buffer, so they could park the cars, get out and make their way to Daryl's office at the back of the lot, without rushing.

Freshmen rush, seniors strut.

They entered like a swat team. Ruby swung the office door open wide and stood behind it, letting the bright, hot sunlight in and the air conditioning out. Daryl looked up from his desk, but there was no one there. This was the panic seconds. The nervous time counted in breaths where you contemplate your plan B. Daryl's plan B was to reach down, under his desk and put his left hand on the stock of the sawed-off shotgun he had strapped underneath it while he reached for the telephone with his left.

"Hello? Good morning? How can I help you?" he said loudly, trying to hide his fear under the vocal spring of commerce.

Bernie appeared in the sunlight, backlit and slowly walked in, without removing her large, drugstore, driving sunglasses.

"Oh, Bernie. It's you," Daryl said, letting the wind out of his distress balloon.

"Whatever is under your desk, could you let go of it?" Bernie said, frankly, then softened. "Please? I like to be able to see both hands of the people I do business with."

Daryl pulled his hand out from under his desk, trying to be casual about it, even though he was spooked by her psychic abilities.

"Were you calling somebody?" Bernie said, stepping forward.

Daryl tried to cover. "Yes actually, as per our agreement, I was about to call the police—you two are late."

Bernie looked at the watch on her wrist. "No, we're early." She turned the watch to face him. "One minute—in fact."

Daryl was sore loser. "Yeah, well clocks differ. Potato, po-tah-to, but my name's on the ownership so—"

"So, you would prefer to explain to the police how two retired women, stole your cars and organized the fraud of not one, but two dead women's license plates to run errands with?"

Daryl was not a fan of her facts. "Cute. You pensioners sure do love to squeeze the blood out of every bill you hand over, don't you? You're always early for dinner, social security and the sample line at the grocery store, but if you're buying, you're sure as hell going to get your money's worth."

"That's because we know what it's like to go without. A great depression and a world war will do that to a person. But you wouldn't know about that, would you?"

BONE PARK

"Where's the other one?"

"Right here," Ruby announced as she entered the office with a cookie tin in her hands, closing the office door behind her.

"Thank you. Thank you for closing the door. Your time obsessed sister here doesn't seem to understand how air conditioning works." Daryl looked Ruby up and down. "Hang on. You're her sister?"

"Yes, I am." Ruby walked up and stood just behind Bernie.

"Really?" He looked her up and down again. "Do I know you?"

Bernie moved over, cutting his line of sight off. "This is for you," she said taking the tin from Ruby and setting it down on his desk.

Daryl looked at the tin and then back to Bernie. "Cookies? I appreciate it but there really is no need to."

"I don't know how to bake," Bernie said straight.

Daryl opened the tin and the white corners of his mouth dropped open—the tin was full of cash.

"That's four thousand there. An advance on the next eight rentals. We are each going to be needing cars, twice a week and we are going to need them on short notice."

Daryl looked up to the sisters from his desk chair, noticing the beeper poking out from under the bottom edge of Bernie's blouse. "What the fuck are you two involved in?"

Ruby smiled. "Meal delivery. There's a lot of hungry seniors with wallets."

Daryl liked the answer, even though he didn't believe it. A good back story was key to survival in his line of work and these two old broads had gotten the memo. "Okay, I think I can handle four rentals a week for you ladies. It sounds like a good cause."

"Glad to hear it," Bernie said, and the two sisters made their way to the exit. Bernie stopped just at the threshold and turned back. "Say, Daryl, if it's not too much trouble, could you try and rotate your stock every month or so? It gets boring driving the same car for too long."

Daryl shrugged. "Demand and supply. You keep up the demand and I'll keep up on the supply."

Happy with the answer, the sisters walked out the door.

Daryl sat digesting it all, looking at the tin of money on his desk, trying to put it all together. The pager, the money, their age, the rotating cars, the—

"Ruby Rain?" he gasped and jumped up from his chair.

He nearly fell trying to get around his desk, tripping over the phone cords, racing to get the door, but as he opened it, it was too late. The taxi with the Buffalo Girls in it was pulling away. As a young man he fantasized about Ruby Rain, most men did, and now his dream was coming true. In a different way then he wished for, but he was working with Ruby Rain. He wished he'd realized it sooner; he was star struck, but for now, his autograph would have to wait.

The next few weeks went without a hitch. Opal, Ruby and Bernie made their runs, twice a week, every week, to and from Miami as requested. Bernie took their cover story and made it tangible. She got all three of them hats, t-shirts and warmer bags with Three Dames' Dinner Delivery branded on them and each woman was starting to build quite the nest egg. Bernie was being diligent. Storing it away, behind a piece of the paneled wall in the trailer hallway, only using what she needed for basics. Food, pad rental and taxis. She knew how to lay low, because that's how she'd always run things. By the end of July each member of Three Dames' Dinner Delivery had pocketed roughly forty-eight thousand dollars. Cash.

BONE PARK

As far as Stan was concerned it was more like three thousand, two hundred, which was more than enough to keep his poker and pony habit going strong. Stan liked this little job his wife had. None of his friends knew about it, it got her out of his hair twice a week and he was free to blow cash like Frank Sinatra. In fact, that's what they started calling him at his favorite watering hole, because ever since Opal started working, he'd end his nights at the bar buying a round for everyone and singing "My Way" at the top of his lungs. Stan was a big deal—in his mind—and that worked out well for everyone.

Ruby was flush for the first time since her bankruptcy. It felt good. It felt like old times only this time, she had all of her clothes on, except for when she was with Benny, which was all the time.

They'd made the old Quonset hut a love nest of sorts. Moved the old rotten furniture out back, swept the floors, hung some Christmas lights that they powered with a car battery and placed a mattress under the large angel painting that Benny had done. Ruby was helping him out with his bills, his sister was doing great in school, and he didn't have to deliver pizzas anymore. He still ran the 'roids' for the vet in Daytona, but the rest of his time was spent in here, painting and making love to Ruby. It was a southern version of a Parisian dream. Tortured artist and infatuated patron. That's what she was, infatuated. She couldn't say she'd ever been that way before, about anyone, but she was about him. Benny was working his way around the hut, painting over all the previous graffiti by others with new, mind-blowing work. The latest of which, was a full nude of Ruby. Twenty feet long and at least ten feet high.

Ruby was laying on her side, naked, still shimmering with the dew of their afternoon session. "Like this?" she asked, adjusting her hips forward.

"That's great. Sorry, this is taking so long."

"Don't apologize. I love it. I love having you look at me like that, uninterrupted for hours."

"And I love you."

Ruby paused, she always paused, every time since the first time he said it. "I love you too."

Benny, who was also naked, climbed up the ladder he had placed in front of the wall and picked up where he had left off. He was using brushes on this painting, not his usual spray paint.

"We should start thinking about after," Benny said making passes with his brush over the neck of Ruby's portrait.

"Are you hungry?" Ruby asked, while trying to stay still for the painter.

"I mean after you stop the running the I-95."

"What should we think about?" Ruby wasn't following.

"Us. We should be planning for us. You're making a lot of money, I know, but we could really build something together. Maybe move to Savannah or New Orleans. We could open a gallery, sell my art, buy a house. Be together."

After wasn't a blip in Ruby's mind. All she had thought about for a long time was the present. That's what happens when you're alone and broke. The present moment is all you *can* deal with, so it's all you *do* deal with, but now she had him. And he was talking about tomorrow.

"I don't plan on mooching off you, Ruby. I figure I can work doing murals for businesses until my own work starts to sell. There are plenty of rich people in Savannah and New Orleans, I just need exposure."

Ruby knew all about exposure. "You certainly have the talent, Ben. But we aren't going to get eyes on your work in here."

"I know." Benny kept painting, letting the ideas swirl around in his head.

"I don't know if a gallery is the right place for your work. It's a little snooty for your rawness. Those kinds of people need to be told you're good. Told that they need to buy your work. They have no taste themselves. That's how Warhol did it. Now, if we could just tell them all. Get you on TV, that would make all the difference," Ruby said adjusting herself on the mattress. "This whole MTV generation would eat your stuff up."

"MTV?" Benny pulled his brush down from the wall. "That's a great idea."

"Okay. Maybe we could make a video of these murals and send it in. I know a lot about making videos."

"No, even better. They do a concert every spring break. Massive show, thousands of people on the beach and it's broadcast all over the USA. If we could get my work down there, they might see it."

Ruby sat up from her pose. "I still know a few people and a few people still know me. We'll tell them that you're great! Ruby Rain could come out of retirement to endorse this racy cutting-edge artist. Sex, drugs and rock and roll! Not much more MTV than that."

The buzzing of Ruby's pager broke their daydream.

"Shit. I have to go."

"Let me do it," Benny said getting down from the ladder.

"No, Bernie would not approve."

"Bernie doesn't have to know. Look, you've been supporting me and my sister and we're talking about building a future together. Together. Let me carry the load a little. I know you're tired."

Ruby sat up and stretched her back a little. "I am a little tired…thanks to you."

Benny gave her a devilish grin as he walked over to the pile of his clothes on the floor. "Then let me do this run. I know what to do. I know how to read the code on the pager. I just go to the pick-up, then drive to the drop-off, collect and don't look at the package."

"I can't help but look at it," Ruby said, returning the devilish stare, straight at his crotch level.

"Come on, let me do it. Let me contribute to our future. I can drop you off at the beach on my way, you could relax for a few hours in the sun, then we can meet up at the tiki bar later. You won't even know I was gone."

Ruby rolled it around a bit. Benny looked really keen on contributing and really what was the harm? The trips had been easy but sitting in a car for six to eight hours was not her favorite thing to do. Ruby knew many things about life, but most of all she knew men. She knew that men needed to feel useful. That it was a vital part of their makeup—even artsy, sensitive guys like Benny. Who knows, maybe after the run, she could tell Bernie and they could add another car to the mix. They could do more runs. Make more money. Have more of a future.

"Okay," Ruby said. "But you're using the car from Daryl's."

Opal waited patiently for her turn at the post office. She had an early drop that day, just after noon, so she planned some running around after. She was a little nervous, a little hesitant to send them off, but she'd made it this far, so she figured she should see it through. She had four envelopes in her hand. Her children were going to be very surprised. They wouldn't be surprised to receive a letter from Opal, she sent them postcards and obligatory birthday cards all year long, but these envelopes were different. These envelopes were fat. Each had five thousand dollars in it. Five large in one-thousand-dollar bills with no card, just a note that said, 'Love Mom and Dad'. She tried to focus on the smiles that would come across their faces when they opened the envelopes. The good it would do for her kids and grandkids. The phone calls that would follow. She'd get to hear their voices, maybe more frequently. She planned on sending more, so maybe this could make everything right, but not this round—she had a fourth envelope. A large, business-sized one. It wasn't going far like the smaller three envelopes. This one just needed a local stamp, because the address was within state lines. It was a heavy envelope, and it was addressed to Reverend Kind.

Ruby seized the opportunity of a 'Benny free' afternoon and turned it into a girl's day. She had thought about inviting Bernie to the beach, but of course that was out of the question because, after all, she was supposed to be on a run, so she called Darcy. Darcy in turn called Nola and Cathy. It was an impromptu, long overdue, reunion on the beach. Four old war buddies from the battle of the sexes, under umbrellas, spread out on lawn chairs, wearing swimsuits that didn't suit their ages. Thongs were illegal on all Florida beaches, but these were darn close. They were pushing the boundaries and they loved it. Together, they were rock stars, a power plant of presence, confidence and uncontrollable laughter. From the delta to the access ramp, they were the main attraction and these four didn't give two fucks if anyone didn't see it that way.

"What are you talking about? There were no VIP sections back then." Cathy, who was sporting white pigtails and had her assets packed tightly into her high waisted two piece, challenged Nola.

Nola adjusted the floral scarf she had around her head that was keeping the blowing sand out of her custom Tina Turner wig and pulled down her sunglasses to the bridge of her nose. "Yes, there was."

"No, there wasn't." Darcy got in on it too. "That club in Erie never had a VIP."

"Yes, it did," Nola replied firmly.

"Nola, I think they're right. I don't remember any VIP there." Ruby added her two cents.

"Oh, yes there was, and I made a fortune in it." Nola stood her ground.

"You got a touch of the dementia, Nola," Cathy scoffed.

"The hell I do." Nola sat up, looking like she was about rumble. "The VIP was in the back of that club, and I made enough money in it to get my first boob job."

"There was no Very Important Persons room at that club!" Cathy snapped.

"Very Important Persons?" Nola winced. "Hell no. There wasn't one of those there, but there was a VIP. *Vagina In* my *Pinto*! I was turning tricks that whole month in my hatchback!"

The girls burst into tear-jerking laughter.

Was it forgotten comradery or maybe it was different now that they were older? Whatever the cause was, it was soul affirming. Same boat. Ruby had never felt a bond like this with anyone in the industry. They all had the same stories, same references, same terminology and same dirty sense of humor. These were the women who survived in the loopholes of male oppression. They had turned dominance into dollars, the keepers into the kept. Yes, they were all single in the last years of their lives, all but Ruby, but they were single on their own terms.

"I still get a few," Cathy said, out into the air, laying back on her lounge, letting her stomach settle where it wanted to, and her pigtails fall to each side of the headrest. "Some younger ones too. They like it when I dance a little first."

Darcy grunted, "Lucky you. Most of the men in my area are the same age as me, but they seem older. Never been into older men."

Nola snorted, "Yes you were. You used to milk them old cows down to the last drop."

"Hustling, maybe, but not for a roll in the hay," Darcy corrected.

"I'll roll with just about anybody these days. If they're prettier than me, then I win and if I'm prettier than them, then they worship me, and I still win. The ugly ones try harder." Nola was preaching.

"How 'bout you Ruby?" Darcy passed the hot potato.

Ruby shrugged, "I've been spending time with someone."

"Someone?" Nola sat up again. "Ruby Rain is spending time with someone? Who?"

Ruby blushed, "His name's Ben, he's an artist."

Cathy pretended to faint. "Oh shit. An artist? Like a painter?"

Ruby nodded.

"Old guy?" Darcy winced.

Ruby shook her head.

"How young? Forty? Thirty?" Cathy was into this.

"Twenty," Ruby squeaked out.

"Twenty!" Cathy shouted and the girls became a sound explosion once again.

Darcy was angry. "That is not fair. We are all out here dodging dentures and homely hombres and you're living some kind of Harlequin Romance."

Cathy calmed down and tried to level with her. "There has to be something wrong with him. Is he ugly? Come on, you can tell us."

"No, he's very handsome and sweet."

"He's broke, isn't he?" Nola dialed in. "He has to be!"

"Yes, he's broke," Ruby relented.

"I knew it!" Nola celebrated, but only for a second. "What the hell am I screaming for? Who the hell cares if he's broke, you're laying down with a young buck—a young handsome artistic buck. Does he have any friends?"

"Me too!" Cathy jumped in.

"And me!" Darcy made sure to be included.

"I'll see what I can do," Ruby said back, half joking, half wanting to see these girls feeling the same way she was.

After their hormones and excitement had settled, Cathy asked, "So, Darcy said you were working at a club?"

"Yes. Not dancing though. Serving drinks and it was hell." Ruby made it clear from the get-go.

"Ruby Rain slinging sodas. That'll be the day." Nola was not having it.

"I wanted to dance. That's why I went into that place. But they didn't want me."

"Well, they should have." Cathy sighed. "I miss it. The good parts. Not the bullshit, the perverts or the pimps, but I miss performing."

"Me too," Nola confessed and so did Darcy.

"Hard to dance if there's no audience," Ruby said. "What we did is a lost art form."

"The ones I've given private dances for would be right in perverts' row," Cathy said confidently.

"We don't have a row." Nola put the whole idea to bed, pointing to a few, shirtless men down by the water, throwing the football around.

The ladies turned their attention to the sweaty, chiseled torsos throwing the ball, and a lot of testosterone around in the waves.

Cathy laughed. "Looks like we're the row now."

BONE PARK

The pick-up was smooth considering the Miami crew weren't expecting a man. They had their reservations for sure, but Ruby told him what to say—and all he had to say was who he knew—Bernie. He didn't look at the package when it was being loaded into his trunk. He obeyed all the rules of the road, following all of Ruby's instructions to the letter and was on his way back to New Smyrna. He kept the Sable rolling down the I-95 at a steady fifty miles an hour and made sure to stay out of the passing lane. He had followed all the rules—accept one. He skipped going to Daryl's after he dropped Ruby off at the beach, but he did it for a good reason. Benny was broke.

Benny was broke, but he didn't avoid Daryl's so he could skim. He didn't skip picking up the borrowed car so he could put some extra money, the rental money, in his pocket. Absolutely not—this was for Ruby. Being broke, he hadn't been able to do much of anything for her. Hadn't been able to treat her the way he wanted to and for a man of passion like himself, this was a big deal. So, he skipped going to Daryl's and renting the car, so he could use the five-hundred-dollar rental fee to get Ruby a gift. Sure, he could have asked her for the money, but that wouldn't have been right. This way, he'd earned it, and he knew exactly what he was going to get her. It was at the Zales in the mall, and he was daydreaming about it all the way back. Picturing it on her while trying to keep his excitement down, the car centered in the lane and his speed steady. He knew she deserved more, that she'd received more in her wealthy past, but it was what he could do. Something he could add to, when his art career took off and it would remind her of their humble beginnings.

She would be waiting at the bar for him, at the tiki bar on the beach where she and Bernie had gone. His plan was to take her down to the beach when the moon was high and give it to her there.

"Ruby, you are moonlight. You are my muse, my soul and my body. You have shone your light on me, and I never want to be out of its glow." Benny rehearsed his words out loud in the car. "This is my heart. I give it to you, now and forever. We never need a ceremony; we just need to feel this, and this is to remind you of that."

There was a loud noise outside the car—behind the car. Benny broke his glazed stare at the interstate ahead and looked up, into his rear-view mirror. It was flashing lights. The unmistakable strobes of a Volusia County cruiser. Benny looked down at his dash, he was doing over sixty-five. He'd let his foot get heavy while he was drifting off.

"Fuck!" he said out loud. Although no one was there, every criminal in the world could hear his words and knew this state of instant self-deprecation.

Benny let his foot off the gas pedal. Maybe the cop was just coming up behind him, about to pass him on his way to catch a speeder, or criminal up ahead? He tried to stay calm. Hands at ten and two and head straight forward, as he brought the car down to a respectable forty-five miles an hour. It only took a second for the cruiser to catch up to him. It got right onto his bumper, letting out two quick, loud blasts from its siren. There was no hoping now, no other speeder or criminal ahead, this cop was pulling Benny over.

Benny put his blinker on, the right one, the one with the shoddy relay that was hit or miss on a good day—and today was not a good day. The blinker stayed solid, betraying its name, giving the cop even more reason to pull over his jalopy. Benny pulled over to the side of the highway and the cruiser stayed tight behind him. He could run. That was a very strong could. He would just have to wait until the cop got out of the car, then he could floor it. Benny knew where he was, it was only a mile or two from there to the New Smyrna off ramp. He could make it— but what then? Where would he go with a cop hot on his tail? His daydreaming had become an escape plan.

The girls had joined her for a while at the bar, while the sun was still out and the happy hour prices were still in effect, but they had long since left. Ruby had moved on to water an hour or so ago but started worrying long before that. Benny should have been back, sitting down on the bar stool beside her, but he wasn't. They should have been making

BONE PARK

plans to leave the car here and get a taxi back to Cicada Hollow where she would do her best to stay quiet, so Bernie wouldn't wake up—but they weren't. Ruby's mind was in full retrospect, fueled by a day of drinks in the sun. Woulda, Shoulda and Coulda—the three most evil demons of regret. They had the power to possess a person and send them screaming to the edge. That's why most people had cell phones. Yes, they were expensive, but it would have been worth every penny and made every one of her raging nerves settle. Maybe he was okay.-Maybe he just stood her up. That didn't wash with her at all. Benny would never do that, but it wasn't like she could call the cops. She'd been down that route once already and that was before she knew who her sister really was. There was only one person who she could turn to now—the one person she didn't want to face.

"So, you're not dead?" Bernie was beside herself, raising her voice. "I have been paging you nonstop, what the hell happened?"

"I don't know," Ruby said quietly, trying to bring her sister's energy down a notch as she closed the door to the trailer and stepped inside.

"How could you not know what happened?" Bernie was seeing red.

"I know what was supposed to happen but—I wasn't there."

"You didn't go? Shit, that would explain why Vergil's been paging me all evening. Why wouldn't you go, or at least tell me? Do you have any idea what kind of shit you have gotten me into?"

"Ben went."

"Benny?" Bernie went full stop.

"He wanted to do the run. I didn't see the harm, but I haven't heard from him! Bern, something is wrong."

Bernie grabbed Ruby by the arm and pulled her towards the carport door.

"Where are we going? Can't you call someone? Find out where he is? There has to be something you can do."

"That's what I'm doing, I still have my rental from today, get in the car and shut up." Bernie opened the side door of the trailer.

Ruby didn't know what her sister was going to do, but she didn't protest. She feared her sister at that moment as much as she did for Benny's safety.

The payphone on the side of the closed ABC liquor store in Edgewater was a petri dish of diseases, but it was the best place for Bernie to call Vergil from. Ruby watched her back while Bernie pressed the sticky, metal numbers on the flat phone box that was decorated in sun dried spit. This wasn't the kind of place two older women should be at 1:00am.

The phone barely rang on the other end and Bernie got the jump. "Yes, it's me. I know, I was trying to get a hold of my sister, but she's with me now. Apparently, there was—" Bernie went quiet and from the other end of the phone, all Ruby could hear was the sound of a deep-voiced male yelling.

"Shit," Bernie said.

The sound of the male's voice got less intense, but Bernie's face did not.

"Okay. Tomorrow," Bernie said, looking down at her watch. "Today—right. Vergil, I'm sorry, I'll make sure—" It was over as abruptly as it started.

Ruby was waiting for a smile, any indication that he was fine. "Is he okay?"

Bernie's face went pale. "Did he have your pager?"

"Yes. How else would Ben know where the drop was going to be? Bernie, where is he? Where is Benny? Does Vergil have him? Do the other people have him? I just want him back. What do we need to do to get him back?"

Bernie feverishly pulled her beeper from her waistband, threw it onto the ground and stomped on it with her yellow flats.

"Bernie, where is he?" Ruby begged her, even though she was startled by her sister's aggression.

"I don't know! I don't know, alright?! Vergil doesn't know either! But we need to go, because wherever he is, he's got your pager and I've been messaging it all day," Bernie said moving quickly back to the rental parked out front of the liquor store. Her and her mind were working way too fast for Ruby, who was still swimming in a pool of questions—but Ruby followed her manic sister, because it was the only path she had that might lead to her man.

Bernie didn't slow down one bit. The sticky, smooth, black asphalt of Cicada Hollow made the tires squeal a little as they left the dirt road and passed under the arched gate entrance. Freda was a light sleeper before all this, but after weeks and weeks of surveillance, Bernie whipping into the park was like an airhorn. Any motion in the park after dusk was.

Hovering in such a light state of sleep, there was no need to adjust; Freda sat straight up in bed, wide awake, swung her legs over the side and started moving. By the time she reached her 'Bernie blind' in the front bedroom, the road around the inner circle was a hive of activity. Bernie had left the rental running, parked askew in her carport and was jogging up the road towards Opal's house. Ruby was a bit behind her, having trouble getting out of the car, because the door was blocked by one of the carport pillars.

It was like a rush to an addict. Freda's body was tingling. Something big was going on and she was mainlining it all. Opal suddenly came rushing out from the lanai side of her trailer, in her trademark pink-chiffon nightie and matching dressing gown. Freda had been leaving the front louvers open so she would be alerted by any shenanigans going on after she'd gone to bed—and right now those open louvers were making it possible for her to hear every incriminating word.

"Where is it?" Bernie said, voice raised and rabid.

"Right here," Opal answered shaken.

Freda focused her binoculars on the small pink square Opal was holding in her hand. The stars had aligned. She'd gotten much better over the last few weeks at keeping the binoculars steady and Opal was standing smack dab in the center of the wash from the porch light. As clear as she could see, Freda had no idea what it was. She struggled to figure out what the heck was in the small pink box that would have gotten Bernie so upset?

Bernie snatched the pink square from Opal's hand, threw it on the ground and stomped on it. Plastic and wires shot out of the sides of it. Freda may not have known what it was, but she knew it was electronic.

"What's going on, Bernie?" Shaken by Bernie's violent action, Opal pleaded for an answer.

"Go back to bed, Opal," Bernie said, bending down to pick up the broken pager on the ground. "I don't have time for this right now."

"I don't understand—what's happened?"

"Nothing. Go back to bed. Everything's going to be alright. Go back to bed, get some rest and we'll talk about it tomorrow."

Bernie didn't wait to convince her further, she just started trudging back towards her trailer, meeting Ruby along the way and turning her around too.

Both Freda and Opal were stunned by this late-night altercation, left watching the sisters' erratic retreat. They were blindsided and buzzing, but on different sides of the window, different sides of the law and for very different reasons.

No matter how old they get, people hate sleeping alone when fear is weighing them down. Bernie had taken the La-Z-Boy and Ruby the sofa. No telling if it was Ruby who needed Bernie or the other way around, but adrenaline eventually gave way to emotional exhaustion and they both fell asleep with the TV on—and within an arm's reach of each other.

There was no point in waking Ruby, when Bernie's eyes were jarred open by 'Good Morning America'. She had someplace to be. Someplace very, very important and she didn't need the added stress that her lovesick sister would add to it. Normally, Bernie would shower before seeing Vergil, before seeing most people, especially after the feverish day and evening that had transpired, but the shower would make too much noise and she was tight for time as it was.

Bernie quietly crept to the washroom for a brothel bath—a light, dry brushing of the teeth, a wipe of her pits with a face cloth and heavy powdering with White Shoulders. Her hair wasn't a mess, but it wasn't Vergil-worthy. Even though she knew that today he wouldn't be focusing on her hair, she took the brush to it anyway. Ruby was worried about Benny, but Bernie was worried about Vergil. After what had happened the last time they met, when he had been roughed up by his suppliers, there was no telling what they'd do to him now. Her imagination was running wild. They said, in no uncertain terms, it was to be six a week. No exceptions and no surprises. Benny was a surprise. How could Ruby be so stupid? If they had Benny, what would be her bargaining chip? How was she going to make this right, for Benny, for Vergil and for—

"Bern!" Ruby yelled from the main room, in a way Bernie had not heard before.

"I'm here," Bernie said rushing out of the washroom and into the main area. "What is it?"

All Ruby could do was point at the TV.

It was the newsbreak portion of the Good Morning America broadcast, where the feed from New York was interrupted by the local stations for news and weather. On the screen, beside the Daytona newswoman who was in the middle of speaking, there was an image of Benny's beat up, red Sable.

"…Volusia County Sheriff's office said that using their profiling criteria, they were performing a traffic stop, when the altercation took place…"

A high school, yearbook photo of Benny came onto the screen.

"Jesus Christ, he's been arrested." Bernie felt like the wind had been knocked out her.

"Twenty-year-old, New Smyrna resident Benjamin Tae was shot by police trying to flee the scene after human remains were discovered in the trunk of his car."

Ruby burst into hysterical tears, crawling towards the television as the broadcast continued.

"Police aren't saying whether this is tied to any other murders at this time. The coroner's office is still trying to determine the identity of the remains found in Mr. Tae's vehicle. Anyone with information is asked to call Crime Stoppers."

CHAPTER

7

An Eye for an Eye

Ruby was clutching the carved edges of the television cabinet as if they were Benny's arms, trying to hold onto his soul, to stop it from ascending. Trying to undo what had been done, to unsee what she'd seen, to unhear what she'd heard.

The phone rang.

Bernie jumped a little, but Ruby didn't, she had disappeared into the darkness and paralysis of sudden loss. Bernie took in the sight of her sister. The unstoppable sadness that was pouring out of her. It was what she had feared from the moment she saw them kiss in his car. The pain that has become her bedfellow. The loss she desperately wished her sister would never have to know. They say that time travel isn't possible, but those who have lost a true love know that is untrue. Time stops, the moment their heart stops and it moves slower than everyone else's. You are thrust onto another track, a line that runs beside everyone else's, but it's in another dimension. A foggier, thicker, heavier place, where you watch the rest of the world from, while you try to hang onto your own life. When a soul attached to yours dies, it pulls on you to join it. Tugs on you to stay in the cloudy track, to give up on it all, because it all has no meaning without them. It is a tethered fate, soul to soul, that draws the living to them and doesn't want anyone to die alone.

The phone kept ringing.

Bernie finally reached for it, still in the haze of her sister's sorrow and her own worry. As she lifted the receiver to her ear, she realized what she'd done—she had no idea who was on the other end. Was it the cops? Benny had Ruby's pager on him. What else did he have that could have led the police to them? The police—looking for her, for Ruby and she just answered the phone.

"Do you know?" the voice asked on the other end of the line. It was a strange voice. A man's voice, but not any man that she knew. Bernie didn't answer back, and it didn't matter because the man continued anyway. "Then it's done. We are content with the outcome. Consider reparations have been paid in blood."

Bernie just stood there holding the phone to her ear. Reparations paid in blood? That didn't sound like a cop, but she was afraid to speak because she didn't know who this was and because she knew better than to talk business where there could be other ears listening.

The man cleared his throat. "Is there anything else we should be concerned about? Verna Hewton? Anything about Ruby Hewton or Opal Murdy?"

Bernie may not have known who this man was, but he knew her and everything that was going on. Only certain types of people reference your family. People you want to keep away from them. "No," she responded. "I don't think so."

"Think," the man said. "Someone in your circle didn't think. I know it was not you. We have been very impressed by you. I trust you will think before letting this happen again."

"What about the package?" Bernie asked.

"They won't find anything. We always think."

"Vergil?"

"You no longer deal with Vergil."

Bernie didn't like surprises. No one in this kind of work did. "And who are you?"

"The people who saved your life. That's all you need to know. There is a package in your mailbox. From here on out, remember—think."

Bernie hung up the phone and turned her attention to her sister, crumpled into a puddle on the floor.

"Ruby. Poob? Sit up. I need you to sit up." Bernie walked over to her and pulled her up off the ground, leaning her back against the sofa. "Ruby, this is beyond awful, but I need you to think, I need you to just stay with me for a moment. Was there anything in Benny's car of yours? Other than the pager, was there anything that could lead the cops back to us?"

Ruby's eyes were as cloudy as pitted glass, her cheeks and nose were cherry red and soaked with sadness. She didn't respond, just sat dazed, tears falling, breath fluttering, mouth drooling.

"Ruby! Please! Think, was there anything in his car—in his pockets? Anything I need to know about? What about the food warmer? Your t-shirt? Your hat? Where are they?"

Ruby was still trapped in her leaking coma.

"Jesus!" Bernie rushed into Ruby's room and started turning it over like a correction's officer on a contraband search. Pulling the closet apart and the drawers. "Where is it?" she yelled, running back into the main room. "Where the hell is your uniform? Pull yourself together and tell me where it is and whatever else you've messed up?! This is your fault. You sent him out there, you put him and all of us at risk!"

Ruby slowly turned her eyes to meet Bernie's. "Body parts?" she said through choked tears. "That's why you didn't want us to look at the package. We were driving around with dead bodies? They shot him. They shot Ben because they thought he was a serial killer or something. He never would have gone if he knew. I'd never had let him—I'd never have done it either."

"They said that he ran." Bernie tried to pull her back to the facts.

"Wouldn't you? He had parts of a body in his trunk."

"He shouldn't have. He shouldn't have been on that highway at all, let alone in his own car. That's how this works. We don't fit the profile! Age, vehicle, gender—race. We are ghosts. You sent a giant neon sign out on the road. A young black man in a beat-up car—this is what happens."

"Go to hell. This wasn't my fault. It was yours."

Bernie crouched down, getting right into her face. "What did you think you were delivering? All those runs, to warrant you making all that money? What did you think, huh? It was sunshine in your trunk? Happiness?"

"Drugs. I thought it was drugs. Marijuana. Cocaine maybe?"

"And somehow that's better? We didn't kill the people we were driving back with. They did. They were *their* enemies in *their* drug war. We're just the hearse. Moving bones. A safe transport for their garbage. Drugs kill people, they kill people, we didn't. We just provided a service to those who did."

"They killed Ben."

"No, Ruby, you did. I told you. I made it very simple and clear.

The rules, the runs, it was all so simple. But you sent him. This is on you and if they trace anything in his car, your uniform or something else with your name on it back to us, that will be on you too." Bernie turned away from her, standing up and walking to the door. "There are three lives still on the line here. I need to talk to Opal."

"Go to hell," Ruby said with every ounce of venom she had.

Bernie stopped at the door. "I know you love him. But burning us all to the ground won't get him back. Ruby, women like us were never meant hold hearts like his."

Bernie stormed out of the trailer and straight for the old-fashioned mailbox that stood at the end of the carport driveway. Every trailer had one, but they were mostly detractive. People only used them for party invites, secret Santa gifts and the occasional advertising flyer. Bernie's mailbox was a crafter's dream, it was handmade, and hand painted to look like a pelican. Its barrel-chested body was the holding vessel for letters that would be deposited into its gullet via its huge bill. Bernie opened the top of the folk-art seabird's beak slowly. She had lost a colleague or two to bombs in the past, usually attached to cars, but mailboxes were always on the table. This was a position she never wanted to be in. Her anonymity was gone. Whoever called her and took care of things with Benny, knew her and knew where she lived.

She lifted the top part of the gull's bill and right there, sitting in the gullet of it, was a phone. A cellular phone. A Nokia 101 to be precise. A flat, black phone, about the size of a hotdog bun, with a small, green screen, simple soft-rubber light-up buttons and a tiny, nipple antenna on the top. There was a piece of paper wrapped around the phone, fixed to it with an elastic band. Bernie pulled the phone out of the mailbox and released the letter from the rubber band. It was a small, folded piece of paper with the words 'You owe us. Leave this on. We'll be in touch.' written on it.

She went to lower the lid, but something else in the mailbox caught her eye. It was not in the gullet of the bill, but just back from it, on the ledge where the body of the box began. She would have missed it entirely, but when she moved to close the lid, the sun coming over her shoulder found the object and it twinkled. Bernie's nerves and body shook as she reached into the pelican box to retrieve it. Opening her hand in the light of day, it was exactly what she feared it would be—a massive, gold bison ring. Vergil's ring. His pride and joy—and it was covered in blood.

Opal hadn't seen the news, but her cage was still rattled from the night before. Her head was telling her it was because she had sinned, as Bernie walked around to the back of her trailer, away from Stan's ears and the neighbors' eyes.

"Everything is fine. Just like I told you. But there was a problem." Bernie held her composure with supernatural calm.

"What problem?"

"It was with Ruby's boyfriend."

"Benny? Is he okay?"

Bernie had to tread lightly. "No. He's not. He passed away—last night."

Opal was stunned. "Died? How?"

"The police shot him," Bernie said to Opal, whose eyes were as big as saucers. "They are saying all kinds of crazy things about it. About him. But the truth is they're lying."

"The police are lying?"

"Yes, Opal, they are. I know it's hard to understand, but some police are not the good guys. They pulled Ben over for some traffic infraction and they shot him."

"What did he do?"

"Nothing, Opal. He did nothing. They are saying he is all sorts of things, a drug dealer, a robber a serial killer, all sorts of nonsense to cover the truth, that they shot a young man in cold blood, because they could. You've met Ben. He was a nice boy, wasn't he."

"Yes. A very nice boy."

"There is no way he could do the kinds of things they're saying, right?"

"Oh, my, absolutely not. How is Ruby?"

"As you'd expect."

"Oh, heavens—poor dear. I should make her some cookies or something."

"No, I think it's best if you just give her some time."

"Oh, right, what was I thinking."

"Your heart is in the right place, as always."

Opal couldn't keep wondering. "Bernie, what was last night all about? Why did you smash my pager?"

"The pager? Yes, that must have been really unsettling for you." Bernie quickly wove her lie. "The pager was totally unrelated. I read an article that they weren't safe to use—they are saying that they can cause cancer. I always worried about it, but when I read that article, I couldn't take the chance."

"Cancer?"

"It's not for sure, but to be careful. That's what I'm all about, being careful. I couldn't be there for Benny, but I'm here for you. For Ruby." Even in the worst situations, Bernie had the gift. A way of dancing with doubt and twirling it around until her partner felt like they could take on the world. "That's why we're such a great team. The three of us. Even in the face of this loss, we take care of each other."

"What about the food runs?"

"I think we could all use a break right now, don't you? I have a feeling Ruby's not going to be up to it for a bit."

Out of the corner of Bernie's eye she caught a glint of something. A flash. Naturally she turned to see what it was, but there was no one there. However, the flash did draw her eye in the direction of Freda's place and the gut feeling that accompanied it was setting off all kinds of alarm bells.

Freda ducked down just in time. She'd worried about this, about the sunlight catching the lenses of her binoculars ever since that episode of Murder She Wrote. She knew that the sun was too low for her to be pointing straight into it, but there had been so much going on, she just had to follow the action into the back bedroom. Even though she was crouching down at that moment, to avoid Bernie's piercing stare, missing what might be happening behind Opal's house, she hadn't missed what happened last night. She witnessed all the frenzy outside of Opal's house and also caught the strange car that crept into the park at dawn. The one that stopped to put something into Bernie's mailbox. She'd gotten a really good look at the man who got out of the fancy car and put it there too. The very tanned, young man, in the silk shirt and pressed slacks. She'd gotten a plate number as well and wrote it down in her notes.

After the car pulled away, Freda left her perch and snuck down the road. She was able to find a few pieces of what Bernie had stomped on left behind on the road and picked them up. She also found what the car had left. Her stealth mission took her all the way to Bernie's mailbox, where she looked inside and saw the phone. She'd even opened the note that was wrapped around it, read it and put it back very carefully. She had seen everything, but she missed the ring.

As Freda stayed huddled under the back window, crouching at the head of the bed, she was still trying to put it all together. She considered the tiny piece of green screen, one of the fragments she'd found on the road and tried to marry it with the words of the note. *You owe us. Keep this on. We'll be in touch.* This was far beyond her first inklings. Far greater than the swingers' ring or pyramid schemes she had envisioned. This was serious. The note was serious. The man who left it looked serious. Serious enough to make her realize that it was time to take this all to the proper authorities.

It had been almost three weeks since Benny was killed, and they had avoided each other the whole time. Ruby stayed in her room for most of it, only showering sporadically when Bernie was out, which wasn't much. The cell phone was left on as instructed but hadn't made a sound. When the battery bars had gotten low, Bernie went out and begged the pimple faced kid at the Radio Shack to help her. He had no idea the importance of the phone and couldn't have cared less about helping her until she made it very worth his while. He got a hundred-dollar bill, and she got a cord for it—a lifeline of sorts, to keep it alive. And it was alive, but Ruby was barely hanging on.

Her days were a mix of tear-soaked naps and cloudy coherence. Benny had appeared in her dreams once or twice, so sleeping was the only thing she wanted to do. Bernie's words weren't wasted on her. She berated herself with them hourly. Benny was a young man who delivered a pizza. Before that day he met her, that's what he was. But he'd met her and like so many other men in her lifetime, he fell under her spell. She'd ruined men before, but never killed any and she had never loved. Bernie was partially right. She had a part in his death, but so did Bernie and until her sister would admit it—until she would take some responsibility for destroying his and her life, they had nothing to say to each other.

Stan wasn't overly happy with the sudden hiatus of Three Dames' Dinner Delivery. It had really cramped the style of his nights out and tarnished his crown. Rounds were not 'on the house' so frequently anymore and the tensions at home reflected that. It wasn't just Stan griping; Opal was not herself as well. She had gotten a small taste of freedom and it was hard to let go of. It was hard to let go of her surrogate sisters too. Ruby and Bernie hadn't been out on an evening trike ride since then. Opal had gone out and joined in on the ride with Maryanne and the others, but it wasn't the same. Getting the mail was the only moment of freedom she had anymore, and she relished it.

The long walk to the community center, where the mailboxes were stacked just inside the front door, was her new drive to Miami. This was her time. It was far shorter, less exciting and unprofitable, but it was solo. No sandwiches or cold beers for Stan, no long stories from him that she'd already heard a million times or complaining about the price of toilet paper. The mailbox did have its periodic moments of excitement though, she had gotten letters from her kids. All three of them. It seemed the money was just the trick, like Bernie had said. One of her kids, her eldest daughter Terry, had written twice and sent current pictures of the grandkids. Opal hoped that the others might follow suit and send more letters too. She also wished she could send more money—that might help elicit more responses, but until the delivery service started again, that wasn't an option. The last few days had been a bust, empty boxes, but she held out hope, because she had nothing else.

As Opal put the tiny key into the slot, she said a tiny prayer. Not asking for much, just a sign from her children and when she opened the door, it was answered. The box wasn't empty! It wasn't a flyer or junk mail, or even a Jehovah's Witnesses' booklet—which she did enjoy reading—there was a letter inside. A greeting-card-shaped envelope and she squeaked with joy. She quickly snatched the letter out and locked the latch on the box. It was a white envelope. A very white envelope, but it had no return address on the back. She'd taught her kids to always do that when they were little and wanted to write Santa or send in a cereal box flap to receive a prize. Maybe they forgot to on this one or not seen the need, because obviously Opal would know who it was from once she had opened it. Opal flipped the envelope over quickly, eager to see which one of her brood had written to Mommy. She didn't recognize the handwriting on the front, but then again, would she? It had been many years since she had sat by their sides and helped with homework and without the other letters in front of her to cross reference, she really couldn't make a clear assessment. She couldn't wait either. This was as exciting as winning the lottery, because it was winning the lottery as far as she was concerned, so she slid her key under the lip of the envelope flap and ripped it open along the ridge. There was a very clean, white piece of paper inside, which she pulled out and unfolded. It was a handwritten letter, in deep black ink. The penmanship was exquisite, not anything like the hurried chicken scratches on letters she had previously received.

Dear Opal,

I wanted to write you and thank you personally for your most generous donation to our ministry. The Word of God cannot get off the ground without the wings of angels like yourself. We were overwhelmed by your commitment to our mission, and I wanted to invite you to join me here at the studio for a future broadcast.

Please accept my invitation by calling the number below and I look so forward to meeting with you and continuing our journey to lighten the hearts of God's children.

Sincerely, Reverend Kind.

It wasn't her children, but it was an answer to a prayer. She had all but forgotten about the money she had mailed to the church, other than when Stan would complain about not having extra cash for poker night. She had sent that money to do some good in this world and she was being given a sign it was well received. The Reverend himself, a messenger of God, was inviting her to come to the show and he referenced her as one of God's angels. Opal had never been one for the Catholic faith, she was a staunch Protestant, but this felt a lot like absolution for her sins, like forgiveness and that felt almost as good as the love she'd bought from her kids.

Ruby was gone. It was midday by the time Bernie noticed. Having not spoken to each other for so long, they'd started to forget that the other was even there. Ruby wasn't in her room. She wasn't in the lanai, or the activity center or the pool. She was gone. Bernie was worried of course, given the events of three weeks prior and Ruby's sudden disappearance did not sit well with her. They were at odds, but it wasn't the first time. She was mad at her sister but not indifferent. She needed to find her.

Every day since Benny's murder she had been on high alert. Whoever left the phone and Vergil's ring knew where they lived. Bernie had tried to reach him a hundred times. She'd paid for taxi after taxi, to take her to different payphones all over New Smyrna. She called every number she had for him, but not one of them was answered. She didn't know what had happened to him. she hoped he was in the wind, but the blood on the bison taunted her with tragic visions.

Coming back to the trailer, after doing her rounds of the inner circle and activity center, she noticed that at the back of the carport, the shed door was slightly open. Bernie's life experience has taught her that nothing is to be ignored and this was no exception. Bernie opened the door slowly, unsure what she would find; a scrounging armadillo, a rat, a gator, a hitman? She could get her gun, but if it was a hit, they might as well take her out, because a gunfight in this geezer park would have the place swarming in black and whites.

There was no rustling, no movement, no bullets, so she pulled the door open wider—Ruby's trike was gone. This meant no taxi, she hadn't run away or ridden her bike the ten miles to the police station so she could turn them all in. This meant she must not have gone far. The trikes were comfortable, but not something you'd ride out on the dirt road with. Bernie pulled her trike out from the shed. Knowing she had to

BONE PARK

be close, she set out on it, to ride around where Ruby could have ridden. Follow her tire tracks. Find her sister. It was one thing to ignore each other, but losing her sister? This whole silent thing between the two of them had gone on long enough. This was the catalyst and Bernie needed to put an end to it.

Way at the back of the park, on the other side of Cicada Hollow, where the oldest trailers sat on the double dead-end lane, Bernie found the red, tasseled trike. It was left by a trail that led off into the forest. The path didn't look well-traveled, it may have even been a game path for all she knew, but Bernie went down it without a second thought. The sight of her sister's trike made a day that so far was fraught with worry, seem hopeful and that was a feeling that had been absent for weeks.

As Bernie walked down the trail, she couldn't believe how dense the forest got. It was an entirely different world than the manicured grounds only a few hundred feet away. What was Ruby doing out here? It was impressive, but Ruby wasn't the nature type. Camping had never been a part of their phone conversations or on her vacation resume, even when they were younger. Of course, there were the passing worries of what some people do in isolated forests—when they feel isolated. The solution some choose when they can't see any other. Bernie had sipped from that cup often, after I left. She drank from the chalice of regret, sipping tequila sunrises to avoid those thoughts, so her worries were founded. The deeper she got into the forest, the worse the worry got. The worse the pictures in her imagination became. All the cliché Edgar Allen imagery took root in her mind. Nooses, trees, vultures, pills—a clearing?

The site up ahead pulled her mind instantly out of the darkness, out of the trail and into the beautiful, open space. It was a cleared circle, decorated by tall trees with streamers of Spanish moss that towered over an old, rusted Quonset hut, that was nestled at the wood's edge on the other side.

"Ruby?" Bernie called out. It was the first time she'd done it since she started searching. She hadn't called it out in the park, because she didn't want to cause alarm and she hadn't called it out in the forest because she was afraid of not hearing a response. "Ruby?"

Bernie walked towards the hut. As beautiful as this secret in the woods was, it was still in the woods. Isolated and away from prying eyes. Just the kind of place a person could make peace with the pain. Just as the horrific imagery returned to her mind, the small wooden front door to the hut opened. It was Ruby.

Bernie may have been relieved to see Ruby, but Ruby was not happy to see her. "Why are you following me?"

Bernie kept her cool. "I was worried. Your trike was at the start of the path."

"You found me. Here I am. So now you can go."

"Ruby, this can't go on. Us not talking."

"Why not? We basically did it for thirty years. I think things were better when we didn't talk."

Bernie did something she never did, but she should have done long ago. "Ruby—I'm sorry."

Ruby looked at her skeptically, wondering how much poison was in this apple.

Bernie pushed on. "I'm sorry about Benny. I should have told you what we were moving. If I had, you would never have sent him, and he'd be alive right now—"

Ruby raised her hand and shook her head for her to stop, but Bernie was in mid confession, her heart was opening. "Please, let me apologize. I need to know how I can make things right between us."

Ruby raised her finger to her lips.

"Everything alright?" a man, with a heavy southern accent called from inside the hut.

"Fine, it's just my sister," Ruby called back.

A short man, in his fifties, wearing a light, linen suit appeared behind Ruby in the doorway. "Well now, Ruby didn't say she had a younger sister." The man spun his tacky yarn as he gently pushed past Ruby, with his hand extended to Bernie. "Barry Montrose."

Bernie didn't know what to make of this. She knew what it looked like, but she couldn't understand how Ruby could do it so fast. So soon after Benny.

Bernie denied the man's handshake. "Hi, Barry."

Barry could feel the cold winds swoop in and turned to Ruby. "Well—I think we're all done here?"

"Thank you, Barry. You know where I'll be," Ruby said.

"The pleasure was all mine. I'll leave you two ladies to your day; I remember the way out," Barry said, stepping past Bernie and heading down the tire tracks that lead back to the main road.

Once Barry was out of earshot, Bernie leaned in. "You told that guy where we live?"

Ruby rolled her eyes. "Don't worry, you're safe." Ruby turned her back on Bernie and walked into the hut.

Bernie followed her, her feathers ruffled. "Ruby. The FBI are looking for me and now…we can't have people coming around."

"I didn't tell him where you lived."

"You said to him 'you know where to find me'."

"I meant here." Ruby raised her hands up wide.

Bernie stopped. She'd been so busy chasing her sister with

questions, she hadn't seen what she had been chasing her into. It was magnificent. The arched metal dome that was covered in elaborate artwork. Bernie was silenced and humbled standing under the paint-plastered metal, a respectful tourist in the middle of an anarchist's Sistine Chapel. She walked the length of the building, taking in every inch of this modern masterpiece. It was raw, unfinished and even vulgar, but that's where all of its beauty came from. As her eyes panned the arched walls, she stopped in front of the massive, unfinished nude of Ruby.

"That's you," Bernie said, with little sound, mostly breath.

Ruby nodded.

"It's beautiful." Bernie was still whispering, as if some curator was waiting to shush her.

"That's how he saw me." Ruby slowly walked up beside her sister.

It took her a few seconds, but Bernie put it together. "Benny did this?"

"Yeah, all of it. That's why I bought it."

Bernie turned to her. "You what?"

"Bought it. This is all I have left of him. That the world has left of him. The real him, not what the news said he was. Barry's a real estate agent. It's amazing how little they want for a shack in the woods."

"You bought it? How? If you put your name on the deed, it could be flagged by the Feds. You're my sister, Ruby. I'm sure they're watching everyone who knows me."

"He's a friend of Daryl's. I paid cash. He's put the land into some lady's name. A living one. Just one that's not all there. She's in a care home and hasn't said a word in years."

"You think you can trust him?"

Ruby looked her in the eye. "More than you."

Bernie took the dig. "I want to change that."

Ruby asked, "How?"

"Ruby, I have no idea. But I don't want us to go on like this. I need you. You're all I have left and neither of us know how much time we have. No one does, but we are definitely on the back end of the odds." Ruby didn't alter, so Bernie kept trying. "Benny's work is marvelous, I wished I knew him better. Seeing these now, I feel I at least know him a little more. Ruby, the blame is mine, but please don't shut me out anymore. We both know now what it's like to not get another chance to talk to them. The regret that comes with all the unsaid. You can hate me, forever if you want, just please talk to me."

"I don't hate you," Ruby said, walking over and sitting down on the mattress where she and Benny used to lay. "I hate this life. The ones you and I made. They're full of this. This hollowness and fight. All we have ever done is fight. Against the world, against each other and it always leads back to here. Why couldn't we be like him? Or Reg and Freda? Or anyone we passed on the interstate? They don't know this. The running, the hustle, the anger."

Bernie sat down beside her. "You don't know that. Everyone's fighting, just different kinds of demons. I don't think there is such a thing as a normal life. Just an uninspired one that people numb themselves into. We can't do that. We can't numb it out, we were born with raw nerves. They don't fight, they just wrestle with their conscience and die slowly. Quietly. But we're the Buffalo Girls, unlike them—we keep swinging."

They treated Opal like royalty. Starting with a designated place for her to park in the studio lot. It was near the door and had a sign with her name on it, stuck to the cinderblock wall. She was greeted at the door by a young woman, who knew exactly who she was and whisked her away to some place called 'the green room'. It was a fancy living room, with leather sofas, refrigerators, flowers, mirrors and three TVs that were hung from the ceiling. Opal was offered all sorts of beverages and snacks, but her tummy was in knots, so she stuck to the glass of water that had *Reverend Kind* written on it.

She had no idea what she was waiting for in there, all she knew was that they had invited her to the show. She thought she might get a tour, or maybe even get to watch the show being taped, like an audience member at Let's Make a Deal. She couldn't figure out how to tell Stan about this and couldn't risk bringing him there, in case they mentioned the money. As far as he was concerned, Opal was grocery shopping, which she still had to do on her way home, so she wouldn't have to lie. That was part of the nerves she was breathing through and part of the reason she hoped this wouldn't take much longer.

"Opal Rose!" The confident, warm voice of Reverend Kind entered the green room seconds before his orange face did. "You made it! I am so excited to meet you finally."

The Reverend walked right into the room and wrapped Opal in a hug. She was not used to this affection and squirmed a little in his arms.

The Reverend released her. "Not much of a hugger I take it. That's alright." The Reverend looked around the room. "Did they take care of you? I specifically told Paula to take care of you. Have you tried the fruit tray?"

"Not hungry. Water's good," Opal said, holding up her branded glass. "Must be holy water," she joked and instantly wanted to shove her foot into her mouth.

The Reverend paused. "Holy water?"

She backpedaled. "It has your name on it."

The Reverend laughed—hard. "Holy water! I get it! That's great, Opal. Really great. I didn't know you were so funny. Holy water! I'm going to use that, Opal."

Opal joined his laughter, although hers was an act of inclusion.

"Well, I'm happy you're settled in here and I'm really looking forward to talking with you on today's show."

Opal went instantly pale. "Oh, my—come again?"

"Paula filled you in, didn't she?"

Opal's blank stare said it all.

The Reverend took Opal's hand. "Nothing to worry about. You and I are just going to sit down and talk. Pretend the cameras and the audience aren't even there. It'll be just you, me and G-o-d."

"What are we going to talk about?"

The Reverend flashed his pearly whites. "Your generous donation of course. Your story will inspire others in the flock to do the same. To give from the heart, not their head."

There was a knock on the door and the woman that brought Opal to the green room popped her head in. "Ten minutes, Reverend."

"Thanks, Paula," he said, then turned his attention back to Opal. "I need to go now, but you can just sit back and relax. Paula will come and get you when it's time for our chat." He moved to the open door. "Here's a little tip that works for me. If you start to feel nervous, just talk to Jesus. He's always listening."

The Reverend left and Opal sat there, in the empty green room, still clutching her glass of water. She took a very deep breath, gently set the glass down on the fancy coffee table in front of her and closed her eyes.

"Dear Jesus. If you're listening—it's me—Opal Rose Murdy."

She sat frozen, listening to the whir of the air conditioning vent as if she might hear the whisper of the divine in it. With no celestial response, Opal's eyes snapped open. "If you're there—I'm sorry." She snatched her purse from beside her chair, jumped to her feet and rushed out of the green room.

Just after dark, Mullet drove his Hyundai Pony away from the park with Bernie riding shotgun. She made sure to call him Tony, even though her head had to convert it every time she spoke. They had always been friendly, but not friends, so he was surprised when she approached him on the lawn.

He was not in his usual Daytona-strip surf-shop attire, as Bernie had requested. With the exception of his mullet, he actually looked somewhat presentable. She didn't like to be chauffeured, but in this case, it was part of the deal.

"Right there." Bernie pointed to the parking lot on the right-hand side, just off the highway.

Mullet acknowledged her instructions and pulled the car into the busy lot.

"Park at the back," she said, and Mullet guided the tiny hatchback to the rear of the lot.

Once it was settled into the empty space, at the back of the lot, he turned off the car. "So, what now?" Tony asked.

"Just what I told you to do," Bernie said matter of fact and handed him a wad of cash.

"Really? This is a lot of cash, Ms. Hewton. You sure that's all you need me to do?"

Bernie smiled. "I'm sure."

Tony folded the bills and stuffed them into his jeans. "Okay, I'll be right back."

BONE PARK

Bernie nodded and he got out of the car. She watched as he crossed the busy, parking lot and disappeared into the building; all that was left, was to wait. If she could have done this in one of Daryl's cars she would have. She didn't like involving others in her work, but Mullet didn't know much. Nothing really. She had kept the instructions simple. Now she waited. There was no telling how long this might take or if it would even work. There was a very high risk in being out in public, after what happened to Benny and a very high risk to this transaction. But it had to be done. Business needed to be settled.

Mullet came out of the building and started running back to the Pony.

Bernie rolled down her window. "Well?"

Mullet spoke fast, "I did it. I said what you told me to say."

"Thank you," Bernie said, opening her door and getting out of the car.

"I still don't know why you wanted me to tell him that?" Mullet asked as he sat in the car.

"It's a prank, Tony. Just like I said. Don't worry about it. But you should get going or you're going to ruin it." Bernie slapped the roof of his car and Mullet started it up.

She stepped back into the edge of the woods, and as he peeled out of the lot, a man came running out of the building. He was exactly what you'd expect to see coming out of a run-down strip bar, and he was exactly who she had come to see.

The man ran over to a large, dark car, packed into the middle of the lot. He walked around it, running his hand over the side panels of it, from bumper to bumper, crouching down, inspecting it.

"Is that your car?" Bernie said, stepping out of the shadows and walking towards the man.

"Quincy said some old broad hit my car, was it you?" the man said, as he stepped into the yellow glow coming down from the light post. He was a dark-haired man, with a patch over his left eye.

"It was me I'm afraid. I sent that young man in to find the owner."

"Where? I don't see any damage?" the one-eyed man questioned.

"It's right there. On the back bumper." Bernie pointed to the back of the car and the one-eyed man stormed around to the back of his car once again.

"You're out of your mind lady. There's nothing—"

The thump was loud and thick. It had the resonance of a hollow stump being struck by a bat and as the one-eyed man fell to the ground, Kurt collapsed the metal asp down and handed it over to Bernie.

"He's out, Ms. Hewton," Kurt said, like he was addressing a teacher.

"Good work, Kurt," she thanked him, putting the asp into her purse.

"I'd be more than happy to do more. Anything you want me to do to this piece of shit—anything," he offered sincerely.

"No, that's alright, Kurt, you've done enough." Bernie dug around in the one-eyed man's pockets and pulled out a set of keys. "All I need now is your help putting him in the trunk."

Bernie opened the lid. Kurt picked up the limp one-eyed man and dropped him into the large trunk, like a rag doll.

Bernie smiled at him. "Ruby will be very grateful."

"I'm sorry I wasn't there for her—will you tell her that?"

"You are here for her now, that's what matters."

"What are you going to do to him?" Kurt asked, not out of a

macabre interest or concern, but in a search for justice.

She climbed into the driver's seat of the dark car and said, "I'm going to make things right."

Two ambulances already that month. August was always a hard time for the elderly and even though the month had just begun, the heat was already unbearable. Two more residents of Cicada Hollow had checked out, involuntarily, taking the gurney ride to the pearly gates. Sirens weren't all that unfamiliar around the park, but always caused a stir. Most of the residents were seeking relief in the activity center these days, spending most of the daylight hours behind the sliding, glass doors of the large, open room. It was a great way to kill the day, sitting in the cool air conditioning, playing cards and shooting the breeze, but Bernie and Ruby chose to tough it out. They preferred to sit in the shade of their lanai, sipping cold drinks, with a good old-fashioned 'red neck air conditioner' pointed at each of them. It was a simple piece of poverty ingenuity. Feet up on a stool in front of a bowl of ice, with a fan blasting behind it. The blast of cool air felt good on Bernie's legs and Ruby's made her sarong billow with sweet relief. Sure, the ice needed to be changed often, but they took turns. They were talking again.

It was Ruby's turn, so she dragged her soaked self into the trailer to get more cubes of sweet relief. As she opened the freezer, which could only be opened for a second, to retrieve two of the cube trays, she saw the peace offering. It wasn't the first time she'd seen it. In fact, sometimes late at night, she had crept out into the kitchen just to look at it. She never asked for it, but her and Bernie were better once it arrived.

She pulled the mason jar out from the freezer and held it up in front of her, so she could look into his eye. Her attacker's eye. The one he had left. The one Bernie took.

Bernie didn't kill him, just left him in the dark for the rest of his life. She could have cut off his penis, but that wouldn't have stopped him. Inside the jar was insurance that he would never creep around another parking lot again.

Ruby returned to the lanai with two fresh bowls of ice, she gave one to Bernie, then took her perch back over at the wicker table.

Bernie had just got the fan pointed perfectly at her, when a police car appeared, slowly driving down the lane, from right to left.

"Poob," Bernie said calmly, raising her chin, prompting Ruby to turn around.

The cruiser was moving very slowly. There were two cops inside and they were taking their time, looking into the side lots of each trailer.

"You think?" Ruby said calmly back to Bernie.

"Don't know, but if they stop?" she said doing her best ventriloquist impression. "Keep calm."

It had been over a month since Benny. Not a word, or a whisper from any authorities that pointed to Ruby. Bernie had not forgotten about the warmer and the uniform, or the possibility that the kid wrote Ruby's name down on something—she hoped it had just been overlooked.

The cop driving the cruiser made eye contact with Bernie, who was sitting in her usual throne all the way at the back of the lanai. They stared at each other for a moment, an odd face-off between an old woman and an officer of the law, that caused the cop to stop directly in front of their trailer.

Ruby looked back to Bernie. "Oh Christ."

"Stay calm," Bernie said watching, as the police officer opened his door and got out.

He was a young officer, maybe thirty and his female partner was about the same. Their faces were unmemorable, not because they were plain, but because Bernie was too busy focusing on her options.

She stood up and moved quickly to the screened door of the lanai to cut them off. "Morning officers, can I help you?"

This was already bad, any interaction with the fuzz always ended up with your name being entered into their little black books.

"Morning ma'am." The female officer took the lead. "We're looking for someone, maybe you could help us?"

Bernie stepped out through the door, making sure the police didn't enter her home. "Who are you looking for?"

Ruby sat with her back to the cops, sweating bullets, but not because of the heat.

The female officer reached into her chest pocket and pulled out her little black book. She wiped a bead a of sweat off her brow as she leafed through the rectangular pages. "It's gonna be a hot one. You two have air conditioning?"

"No, but the activity center does—we were just on our way there," Bernie said.

Ruby took her cue, getting up and going into the trailer.

"Good idea." The male officer nodded. "You snowbirds aren't built for the heat of the glades."

"Who was it you are looking for?" Bernie wanted to cut to the chase, the less they said to each other the better.

The female officer placed her finger on a page in her book. "Reg Hall? Do you know him?"

Bernie was instantly relieved. "Reg Hall?" She was relieved but she was no snitch. "I'm afraid not. Don't know anyone by that name. But then again, we're new to the park." Bernie cut the conversation off right there. "If that's all, it's getting a little too hot for me out here."

"Right. Best you get to the air conditioning," the policewoman agreed. "Thanks for your help."

Bernie waved and walked back to the trailer.

Inside she found Ruby in her bedroom, tucked tight to the wall by the front window. "What did they want?"

"Reg," Bernie replied, moving quickly into the bedroom to join her sister at her lookout.

The two of the watched through the side of the curtains as the police got back into their cruiser.

Ruby couldn't fathom it. "Reg? Freda's husband? Why?"

"I don't know. Didn't ask."

"Did you tell them where he was?"

"Nothing good ever comes from talking to them." Bernie said the oath, "I never tell them anything."

"Well, she might." Ruby sighed, seeing Maryanne walking up to the cruiser.

It only took a few seconds of interaction for Maryanne to raise her finger and point down the rounded road, directly at Freda's place.

It was hotter than sin that day, but Freda wasn't in the activity center either. Not because of her anti-social personality or her nosey Neighborhood Watch addiction, she was taking care of Reg. It had been three days since he was able to get out of bed, with the exception of a heavily aided trip to the bathroom, here and there. Freda didn't know what was wrong with him and he refused to let her call a doctor. He wouldn't give her an explanation as to why, but she loved him and his were the only wishes she respected. So, she sat by the bed, doting, devoted, keeping her loving husband cool with cold cloths and hand fans.

BONE PARK

There was a loud knocking outside the trailer and Freda ignored it. She thought it was probably just the neighbors or Mullet doing yardwork. It happened again. Then again, and again. Privacy was not something Cicada Hollow was big on. Freda placed the cold towel on Reg's forehead, set down her Japanese fan and walked softly out from the back bedroom. She kept her movements light, because she didn't want to wake him or alert whoever was pounding on their door that they were home. Freda was in no mood to chat.

By the time she reached the door, the knocking had stopped, so she looked out the tiny square window on the upper half of the door. It wasn't a neighbor; it was two officers—they were leaving the lanai and walking back to their car. Officers? She was suddenly atwitter. Had they finally come about all the shenanigans with Bernie and Opal? But that was a month ago? Was there new information? Did they need her information? How did they know she was watching them? Freda frantically unlocked the door as fast as she could and rushed down into the lanai.

"Excuse me? Officers, were you looking for me?" Freda called out as she ran out into the road after them.

The officers stopped short of their car and turned back. "Who are you?"

Freda quickly lowered her voice, realizing she was out in the open. "I'm Freda."

The male officer took the lead. "Oh, okay, sorry we disturbed you, Freda."

"Why were you knocking on my door?"

The female officer stepped forward. "We are looking for someone. One of your neighbors said that Reginald Hall lived here."

"He does," Freda answered, confused. "Reg is my husband. What do you want with Reg?"

The female officer looked at her partner. "This is probably something that we should be speaking with Reg about."

Freda squared her shoulders. "Well, you can't. He is very sick. He hasn't been awake for more than five minutes at a time the last day or so."

"Should we call an ambulance?"

"No. He'll be okay; he just needs his rest. Now, please tell me what this is regarding." Freda was getting spicy.

The female officer lowered her voice, stepping closer to Freda. "Ma'am, this is very awkward. You see this isn't where these things typically happen. We had no idea that Mr. Hall was here, in this—kind of community. I am going to give you my card and as soon as your husband feels better, I need you to have him call me." The officer handed Freda the card. "I really think it's best if he tells you himself. Once you've had that talk, call me. But if I haven't heard from him by Friday, then we'll be coming back."

Freda took the card. It was surreal for her, she'd never been in trouble with the law, Reg either. This had to be some kind of mistake. She couldn't believe that the police weren't there for Bernie. That they were there for Reg. Her Reg. Why? What was so bad that they had to come here and why wouldn't the woman tell her?

The police got back into their car and slowly drove away, leaving Freda standing on the side of the road with the card in her hand. She was exposed, out in the open and Bernie saw the whole thing.

By the time the sun had set, and the air had cooled down a little, most of the park was in bed, but The Three Dames weren't. They were riding around the park on their trikes, catching the cooler wind in their hair and catching up. They'd been doing this for a week or so by then— riding—just the three of them, away from the snide looks and comments of Maryanne's minions. They had become their own chapter of the trike gang. The new set up was prompted by Opal, she had really been missing her time with the girls and they missed their little sister as well.

"So, the Reverend invited you to the show?"

"Uh, huh. I felt like a movie star. Got to see backstage and everything."

"How did you wrangle that?" Bernie inquired.

Opal got very quiet.

Bernie huffed. "You're not giving that shyster money, are you?"

"Oh, my. Oh, dear, no," Opal replied quickly but her mouth rejected the lie, instantly turning down like a sad stroke and her eye started to strobe like Studio 54.

"You're giving him money?" Ruby was appalled. "My word, how much?"

"Not much," Opal said, her eye was already doing the Macarena, so she didn't have to worry.

"Opal. It's your money, you can do what you want with it, but there has to be better uses for it than to give it to that crook. He's worse than the people we got it from." Bernie scolded her.

"We got it from meal delivery, remember?" Opal stated as if her mind needed a refresher of her truth. The paper-thin truth that her soul rode the edge of.

"Right. Well, all those deliveries shouldn't be going into his pocket." Ruby backed her sister up.

"They aren't. I actually sent some home to my kids."

"Atta girl," Bernie said, swerving her trike a little towards Opal—the bicycle version of a pat on the back.

"Can't wait to send more," Opal said, and her eye stopped blinking.

"You should look at property," Ruby stated like some kind of Wall Street insider. "Equity. That's what I've been doing with mine."

"That shack in the woods is sentimental—not an empire, Ruby." Bernie tried to pull her gently down from her high horse.

"Well, it's not just that. I bought Matilda's place too."

"Matilda? She just died last week, poor thing," Opal said, a little bothered by the whole idea.

"Yes, she did. She moved onto a better place and so am I." Ruby seemed very pleased.

"Why haven't I heard about this?" Bernie tried her best to speak calmly, although she wanted to scream. "We all need to be very careful what we invest in. Property and anything like it, has a paper trail and our profits don't do well with those."

"Nothing to worry about, Bern. Barry took care of it for me. Handled the deed just like the hut," Ruby said with a wink.

Bernie knew what her wink meant, that it was put in some catatonic woman's name, but she still didn't like it. "So, what does that mean? Are you now a landlord, or are you—"

"I believe so," Ruby said plainly, cutting Bernie off, then turned her conversation to Opal to put a stop to any further digging. "The price is usually lower if you pay cash, Opal, and there are places coming up all the time around here. Contrary to what Bernie said, I think we could build an empire. You have to start somewhere. You should really look at scooping up some property too."

"No, she shouldn't," Bernie snapped, "and when were you planning on telling me this?" Bernie was fired up.

"Bern. I love you, but don't you think it's best if we have our own places? We're still in the same park, just not under each other's feet."

"Don't you mean thumbs?" Bernie corrected her.

"That too," Ruby retorted with a layer of malice, silencing Bernie and they all pedaled along in an uncomfortable silence that Opal wasn't used to.

As the trio rounded the top of the inner road, the circle they all lived on, that wrapped around the pool and courts, Ruby stopped pedaling. The clicking sound of the red beads she'd attached to her spokes slowed their repetition and she steered her trike towards the activity center.

"What the hell?" Bernie said, slowing down too and pulling up beside Ruby—who had stopped at the rear bumper of a beat up, red, Mercury Sable. "That's Benny's car, isn't it?"

"You see it too? Oh, thank God. I thought I was losing my mind." Ruby stepped off her trike and slowly walked around her boyfriend's car. "But the police impounded it, didn't they?"

"I would have thought so." Bernie looked suddenly worried. "Could be a message—from them."

"Who?" Opal wanted in on this ghost story.

"Never mind, Opal." Bernie squashed her inquiry fast. "Why now? What's the message by bringing Benny's car here?"

"You knew Benny?" A young woman, maybe twenty years old, came out from around the side of the activity center. "Everything's closed," she said, pointing to the building. "I'm looking for someone named Ruby?"

Bernie turned to her sister, giving her the subtle, but stern 'don't' look.

"She's Ruby," Opal said, friendly and helpful.

The young woman looked a little bewildered. "You're Ruby?"

Ruby did her best to smile. "I am."

The young woman didn't smile back, she just walked around to the trunk of the Sable and opened it. "Then these must be yours."

The young woman slammed the trunk closed, revealing she was holding the Three Dames' Dinner Delivery warmer pouch, hat and t-shirt in her hands.

"Yes—they are," Ruby said skeptically as she took the uniform and bag from the girl, "and who are you?"

The girl dead eyed her. "Natalie—Benny's sister."

Natalie, Bernie and Ruby sat facing each other in the main room of the trailer. It was too hot to be inside, but this conversation was too hot to be outside. Natalie sat on the couch, across from Bernie and Ruby, who had turned two of the three kitchen chairs around to face her. Bernie did this on purpose, because of the optics—the height difference between the sunken cushions of the sofa and the tall, firm, chrome and vinyl chairs, gave the sisters the higher ground. An important tool in Bernie's kit from years of dealing with people. Good people, bad people, it didn't matter, the upper hand was the upper hand. They needed it too—this girl's brother was dead. Murdered by police with a body in his trunk. Both Bernie and Ruby were aware of what she wanted—it wasn't Ruby—she was looking for answers.

"How did you know my brother?" Natalie hadn't taken a sip of her beer since they gave it to her. She just watched as these two old women rushed around this place and around the topic.

Ruby was having trouble staying calm. Natalie looked just like her older brother, the female version of Benny. She was a beautiful, brown-skinned girl, with hazel eyes and attitude braided into her hair. It was hard for Ruby to have such a beautiful version of Benny sitting right in front of her.

Ruby stumbled a little. "Uh, we—were—friends."

"Friends?" Natalie looked her up and down. "Is that so? How did you meet him?"

"He delivered a pizza to my work," Ruby said matter of fact, trying to cover her previous word acrobatics with smooth, stutter-free sentences.

"To your delivery service?" Natalie raised an eyebrow.

"My what?" Ruby was caught off guard, forgetting what was written all over the warmer bag, t-shirt and hat the Natalie had just returned to her.

Bernie jumped in. "No, they met at her previous job."

"Where was that?"

Ruby pulled in the reins. "A bar."

"A bar? That's pretty general." Natalie was stone.

"A little bar over in Edgewater—you probably wouldn't know it." Ruby played it down.

"Shakers?" Natalie said, pulling a Shakers branded matchbook from her pocket. "I went there today too and asked if they might know who Ruby was?" She opened the matchbook and showed them Ruby's name, written in pen on the inside cover. "You worked at a strip bar?"

"Waitress." Ruby got in front of her next question.

"I know. They told me all sorts of things—Sugar, I think her name was. She really doesn't like you, does she?"

Ruby pulled her shoulders back. "Feeling's mutual."

Bernie had about enough. "What's with the third-degree kid? If you already knew that, then why the hell did you ask? We have been nothing but kind and hospitable and you've been nothing but rude. I'm about ready to throw you out on your ear."

Natalie turned her head a little to make full eye contact with Bernie, she wasn't intimidated in the least. "You throw me out and I call the police. You do realize that you gave an eighteen-year-old alcohol…" she said as she held up her beer, "pretty sure that's against the law. You want me to get to the point? Fine, let's stop fucking around. Benny didn't have a mean bone in his body. There is no way what they are saying about him is true. That morning, as I was leaving for school, he came home in a rush and changed. Showered and he put on a shirt and tie. When I heard the news, I raced home. Right before the police showed up, I found your delivery stuff in his bedroom, he must have brought it in when he changed. I hid it along with some other of his things. Didn't know whose it was, but I knew it wasn't his and I didn't want the cops to find it. Pigs twist everything around on people like us. I'm starting to think that I wasn't helping him by hiding it, I was doing you a favor. You seemed very relieved to see it when I pulled it out of the trunk. Now, you old ladies don't look like the kind of people who would kill someone and put them in a trunk. I know my brother did odd jobs for people to make extra money, sometimes some shady shit, but not this. I don't know if you're involved in it, but you're lying to me, that much I know. I just can't figure out why?"

Bernie turned to Ruby. "Tell her."

Ruby's eyes widened. "Excuse me?"

"Tell her how you really know Benny." Bernie nodded, leading Ruby. "She deserves that much." Bernie then stood up. "I'll leave you two alone."

As Bernie walked out the door to the lanai she gave Ruby a look, a look full of instructions that only a sister would understand. The same kind of look she gave Daz as they left the hotel room.

Ruby moved her chair closer to Natalie. "I did meet your brother at Shakers. That's true. The stuff in his room is mine, that is true as well, but we weren't friends. We were together."

Natalie shook her head a little, like the words didn't land right in her head and she needed to help them fall into the right spots. "Together? How?"

Ruby took a very deep breath. "We were—dating."

"Fuck off," Natalie said sitting back, not buying it.

"I know I'm older—"

"Older? You could be his grandma."

"That there!" Ruby was insulted. "That's exactly the reason you didn't know. Because of immature bullshit like that. I loved Benny!"

Natalie's face softened. She could see the truth in Ruby's glassy eyes.

"I loved him. Really, really loved him and he loved me too." Ruby couldn't hold her tears back any longer. "I still can't believe he's gone."

Natalie couldn't hold hers back either and her tough girl shell melted away with the tears rolling down her cheeks.

Ruby didn't wait for an invitation; she just leaned in and wrapped the breaking girl in her arms. She nestled Natalie's head against her chest, mothering her sadness, something that this young woman needed so desperately and hadn't had for far too long.

The electricity had been reconnected thanks to Barry, but the fluorescent ceiling lights in the hut were toast. Natalie pointed the flashlight up, washing the top of the arch with light, revealing the masterpieces that were hiding in the darkness. As Natalie stared up,

Ruby made her way over to the temporary flood lights that she had set up on stands, scattered around the hut.

A few clicks and the Quonset Hut came alive.

"This is all him," Ruby announced with pride.

Natalie slowly turned around, taking in the wonder that surrounded her. "I knew he drew. He was always doodling when we were younger, but since mom died—" There were too many conflicting emotions to end that sentence, so instead she absorbed his art. Took in her brother's spirit, that was alive on the walls. "It's like I can feel him. He's here, isn't he? I can see him in it."

"That's why I bought it. To keep him close."

Natalie brought her eyes down from the arched roof to meet Ruby's. "You did love him."

"No—I do," Ruby corrected her, but not to be smart, just to be honest.

Natalie turned her attention to the massive painting of Ruby. "That's how he saw you?"

"I guess." Ruby was humbled, having her nudity, their love, on display in front of his family.

"It looks like he really loved you too," Natalie said with the birth of a smile coming to her lips. "So, what happened? This is the Benny I knew, not what they said about him. If you know, please—please tell me."

"I know part of it." Ruby shouldn't say another word, but she couldn't leave this girl hurting like this. Thinking and wondering about her brother. Benny would never have wanted her to be burdened with all those questions. "Your brother was just doing a delivery. You said you knew he did some odd jobs on the side. This was just one of them. He had no idea what he was delivering. Neither did I. It was my run he was doing. It was supposed to be me that day, but he wanted to do it and it paid really well. I swear I had no idea what the cargo was."

"You sent him out?" Natalie was surprised.

"We do deliveries. The person who hired us, lied to us. There is no way I would have ever let him do it otherwise. I would never have done it either if I knew. I'm sure that's why we were never told. What we delivered was always a secret."

"You have to call the police." Natalie was ignited.

"Don't you think I wanted to? We can't. You can't. The people we work for, are bad people. Very bad people. The kind that kill and put bodies in trunks. If we say a word, they'll kill us all, even you."

"I don't care. He's dead. I've got nothing now."

"Ben did everything for you, so that you'd have a future. Calling the police will make sure you never have one. You said it yourself—you know how pigs twist things. For all we know they're in on it. Don't you think it's strange that it all disappeared? How many times did they talk to you?"

Natalie is confused. "Once."

"Once? Your brother was shot because they thought he was a murderer and they only talked to you about him once? Doesn't that seem strange? And his car, they just gave it back to you?"

"A few days after."

"A few days? If they really thought he was some kind of Jefferey Dahmer, don't you think they'd have torn it completely apart? Yet you're driving around in it, and it looks exactly the same as the last time I saw it."

"It's all I have left of him."

In all the commotion and emotion, Ruby hadn't clocked the signs. Natalie's dusty runners, her greasy hair, the dirty fingernails.

"How are you getting by?"

"Benny had a shoebox of money, not enough for rent, but enough for gas and food. I was lucky, the same day they kicked me out of our apartment, the cops dropped off his car. It was a sign."

"You believe in signs?"

"Yeah. I guess. It's like he brought his car back for me, so I had a place to stay. It's all I have left."

"That's not true. You have me. I think this is another sign. Benny brought us together; the uniform, the matchbook, he led you to me, so I could look out for you."

"I came here to find out what happened to him."

"And you did. But you also found me. Now, you can either go, call the cops and go it alone, or you can stay with me. It's up to you, but I would ask you, to ask yourself—what would Benny want you to do?"

It wasn't the worst pull-out sofa, but the mattresses on pull-out sofas are always thin. Too thin for any back over 20. Ruby gave Natalie her room for the night. It was a double pronged gesture. One, she thought a teenage girl deserved her privacy and a good night sleep after living in her dead brother's car for weeks. And two, she wanted to make sure she didn't leave. Ruby had told Natalie a lot. More than even Opal knew, and it could put them all away for a long time—or underground for all of time.

"I can't believe you let her stay here?" Bernie grumpily sipped her Sanka, scowling at her sister from the kitchen.

"Keep your voice down." Ruby hushed her as she struggled to get up from the 'mostly spring' mattress of the hide-a-bed.

Bernie couldn't take seeing her sister flapping around like a beached snapper, so she went over to lend her a hand. "I made you a cup. It's on the counter."

After getting Ruby to her feet, Bernie stepped down into the lanai and Ruby wasn't far behind her. "Listen I know you're not big on strangers but—"

"You shouldn't be either." Bernie was waiting for her chance. "I can't believe you told her everything."

"My word, I must be full of surprises, because there seems to be a lot of things you can't believe this morning," Ruby jabbed as she sat down into the wicker chair by the table.

"Ruby, if she tells the police, we're done. She's probably done too, once they find out. Heaven knows what they did to Vergil, and he was on their side."

"She's not going to say anything." Ruby casually sipped her coffee.

"How do you know?"

"Because I know. I know girls like her. So do you. She's grown up like us. She's tough. A lot tougher than Ben. She's angry about what happened to him, but she's not stupid."

"Well, you certainly have been. Jesus, it's just one thing after another with you, isn't it? How am I supposed to protect you, if you won't protect yourself? That girl cannot stay here." Bernie was doing her best to contain her frustration, but her best wasn't very good.

"She's not going to stay here."

"Good. Now you're talking sensibly."

"She's going to stay at my place. I was waiting for the right time, and it looks like this is my cue. Another sign."

Bernie went to speak, but Ruby ran right over her. "Before you ask—I don't need anything from you—I'm set. The place comes fully furnished. It's crazy—Matilda loved red as well. Call it all coincidence, but the signs continue to point in that direction—away from you," Ruby said smugly.

"Shhhh," Bernie said raising her finger.

"Don't shhhh me!" Ruby was ignited.

"Listen." Bernie turned her ear to the open inner circle behind the trailer. "Do you hear that?"

Ruby silenced her rage and tuned in on the faint sound in the distance.

"Ambulance?" Ruby whispered.

"No," Bernie said back, concerned.

The sirens got louder. Closer.

"You're sure she didn't call the police?" Bernie glared at Ruby as a cruiser with its lights flashing and its siren blaring came tearing down the curved road towards their place.

CHAPTER 8

The Lottery

Bernie burst through the door of the front bedroom and Natalie screamed, she was still a prisoner of the natural sleep drugs that separated her from the waking world. She had no idea what was going on and where she actually was.

"What did you do?" Bernie shouted as Ruby raced in after her, getting between her and the bed.

"Slow down!" Ruby shouted, cautioning her sister.

Outside the trailer the sirens shrieked.

"I don't know what you're talking about!" Natalie reached out and pulled on the back of Ruby's nightie. "What is she talking about?"

Outside the sirens reached fever pitch, but they were on the move.

Bernie ran around the bed, over to the window and looked out through the curtains. "They stopped at Freda's house."

Ruby was pissed. "I told you."

"Well maybe Freda called them! You saw her the other day? She took the card from those cops."

"They were asking for Reg, you said as much."

"Maybe he called them?"

"You're paranoid, Bern." Ruby warned her then took Natalie's hand. "Hey, I'm sorry about all this. Everything is fine. Why don't you grab your things." Ruby let go of her hand and moved over to her closet where she pulled out a couple of suitcases and started putting clothes in them.

"Are the police here for you?" Natalie gasped.

"Probably," Bernie said storming out of the room.

She walked straight though the main area, past the kitchen and into the bathroom. She stood in front of the toilet and lifted up the middle, crocheted-skirt-wearing doll, revealing the snub-nosed revolver hidden in the can underneath. She reached for it—but stopped. Something outside stopped her. It was another sound. Another siren—but this one was different. More whine, more repetition to it. It was an ambulance.

Bernie ran out through the lanai in her robe, not dressed for the public, but just in time to see the ambulance go streaking by her place. From the front corner of her trailer, she watched as the paramedics ran into Freda's trailer. There were more sirens in the distance—fire trucks—Bernie knew their distinctive sirens too. This wasn't a raid; it was a 911 call. All branches dispatched. Whoever called, must not have said what they needed, just that they needed help.

Down at the end of the curved road, Reg emerged from the trailer, being carried out on top of a gurney. Freda was rushing right alongside him.

"I'll come back for the rest," Ruby said emerging from the trailer with her suitcases.

Bernie turned around, startled and embarrassed. "Poob, please, I just..."

"I hope they're okay," Ruby said, ignoring her attempt at an apology and focusing on the real catastrophe happening at the end of the road.

Natalie came out of the lanai, stepped up to Bernie and said calmly, "I don't snitch."

With that, Ruby and Natalie turned and walked between the trailers, heading off to Matilda's old place, the one with the red stripe around it, on the other side of the open inner circle.

It was hours of nothing. Nothing but blank faces, blank coffee and blank reruns on the TV suspended from the ceiling in the waiting room. No one had told Freda anything. They let her ride in the ambulance, but that's only because she begged them—and Freda didn't beg. She hated herself for letting it come to this, but it hadn't been that bad until this morning. He'd had a few rough days a couple of days ago, but he was on the mend. Yesterday he was doing great. They even sat outside most of the afternoon. They had a drink last night—he'd made love to her—and this morning he was barely breathing. His lips were crusty. Why did she fall asleep? Normally she sat up most of the night, watching him. It had been easy to watch over him, because she'd gotten so used to staying up most of the night to watch Bernie's activities. But they had made love. She always got tired after. She liked getting tired after so he would hold her in his arms. Big Spoon.

He never called her little spoon. She was Sugar Spoon to him. She always fell asleep, her right ear on the inside of his big, right arm. His arm always fell asleep under the weight of her head, but he never moved it. Big Spoon liked to watch his Sugar Spoon sleep. She was a tightly wound ball of energy, that bounced around from problem to problem, so any time that she would rest, he cherished. They cherished each other, but there would be no rest for her today—no rest for a long time.

"Mrs. Hall?" The nurse behind the desk called out her name over the PA system.

Freda was quick to her feet, they were numb from sitting so long, so it took her a few steps before she started to walk right. "That's me. I'm Mrs. Hall," she said putting her hands on the top of the reception desk, bracing for what might be next.

"Mrs. Hall. Your husband is out of the ER now and is stable."

"ER—stable?" Freda was just repeating words, nothing was sticking.

"Yes. He's stable. The doctor would like to talk with you. He'll meet you in room 1013. That's where your husband is."

"10—?" Freda struggled.

"13," the nurse repeated kindly. "Room 1013, just down this hall."

Hermes had nothing on Freda, her sandals practically flew down the hallway to room 1013.

"Reg!" she said, rounding the corner of the doorway, way too loudly for a hospital ward, but she didn't care.

Her flying Greek feet suddenly lost their flight the moment she stepped into the room. Reg was there, but not awake. There were more tubes and wires coming out of him than hairs on his balding head. He didn't look good, even worse than he did at the trailer. Freda walked slowly up to his side and took his hand in hers, being careful not to disturb the medical spaghetti attached to it.

"Mrs. Hall," a man said behind her, but she didn't turn—didn't let go of her Big Spoon's hand. "I'm Doctor Noth." He walked around to the other side of Reg's bed, so he could face Freda.

"The nurse said he was stable." Freda was angry.

"He is." The doctor tried to diffuse her. "Stable, but not conscious. Mrs. Hall, how did it get this bad?"

Freda felt attacked, just like when the police were digging around. "He didn't want me to call a doctor or an ambulance—and he was doing much better just yesterday—these summer colds usually go away in a few days."

"Summer cold?" The doctor paused. "Mrs. Hall, your husband has cancer."

Freda felt the world spin, her feet go out from under her, and the ceiling take over her view.

There was a lot of yelling and many hands on her, but she eventually found herself sitting upright, in a chair across from Reg's bed.

The doctor crouched down to speak to her. "Have some water," he said handing her a tan Melmac cup. "Are you alright?"

Freda nodded, sipping the water. It was basically the only thing she'd ingested since Reg was unresponsive.

"I take it from your reaction that you didn't know."

"No. He must not have either."

"He had to have. The tumor on his prostate is enormous. It didn't grow overnight. It had to have been very painful for him."

"Then why did he hide it from me?"

The doctor tread lightly, "Well, do you have insurance?"

"Of course—made the payments for years—I gave the card to that nurse."

"Yes, they checked it, and it seems that it lapsed a few years ago. I'm not certain, but a lot of people avoid things they think can wait, because of the cost."

"Reg would never do that."

"Well, whatever the reason, it's spread. Everywhere. Mrs. Hall, your husband's in a medically induced coma. The pain he would be in if he was awake is unmanageable, even with our heaviest medications and they would make him just as unresponsive."

"What then? What can you do?"

The doctor adjusted his stance, bracing himself for the weight of his words. "This. This is all we can do. Mrs. Hall, your husband is dying. He was already…we resuscitated him when he arrived, but now he's with us only because of these machines. If he had come to us earlier, when this started—"

"Stop. Please stop. I just did what I was supposed to do. I was obeying my husband. He clearly didn't want to come here, so I respected his wishes."

"I understand. But now it's your call. He can't tell us what he wants, so we need you to."

Freda nearly strangled the doctor. "I'm not pulling the plug if that's what you're asking."

"That's not how we put it, but it is the question."

"The answer is no."

"I sympathize with you, but I need to advocate for both him and yourself. Mrs. Hall, your husband is not there. He has suffered for a very long time and keeping him on these machines, in here, is very expensive. I don't think that a man who wanted to spare you the worry of his health, would want you to carry the burden of this expense."

Freda stood up. "I said no."

The new digs suited Ruby well. The late Matilda did in fact have a crush on crimson. Ruby's favorite color was everywhere; lampshades, pillows, toaster, kettle, cups, plates, even the bath towels and knitted toilet seat cover were red.

"Front bedroom's yours," Ruby said to Natalie as she headed to the bedroom at the back.

The room was nice. Simple, but tastefully decorated. It was the only room in the house that wasn't plastered in red. Simple white bed set, white curtains and framed portrait on the wall of an Asian woman, painted in tones of green.

"Thanks, Ruby. Should only be for a few days. Once I get my head on straight. Been a bit of a trip since Benny," Natalie shouted, setting down her small gym bag on the bed.

Ruby called back to her from the other end of the trailer, "The room is yours, for as long as you want it."

Natalie took the room in again, through new eyes. Eyes of someone welcome, not temporary and her jaw unclenched.

Ruby left the back bedroom and walked down the hall, into the kitchen. She opened the fridge door and immediately slammed it shut. "Oh shit!"

Natalie came running out of her room. "What is it?"

Ruby laughed. "This fridge smells like an outhouse." She frantically opened drawers until she found some rubber gloves and a couple of dish towels. "I only looked in it for a second, but everything is black. They must have turned the power off when she died."

"Is it really that bad?"

"My word—it's worse." Ruby pulled on the gloves, tied one of the dish towels around her face and held the other one out to Natalie. "I suggest you wrap this one around your face. It's the only way we are going to get through it."

"Me?"

"Yeah you. This is your house too now. I'm not cleaning it alone."

Ruby opened the fridge door and the smell that emanated from it reached Natalie's nose. She gagged then snatched the towel from Ruby's hand. She tied it tight around her face, just like Ruby, but it wasn't because she had a weak stomach, or because she was afraid of breathing in the putrid, toxic fumes—it was because she liked the sounds of having a home.

A yellow top taxi pulled over to the side of the lane in front of Bernie's place and she was already outside waiting for it. She was dressed for it too. Sunglasses, slacks and a blouse. This well-dressed version of the Buffalo Union Boss wasted no time getting out of the sun and into the air-conditioned car.

"Daryl's Deals on Wheels," she said to the cab driver as she closed the door.

The cab pulled out from the front of her trailer and made its way around the inner circle's one way road. As the cab rounded the other side of the circle, Ruby and Natalie, came running out of the trailer with the red stripe. They were holding garbage bags, laughing and gagging under the dish towels they had wrapped around their faces.

Ruby caught Bernie's eye as the cab passed by. She wondered what Bernie was up to, but she was also glad that she didn't know. She was happy that she was there, on the other side of the circle, laughing and letting go.

Inside the taxi, Bernie's waves of jealousy were squashed by the abrasive ring of her cell phone. *The* cell phone. Bernie held the phone out in front of her and pressed the answer button with her middle finger. The finger now wearing the large, gold, bison ring of Vergil.

"Yes," she said into the phone. "I'm on my way."

There were a few taxis called to the park that day, but the next one rolled down the inner circle road much later. It was dark when Freda paid the driver and peeled herself out of the backseat. There were no lights on in her trailer. She'd left first thing in the morning, in a blur of panic and as the cab pulled away, the trailer was as dark as her heart—and just as empty.

She didn't bother turning on any lights as she stepped up into her rectangular home. She had left the solid doors open, just the screen one was closed, but the house still smelled of sweat. That hot, sticky, sweet smell of heat and sickness. Freda walked straight to the bathroom and opened the medicine chest. She grabbed the bottle of Old Spice after shave, poured some on her hands. She watched as the liquid ran through her fingers then placed them over her face. Her body started to convulse as she breathed in her husband. His smell, his healthy better days, not this sickness. She broke—completely, sobbing to the edge of sound, holding the scent of their dates, their wedding, their nights, and her Big Spoon, the love of her life, in her hands.

The next three taxis arrived one after the other, letting their loud, slightly inebriated passengers out at the front of the trailer. This wouldn't fly at Bernie's, but the trailer wasn't Bernie's—it was all Ruby, and it was swinging. Darcy, Nola and Cathy had come to the park, on Ruby's invitation and dime, for a housewarming party. It was the opposite of what was happening on the other side of the circle. It was alive and fun and just what Ruby and Natalie needed.

Natalie had never had this kind of connection with other women. She kept her nose down in school, because Benny said it was the only way for her to go to college. Scholarships. The other girls didn't take too kindly to focus, so she became the brunt of popular jokes. She was easy pickings. Poor, quiet and smart. Sure, she was strong, but as another poor black kid, with a dead drug-addict mother, administration had already placed a target on her back. She needed to bite her lip and toe the line. There were no slumber parties or double dates for her, so being a part of this group of ex go-go dancers was exciting.

Ruby let her drink, but kept an eye on her, making sure the other girls didn't top her up too fast.

"So, you realize you are sitting in the midst of legends, right?" Darcy was the first to put Natalie under the lamp.

"Uh, yeah?" Natalie was clearly not in on this joke.

"She doesn't know?" Darcy was aghast. "This here is Ruby Rain! Dancer extraordinaire."

"Dancer?" Natalie turned to Ruby. "I thought you were a waitress?"

"I was, but that's not what she means. I used to be a stripper—"

Nola climbed onboard. "Stripper? Hell no. You were a dancer—and a model, and the first—wait—not just the first, the *only* female owner of an adult video company to date."

Cathy was all for it too. "She was a pioneer in VHS and was a Playboy centerfold."

Darcy added, "and Hustler and Swank."

"Hell, she was the first winner at the AVN awards." Nola was practically cheering.

"The what?" Natalie was being bombarded with this crash course in Ruby.

Nola looked at her sideways. "AVN awards, the Adult Video News awards. Young lady, where have you been?"

"Nola, I will have you know that I didn't just win it first, I helped create those awards. I'm the asshole who moved them away from the AFAA." Ruby patted herself on the back. "But it's not just me Natalie, all these ladies are legends. Allow me to introduce to you—"

"No," Darcy said all excited. "Do it right."

Ruby giggled and then raised her beer to her mouth, speaking into it like a microphone. "Ladies and Gentlemen, now coming to the stage, for your viewing pleasure—Naughty Nola, Cathy Cutie and Darcy Dimples!"

All three women stood up and strutted around the main room on an imaginary catwalk, blowing kisses to their forgotten fans as Natalie applauded.

"You all must have been something." Natalie was in awe.

"Must have been? I beg your pardon?" Nola was not happy with the past tense.

"Not what I meant." Natalie was quick. "I just wish I could have seen you dance. My mother was a dancer—for a while, before us—before the drugs."

The women stopped prancing.

"Oh baby. So then, your mama was a legend too. We've lost too many legends to those demons," Darcy said, laying a hand on her cheek.

"Did you like it?" Natalie asked Ruby honestly.

"The dancing? Yes. I loved it. But the rest? The videos and the company, I could care less about, but I did love to dance."

"Me too." Darcy latched on, as did the other two women.

"So why don't you dance?" Natalie took a big swig of her drink.

"Now? We're retired," Nola stated the obvious.

"Why? If you love it, why wouldn't you keep doing it?"

"I would," Cathy said. "But there's nowhere to dance. No one's hiring dancers our age, sweetie."

Ruby laid out the cold, hard facts. "She's right. That's why I was waitressing. Even with everything I've done, they didn't want me."

"You could open your own place. You were a big businesswoman."

"That would cost a lot of money and we're all on social security. Not a lot coming in other than the government checks and cash I was able to squeeze out of my last husband." Darcy shot it down.

"Ruby has a place," Natalie said, nodding to Ruby.

"I think you've had enough to drink. This is a trailer and it's in an old folks park, not a whole lot of potential for a strip bar." Ruby got up to take the beer from Natalie.

Natalie held her beer out Ruby's reach. "Not here. The shack. Benny's shack. You could dance there."

Ruby stopped reaching and started thinking.

"Ruby?" Darcy asked seeing the wheels turning behind Ruby's eyes. "What is she talking about?"

Ruby turned to the three old women—suddenly sober and dead serious. "Do you legends really want to dance?"

BONE PARK

The drive to Miami seemed longer this time. Maybe it was the uncomfortable seats of the Nissan Daryl rented her or the guilt she felt every mile along the way. Bernie couldn't help it. She saw Benny's face at every mile marker, in every car pulled to the side of the road and every cop she passed. It haunted her as much as the ring on her finger. Both their blood was on her hands, and she was about to meet who cleaned up one mess and made another.

When the phone first showed up in her pelican mailbox, she thought it would ring the next day. Impatience was a typical trait of most gangsters, that's why they got caught. But the phone didn't ring the next day or the day after that. It didn't ring until that morning. Over a month later. This was unlike any gangster she'd ever dealt with before. Of course, she had questions, the first of which was how the hell these people found out she was working with Vergil. He told her that they knew, just not how. No matter what they had done to Vergil, she knew that he would never have told them. Just as she wouldn't have, if the tables had been reversed. They were old school. Cut from a different cloth that was stitched with a code. Honor and loyalty. These things that seemed to be in very short supply these days.

The address she was told over the phone was vague. As best she could make out on the gas station map she'd bought, the meetup was on the ocean. It looked like an industrial area to her, but then that wasn't strange at all for these sorts of meetups. But what was this meetup exactly? What did they want from her? There was no way she was running bodies anymore, so that discussion would be quick. Besides the police and the public being aware of it, it was the precedent. Bernie wasn't into signs, but she was still superstitious about certain things and a dead run—was a dead run. No way she was going to tempt the fates twice. As far as she was concerned that angle had run its course.

It was an old shipyard like she thought. Giant abandoned buildings made of steel and broken glass that lined the water's edge. It was so on the nose, that she started to get worried. The cliché of it all reeked of undercover. Sometimes the rookies on a squad got eager and set these kinds of things up, hoping for a big collar that they could climb the ladder with. Those setups always looked way too good. Like they had watched too many Hill Street Blues and Miami Vice episodes. A good crook, a real crook, could sniff out these setups a mile away. That's why the only good undercover cops, were crooks themselves. They had to kill and snort lines like their marks. Rub the stink of bacon off of them with sin. They were the same as their busts, only their crimes were swept under the rug when the cuffs went on their perps.

Bernie drove slowly. There was no sign of anyone, just more broke-down buildings. It was the ghost town equivalent of maritime industry, spooky and quiet—that is until she reached the end of the row—and the scenery changed. There it was. The most expensive-looking sore thumb she'd ever seen. A giant, white yacht. Four, maybe five stories tall, docked behind the last building. It had a long, steep gangplank extended down to the pier and two, very big men with guns standing at the end of it. These people were not trying to hide. They were doing the exact opposite. Bernie parked her loaner at the end of the ghost building row and got out. The armed men didn't budge, the Miami version of the Queen's guards, just without the bearskin hats.

As she walked towards the gangplank, a man appeared at the top of the ramp who had a forgotten, but very recognizable face. It was Donnie, the well-dressed gangster that held her hostage all night in the hotel room, after she, Ruby and Daz had helped that drunk kid.

Donnie motioned with his fingers for her to come up and Bernie obliged, walking right past the stoic guards and up the long ramp.

"You're taller than I remember," Donnie said.

"You're shorter." Bernie smiled.

Donnie chuckled. "But you're still a bitch."

"Thank you—Donald," Bernie snarled. "So, this is all you? What do you want with me?"

Donnie shook his head. "I don't want anything." He turned his back and started to walk away from her, down the walkway, towards the bow.

Bernie was left alone there, with no choice but to follow, so she did. The light-stained teak deck boards and white caulking of the exterior walkway seemed to stretch on forever. It was a kind of wealth Bernie had never known. It was even beyond Vergil's opulence. This floating fortress was so big that Donnie completely disappeared at the end of the walkway. Bernie took her time catching up though, still unsure of what was going on, even though she didn't like losing eyes on her potential assassin.

The covered walkway ended at the beginning of an open deck that looked like a full-size cocktail lounge. There were gas fire features, white sofas and chairs, umbrellas and a full-size fully stocked bar, complete with a bartender, who was standing behind it.

"Verna," the old woman, sitting alone on the long sofa sipping a martini said, as if she'd known Bernie her whole life. "Punctual. I expected as much."

Bernie looked the woman over, but she had no idea who she was, other than she could be Donatella Versace's grandmother. Silky, white, flowing pantsuit and long, straight, white hair.

"Please come join me," the woman said, gesturing to the sofa beside her.

Bernie couldn't help but get Vergil vibes from the whole thing. The white outfit, the white couches, the open view of the ocean and skyline.

"Why did you kill him?" Bernie didn't move, but her lips did.

"I didn't," the woman said. "Please come sit down, that's the whole reason you're here, so we can talk."

Bernie sat down, but not beside the ivory woman; she chose a large chair a few feet away from her.

"I would like to begin by thanking you for taking care of my grandson. Kenneth is just like his father, it's not his fault, but I appreciate your concern for him."

"What about Vergil?"

"I told you, that was not us. We found him like that. His partners did that. We sent you the ring, because we knew you were fond of him and of it."

"How did you—"

"Verna, please. A magician never tells her secrets, just know that those former bosses you were working for have been dealt with. What they did to your friend was inexcusable and not the way we do business."

"What is your business?"

"It's not moving dead bodies, that I can assure you. We are in the import-export business, and we've been watching you. I have been watching you ever since Donnie told me you were out here. I was very surprised to hear that you came out of retirement, what with the federal attention and all."

"They've got nothing, and I said nothing."

"I know. I always do my homework. I was very impressed with your little business. Brilliant actually. I was however surprised at your choice of suppliers. Those Cubans are unstable and ruthless. It's a shame what happened to that boy. Benjamin? We did our best to make it disappear."

"That was you?"

"Yes. Would have been quieter but every reporter these days seems to have a police scanner. We couldn't do anything about the spin they put on it. I understand his sister is living with yours now."

Bernie tried to hide her concern. "She is."

"That's the kind of people you are. You take care of the Kenneth's and the Natalie's of this world. You keep your mouths shut and you have manners. That's why I want to do business with you."

"What business? I'm done. That boy was killed because of me. It's over."

"Verna, tell me, why did it work? Before the boy? How were you able to move that many dead cartel bodies up and down the I-95? Under the nose and aggressive program of the Volusia County Sherriff?"

"You know why."

"Yes. That's the genius of it. *Your* genius. The trojan horse, under the Sheriff's watch. My product is having a very hard time getting up and down the I-95; do you know why?"

"Because you don't have a fleet of old women driving for you?"

"No. I can get old women. But there is only one of you."

"I'm not moving your drugs down the highway," Bernie said, holding her ground.

"Why not? What have you got to lose? By my calculations, you only have enough money to get through a few years."

"That's all I need."

"What about your grandchildren? Do they have everything they need?"

Bernie's face went pale.

"I'm not threatening your grandchildren. I don't work that way; what I am asking is wouldn't you like to leave them more? Give them more? I can help you do that. If you help me. You saved my grandchild, together we can save yours. Verna, you can walk away from this boat, and I will never bother you again. I give you my word. I have that much respect for you and all your years behind you. But if you would work for me, I will make sure your grandchildren and their grandchildren never have a worry in the world. You can give them what your son can't."

Bernie locked eyes with the woman. "Gary."

She said it. The forbidden word. My name. The one my mother hadn't spoke for seven years.

There was no sleeping, no matter how exhausted Freda was, she couldn't let go. How could Reg have kept this from her? Were they really living without insurance? Freda had spent most of their life together crunching his numbers, right up until he retired, so this couldn't be right. Like she had told the doctor, she'd cut the checks. That's what had her tearing apart the closet, looking for a bank statement. Reg had taken over the money side of things since he'd bowed out of the rat race, so she really had no idea where they presently stood. The last time she saw their financials was in the last month of his career, when she was tidying things up, closing accounts and settling invoices, but she hadn't looked since.

Freda pulled apart everything in the tiny trailer. They hadn't brought much from Worchester, just what would fit in the wagon and U-Haul, the rest was Connie and Merle's things. Most of their business files were in a storage shed back in Massachusetts. She searched harder than a bloodhound, but she found nothing in the dark tin can, no smoking gun, no Hail Mary. Nothing, except for the card on the kitchen table. The one she'd put under the phone book—the one from the police officer.

It was the middle of the night, but not for her. For her it was the middle of a nightmare and she needed someone to wake her out of it.

The ladies had left, but only after much more booze, laughter and shimmying. Ruby was spread out on her new bed, but she couldn't sleep either. Her head was racing, but not with worry, with possibilities. Natalie had made a very valid argument that had all of them talking the rest of the night. She had planted a seed in the ground that the ladies thought was long dead, only to discover it was just lying fallow. They shot ideas around that main room, spitballing like New York advertising execs, planning décor, lights, cocktails, music and costumes. They all had been given a shot of youth and it felt incredible. Ruby felt incredible, the thought of being able to possibly do it, with these women, to share that joy with them at this point in their lives, was irresistible.

"You asleep?" Natalie's voice whispered from the open doorway.

"No. I'd ask you, but you're standing in my doorway. Everything okay?"

"Everything's fine. I have something—something I think belongs to you or was meant for you." Natalie held out her hand, but the bedroom was too dark to see what it was, so Ruby leaned over and turned on her side table lamp.

Natalie brought it over to her. It was a small piece of paper. "I saw it on his dresser, the day he died, when I grabbed the other stuff. It has your name on it."

Ruby looked at the small piece of paper, through her tipsy, tired eyes. It was a receipt. A deposit receipt of forty dollars at Zales and Ruby's name was written across the top of it.

"Do you know what it is?" Natalie asked.

"I haven't the foggiest," Ruby replied. "But there is one way to find out."

"Can I come?" Natalie sounded vulnerable.

"Sure thing. We'll go tomorrow."

"Alright." Natalie turned very slowly to leave..

Ruby picked up on her body language. "Hey. Hop in," she said, scooching over and pulling back the covers on the empty side of the bed.

Natalie took the offer and jumped in. Ruby leaned over, turned off the light, and the two of looked up at the ceiling.

"So, do you think you'll do it?" Natalie whispered.

"Of course, like I said we'll go to the mall tomorrow."

"Not that. The club."

"It's a very exciting thought, but it would cost a lot of money."

"I guess. If you won the lottery, would you do it?"

"In a heartbeat."

"If only you knew how to win the lottery."

It was the crack of dawn when Bernie pulled into the carport. Not even the incontinent residents of the park were awake yet, but as Bernie got out of the rented Nissan, she heard a very strange sound. She stepped to the end of her driveway, listening to it, trying to find out where it was coming from. It was a repetitive clicking and whining. Not morning friendly, but mechanical sounding.

Bernie walked down the curved road, following the grinding noise. It kept getting louder so she knew she was on the right track. Just past Opal's, on the same side of the road as her trailer, she saw the culprit. She stopped walking, slowly backing away a little, just out of sight and watched for a moment. It was peculiar, Freda was sitting in her lanai, with a lit cigarette dangling from her lips, pounding the keys of a paper-fed adding machine. Whatever she was calculating, it looked painful because her face was puckered up like the knot of a balloon. Bernie didn't want to get caught, like some kind of common peeping Tammy, so she quietly moved back from Freda's line of sight.

BONE PARK

As Bernie returned to her trailer, she couldn't help but think of Reg and what this all-night accountant routine might have to do with it. She'd wanted to say something to Freda. She wanted to ask how Reg was, if he was home from the hospital or not, but Bernie knew not to pet an injured animal, and Freda wasn't just licking her wounds, she was damaged.

The mall was a 'love hate' for Ruby. When she had money, or when some follicle cul-de-sac was trying to buy her affections, she loved it, but without cash, it was bleak. On the broke side of that tumultuous retail relationship, she and Natalie felt the same about it. Overwhelmed. It was so much in one place. So many things to buy, so many people buying them and if you weren't there with a thick wallet or an empty card, the whole thing was pretty depressing.

Ruby was far from rich, but she had a couple of bucks still left from her runs, so she was able to walk through the upper levels of this teen hangout with her head held high. Natalie was unaware she was doing it, but she was mimicking Ruby's confidence and it felt good. They didn't bother to look at the map at one of the kiosks when they arrived, instead they chose to make the rounds. It was like a living copy of 'Gator Vogue', seeing what was in this season for the hip mall rats of southern Florida.

Ruby could see the glances Natalie was giving to the girls her age that passed by in their brand name clothing, and the longing she showed for the mannequins in the store windows. Ruby wanted to give her a pep talk, a speech about worth from a woman who's been there, done that, but she knew it would do no good. She'd only hear 3% of it anyway. It's what she'd expect, what is written in the back pages of fashion magazines, the afterthought articles, composed to appear feminist and progressive. To confuse women in visual versus literary gaslighting of 'do what we write, not what you see'.

They eventually stumbled upon Zales, the over lit glass-case-filled jewelry store, with a salesperson behind every display. The clerks all wore black, and condescending looks on their faces. Ruby knew the good stuff and this place didn't have it. It was the same corporate, semi-precious dumping ground that owned Kays and Jareds. The lights were so bright and strategically placed that this was the best these polished baubles would ever look. Presented in the perfect way to make the lower and lower-middle class feel like they were buying treasured heirlooms, when really, they were being fleeced.

Ruby walked right up to the least snooty-looking, tight-ponytailed employee and presented her receipt.

"Hello, I'd like to pick this up," she said as she held the wrinkled piece of paper out over the smudge-less glass case.

After briefly perusing the scrap of paper without contact, the woman took the receipt from Ruby using only two fingers, as if she might catch something from it. The woman didn't say another word, just walked away into the backroom. If this were Tiffany's, Ruby would expect this kind of arrogance, but this was not Tiffany's.

A few moments later, the woman returned from the bowels of the backroom holding a small box in her hand. "There is a balance still owing on this. A majority balance," the woman said as if it should have shocked Ruby into the vapors.

"That's fine. How much?" Ruby asked, matter of fact.

The woman did her sales smirk. "Four hundred and fifty dollars."

Ruby didn't bat an eye and opened her small red purse, with the long tassels, and pulled out a large roll of bills. It was the last of her 'bone running money', the job that got Benny killed, and she couldn't get rid of it fast enough. Without saying anything, she began peeling bills off the roll, one by one and laid them down on the display case in front of the woman. Once the simple, visual math was done for everyone to see, she paused, then laid down one last fifty-dollar bill.

"That's for you," Ruby said to the woman. "So that maybe you won't be such a cunt to the next person who walks in here."

The saleswoman was stunned by Ruby's words, but also humbled. She pushed the bill back towards Ruby, saying under her breath, "My bosses are assholes. They want us to be like this. I'm not a cunt. I just hate my job."

"Even more reason for you to keep the fifty." Ruby pushed the extra bill back to her.

The woman put her hand on the bill and slid it back towards her, pocketing it like a poker shark. "Thank you." The woman smiled, but for real this time as she handed Ruby the small box. "You know, this is the one that boy kept coming back for."

"What boy?" Natalie jumped at the bait.

"Twenty maybe, looked a lot like you. Thought he was casing the place until he finally picked something—no offense."

"Taken," Natalie snarled.

"He didn't have the money for it, but he kept coming back and putting a few dollars on it every week. My boss was pissed because I let him put three dollars down on it to start. It's been in lay away for a while now, I'd forgotten about it until today."

"I knew you were a good person," Ruby reassured the woman.

The woman motioned to the small, closed box. "Aren't you going to open it?"

Ruby was at a loss for words, she just took Natalie's hand and lead her out of the shop.

Once they got far enough away, Ruby let go of Natalie's hand. "I just couldn't take any more of that. Of her talking about him like he was still here." Ruby dug around in her purse again and pulled out a few bills. "Get anything you want," she said to Natalie, handing her the money.

"No, Ruby. I don't need anything."

"I didn't say get what you need. I said get what you want." She dangled the cash from her fingers like she was teasing a kitty.

Natalie grabbed the potential shopping spree with a sudden excited grin on her face.

"Go on. Don't need me cramping your style. I'll wait here," Ruby said walking over to the empty bench that backed against the glass railing. "Go on."

Natalie was done looking this gift horse in the Chiclets, so she skipped off into the mall, leaving Ruby alone on the bench. She sat there for bit, watching the people pass. The families, the couples, the 'nuclear normal' Normans, captured in every Kmart studio portrait all over the USA. She didn't fit into those portraits. Never had and Benny loved her for it. She looked down at the small box in her hand and the receipt with her name on it. The total had come to five hundred dollars.

Five hundred dollars. She kept thinking about the number. So even—half of a thousand. You could buy whatever this was for that, or a flight anywhere in the USA, or even rent a car from Daryl for that—

She had to remind herself to breathe. Five hundred dollars was the cost of renting the car from Daryl. Is that why Benny wanted to do the run so bad? So he could buy this?

Ruby slowly lifted the lid on the small box in her hand. As lid came off, the light coming in through the skylights above her, caught the angles of the jewelry inside. Her heart stopped. Not figuratively—actually. The beating paused at the sight of it. Inside the box, was a heart-shaped ruby pendant, with diamond chips all around it and a small, crescent moon at the bottom.

"You're moonlight, Ruby." She could hear Benny's voice in her ear. "Yes. Moonlight. You took my heart and lit up my little dark world."

Ruby curled over the box, trying to hide her face from the

passers-by. She pressed the pendant against her chest, hard, digging its sharp edges into her skin, as if she could push the heart-shaped gem inside of her and replace the one that was broken.

This was easier than the bodies, because Bernie designed it that way. Her new partner—that's what Hellsa insisted she be called, because women like them didn't have bosses, they were bosses—gave Bernie full control. Bernie had sat most of the night on that yacht hashing out the details while Hellsa listened and supported all her ideas. This was a new way of doing business. Without all the dicks waving around, these women could actually get things done.

Overnight, a warehouse that Hellsa owned in Miami began supplying adult diapers. Adult diapers that were shipped to a small drugstore in Little River, a neighborhood on the edge of Miami, but still within the city limits. Hellsa's issue was getting their product out of Miami but moving it around in the city was not. The small drugstore in Little River now had a great deal on diapers, such a great deal that they started running sales on them and even put it in the overnight flyer.

Bernie went all the way to Miami for the deal. Old folks love a good deal, everyone knows that. Bernie bought three boxes of adult undergarments from the nice clerk who worked Mondays, Wednesdays and Fridays and who also happened to work for Hellsa. Once done paying for the items and receiving her receipt, Bernie had the nice clerk put the unusually heavy boxes into her car. She then headed off, with the boxes in plain view, receipt in hand and sale confirming flyer displayed beside her on the passenger seat. The drive was longer though, it was eight hours one way from Miami to Georgia. It was now Georgia, not New Smyrna where Bernie did her drop-offs. She went over state lines to drop the boxes off at another warehouse, that overnight had begun shipping adult diapers all over the USA. It was a longer drive—but it was a better plan.

Hellsa had set up a small apartment where Bernie could sleep and then return in the morning, fresh, safe and well rested. This was a partnership. This got the drugs down the I-95, out of Florida, out of the Dade and Volusia County Sheriff's districts. Out of their corridor of profiling and back into Hellsa's distribution network. It was a good plan, with good optics and simple moving parts. It had story-validating documents and cargo that most police would never go near, let alone question. It also paid Bernie triple what the 'bone runs' had. There was just one problem. Frequency. The only part of the plan that didn't look right, was how many diaper runs one old woman needed to do.

The small apartment just inside the state lines of Georgia was nice. It was comfortable and stocked with Sanka and cereal. Bernie left the bachelor suite just after dawn and pulled into Cicada Hollow around 10:00am. Daryl was on retainer now. Bernie could rotate her cars when and how she wanted without the twenty-four-hour restrictions. Daryl didn't ask questions; he was just happy to have the business back.

Bernie shut the door on the sedan and as she walked around the front of her trailer, even over the buzz of the warmed cicadas, she could hear the clicking again. The same clicking she heard the other night.

Freda hadn't slept at all in the last two days. She didn't need to say it, she looked it. She hadn't moved much either, the overflowing ashtray, empty beer cans and twinkie wrappers told that story. There were boxes of paperwork and ribbons of number-filled calculator tape all over the ground of the lanai. Bernie stood at the screen door for a moment, waiting for Freda to notice her, but Freda never looked up.

Bernie knocked on the frame of the mesh door. "Freda?"

Freda jolted her head up, looking bewildered at the sight of another human.

Bernie was cautious. "You okay in there?"

Freda picked up the cigarette smoldering on the top of her butt pile and took a drag. "What's it to you?"

"Well, I heard you out here a couple of nights ago and from the looks of things, you're still out here."

"You spying on me?" Freda stopped calculating with her right hand and sat up straight.

"No. Not like you were spying on me," Bernie said, pulling Freda off her elevated saddle. Freda was caught in a web that she was too tired to climb out of, so Bernie opened the screen door and invited herself in. "How is Reg?"

Freda was reluctant to speak but had nowhere to run to. "He's still in the hospital."

"Oh, I see."

Freda shook her head, and a small tear came to the corner of her eye. She wasn't a crier, she was tired—sick and tired. "He's got cancer. The only thing keeping him alive are the machines and drugs they have him on."

Bernie looked around at the papers and receipts on the ground. "Is that what all of this is about? Money?"

"Partially. I didn't know we didn't have insurance until he was in dreamland, and I was left holding the bag."

"Is there any family that can help?"

"We never had kids. Well, I didn't—"

"Freda, I'm—"

Freda broke. Nothing to lose and no one else to vent to. "He had a whole other family. Three kids—a wife—a house and dog!"

There was nothing to say, nothing for Bernie to do, but just listen.

"He traveled all the time for work. Turns out I was the other woman. She was the home—I was the hussy. The police came here looking for him. I called them the other night, trying to find out what was going on. None of this makes sense. We are well off! They came here because there was a warrant for his arrest. At first it was missing persons, but then it turned into a bench warrant. He's in debt—in arrears for support. Child support, spousal support. He just left an entire family one day and never went back. The courts have taken everything they could. That's why we don't have insurance. That's why I now have two hundred dollars to my name and this place. From Worchester to this shithole! He's on life support and so am I."

Bernie brushed some papers onto the ground and took a seat, occupying the silence with Freda. Freda didn't look at her, just lit another cigarette and dried her single tear.

"I might be able to help you," Bernie said, humbly.

"You have a cure for cancer?"

"No, but I might have a cure for your money trouble."

"Thanks, but I don't do handouts."

"No handout. You'd have to work for it, but it pays well. Enough to keep him plugged in and these debts to go away."

Freda slowly turned to her. "What kind of work?"

Bernie's face stayed still, direct. "I think you know what kind of work."

"I have an idea."

"Truth is, I need the help and it looks like you do too."

"Why me? Why would you tell me? You say you know I've

been watching you. How do you know I didn't tell the cops?"

"You didn't. I thought you did, but you didn't. My partners are very thorough. If you had snitched, we wouldn't be sitting here."

"You'd be behind bars."

Bernie curled her lip. "No. You'd be on life support too."

Freda didn't spook easy, but Bernie's eyes were steel, forged in the endeavors of evil and Freda could see it. "Fair enough, but why me."

"You know what they say about keeping your enemies close? It's that and you seem to be a wiz with numbers. You were Reg's accountant, right? Well, if we are going to move the kind of money that's going to be coming in, I'm going to need someone who can work the numbers."

"I don't know. I missed this! All these years and I didn't see this happening with Reg."

"He lied to you. That's what men do. But how was his business? How were those books?"

"Spotless," Freda said with a surprising amount of pride.

"That's what I want."

Freda looked around at the shrapnel on the ground. The mess left by the explosion of a life she thought she had. "Fuck it. What do I have to lose?" she said extending her hand to Bernie, who shook it right away.

"Are you expecting them?" Freda said finishing the shake, looking over Bernie's shoulder.

Bernie turned around to find Ruby standing on the road outside Freda's trailer, with Natalie and Opal.

"There you are," Ruby said. "We've been looking all over for you. Can we talk?"

Bernie shrugged. "Absolutely, come on in."

Ruby was skeptical. "Yeah, I think this is something we should talk about at your place." Bernie wasn't moving, so Ruby tried to be a little more pointed. "I saw your rental car. I think we need to talk about that."

"I agree," Bernie said. "So, come in. Freda knows."

"She does?" Opal said, worried.

"She does. I'm surprised to see you here, Opal—does Stan need new clubs already?"

"Something like that," Opal said, slightly embarrassed.

Bernie let her off the hook. "We all have our reasons, but you both need to know, a lot has changed."

"Changed about what?" Natalie was trying to keep up.

Bernie shot Ruby a look and Ruby understood. "Natalie, you need to go back to the trailer, alright? This is a private matter."

Natalie responded, "Why? What are you doing?"

Ruby winked at her. "Remember what you said about the club? I know how to win the lottery."

That moment in Freda's trailer, that's what Bernie was thinking about as the sirens got closer and she walked back to her trailer, leaving Opal out in the inner circle grass. Opal was catatonic in pink chiffon, staring at Mullet who kept trying to pull her dead husband's body out of the pool. Bernie wasn't thinking about the approaching doom. Not the fear of imprisonment or a shootout with the law; she was thinking about that moment, when the four of them finally came together. When it all really started, and it was good.

A scream.

There was a lot of screaming coming from out in the open grassy area, but this wasn't Mullet. It was Ruby. Bernie turned on her heels and rushed back out to the grassy area, where Ruby was running towards her from the other side.

"Natalie! It's Natalie!" Ruby could barely get the words out, but Bernie didn't need any more words than that. She knew.

Bernie reached Ruby in the middle and the two of them ran back to Ruby's trailer, passing the sculpture of Opal, forcing Bernie to let go of her romanticized memories. Quieting the fleeting thoughts of that day in Freda's lanai, when the four women decided to do something big. Something they hoped would last long after they were gone. Something bigger than each of them, but only possible with each other. Something that their enemies would fear, that the authorities would hate, and the papers would make infamous. Something the world would soon come to know as The Grand-mafia.

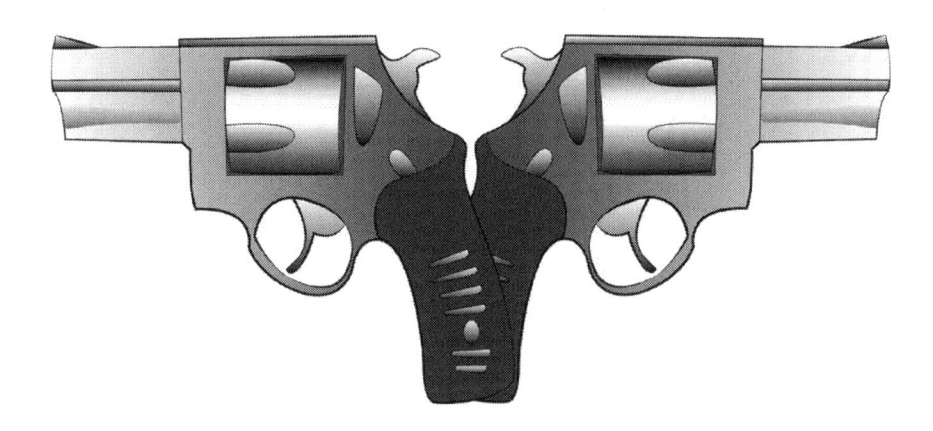

ABOUT THE AUTHOR

Sandy Robson is a Canadian author/writer/filmmaker/actor/artist and ginger. He strives to create worlds around characters, not the other way around, stories that put us in their shoes and let us take a moment out of our own realities, to run away in theirs.

For a deeper dive into Sandy Robson's writing, The Trine Trilogy, Sandy's weekly blog, release dates, other books and more visit:

www.sandyrobsonbooks.com

Manufactured by Amazon.ca
Bolton, ON